TRIFLES AND FOLLY

A DEADLY CURIOSITIES COLLECTION

GAIL Z. MARTIN

TRIFLES AND FOLLY

A DEADLY CURIOSITIES COLLECTION

by Gail Z. Martin

ISBN: 978-1-939704-51-1

Cover art by Lou Harper
SOL Publishing is an imprint of DreamSpinner Communications, LLC

INTRODUCTION

WELCOME TO MY world. This collection of short stories is from the Deadly Curiosities' universe, and as odd as it sounds it began with real life. Authors take inspiration from many places and for me, life events took me down a dark and mysterious road. It all began with *Buttons*, I was asked to participate in the Solaris anthology *Magic: The Esoteric and Arcane* and had to come up with a new story. I'd written several involving Sorren set in earlier times but I wanted a fresh take and a modern setting, and Cassidy was born.

At the time I was dealing with the recent death of my father and my husband and I were settling his estate, dealing with auctions and appraisers and sorting through a life-long collection of stuff. Not ordinary stuff, but the kinds of things that provided fodder for ghost stories. Though obviously, I took some creative liberties, some everyday items do have unusual providence, and oh, the things they've seen!

Over the course of the short stories and novels, the characters grow and change, as you'd expect if they were real people. When we first meet Cassidy in *Buttons* and in *Deadly Curiosities*, she is very new in using her gift of psychometry, and the visions often throw her for a loop. As time goes on, she gains more skill—both in controlling her magic and in using it defensively. Teag also grows in his magical abilities, and Sorren proves that continued growth and change are part of a successful long existence.

I hope you enjoy these stories and if so, there are more available and more to come, including the full length novels: *Deadly Curiosities, Vendetta,* and *Tangled Web.*

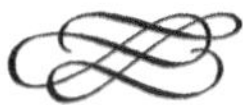

"More buttons, Cassidy? I swear, you read those things like a steamy novel." Teag Logan sailed into the shop and never even slowed his pace.

Some people read novels. I read objects, especially buttons. I can glimpse the dizzying highs and shadowed lows of a stranger's life in a single, beautiful button.

I'm Cassidy Kinkaide, and I own Trifles and Folly, an estate auction and antiques shop in beautiful, historic, haunted Charleston, South Carolina. Truth be told, we were also a high-end pawn shop on the side. I inherited the shop, which has been in the family since Charleston was founded back in 1670. We deal in antiques, valuable oddities, and very discreetly, in supernatural curios. It's a perfect job for a history geek, and even more perfect for a psychometric. My special type of clairvoyance gives me the ability to "read" objects and pick up strong emotions, sometimes even fragments of images, voices, and memories.

"Shipment from the weekend auction just came in," I called to Teag. "I love Mondays."

"Let me know if you find any 'sparklers' or 'spookies,'" Teag answered. "I'll get the 'mundanes' out on display." In our time together, Teag and I developed our own private language. 'Mundanes' are items that are lovely but lack any psychic residue whatsoever. 'Sparklers' resonate with the psychic imprints of their former owners. I'll set those aside until I can go through them. 'Spookies' reek of malevolence. They go into the back room, until Sorren, my silent partner, and patron, can safely dispose of them.

Most people think Trifles and Folly has stayed in business for over three hundred years because we're geniuses at offering an amazing selection of antiques and unique collectibles. There is that, but it's only part of the story, a small part. It's the back room that keeps us in business. We exist to find the dangerous magical items that make their way onto the market and remove them before anyone gets hurt. Most of the time, we succeed, but there have been a few notable exceptions, like that quake back in 1886 that leveled most of the city. Oops.

"This is all from the Allendale house south of Broad Street, isn't it?" Teag asked, coming back in with a steaming hot cup of coffee.

"The house itself was impressive," I answered, "but it was packed to the gills. Old man Allendale was a collector and a hoarder."

"Bad for the family; good for our business," Teag replied. "It's not often we need four full-day auctions to clean a place out, and that was after the family took what they wanted and got rid of the trash."

"The crowds came for the Civil War relics," Teag pointed out, brushing a strand of hair out of his eyes. He's in his mid-twenties, tall and skinny, with a skater-boy mop of dark hair, and a wicked sense of humor. He looks more like a starving artist than an aspiring art history Ph.D. candidate, but he's ABD (All But Dissertation) at the University of Charleston. Blame Trifles and Folly for derailing his ambitions. One summer's part-time job working with the amazing antiques and oddities that come through this store, and academia lost its attractiveness. Now he's my full-time assistant store manager, as well as assistant auctioneer, archivist, and occasional bodyguard.

"The guy spent a lifetime wandering around battlefields, since he was a kid in the Twenties," I replied. "If you think the pieces we got for auction were good, imagine what the museum took. They got first pick, for the new *Edward Allendale Memorial Exhibit.*'" I glanced at the pile I was sorting. Mostly small stuff, like musket balls, belt buckles, old postcards, and buttons. A big glass jar of buttons.

I shifted in my chair, trying to get more of the draft from the air conditioning. Summer in Charleston was brutal between the heat and the humidity, and my strawberry blonde hair was more frizzy than usual. I tucked a lock behind one ear because it refused to stay in a ponytail. One look at me and you could guess my ancestors' Scots-Irish background, with the green eyes and pale skin that had a tendency to burn the instant I stepped out into the hot South Carolina sun.

"Be careful, Teag. We've got at least one 'spooky' in the pile that came today. I can feel it. I'm getting a very strong sense of something… evil. I just haven't found the damned thing."

Teag looked at me and raised an eyebrow. "Dangerous?"

I frowned. "Dark. Consider it dangerous until proven otherwise."

Teag leaned against the doorframe. "Didn't Sorren say there were stories about old man Allendale? About the house?"

I nodded. "Yeah, but there are stories about most of the old homes south of Broad, and most involve ghosts. Sorren wanted us to take this auction because he was certain there was more to these particular stories."

"Grumpy old man with no close family, hoarder, has a heart attack and dies," Teag recapped. "Happens every day, somewhere."

I tried to split my focus between my inner sense and paying attention to Teag. "Not quite like this. Neighbors complain about a shadow watching from an upstairs window. Reports of strange noises. People say their dogs don't like to walk near the house." I let my hands hover a few inches above the large boxes yet to be unpacked.

"There's a… residue that clings to everything, like old cigarette smoke, but it's not physical, it's spectral. I can feel it. Everything's tainted."

Teag looked at me over his trendy eyeglasses. "If it's so dark, how come we let it go to auction?"

"Sorren and I went down to the auction site while you were busy dealing with the rest of the event details. We tagged everything he and I thought had a powerful enough resonance to warrant a second look, and had it taken out of the auction until we could go through it."

"So what you're saying is, we've got a whole shipment of 'spookies,' or at least 'sparklers,'" he replied dryly. "Wonderful."

"Sorren says he'll be here after sundown to help us go through everything," I said. "All we need to do is catalog what came in, and let him know if anything in particular, gives off a strong vibe."

"If anything gives off a vibe strong enough for me to feel it," Teag replied, "it would probably knock you flat on your behind. You might want to let me open the boxes and have a first look."

"Fine by me. I'm going to start on the buttons." Buttons speak to me more often than most objects. I've always thought it was because they were worn for long periods of time, day in and day out, often close to the skin.

I reached for the large tray I use to sort buttons, and picked up the jar to dump it out. I felt a tingle in my hand, and I knew that I'd be picking up strong images from some of these buttons. Strong… but nothing felt evil. I promised myself I would be careful.

I watched as a river of old buttons spilled out onto the tray. Mid-Twentieth Century and older, I guessed, watching the array of colors and shapes waterfall out of the jar. Some, made of metal, wood, and bone, looked much older.

I picked up a pencil and used the eraser end to poke the pile of buttons. Using the pencil insulated me from the full strength of the impressions, but didn't block them altogether. That was helpful when I wanted to keep my wits about me.

Images flashed through my mind on many of the buttons. The echo of a child's laughter sounded in the distance when I touched a plastic, heart-shaped button. A round ivory disk yielded a woman's voice, humming to herself and an image of rolling out dough in a kitchen. My pencil flicked among the buttons, and in my mind, I saw the blackboard in a long-ago school room from a shirt button, memories of a heavy winter storm from a coat's fastener, and the distant strains of an orchestra from a dainty pearl ball. It went on like that for a few minutes, glimpsing fragments of long-ago lives, until my pencil hovered above one particular button.

An image came to me so clear and strong that it transported me beyond the back room of my shop.

Tall grass, dry from the summer heat, slapped at my legs. The air smelled of sweet honeysuckle, mixed with the acrid stench of gunpowder. Not far away, I could hear the thunder of cannons. My heart was pounding, and my palms were sweaty. I gripped my rifle more tightly, comforted by the smooth wood of the grip, and the cool metal of the barrel. Hoof beats pounded closer, not just a few men on horseback, but a cavalry unit on the move. Men would die today. The fear that I might be among them seemed to freeze my blood.

"Cassidy! Come on Cassidy! Snap out of it!" Gradually, Teag's urgent voice intruded, and the vision receded. I shook my head and came to myself. Teag stood over me, worried but not surprised. He'd seen me "trance out" enough times to know what to do.

"I'm okay," I said, still reorienting. Teag's glare meant he knew damn well that I wasn't all right.

"Do you know which button sent you day trippin'?" He made an effort to sound flippant, but I could hear genuine concern beneath his words.

"That's the one," I murmured. "I'm certain most of the resonance is coming from this button."

Teag frowned as he bent over the tray, then picked up the button and held it between thumb and forefinger. "It's old. Looks military. Might even be Civil War."

"I'm almost certain it's Civil War," I replied, remembering the images I had seen. "The question is, why are the impressions from this button so much stronger?"

Teag sat on the edge of my desk. "Did you pick up on anything when we were at the house? Get any visions?"

I shook my head. "I never went inside, remember? I was working the Oliver estate, and I left the Allendale house in your hands. Other than a peek in the front door, I never got close."

"The crew was uncomfortable working there, particularly after dark," Teag replied. "The lower floors weren't a problem, but they really didn't like the attic." He paused. "A couple of times, when the men were loading the truck, they said they felt like someone was watching them from an upstairs window, even though no one was in the house. And Jorge, one of my best workers, called off sick the last day. He never gets sick, but the day before, he swore he'd been chased by a shadow. I don't think he wanted to go back in there."

"I don't think this button is a full 'spooky,'" I said, daring to let the pencil hover a bit nearer to the worn metal button. "Spookies" were malevolent items or objects with a dark magical history. I knew better than to touch "spookies." I turned them right over to Sorren, and he locked them up, neutralized their magic, or sent them off for further study. Sorren had been at this for a lot longer; I was happy to leave those details to him. "Maybe just a strong 'sparkler.' He doesn't feel angry just… terribly sad."

"Wandering around for more than one hundred and fifty years without being able to rest would make anyone sad, and a mite cranky, too." Teag looked around the back room and through the door to the loading dock. "Get readings from anything else we brought back?"

I got up and began to wander among the boxes, letting my hand trail along their sides. I felt the residue of daily life, hopes, fears, hunger, and exhaustion, but one box made me stop and examine my impressions. "What's in here?"

Teag bent to look at the label, since only he could read his scribbled writing. "Antique baby items. Very good condition."

"That's because they were never used," I said quietly. "There was a christening gown, embroidered linen with eyelet lace?"

Teag nodded, his eyes widening. "Yes. Very pretty."

"Set it aside for Sorren. The child died right after the baptism. I'd hate to think someone might purchase that and carry the resonance forward to a new baby."

Teag moved the box away from the others. "Consider it done. How about anything to go with that button?"

I had moved among all the new boxes, and none drew me in or offered up impressions that matched those of the button. It's hard to explain, but when I pick up on "residue" from an object, it's as if that impression has its own special frequency. Nothing else was on the button's frequency.

I shook my head. "Nothing." I paused, thinking. "Of course, I don't know what I would have picked up from what the museum took. Maybe that button came from a uniform that was in the boxes for the exhibit."

"I am not taking you in the museum again. No how, no way," Teag said, holding up his hands. "Do you remember what happened when we accidentally ended up in the *Plagues and Pestilence* exhibit?"

I shuddered. Yellow fever, smallpox, malaria, diphtheria, and cholera all wrote their own bloody lines of the city's history. The impressions from that display were so overwhelming that I passed out and didn't regain consciousness for a full day. Even then, it had taken some of Sorren's arcane know-how to bring me out of it. I was happy to donate money to the museum, but there was no way in hell I'd step foot inside again.

"I remember," I muttered. "But maybe a family member could provide some details."

"Not much family to speak of," Teag said, consulting the file he accessed on his smartphone. "There's a niece who drew the short straw, so to speak, on having to clean up after him. No other living relatives."

"Got an address?"

Teag looked at his watch. "What's it going to be for the rest of the afternoon, until Sorren gets here? Unpack boxes or play button, button, who's got the button?"

"Button hunting," I decided. "I don't think the resonance is dangerous, but I'd hate to be wrong about that." I'd learned the hard way to play it cautious after an unfortunate incident with a trunk full of antique porcelain dolls. I shuddered. That was going to show up in my nightmares for a long, long time.

"Okay then," Teag said, mustering good spirits for the hunt. He put the button into a plastic box, and he put the box into his pocket. "It's a pretty day. Let's head out to see the niece. My notes said she works nights, so if we head over right away, odds are good we'll find her at home."

Teag's phone had all the contact information, so he handed it over while he drove. It was a glorious day, though hot and humid, something that comes with living in Charleston. If you didn't grow up here, you either loved the weather, adapted quickly, or packed up and left.

I called Sullivan Michaels, Mr. Allendale's niece. She was surprised to hear from me, but agreed to see us, especially when I hinted that we had found something of particular interest among the "junk" she had been happy to sell at auction.

Teag made a few turns and pulled into the driveway of a modest, one-story ranch house. Sullivan Michaels' house dated from the 1950s rather than the 1850s, but it looked neat and well-maintained, a far cry from the run-down state of her elderly uncle's home. Teag and I walked up to the door and knocked.

Sullivan Michaels was a plump woman in her middle years. She looked as if she was just getting ready for work, and judging by her clothing; I was guessing something in the hospitality business, maybe the night manager at a hotel or restaurant. She had a broad, intelligent face, but there was no spark that suggested passionate curiosity. "You made good time," she said, welcoming us into her home. "I set out some sweet tea and cheese straws if you'd like a bite."

I left the cheese straws for Teag, and poured two tall glasses of sweet tea. The dark amber liquid crackled as it flowed over the ice, and I knew that if it had been made to true Charleston standards, it would be strong as a hurricane and sweet as a honeycomb.

"Thank you again for using Trifles and Folly for your uncle's estate," I began. "We were going through the boxes, and we came across something interesting. We wondered if you might know more about it."

On cue, Teag held out the box with the uniform button. Sullivan examined it, and then shrugged. "I'm sorry, but there was just so much in the house, I don't remember things like individual buttons." Despite her words, she kept turning the button this way and that in the light.

"Did your uncle keep any records of where he found the items in his collections?" I pressed.

She gave a weary chuckle. "He picked up a lot at flea markets, and he scavenged other people's estate sales. When he was younger, he walked battlefields, poked through abandoned houses, and meandered through the woods near where the armies had fought." She paused. "But for all that, he was almost obsessive about noting down what he got and where he got it. Usually he jotted a note on a scrap of paper and put it with the item. I passed everything to the museum that went along with the items they wanted."

"Did your uncle leave any journals or diaries, something that might have recorded his ramblings?" I tried to keep my tone light, but my inner sense told me we were onto something, and that Sullivan held the key.

Sullivan looked uncomfortable. "He kept a journal throughout his adult life," she said. "Stuffed them full of newspaper clippings, photos, even letters. I haven't looked through them, and I don't know if I'll even try." She sighed. "We weren't very close. My uncle kept mostly to himself and had a rather sour disposition. He'd probably come back to haunt me if he knew I'd donated his belongings to a museum rather than holding out for top market price."

Her comment sent a chill down my spine. Hoarders and misers were the most likely to retain an otherworldly attachment to their worldly goods. "I know I'm asking a great deal, but would you be willing to lend me the journals, just for a little while? We try to know the provenance of all the pieces we sell at Trifles and Folly, and something as trivial as where a button was found or purchased means so much to our clients."

"My uncle's life revolved around acquiring items for his collections," Sullivan said. "I'm guessing you'll find little more than a journal of his shopping trips, but good luck hunting." Sullivan looked at turns guilty and relieved. I could guess why. She probably felt a bit guilty turning over a man's private papers to a total stranger. At the same time, I wondered if, subconsciously, Sullivan picked up a disquieting resonance from the old man's things

"I'll go get the journals," she offered and jumped up. Teag went to help, and a few minutes later he emerged with two mid-sized cartons.

"One more question, Ms. Michaels," I said. "Would you mind if we went back into the house, just to see if there's anything we missed, like a button or two?"

"I can't imagine that you'll find anything, but you're welcome to go. Just drop the key off when you're finished."

Teag put the boxes into the trunk of his car, and we started back to the shop. "You've got a feeling about those journals, I can see it in your face."

"The button is a clue, but by itself, it's not dark," I replied. "But the more I think about it, the more I'm sure that something Edward Allendale brought home with him for his collections turned into a nasty surprise."

"There are an awful lot of journals. It's going to take forever to go through them all."

"I have a hunch that the button will narrow it down for me."

"Which is why I don't think you should do it alone." Teag might be a couple of years younger than me, but he acts more like the big brother I never had. "Let's take them back to the shop, order in pizza and a six-pack while we wait for Sorren, and work our way through the journals."

I tried not to look as relieved as I felt, but I knew Teag was wise to me. "Okay, twist my arm," I laughed. "But are you sure you don't have something better to do?"

"I could footnote my dissertation," Teag replied dryly. "Other than that, no."

Within the hour we had journals spread across my office. Good ol' Edward had been a compulsive journal writer, and the slim tomes stretched all the way back to the 1930s. We ate, and as the afternoon shadows lengthened, we tackled the stack of books after setting them out in chronological order.

"Where does your hunch tell you to start?" Teag asked.

"The early years," I answered without having to think about it. "I'll take the oldest ones. He's got more than seventy years' worth of books; more than enough for both of us."

I cheated and didn't start with the oldest volume, but instead, I turned my senses inward and waited to be led. Eyes closed, my hand came to rest on two of the journals. The leather bindings were scuffed and cracked, and the pages had yellowed. Inside, scrawled in a young man's handwriting, entries had been inked with a fountain pen.

June 14, 1939. Spent the day down along the river. I know General Beauregard's troops marched through here, or close to this spot. The man who owns this land says it's been in his family since the war years, but no one ever did much with it. He thought there were a few skirmishes hereabouts. Wouldn't I love to find something they left behind!

I read on, caught up in the old entries. I had braced myself for negative impressions from the journals, but from this volume, I sensed only curiosity and enthusiasm. As soon as I picked up the next journal, the feeling changed. There was a darkness to the journal's resonance. Something had changed Edward Allendale between 1939 and 1940. I had a feeling our button had something to do with that shift.

I flipped through it, scanning the dates. Then I realized something. The first half of the book still had the positive feel of the first journal, but toward the middle, a heaviness hung over the pages. I flipped back and forth, trying to find out where the feeling shifted, and this passage caught my attention.

July 17, 1940. I just don't seem to be able to leave off walking along the river. I think there's something here to find, almost like I'm supposed to find it. I can barely sleep at night, thinking about when I can come back and poke around some more.

On the next page, it felt as if a dark curtain descended. I knew I'd found what I was looking for.

July 18, 1940. I saw a little cave I'd never noticed before. It was shallow and filled with rocks, but I found bits of an old uniform, mostly gone to mold except for a button, a gold coin, some yellowed bones and a skull. I'm certain one of our boys in gray made this his last resting place. I left the bones, but I took the button, the coin, and the skull. I'll figure out who to tell about it. Maybe they'll give old Johnny Reb a memorial parade, and pin a medal on me for finding him.

"But you didn't tell anyone, did you, Edward," I murmured. I riffled through the pages of the journal, and two yellowed letters fell out. I bent down, curious.

"That's odd," I said. "These letters are much older than the journal." I looked to where the journal had opened, and read another entry.

September 5, 1940. I think I may have figured out who the Johnny Reb was in that cave. Mr. Johnson at the Historical Society has been letting me go over the lists of the missing and dead from the battles fought near where I found the skull. I could narrow it down some from the type of button, and today I think I found my man. Some of the dead soldiers' families bequeathed items to the Historical Society. Mr. Johnson let me go through those, too. When I found the letters, I knew it had to be the man whose bones I found. His name was Jonah Macaulay. I kept the letters for safekeeping, and I'll give them back to Mr. Johnson along with the skull and other things once I can figure out how to get old Jonah his final rest.

"Find something?" Teag asked.

I showed him the entry, glad to get the book out of my hands. The darkness that found Edward Allendale had started closing in around me. "It changed him," I said. "Before he found those things in the cave, he was just a young guy looking for treasure. But the sense of him shifts from the time he found that grave."

"So Edward stole the letters, huh?" Teag said when he finished reading.

I nodded. "I think he was used to bending the rules, and maybe by this point, the items he found were already getting a hold over him."

I fingered the old parchment, but by themselves, the letters had no special resonance. Carefully, I unfolded the yellowed paper. Bold pen strokes told me that the handwriting probably belonged to a man, and the signature confirmed it. "Jonah Macaulay," I murmured.

"So what's in those letters?" Teag's eyes shone with the love of the hunt.

I struggled to make out the faded lines. "They were written by Jonah to Elsabeth Bradley, and it appears they were engaged," I said, working my way through the cramped paragraphs.

"My dear Elsabeth," I read aloud. *"The sentiment of your gift pleases me, but I am concerned when you speak of its origins. I know that your people come from New Orleans, and many things are done differently there than in Charleston, but I would be a bit more comfortable with the gift of a small cross or even a medallion of one of the saints, like those the Catholic soldiers carry. Nevertheless, I know the intent of your heart, and you may be assured I will carry your token with me into battle, as did the knights of old."*

"She gave him something as a good luck charm," Teag said, staring at the button. "And it made old Jonah uncomfortable."

I unfolded the second letter and noticed immediately that the writing was different. Smaller, graceful, meticulous penmanship hinted that the writer of this letter was female. "That's interesting," I said. "There's a note in pencil on the outside of this letter, saying it was found with the kit bag of a missing soldier."

I scanned down through the letter. "Here it is," I said, feeling a thrill of triumph.

"Darling Jonah,

How I pray for this war to be over, and for you to return safely. I know you sent me back to my parents in New Orleans for my safety, but I now feel doubly parted from you. I cannot sleep for fear that something might befall you. I implored my maid to take me to the French Quarter, where a Creole woman sells amulets that bring good fortune. Please do not think me unchristian, but I fear my prayers alone may not be enough to bring you home again. The Creole

*promised me that if you keep this gold coin near your heart, you will
not die. I beg of you, my love, do this for me.*
    Ever yours, Elsabeth."

"I learned long ago that the devil is in the details when it comes to
contracts." Sorren's voice made me jump. He stood in the doorway,
and I realized that we had been at the journals long enough for the sun
to have set.

"You heard?" I asked, clearing journals off a chair for Sorren to
have a seat. Sorren looked to be in his late twenties, but I knew he was
older. He had dark blond hair, blue eyes flecked with gray, like the sea
after a storm, and a slim, wiry build. Once upon a time, he had been a
jewel thief in Antwerp, but that was before the Alliance had recruited
him. Now, he put his talents to better use, keeping dangerous magical
objects from falling into the wrong hands.

"I heard enough to make me suspect that perhaps Elsabeth should
have been more careful with the way she phrased her request," Sorren
said. His gaze rested on the old letters.

"If you keep this gold coin near your heart, you will not die," I
murmured. I looked up, meeting Teag's gaze. "Could an amulet keep
Jonah's spirit from crossing over?"

"Your phone message left a good bit out," Sorren interrupted. "Perhaps you could recap a bit for me." After all this time, his voice still
held a trace of a Dutch accent.

Teag and I took turns filling Sorren in, ending with the discovery
of the journal and the letters. Sorren listened quietly, but I could see
the spark in his eyes that said he was mentally cross-referencing
everything we told him against his considerable knowledge of magical
lore.

"So Elsabeth asked a Voudon to make an amulet for her beloved,"
Sorren said. "That kind of magic should not be dabbled in. It's powerful, and the spirits that give the Voudon power, the Loas, do not make
simple bargains."

I moved around the room, letting my hand hover over the journals,
decade by decade. "Something isolated Edward, filled him with

despair. I can feel how it grew over the years. By the end, it consumed him."

Sorren nodded. "Edward found Jonah's skull – and the button and coin – in a cave. Caves are liminal space, thresholds between our world and other realities. That would have heightened the power of the spell on the coin, and lying there for more than a century would have strengthened it even further. Then Edward happens upon the bones and takes them home with him, to a home built on land reclaimed from the sea – another sort of liminal space. He brings it into a home that already had a history of haunting, so other spirits had found an easy passage from their world to ours."

I shook my head as the horror of the situation became clear. "Jonah, or the coin, fed on Edward's life energy until Edward weakened and Jonah grew stronger."

"I fear Jonah has been a tool of the coin's curse for many years now," Sorren replied. "If anything of Jonah still remains, it's what left after the coin drew the power it needed to fulfill the spell."

"We didn't see a skull or a gold coin in the house," Teag said. "But before the house passes on to another owner, we're going to need to find them, or Edward won't be the only victim."

Sorren nodded. "The coin – or rather, the curse on the coin – is strongest in liminal space. So you'll have to go in daylight, avoiding the threshold times."

"Noon, midnight, dawn, sundown," I replied. "And nighttime."

"Exactly. And my magic makes *me* liminal space," Sorren added quietly, meeting my gaze. Magic had kept Sorren alive long beyond a normal lifespan. "So I won't be able to go with you on this one. My presence will only make the curse stronger." He paused. "Don't worry, Cassidy. Teag and I will still get the items to the Alliance. I just need you to find them."

"How do we get it out of there?" I asked. "I don't dare touch it, and I don't want to put Teag in danger."

"Agreed," Sorren replied. "Give me a couple of hours. I need to pay a visit to an old friend."

Sorren left the shop, and Teag and I passed the time cleaning up the pile of journals and unloading a few of the boxes I could assure contained nothing except "mundanes." Before long, we heard a knock on the door and rushed to let Sorren in.

"I went to see a friend of mine, one who knows something about Voudon. Mama Nadedge," he said.

"Why didn't you take us with you?" I asked, intrigued and a little put out at being left behind.

Sorren chuckled. "Mama Nadedge died many years ago, Cassidy. Her spirit lingers, if one knows where to look. I asked her guidance, and this is what she gave me." He withdrew a piece of paper marked with a complicated, stylized pattern of crossed lines, stars and a heart, something I recognized as a *veve*, a Voudon symbol.

"I took these to a jeweler I know, someone willing to stay open late for a good cause," Sorren said. "He made these for you and Teag." Sorren reached into his pocket and withdrew two silver disks engraved with the same pattern as the paper, each on their own silver chain.

"I know enough about Voudon to know each spirit, or Loa, has its own *veve*. Whose is this?"

Sorren smiled. "Very good, Cassidy. This is the *veve* for Maman Brigitte. She's the spirit who reclaims the souls of the dead and helps them cross over. Believers say she's powerful, and she appears as either a bride or a veiled old woman. She is very near the top of the Loa hierarchy, which means that whatever spirit placed the curse on Jonah's coin is less powerful than Maman Brigitte."

"At least, we hope so," I muttered under my breath, taking the amulet and slipping it over my head.

THE NEXT DAY, when we reached the Allendale house, I let Teag go on ahead to unlock the door and turn on the lights. I lagged behind, turning my senses inward, listening for the button's owner. There was a presence here. I followed Teag to the attic.

"Teag, let me hold your jacket, please," I said.

I was hoping that having the button close to me would heighten my senses. It did. As soon as I held Teag's jacket, the connection with the button grew stronger. As Teag began to wander around, looking at the attic walls for hiding places, I let my senses focus on the box, let it draw me toward one particular corner.

Against one wall was a large, empty armoire. I stood in front of it, wondering why the button had steered me here.

"I emptied that myself," Teag said, coming up behind me. "We went through it completely. There aren't any hidden compartments, no extra drawers." He shook his head. "We left it here because frankly, no one could figure out how to get it down the stairs."

I looked down toward the floor. "Casters," I said, pointing. "It can be moved. Did you look behind it?"

Teag shook his head. "It was pretty clear no one had moved it for decades, and it's flush against the wall. Never occurred to me."

I went to one side and put my shoulder against the armoire. "Come on. Let's see what's behind it." Teag joined me, and we started to push. The heavy wooden armoire didn't want to roll, but finally, the casters creaked, and we inched the heavy box down the wall.

"There!" I said and pointed. The wall behind the armoire was filthy, covered in dust and a shroud of old cobwebs. Down where the wall met the floor a piece of wood covered a hole in wall, and above it, a thin dark crack separated two wide boards.

Teag pulled out a pair of work gloves from his messenger bag, along with a screwdriver. He knelt next to the opening and began to pry at the wood. I could hardly think straight because the sensations from the button in my pocket had gone off the charts.

The attic walls melted away, and once again I saw the sunlit battle-field I had glimpsed before through the eyes of the button's owner.

Fear coursed through me, making my heart pound. All around me, I heard the sharp crack of rifles and in the distance, the steady, deadly pounding of cannons that shook the ground beneath my feet. The uniform I wore was gray, or had been once. Now, it was faded from the sun, stained where it had been splashed with the blood of other men, brown from the red clay dirt. Just as I raised my rifle to my shoulder, I heard another loud crack, closer this time, and staggered backward as if someone had shoved me. My own shot went wild, with the rifle barrel pointed toward the sky as I nearly fell. When I put my hand down to my side, my fingers came away stained with blood.

"It's open!" Teag shouted in triumph, setting the board to the side. A dark hole gaped in the wall. From that hole, Teag drew out a small bundle wrapped in old rags. He unwound the rags and withdrew a yellowed skull. He jostled it, and the lower jaw fell away, revealing a gold coin that had been placed in the mouth.

I stared at Teag and the bundle, then my gaze shifted behind him, to the wall. The thin dark crack had grown wider, and from it, a shadow slipped out like smoke.

"Get back, Teag!"

Teag followed my gaze, but I could tell from the look on his face he didn't see what I saw. Still, he acted, scrabbling backward, clutching the skull and coin. The shadow grew larger, briefly taking the form of a man and then shifting, with tendrils that unwound themselves like a black kraken uncoiling. Behind me, one of the light bulbs flared and then burst with a crack like gunfire. I searched with my senses and knew that the dark crack was a fissure between more than the attic siding. The Allendale house had been rumored to have been a hotbed of paranormal activity for long before Edward brought home his battle-field treasure. Now I knew why. The dark space was no ordinary splintering of old boards, no settling of the foundation. It was a threshold between the world of the living and the place of the dead.

"Get out of here." I could barely make words come from my throat. The dark shadow was growing larger.

"The hell I will," Teag said. "Maybe it wants the button."

But I could feel what the darkness really wanted; it wanted fresh meat, warm blood, and the life that animated our beating hearts.

My gaze went again to the crack between the boards. I reached for the amulet around my neck for moral support and pressed the smooth silver disk against my palm.

An image formed in my mind of a woman in an antique bridal gown. A heavy lace veil covered her face. I could sense an aura of power around her.

Leave the shadowed one to me, my child. Send the curse where it belongs, and close the rift.

How? I wondered. How do I close the rift? I looked again at the dark crack, a thin opening, or a small rip. Or a buttonhole.

"I've got an idea," I said, eyeing the skull Teag still held and the distance between me and the wall. "Can you get the coin out of the skull's mouth?"

Teag juggled his macabre charge. "I think so. Dammit! Someone wired it in here."

"Try not to handle the coin if you can help it. Put it on the floor, where it's easy for me to get it," I instructed, keeping my eyes on that damned shadow.

A coin in the mouth of a corpse, a penny for the ferryman, I thought. Perhaps at some point, Edward Allendale had tried unsuccessfully to send his unwanted visitor to the great beyond.

"Got it," Teag said

I reached into the pocket of Teag's jacket, and my hand closed over the plastic box with the button, and I fumbled with the latch to open it. The box gave way, and the button tumbled into my palm.

For that instant, the contact with the long-dead soldier was complete. Darkness washed over me, drawing the warmth from my blood. Anger and despair filled me, and my gut contracted with the pain of a rifle wound that was more than one hundred and fifty years in the past. Then another presence filled me, and the image of the bride grew brighter and brighter, becoming a light that flared and forced the shadow to retreat.

Now! The voice shouted in my mind. I dove across the floor, grabbing the coin with my right hand and clenching the button in my left. I skidded toward the wall and used my momentum to thrust both the coin and the button through the crack.

Maman Brigitte's light struck the shadow man, just as I forced the coin and the button into the darkness. I heard a scream, although I could not tell whether it came from the shadow or whether it was my own.

The darkness vanished, and I slumped to the ground, too spent to move. In my mind, I saw the image of the bride again, bending over the rift, sealing it with her veil. Teag grabbed my wrist, yanking me to my feet, and together we barreled down the stairs and out of the house. We reached the other side of the street and looked back, half expecting the house to disappear into a vortex or tumble to the ground. It did neither, although, for an instant, a light flared brilliantly from the attic window, then went dark.

"Want to bet no one sees a shadow at the window again?" Teag asked. I looked down. He was still holding that damned skull. He caught the direction of my glance and shrugged. "Poor guy is long overdue for a decent burial. Without the coin, it's just a skull. I have an old friend who works at the mortuary. I'm betting he can make sure old Jonah gets a proper burial."

Teag might have said more, but my head was swimming, and I swayed on my feet. He reached out to steady me as I passed out, but there was someone else as well. In my mind's eye, I saw the veiled bride standing over me. She bent down and touched a finger to my amulet, and the metal disk felt warm on my skin. As consciousness faded away, so did her image, but I had the feeling she approved.

I woke on the couch in my temporary apartment over the shop. Consciousness returned slowly, and with it, warmth. I felt a presence, safe, reassuring, and it carried a honeyed compulsion to rest. I opened my eyes, and found Sorren, looking down at me, concern clear in his features. He helped me sit up enough to sip some sweet tea, and then eased me back onto the pillows.

"Rest," Sorren said, and his voice felt like balm poured over a throbbing wound. "When you're feeling better, there's a new situation to discuss."

"Oh, goody," I murmured, but as I drifted off to sleep, I knew the truth, and so did Sorren. Trifles and Folly was far more than just another antiques store. It helped make the world a little safer, one haunted item at a time. I couldn't walk away from that, not when my gift could make a difference. Not for all the damned buttons in the world.

THE RESTLESS DEAD

"What do you make of it, Cassidy?"

I looked at the piece of metal that lay on the counter and frowned. "Off-hand, I'd say it looks like the balance wheel off an old Singer sewing machine, probably from the late 1800s," I replied. The old wheel was dirty and scratched, but on the whole, not in bad shape for something that might have been made that long ago. "Where did you find it?"

Blair Hunt had been leaning across the counter, intent on the old machine part. He stood up and sighed. "We found a bunch of stuff in the sinkhole that opened up behind the Palmetto View Plaza."

I let my hand hover above the old sewing machine part, but I did not touch it. Even at a distance, I could feel tragedy and betrayal, and knew its former owner had come to a bad end.

I'm Cassidy Kincaide, and I'm a psychometric—which means I can read the history of objects by touching them. I'm the most recent in a long line of my relatives to be the proprietor of Trifles and Folly, an antique and curio store in historic, haunted Charleston, SC. Most people think the store is a great place to pick up a one-of-a-kind vintage gift. Our real business is much darker. For over 350 years, nearly since Charleston was settled, this store has been part of a conspiracy to get dangerous magical objects off the market and out of the wrong hands. When we do our job right, people remain blissfully unaware of the danger that surrounds them. And when we screw up, lots of people die.

"In a sinkhole?" I mused. "That's odd." I examined the wheel more closely. It was steel, made with the kind of graceful design most things today lack. The outer rim was gleaming silver, and the spokes inside were black. Built to last. I'd have bet it came from a Model 15K, circa 1879, a real workhorse of a machine. Rumor had it travelers spotted the old machines still at work in remote areas of China and India. The body of the machine was heavy steel, painted black with gold embell-ishment, run by a foot pedal, so it didn't need electricity, sturdy enough to sew winter coats, delicate enough to make wedding dresses. Not much could break one, and they almost never wore out on their own.

"No idea how it got there," Blair said. "I'm with the architecture firm trying to update the plaza's look, get it back on its feet again. The sinkhole opened up out of nowhere on Friday, swallowed a large part of the loading dock area. We were lucky no one fell in." Blair ran a hand back through his red hair. From the side, he looked like an older version of Britain's Prince Harry. Normally, he had the prince's jovial manner, too. Today, he looked like he hadn't slept well.

"Problems on the site?" I asked. "I mean, other than the sinkhole?"

Blair shrugged like he didn't want to talk about it. "That plaza has been down on its luck for a while. It's been standing empty now for several years. Turning that around was already going to be a major challenge without something like this. Now we've got to stop work until the engineers can make sure there's no structural damage." He shook his head. "Some days, I think it might not be a bad idea if the earth did open up and swallow the whole damn place."

I knew where Palmetto View Plaza was. It had been new back in the 1970s, and then lost out to bigger, better, fancier retail centers as the years went by. Charleston is lucky to have a vibrant downtown shopping district, but many of those shops are for tourists. For necessities like everyday clothing and shoes, residents headed for the nearby malls. Palmetto View was a relic of a bygone era, and I figured Blair had his work cut out for him.

"If you find the rest of the sewing machine, I'd love to take a look at it," I said. Something about the piece that lay in front of me made me terribly sad, and I wanted to know its story. I didn't hold out much hope that even a vintage Singer machine found in a sinkhole would be in working order, but stranger things had happened.

"Sure," Blair replied. "I've given the guys orders that anything antique-y they find needs to be boxed up to come over here for appraisal. But I still don't know what stuff like this is doing in a hole in the ground."

"When you figure it out, let me know," I said. "You've got me curious." Blair agreed to keep me in the loop, and the bell over the door jangled as he headed out.

Teag Logan, my assistant store manager, best friend, and occasional bodyguard, sauntered over. "For all your curiosity, I notice you haven't touched it," he observed, raising an eyebrow. Teag knows about my psychic gift, and he's got some gifts of his own. He's a Weaver, able to weave magic into the warp and woof of fabric, and able to weave data streams together to find information. It makes him an unbeatable researcher and an unstoppable hacker.

It was the middle of a cloudy autumn afternoon, the day before Halloween. The main tourist season was over, and since clouds threatened rain, walk-in traffic had been sparse. I left Maggie, our part-time assistant in charge of watching the door. Teag picked up the hand wheel, and we headed to the break room in the back.

"I still can't figure out why a sewing machine piece would be in a sinkhole," I said. Teag put the steel wheel on the table and poured me a glass of ice-cold sweet tea. The tea was just the way we like it in Charleston, strong as love and sweet as passion. We both knew the tea was there to revive me in case the impressions I read from the wheel were overpowering.

Teag shrugged. "Maybe it was the basement of an old house that got forgotten and built over top of," he said. "Maybe they unearthed an old garbage pit."

I shook my head. "Nobody just threw out one of those Model 15s," I said. "Folks back then made use of something until it fell apart, and then figured out how to use the pieces."

"Touch it and see," Teag prompted. We both knew I was stalling. My visions could be intense, depending on the emotions connected to a particular antique. Most people don't realize that the strong emotions of their lives are recorded in the objects around them. Not every emotion or every old piece, but the resonance is especially strong either in items used every day or things associated with a major life event. When the circumstances are good, the piece gives a happy, calm reading. But when the circumstances were bad—well, like the rhyme about the little girl with the little curl, it can be very, very bad.

I drew in a deep breath. One hand went to my agate necklace, which is supposed to have protective properties. So many of the readings I had done on objects with an upsetting past had ended with me flat on my butt or passed out cold that Teag and I had a routine. I had the sweet tea near to revive me. I was sitting down, so there wasn't far to fall, and Teag was there to catch me. It was as good as it was going to get.

I laid my hand on the cold, dirty steel. Memories flooded my senses—and none of the memories were my own. *Green rolling hills, and the crash of the sea on a rocky coast. The stuffy, cramped confines of a ship packed full of hard-scrabble people in Victorian-era clothing. Fear, Loneliness. Courage. Doubt. Resolve. I saw hands—my hands— working the sewing machine with skill. Whatever else happened, whatever hardships came my way, fabric, needle, and thread made me feel safe, confident.*

The scene wavered and changed. I heard a rhythmic click-clack, like a train on the tracks only quieter. I saw the sleek, black and gold body of a Singer Model 15, saw the needle move up and down in a blur, felt the steady pressure of my foot against the treadle. Once again, fabric slid beneath my hands. The rhythm of the needle was comforting as my mother's heartbeat in this strange and unforgiving place. Outside the dimly lit workroom, the world was beyond my control. Here, I was the master. And soon, I would be free...

"Come back, Cassidy." Teag's voice coaxed me back to the present day, and he pushed the cold glass of ice tea into my hand. As visions went, that wasn't bad. I hadn't passed out or thrown up. But the sense of loneliness and longing, of fear and purpose, remained.

"I saw a woman using the sewing machine," I recounted when I had recovered. "That machine wasn't just her livelihood—it was her life. She was afraid of everything, but there was something else—a big dream—and she was determined to make it happen." I shook my head.

"I want to find out who she was, Teag," I said. "She would never have let someone put her sewing machine in a hole. She would have died first. It was her ticket to… something else, something bigger. Freedom."

Teag crossed his arms over his chest and leaned back against the table. "Let me see what I can find," he said. I knew he meant the Internet. Teag can hack any database—even the government and the sites no one is supposed to know are out there. He knows his way around the Dark Web, the hidden websites where a lot of unsavory activity goes on, but he's also right at home on the Darke Web, the ensorcelled-encryption sites used by the supernatural, immortal and magical communities. If it's out there, no matter who's trying to hide it, Teag will find it, given enough time.

"Maybe we ought to put in a call to Sorren," Teag said.

Sorren is Trifles and Folly's other secret. He's my boss, a nearly six hundred-year-old vampire, who's been the business partner for every one of my relatives who owned the store for the last three hundred and fifty years. Sorren is part of a hidden Alliance of mortals and immortals who try to keep those malicious magical items from hurting anyone. He traveled a lot on Alliance business, but he was due back to Charleston any day now.

"I'll leave him a message, and send an email just for good measure." Yes, my vampire boss uses modern technology. Sorren says that vampires who don't adapt don't live long. He's made it this far, and I suspect he'll be around for a quite a while to come. "No telling when we'll hear back from him though."

Even without Sorren, I had my own sources. "Since the store isn't busy, I think I'll head over to the Historical Archive," I said. "It's been a while since I've paid a call on Mrs. Morrissey."

Mrs. Benjamin Taylor Morrissey was a true Charleston blue-blood and the director of the Historical Archive. She was a real history buff as well as a patron of many Charleston museums and arts institutions, and it probably didn't hurt that the Archive occupied one of her ancestor's former homes. She was one of my go-to people when I needed to dig up information about old objects gone bad.

I brought Mrs. Morrissey a latte, which I know she loves. Maybe that's why I got such a big smile when I walked into her office, but I prefer to think she just likes me. She knew my Uncle Evanston, who willed Trifles and Folly to me, and I sometimes wonder if she has her suspicions about what we really do.

"Cassidy! How nice to see you!" Mrs. Morrissey is in her seventies, with the kind of runway-model slender figure St. Johns suits were made for. She didn't believe in things like Botox or face-lifts, so she looked her age in the nicest of ways. Understated jewelry—all of it real, and expensive—completed the outfit.

"And you brought a latte," she said with a grin. She gave me a broad wink. "Does this mean you're doing some detective work about one of your new pieces at the store?"

If Mrs. Morrissey wanted to believe that we were more P.I. than paranormal that was okay with me. "You got it in one," I said, chuckling. "But it's really more a question about a part of town, instead of an acquisition."

Mrs. Morrissey waved me toward one of the two lovely Queen Anne-style chairs that sat facing the room's old fireplace. I suspected this was where Mrs. Morrissey chatted up prospective patrons for the Archive.

"Ask away!" she invited, sipping her latte.

"What can you tell me about the area over by the old Palmetto View Plaza?"

Mrs. Morrissey thought for a moment, then frowned. "What time period?"

"Doesn't matter. The item's owner found it in the sinkhole that opened up behind that empty big box store."

Mrs. Morrissey motioned for me to follow her into the next room, where several computers were set up for browsing the Archive's collection. She sat down at one of the stations, and her fingers flew across the keys as she searched for what she was looking for in pages of old documents that had been imaged.

"Here," she said, pointing at the screen. I saw a photo of the plaza in better days before its tenants had deserted it. "Is this the place?"

I nodded. "That's it."

Mrs. Morrissey called up several old newspaper clippings and scanned down through them until she found just what she wanted. "That area's had more than its share of bad luck," she said finally. "The plaza was quite the place when it first opened, but one thing after another went wrong. Electrical fires, burst water pipes, a couple of muggings in the parking lot—they just couldn't seem to get a break."

That kind of bad luck didn't usually happen by accident. Often, some kind of unresolved supernatural power created havoc on that scale, and when the ill-fortune lasted for decades, I started wondering about curses.

"What about before the plaza was built?" I asked. "Do you have any records about what used to be on that location?"

Again, Mrs. Morrissey played the computer keyboard like a concert pianist, coaxing details from the Archive's database. More old newspaper clippings appeared on screen, along with grainy photos from the past. "As I recall, Palmetto View Plaza was an attempt by some of the city's developers to reclaim that area from decline and turn some of the real estate values around," she said, tapping a pencil against the desktop as she thought.

"Lots of areas have their ups and downs," she said, "but that area never really took off. Back in the 1700s, there were taverns and brothels and barracks for soldiers." She scrolled down through articles too quickly for me to read them. "In the 1800s, the brothels were there, along with cheap rooming houses and more taverns. Later on, there were piecework shops and cotton mills—deplorable conditions—until it all washed away in the Hurricane of 1885."

"Piecework shops?" I questioned. "You mean, places with seamstresses?"

Mrs. Morrissey nodded. "Nowadays they call it 'vertical integration.' Some of the big cotton farmers also owned the mills that turned the cotton into thread and the thread into cloth. Then a few enterprising folks went a step further and brought over hundreds of indentured servants from Ireland and England to use the new-fangled sewing machines and turn out off-the-rack clothing working people could afford," she said.

Interesting, considering that I had a piece of one of those antique sewing machines back at the shop. "What happened in the Hurricane of 1885?" I asked.

This time, Mrs. Morrissey called up old photographs. Charleston is near the coast, so it's been slammed by its share of hurricanes and storms. People still talk about what happened when Hurricane Hugo came to town. New tragedies happen, and old ones slip out of memory. As I looked over Mrs. Morrissey's shoulder at the images of flattened homes and buildings, I got a chill down the back of my neck.

"The high winds pushed the flood waters pretty far into the city," Mrs. Morrissey said. "All the way to the area around where Palmetto View stands now. The land rose a little there, and the flood tide carried all the debris to that part of town, and then dumped them as the water receded."

"What did they do about it?" I asked, my skin tingling with the certainty that I was onto something.

Mrs. Morrissey shook her head. "Not much they could do about it, with how bad the damage was everywhere. Most of the folks in that neighborhood were too poor to rebuild, and a lot of them died in the flooding or just left and didn't come back. From what I've read, the city just covered up the debris with dirt and built over them."

"So when the sinkhole opened behind the plaza, it might have exposed some of that debris, if it went deep enough?"

Mrs. Morrissey nodded. "I guess that's possible. Assuming anything was left—it's been more than one hundred years."

I acted on a hunch, although I wasn't entirely sure why. "Do you know if there are any lists of the people who died in that hurricane?"

"Probably—although they're likely to be incomplete," she replied. "There are always folks who don't get counted when things like that happen—transients, homeless people, you know what I mean."

Indentured servants, I mentally added to the list, resolved to find out more. "I realize that," I said. "But if you can find a list—if it's not too much trouble—I think it might help with provenance for the piece."

Fifteen minutes later, I left with an invitation to the Archive's next gala and a print-out of the known dead from the Hurricane of 1885.

THE SHOP WAS BUSIER than I would have expected for an autumn after-noon when I got back, so I didn't get a chance to talk with Teag until we closed up. "Blair dropped off another piece of a sewing machine," he said, pushing a lock of dark hair out of his eyes. "If you want to take a look at it, I've got a fresh pitcher of iced tea in the break room."

I mock-glared at him. "Very funny." Unfortunately, Teag was right. The iced tea helped me recover from strong readings, and I had the feeling that the sinkhole behind Palmetto View Plaza was a supernat-ural hotspot. But I couldn't shake the feeling that there was more to it than that. I wagered that the "debris" Mrs. Morrissey said were jumbled up and built on top of probably included bodies of flood victims that were never found. If so, that kind of improper burial and restless dead might account for some of the problems the plaza and the surrounding area had experienced over the years. But intuition was telling me to look deeper, although I had the suspicion that I wouldn't like what I found if I did.

"Before we get to that," I said, stalling, "let me fill you in on what I found out at the Archive." Teag listened as we finished putting things in the front of the store away for the night, and then followed me to the break room.

"I think you're onto something," Teag said, pouring a glass of iced tea for each of us. "I talked to Ryan Alexander—the urban explorer guy you met a while back?"

I nodded, remembering. Teag and I had gone out with Ryan's team when we were trying to stop a dangerous ghost, and just for fun a few times since then. Urban explorers like to go through old buildings, abandoned factories and institutions, even old storm drains and forgotten subway tunnels, for the thrill of finding the ruins civilization leaves behind. Teag, Sorren, and I often found ourselves poking around the same kind of places for entirely different purposes. That's why Teag and I figured that going along with the UrbExers was good exercise, and we might get a look at odd places that could come in handy later on. "What does he have to do with this?" I asked, taking a sip of my tea.

"That plaza has been abandoned for a while now," Teag said. "I figured if anyone had been inside lately—anyone who would talk to me—it would be Ryan's folks. And I was right."

"And?" I reached for a couple of cookies, too.

"Ryan said they did go poking around there about six months ago, and got into the big box store on the end. He said that they cut the exploration short because something didn't feel right."

"Interesting," I said with a mouthful of Oreos.

"Interesting enough that Ryan got in touch with his friends at the Southern Paranormal Observation and Outreach Klub—that's 'club' with a 'k,'" he replied.

I rolled my eyes. "Seriously? They go by SPOOK?"

Teag chuckled and nodded. "Yeah. But according to Ryan, they know their stuff, at least the core members do. That's why we're meeting him for pizza in an hour." He reached for a lumpy parcel wrapped in cloth that was in the center of the table and slid it toward me. "So you'd probably better see what you make of this, so you can get your second wind before we connect with the SPOOK guy."

I nodded and took a deep breath, preparing myself. Teag

unwrapped the bundle, and I saw the battered body of an antique Singer sewing machine. Time and exposure to the elements had badly scratched the black and gold paint. All of the smaller pieces were missing. But considering that the machine had probably been at the bottom of those flood debris for a very long time, it wasn't in bad shape.

I rested my hand on its cold, smooth main arm. *Time shifted. I saw what the last owner of the sewing machine had seen, rows of tables, all outfitted with similar machines, in a large, stifling room. Women sat at the machines, eyes downcast on their work, guiding fabric beneath the click-clack of the needles and bobbins, feet pumping the treadles in steady rhythm. They were dressed in neat but plain clothing like household staff in a manor or hotel. All of the women looked very young, teens and twenties, and most had a gaunt, underfed appearance.*

"Clara—watch that hem, it's not straight! Mary, adjust the bobbin. Your thread is puckering. Bess, pick up the pace, girl. You haven't finished anything all day." A stern-looking, older woman walked up and down the rows. She stopped now and then to chide the workers. No one looked up at her, and I could feel myself tense with fear as she walked by.

High overhead, a few windows were cranked open, not enough to combat the heat. One of the other seamstresses collapsed at her machine, slipping bonelessly out of her chair. Two of her co-workers stood to go to her aid.

"Leave her!" the matron snapped. "She'll wake up. Stay at your machines." The others left the girl where she lay, glowering at the matron, who brought the girl a glass of water and helped her back to her seat.

Outside, the wind had picked up. Now and again, the young women dared to glance up from their work toward the small windows up above. The sky was gunmetal gray, and gusts of wind rattled the doors. "Keep your eyes on your seams!" the matron said, but I could hear an edge of nervousness in her voice. "Storm'll likely be over by the time the workday's done."

I heard the distant sound of church bells ringing the hour. Another blast of wind shrieked as it tore past the building's roof, and one of the other girls cried out in alarm. Several of the women bowed their heads, and I heard voices whispering the Hail Mary with a distinct Irish accent. Some of the others quickly crossed themselves without slowing their machines.

Rain began to fall, loud on the tin roof. It grew louder, hammering like a blacksmith, as the wind slammed against the building's brick walls, rattling the panes of glass high above. Inside, the temperature fell as cold wind blasted through the open windows overhead. The vision blurred, and time passed. When my sight cleared again, the rain lashed the building so hard it had broken out some of the panes of glass in the windows near the roofline, and water was running down the walls in rivulets.

I pricked my finger on a pin and drew a bead of blood. "Emily! Be careful. Don't stain the fabric, or it comes out of your wages!" the matron warned me. I thought her voice was sharper than usual, and I wondered if she was afraid, too.

The sky outside was dark, and it was too early in the day for the gas lamps to be lit. I blinked, trying to see the stitches in the dim light. My hands were shaking, and my heart skipped a beat every time the wind battered the building. But I knew better than to ask if we could go home. A full day's work for a day's wages; that was the contract. I listened to the wind howl and shivered. Truth be told, the brick-walled factory was sturdier built than the ramshackle rooming house where we all stayed.

Outside, there was a crash, booming like cannon fire. I jumped, and my fabric veered crazily, but I wasn't the only one. Another crash, and then another echoed nearby. The matron shouted for order, but it was too late for that. The sewing machines stopped their clicking, but the sounds of the storm filled the large room.

"Get back to work! It's just rain," the matron ordered, but she didn't sound certain.

Just then, a sheet of metal from the roof tore loose with the screaming sound of ripping steel. Water poured into the center of the room, soaking us and our machines. The wind snatched at the remaining roof panels, and the huge pieces of metal wobbled and groaned.

Work was forgotten as we ran screaming toward the far end of the building, and the matron ran with us. The sky was dumping water down so fast that the rain fell like a waterfall. We ran toward the doors, pulling and pushing, but chains on the outside held them fast.

"The key! Please open it! Use the key!" We shouted, but the matron shook her head, and I read our doom in her face.

"I don't have a key, girls. We'll have to make the best of it."

The rear wall had begun to bow, and then as we watched in horror, the bricks gave way and tumbled to the ground, bringing the sagging roof down with it. We screamed, but the wind and rain hid the sound, and the rising water weighed down our heavy dresses until it could take our breath. I flailed, but I never had learned how to swim…

"Cassidy! Cassidy! Come back." Teag urged. He was watching me with concern as I came back to myself, shaking my head as the terrified screams of the drowning women faded in my memory.

I lifted my head to meet his gaze. "They drowned," I said quietly. "They were locked in, and a hurricane destroyed the building. Indentured servants. No one cared. Her name was Emily."

Teag pushed the sweet iced tea toward me, and I sipped it to recover my strength, but I grieved for those long-ago lost women. Locking workers into factories was a common practice until a devastating fire in the 1920s forced changes, almost forty years after the Hurricane of 1885 hit Charleston and killed Emily. My hands stopped shaking, but I knew I would grieve Emily's death for a long time.

Teag was already scanning down the list of the hurricane's victims. "Emily O'Connor. Indentured servant, age twenty-two. Lost, presumed dead," he said. "There are about fifteen girls, all with Irish surnames, all marked as indentured servants, near the same age," he added.

I shook my head. "There were double that many, at least," I said. "They never found them all, or didn't think it was important enough to update the records." I sighed. To the city's wealthy and powerful, poor immigrant seamstresses were nobodies, far from home and without family nearby to make a fuss. Whoever had owned the sweatshop probably just sent over for more and started again in a different building. I looked at the battered sewing machine. Whatever happened, I wanted to do right by Emily's memory.

"Let's go meet the SPOOK guy," I said, draining my iced tea. "Maybe dinner will make me feel better." I doubted it.

Charleston loves Halloween. We're not as over-the-top as New Orleans, or as understated as Savannah. Charleston knows how to put on a party with class, even if it's for All Hallow's Eve. Pumpkins and decorative pots full of golden mums adorned the more sedate entranceways, peeking from behind wrought iron gates. Door wreaths of colored leaves and rainbow-hued small gourds added a touch of seasonal zing to other homes and businesses. Jack-o-lanterns glowed from windows and porches. Folks from up North might still think it was warm, but for us, the nights had gotten downright chilly.

Still, I couldn't avoid a shiver that was more to do with fear than temperature as Teag and I headed for Jocko's Pizzeria, our favorite place. Something unsettling was in the air, a vibe that felt like discordant music to my magic. Even without touching anything, I felt uneasy, like a storm was brewing.

Two men were waiting for us when we arrived. One I recognized as Anthony Benton, a young lawyer who was Teag's long-time steady romantic partner. The other man I didn't know. Both Anthony and the stranger rose when we approached.

"Figured you wouldn't mind us getting a table since it gets crowded fast," Anthony said with a grin, greeting me with a hug and Teag with a quick peck on the cheek when he thought no one would notice.

"Cassidy, this is Kell Winston, founder of SPOOK," Teag said, introducing the newcomer.

Kell was as tall as Anthony, with blue eyes, light-brown hair and a tan that looked like he had been out on a sailboat all summer. Anthony was *GQ* to Teag's hoodie and jeans, and Kell's style was somewhere in the middle, not quite the up-and-coming-young-lawyer look that Anthony rocked, or the insouciant grad student look Teag pulled off.

Kell wore a tweed jacket in an updated cut over a black t-shirt and jeans over sneakers. Professional, but not stuffy.

"Hi, Cassidy," Kell said, as Teag joined Anthony on one side of the booth. "Nice to meet you." He slid across the booth seat to let me have the outside. "Anthony's said a lot of nice things about both of you."

I glanced from Anthony to Kell. "You know each other?"

Anthony grinned. "We went to University of South Carolina together. Pledged the same fraternity. I went to law school, and Kell went into TV production."

"Gadgets," Kell confessed. "It's my weakness. And it's a passion that crossed over from my day job to all the paranormal investigations we do at SPOOK." He slid two business cards over to me, one for SPOOK, and one from a local video production company.

"Let's order, then talk," Teag said. "I'm starving." My stomach growled, and I blamed it on the delicious aroma of the pizzas. Giacomo Rossi—Jocko—is a friend of ours, and he waved from his spot behind the counter as I looked up. Teag and I ate there so often Jocko knew what we wanted without us needing to order, but the server stopped by anyhow.

"I hear you're interested in the old Palmetto View Plaza," Kell said, cutting a glance my way.

"It keeps coming up," I replied. "Have you been out there?"

Kell sat back and took a sip of his Coke. "A couple of times."

"No activity?" I probed.

Kell shook his head. "No. Too much going on. We were just out there a couple of weeks ago, and the whole feel of the place had changed. Juiced up."

"How?" Teag asked, leaning across the table.

Kell paused as if searching for the right words. "Look, I know that most people think we're loony for going through old buildings looking for ghosts. Then again, Charleston promises the tourists more ghosts per square foot than just about any city in the US, so if believing in ghosts make you crazy, my team and I have a lot of company."

"We don't think you're crazy," I said, with what I hoped was an encouraging smile. "We just want to know what you've seen."

He gave me a look as if he doubted that, then let out a long breath and ran a hand back through his brown hair. "The first time we went was over a year ago. We walked around the outside, and then Ryan's folks got us into some of the buildings. We got some low-level EMF readings, nothing spectacular. It was enough to want to go back."

He sipped his Coke again as he considered what to say next. "The second time was about six months ago. This time, the readings were a lot higher, and we didn't just get spikes on the electro-magnetic frequency meter, we got recordings that sounded like garbled voices, and video of movement where there shouldn't have been anyone around."

"So we let a few months go by, and went back a couple of weeks ago. Ryan told me his group had some freaky experiences over there, and we wanted to see if things had gotten more intense." He let out a rueful chuckle. "Hey," he said. "Ghost hunters rush in where others fear to tread."

"And you got more than you bargained for?" I leaned forward, watching him as he spoke. I've always been leery of ghost chasers, since some of them are just in it for the thrills. In our business—our real business of dealing with dangerous magical objects—amateurs can get in the way. But I had the feeling that Kell was on the level.

Kell nodded. "The front of the property wasn't too bad, but the closer we got to the back, the more the instruments lit up with readings. Then we got hit with stones; only no one was around. The air got freezing cold, and we started to see shapes in the shadows that were moving toward us. That was freaky enough. But all of a sudden, it just seemed like some kind of power rose up and it didn't want us around." He shivered. "I've never felt something like that before, and I hope I never feel it again."

"You were close to the back, near where the sinkhole opened up?" Teag asked.

Kell nodded. "Our readings were off the charts, but we didn't get any photos, nothing that would prove what we saw." He shook his head. "All I've got to say is, I'm not in any hurry to go back there."

Jocko sent out our pizzas then, and for a while, nobody talked as we chowed down. Jocko serves up real New York pizza from a family recipe. I swear it's the best in town.

"When Teag told me about your interest in the Palmetto View property, I took a look at some of the filings about it," Anthony said when we were down to the last few bites. "That land has changed hands an unusual number of times over the years, always in unfortunate circumstances. Fire, bankruptcy, structural collapse—if I didn't know better, I'd think the place was cursed or something."

I winced, but I don't think Anthony saw it. Teag did, and he understood. The plaza was literally built atop a tragedy, and the restless dead might not have been able to actively haunt it throughout those years, but their presence would throw off the area's energy, make it vulnerable to bad things. The sinkhole—or something—had magnified that. Somebody was likely to get hurt.

"Thanks for looking into it," I said to Anthony. Then I turned back to Kell. "Is there anything else about the plaza that seemed off?" I asked. "Anything at all?"

Kell looked as if he were debating with himself over how much to say. Finally, he seemed to come to a decision. "I didn't realize it until just now, but every time we went out there, the same member of our team put in the request. Danny Thompson." He shook his head.

"Danny's an odd sort. Not very social. I've often wondered if our group is the only thing he belongs to. He's kind of awkward," Kell said, looking a little embarrassed. "I mean, we're all geeks, but the rest of us navigate the outside world pretty well—jobs, family, significant others. I have the feeling that Danny doesn't have anyone else."

"Why do you think he was so interested in the plaza?" I asked.

Kell sighed. "I don't know for sure. I asked, and he said something about having worked there, but I don't think he was telling me the truth. He's too young to have worked there. Ryan told me once that Danny tried to join his group and went out with them a couple of times, but all he was interested in was ghosts, so Ryan steered him over to us."

He drank the last of his Coke. "Danny's interest is—different— from the rest of us. A little on the obsessive side. I got the impression from some of the things he said that he was really into the occult—magic, that kind of thing. He used to talk about doing rituals to call up the spirits. That made everyone a little nervous. We're about scientifically documenting paranormal phenomena, not pretending to be wizards."

"Did Danny go with you the last time?" Teag asked.

Kell shook his head. "No. He told one of the guys he had to work. But then we saw his car a block away. I'm sure it was his. So I don't know what game he was playing. I'm not going to go looking for him. We're a pretty laid-back group, but Danny weirded us out."

"Did you get any other impressions of the ghosts over by the plaza?" I asked.

Kell fiddled with his napkin. "You're not going to believe me, but the second time we went out, we all heard someone humming a song. We didn't realize until we got back in the van that none of us had been doing the humming. But we all heard the same song. *The Wearing of the Green*. It's an old Irish tune."

Teag and I locked gazes, and I knew we were both thinking of Emily and her doomed friends. "Did you know that the plaza was built on top of wreckage from the Hurricane of 1885?" I asked Kell. "Wreckage that probably included more than a few bodies?"

Kell's eyes widened. "No. I'd never heard that. But it would make a lot of sense why the area seems so unlucky." He frowned. "Is there a reason the ghosts would have gotten more active? Like an anniversary of the storm?"

"No idea," I replied. "But it would be interesting to find out, wouldn't it?" Again, Teag and I looked at each other. Kell might think our interest was mere curiosity, but I had the feeling something had stirred up a supernatural hornet's nest, which made it our business to take care of.

Anthony had to go back to the office to finish up work on a legal case, so after we said good-night to Kell, Teag and I decided to swing by Danny Thompson's apartment and see what we could find. Teag got us the address, and we drove down a side street in a low-rent part of town. Danny lived in a walk-up flat in a run-down old home that had been converted to apartments. We rang the bell, but no one answered.

Sorren had taught us a few tricks about picking locks. Teag had the front door open in a few seconds, and we stood in the depressing entranceway. The paint was faded and stained. The floor sagged, and one dim bulb illuminated the corridor. Teag glanced at the mailboxes and nodded. Room 21 was at the top of the stairs.

I tried to come up with a good excuse in case someone demanded to know why we were there as we made our way up the creaking steps toward the upstairs hallway. No one seemed to notice or care. I smelled pizza and beer and pot in the air as I climbed the steps. Maybe that accounted for Thompson's neighbors' lack of interest. Or maybe they just didn't get involved.

We rapped at his door, and waited. No one came, and nothing stirred. Teag knocked again, a little louder this time, but when there was no answer again, he pulled on one of the linen gloves we use in the shop to handle old paper, worked the lock and let the door swing open.

"Not much of a housekeeper, is he?" Teag muttered as we stepped into a filthy apartment. From the smell, no one had taken the garbage out in quite a while, and without air conditioning, it smelled like a dumpster in the sun. Clothes were strewn across furniture and floors. Dirty dishes wallowed in fetid dishwater in the sink. We moved through the small apartment carefully, trying not to touch anything.

"There," I said, pointing. Teag followed my gesture. Next to Thompson's unmade bed was a stack of books on magic and spiritualism. He had enough candles and cheesy pseudo-magical paraphernalia to have kept an online spellcraft store in business for a year. I knew from experience most of the items were fake.

"Looks like Kell was right about Danny's interest in magic," Teag said.

I turned to look around the rest of the room. No family pictures, nothing that suggested Thompson had much of a life beyond his work. Even without touching his possessions, the room filled me with a deep, penetrating despair, a hopelessness that verged on madness. And beneath the gloom, I sensed a desire for vengeance.

"Look," I said in a whisper as I turned back toward the door. Thumbtacked to the wall were grainy pictures of at least twenty people who looked like they had been photographed by a paparazzi. A large, black "X" had been drawn through each person's image. It wasn't hard to get the point. Danny had a hit list. And the longer we stayed in his apartment, the more of the vibe I picked up.

"He's angry, and he's unstable," I said. "He's looking for a way to get back at people who've hurt him."

"We need to get out of here," Teag said.

"Wait." I wanted to get a better idea of who Danny Thompson was. Not the fake magic items, but the man who wanted vengeance so bad he could taste it. Just the contact I had with the floor, stepping around Danny's clothing, gave me a filtered reading. I saw a selfie Danny had snapped and printed out. He was a gawky, stoop-shouldered young man in his early twenties wearing a t-shirt and Levis. The graphic on the t-shirt was a hand with the middle finger up. Danny had a cocky grin, and he looked like a loser who thought he was on a lucky streak. That worried me.

Then I saw a cheap plastic obelisk with a stick-on metallic disk that said "Best Effort." It was the kind of trophy someone won if the organizers were determined to give something to everyone, no matter how pathetic the level of participation. "Grab the obelisk," I said, unwilling to touch it myself until we could get somewhere safe. Teag grabbed it and stuck it into the front pouch of his hoodie.

We pulled the door shut after us and made our way down the stairs without being accosted. I didn't know whether to be grateful that we didn't get caught, or appalled at the lack of security. I settled for grateful. Since neither of us had anything better to do, I invited Teag back to my place to see if we could figure out what was going on. On our way, I got a text on my cell phone from Sorren.

"He says he has information for us, and that he'll be over in a little while. Oh, and he's bringing friends." Sorren's messages and emails were usually cryptic for security reasons, so I wasn't surprised that he left me wondering.

"Friends?"

I shrugged. "With Sorren? Who knows? Could be a Voudon mambo or a Hoodoo high priest—or something else entirely. I'm past the point of guessing," I said. We picked up my Mini Cooper at the store and Teag followed me back to my place.

I live in a Charleston single house, which has the narrow end of the home facing the street and the wide part of the house facing a fenced-in private garden. In fact, the "front door" to the street doesn't lead into the main house; it leads onto a porch—what Charlestonians call a "piazza." The autumn air was pleasant, and I could smell wood smoke from a neighbor's fire pit wafting on the cool breeze. A huge moon hung in the sky. It was definitely Halloween season.

Baxter, my little Maltese dog, barked and yipped as I unlocked the door. He ran in circles around our feet, then danced on his hind legs to greet us, refusing to settle down until he had been duly fussed over by both Teag and me. Teag had brought the pieces of the sewing machine with him, and he headed toward the dining room while I made sure Baxter got his dinner and put the leftover pizza in the fridge.

"Let's see what I can get from Danny Thompson's sorta-trophy," I said. Teag took out the hard plastic obelisk and set it on my dining room table. I noticed that it was from a couple of years ago. Taking a deep breath, I got myself settled and then reached out to touch the award.

This time, I saw the scene as an observer, not through Danny's eyes. A roomful of people in restaurant uniforms were seated in front of a stage as a sales manager gave his rah-rah pitch and started handing out prizes. Members of the audience came up to the stage to accept awards for customer service, attendance, speed, and accuracy. More and more of the audience stepped up to take their awards, and pretty soon it looked as if everyone except Danny would go home with a trophy.

"Danny Thompson." The sales manager's voice faltered, just slightly, and he seemed to struggle to keep a straight face. The audience murmured as Danny lumbered to the stage. "Best effort," the sales manager said, barely keeping the laughter out of his voice. The audience tittered, but no one laughed out loud. They didn't have to.

Danny slumped back to his seat clutching the award, sinking as deeply as he could, looking as if he wished he could disappear. But the scowl on his face said something more. In that moment, if he had the means, Danny Thompson wished he could make all of his coworkers pay for his humiliation.

"Snap out of it, Cassidy!" Teag was patting my hand, pressing a cool cloth against my cheek. I came back to myself groggily, and it took a whole glass of sweet tea before I could relate what I had seen.

"So Danny's a guy on the verge of snapping," Teag summarized.

I nodded. "Big time. I think that's what he wants the magic for."

"Then we've got real problems," Teag said. "Mind if I borrow your computer?" Teag asked. "I want to see what else I can find out about Danny Thompson."

"Be my guest. I agree—I think he could be the link in all this," I replied, and Teag disappeared into my small office.

A knock at the door brought me back to the entranceway, where Sorren and two other people stood on my piazza. "Sorry for the short notice," Sorren said. He's tall and slender, with blond hair and light gray eyes the color of the sea before a storm. He was turned back in the 1400s, but he'll look like he's in his twenties forever. Tonight, he had a dark hoodie over a black t-shirt and jeans. His hair was cut in a trendy style, playing up his European features. Before he was turned, Sorren was the best jewel thief in Antwerp. Now, he works through intermediaries to acquire and neutralize weapons of magical destruction.

"Hi Sorren, Caliel," I said, with a nod to the other man. Caliel was just a little shorter than Sorren, with short-cropped dark hair, skin the color of night and a broad, gleaming smile. He was dressed in white linen, with several colored strings tied at his left wrist, and a couple of *veve* charms on leather straps around his neck. Caliel was a Voudon *hougan*, and the descendant of a very powerful mambo. We had worked together before.

"Greetings to you!" Caliel said with a broad smile, his accent thick with a Caribbean lilt. "It's good to see you, but even better if it could be under different circumstances."

Baxter heard the newcomers at the door and came running full-speed, barking his fool head off. Sorren bent down and met his gaze, and Baxter dropped to a seat and went silent, his tongue hanging out of his mouth, looking at Sorren with a goofy glazed expression.

"If you're going to keep glamoring my dog, I wish you'd teach me how to do it," I said in mock exasperation. Sorren could use his vampire mojo to become Baxter's best friend and bring the yipping to a halt. It was a handy trick.

"Cassidy, I'd like you to meet Alicia Peters," Sorren said, introducing the third member of their party, a woman I did not recognize. Alicia looked to be in her late thirties, plump and unassuming but dressed in a pulled-together casual style that said she was comfortable with herself. She had a pleasant face and light blue eyes, with black hair that fell in waves to her shoulders. I met her gaze and felt a frisson of magic. I wasn't sure what Alicia's gift was, but I knew that she had power.

"Very pleased to meet you," Alicia said in a quiet voice with a strong Lowcountry accent.

"Come on in and sit down," I said, standing aside. After I had put out some chips and offered everyone something to drink, I sat down in an armchair in the living room with the others.

"You got my message?"

Sorren nodded. "And I may know what's behind the problem, although I sincerely pray that I'm wrong." I could hear a hint of a Dutch accent in Sorren's voice, something that only comes out under stress. That worried me.

"Did you bring the pieces of the machine with you?" he asked. I gestured toward the dining room table.

"Alicia is a very powerful medium," Sorren said. "My hope is that she can connect to the former owner of that machine in the spirit world and provide information on why the spirits have grown restless."

"You've been involved with Trifles and Folly since the 1670s," I said. "So you were around for the Hurricane of 1885. I think it has something to do with the problem at Palmetto View."

"I'm almost certain of it," Sorren said. Most people couldn't meet a vampire's gaze without being glamored like Baxter, but maybe it was my gift, or perhaps the long family affiliation, but it didn't affect me. I looked him in the eyes and saw concern. And when a six-hundred-year-old vampire is worried, it's time for mortals to be very afraid.

"Is Teag here?" Sorren asked.

"He's in my office, using the computer, following up on a lead," I replied.

"Then let's start without him," Sorren said. We moved over to the dining room table and seated ourselves close to the broken sewing machine.

Alicia settled herself into her chair and took a few deep breaths. Then she pulled the sewing machine pieces toward her, laid her hands on them, and closed her eyes. For a few moments, nothing happened, and we all stared at Alicia. Gradually, I noticed how rapidly Alicia's eyes were moving beneath her closed eyelids, and realized that her breathing had grown shallower. A subtle change came over Alicia's features, making her look less like herself somehow.

"I couldn't swim," she murmured. "Never learned. Made it across on the ship, didn't like the sea. Hate the water." All traces of Alicia's Southern accent were gone, replaced by a thick Irish brogue.

"Emily?" I asked quietly. Sorren frowned, but followed my lead and gave me an encouraging nod. Caliel's eyes were closed, and although he was silent, his lips were moving. In the distance, I heard a dog bark. I caught a faint whiff of pipe tobacco. That told me Caliel was calling to Papa Legba, the Voudon Loa who opens the passage between our realm and the other side.

"I'm Emily," the voice replied.

"Do you remember your sewing machine, at work?" I tried to make my voice as gentle as possible.

"Oh, what a beauty!" Emily said. "An' I was good with it, too. Fast. Careful. Nearly had my contract paid back early, just a few more months—" So that was the "freedom" I had sensed. Emily was going to buy back her indenture contract, become a free woman, maybe even become an independent seamstress. She had been so close to her goal when she died. Yet another reason her spirit didn't rest easy.

"What happened, when the rains came?"

Alicia didn't answer right away, "Couldn't get out. Couldn't swim. Water kept coming. So high, so cold. The walls fell, and the water washed us away."

"That was a long time ago, Emily. You slept. What woke you up?"

"The man," Emily replied, and I heard both fear and dislike in her tone.

"What man?"

"The gray man. He woke us. Then he left us alone for a long time. Now he came back. I don't like him. Don't want to do what he says."

"What does he say?" I pressed, sure we were close to the key.

Emily screamed. Alicia's face contorted in agony, and she grasped her temples with both hands, then fell forward, suddenly limp. Sorren caught her before her face smacked into the table. I held out her glass of sweet tea, and Alicia roused enough to take a few sips.

"Something cut her off." The voice and manner was Alicia's own. "I felt it. Someone didn't want Emily to talk to us." Alicia managed a wan smile and Sorren removed his supporting arm from around her shoulders.

"Did you sense anything else, in the instant the other presence was near?" Sorren asked. His tone was urgent, and my worry-meter ticked up a few more notches.

"Power," Alicia said, thinking back. "It felt unclean. Rage. I had the feeling that whoever was using the power might lose control at any second."

Just then, Teag burst into the room. "Y'all need to hear this," he said. "From what I can find on the Darke Web, Danny Thompson is a necromancer wanna-be."

We moved back into the living room, and Alicia lay down on the couch, while Sorren, Caliel, and I drew up armchairs. Teag perched on the arm of the couch. "Danny Thompson is the stereotype of the kind of guy who shows up to work one day with a sawed-off shotgun and wipes out everyone in the office," he said.

"Twenties, no close friends, barely got out of high school. Worked a bunch of low-paying jobs—food service, janitor, night clerk at convenience stores—none of them for very long. All the company databases I could hack said he had 'attitude problems.' What I saw on his Facebook page told me has a chip on his shoulder bigger than the Empire State Building."

"Where does the necromancy come in?" Caliel asked. I noticed that Sorren was being very quiet.

"Danny has been hanging around some bad places in the Darke Web," Teag replied. "Asking questions, trying to meet people. All of it about raising the spirits of the dead." He flicked a stray lock of hair out of his eyes. "Lots of people are posers, but Danny knew enough to ask the kind of questions that got people talking on the Darke Web, where the real supernaturals hang out."

"Why did he want to raise the dead?" Caliel asked, his dark eyes growing worried. "That's bad stuff. He lose someone?"

Teag shook his head. "I don't think Danny's looking for a family reunion. The people on the Darke Web thought he knew enough to be dangerous, so they refused to talk to him. I was able to hack into his computer—lousy firewall." He looked like he was going to be sick.

"What?" I asked.

"He had pictures from Columbine. From Virginia Tech. From Aurora. All the rampages of the last couple of decades, he had the photos, like a shrine to the shooters. And he had an enemies list that matched the photos we saw. Best I could figure it was his bosses at all the places he'd worked." He paused, pushing his hair back from his face with both hands in a gesture of desperation. "He's planning to make them pay, kill dozens of people—and he's going to use the restless dead to do it."

We sat in stunned silence for a moment. Then Sorren spoke. "This is my fault."

I stared at him. "How do you figure?"

Sorren looked worn. "The second Hurricane of 1885 wasn't an entirely natural phenomenon. That *was* a bad year for storms. There was a lot of dark energy loose, and if it doesn't get tapped and used, it builds into storms, earthquakes, that sort of thing. Wild energy like that attracts madmen. Jacob Hitchens was a freed slave who came from the sugar plantations in Haiti. He was a *bokor*—not a true Voodoo *hougan* or mambo, but someone who would cast curses for pay."

Anger sparked in Caliel's eyes. "I've heard of Jacob Hitchens. We disavow him. He's bad seed. Not real Voudon."

Sorren nodded. "The Alliance knew Hitchens was trouble. We had managed to shut him out of artifacts he tried to get on other occasions. He fancied himself a necromancer, and word reached us he had made a zombie of his own in the old ways. I went to shut him down."

"But something went wrong," I murmured, and Sorren looked stricken.

"Hitchens was powerful," Sorren said. "I went up against him with some others from the Alliance. We thought we had destroyed him. Then, many years later, I heard rumors that Hitchens had stored some of his power in a talisman, and that he sent his soul into that talisman when he 'died' during the battle. No one knew one way or the other. I tried to learn more, but I hit dead ends."

"You think that somehow, Danny Thompson found Hitchens's talisman?" Caliel asked.

Sorren nodded. "And that either Thompson was able to take what was stored of Hitchens's power, or that Hitchens really did hide his soul there."

"And if Hitchens was a real necromancer, he might have been able to pour his soul into Danny Thompson, control him, guide him," Teag finished. "Shit."

"How do we stop him?" I asked. "If Teag's right, Danny is planning to go postal on everyone he had a grudge against. People are going to die."

"Gonna be Halloween tomorrow," Caliel said. "If he's going to do something with the spirits, likely to be then."

"Danny wanted the UrbEx people and SPOOK folks to go out to Palmetto View because he knew about the flood debris," Teag guessed. "He figured those unclaimed dead could boost his power." People like Emily, and the young women I had seen in my vision, who died because they took a chance on building a better life.

Sorren nodded. "I'm afraid you're right. And if so, we've got very little time to prepare."

"We can stop him, right?" I said. "I mean, you stopped Hitchens."

"I didn't do it alone," Sorren said. "I worked with the Alliance. So I believe we can beat Thompson. But we've got to hurry. He's likely to make his move tomorrow, on Halloween."

"This Thompson fellow means to do some killin'," Caliel said. "We're going to shut him down."

Normally, Halloween is one of my favorite holidays. I love the costumes and the parties for kids and grown-ups. Even before I knew that some of the things that go bump in the night are real, I loved the ghost stories and monster movies. Now that my job involves protecting people from dark magic and supernatural bad guys, I still like Halloween because it's make-believe. The real stuff is a lot scarier.

HALLOWEEN WAS GOING strong when we headed out. Kids were out Trick-or-Treating in the neighborhoods, and lots of houses had put up spooky decorations. Even the stores, restaurants, and bars we passed got into the act. It was just after eight. The real denizens of the dark wouldn't come out until midnight, when the veil is thin between the world of the living and the places of the dead, and magic is strongest. I'd bet money that Danny Thompson would be out late tonight.

Teag and I drove over to Palmetto View Plaza together. Caliel and Alicia came in a second car. Sorren said he would meet us there, and I figured he would scout the area. Even so, Teag circled the block looking for cops, vagrants, or loiterers who might cause problems. Maybe it was because people had better things to do, or perhaps it was the uncomfortable vibes the old plaza was giving off, but no one was around.

We pulled into Palmetto View Plaza's parking lot. It looked like a lot of 1970s strip malls: uninspired and ugly in a mass-produced way. A long time ago, each end of the strip had a big department store with specialty shops, restaurants, and dry cleaners sandwiched in between.

Now, the storefronts were boarded up, the asphalt in the parking lot was broken and wavy, and trash blew across the huge, empty lot like tumbleweeds. Only a couple of the parking lot overhead lights still worked, but they were down on the other end of the plaza. Here and there, weeds poked up through the holes in the asphalt. It looked like something straight out of a Hollywood back lot for a zombie movie, so heading out to stop a necromancer didn't seem too far off.

"Got everything?" Teag asked, and I checked my gear. I wore an agate necklace and a bracelet with small brass bells, all good for protection. Different types of magic or supernatural bad guys required different weapons or protections, and we were starting to collect quite a variety. I had a smooth chunk of obsidian and a piece of black tourmaline in my pocket, along with a pouch of salt, good for neutralizing a lot of bad magic. And just in case, I had a smooth glass *nazar*, a flat disk that looked like a blue eye inside a dark blue border. At the last minute, on a hunch, I wrapped a cloth around Danny Thompson's "Best Effort" award and took it with me.

Teag had an obsidian ring and his own salt and tourmaline. On a strap around his neck, he had a Philippine *agimat* charm, and a *hamsa* to ward off evil magic. His worn birch staff from his martial arts training was in the back. The staff was scarred from use, and the top was carved with protective runes, and several short bits of rope with macramé knots were tied to one end. Teag's Weaver magic let him store power in knots. He had a small backpack with him, and I knew he had brought some other magical weapons, just in case.

In the backseat, we had the pieces of Emily's old sewing machine in a sturdy tote bag.

We parked close to the empty big box store nearest the sinkhole. Odds were high that was where we'd find Danny Thompson if he really was going to try to raise the spirits of the hurricane's victims. Teag and I waited in the car until Caliel and Alicia pulled up a few moments later. Sorren walked out of the shadows just as they turned off the engine and cut their headlights. Overhead, the moon was nearly full. Good thing, or we wouldn't have been able to see at all.

"Ready?" Sorren asked. I glanced at Caliel, who was dressed in white. He had a backpack with him, and I guessed it had all the items he needed to summon the Loa and fend off a necromancer. He had a small hand drum, and a gourd rattle as well, tools of his calling as a *hougan*. Alicia wore a small silver crucifix and citrine earrings, but if she carried other protections, they were hidden. I noticed that tonight, Sorren also wore an iron disk with carvings I could not read.

"Is Danny Thompson here?" I asked.

Sorren shook his head. "There's no one around except us. Let's hurry." We followed him around to the side of the old department store. Sorren jimmied the lock like an expert, but then again, he was a jewel thief when he was mortal. The store was a public place, so he didn't need an invitation to enter. We slipped inside quickly and closed the door, leaving it unlocked in case we needed a quick exit.

You never realize just how big stores are until they're empty. The old big box store seemed to stretch on forever. Moonlight streamed down through skylights and the unboarded upper windows, making it possible to see at least part of the store. The merchandise was long gone, and so were the best fixtures, but dirty glass display cases and dozens of clothing racks stood where they had been abandoned. The tile floor was littered with old price tags, torn bits of paper, and a couple of creepy discarded mannequins. Overhead, faded "Clearance Sale" banners hung askew. The floor was dirty, and in the distance, I could hear water dripping from somewhere. The moonlight only reached part of the sales floor, leaving the walls deep in shadow.

We all knew the plan. Alicia and I found a place in the shadows halfway toward the back wall where we could have a pretty clear view of what was going on. I used the salt to make a circle just large enough for Alicia and me to stand inside, along with the old sewing machine. At the four directional points, I set out the chunk of onyx and the piece of tourmaline, the brass bell bracelet, and the *nazar* to strengthen the protective energies. Outside the circle, I laid the cloth-wrapped plastic obelisk, Danny Thompson's one award.

Alicia carefully removed Emily's sewing machine from the tote bag and set it in the center of the circle. Then we both stepped inside and waited. I didn't close the circle yet because we didn't want Danny Thompson to sense the magic.

Teag, Sorren, and Caliel moved cautiously toward the back of the store, alert for traps—supernatural or otherwise. I knew that Caliel would need to make some preparations if he meant to call the Loas, and I wondered how he would hide what he was doing from Thompson —or Hitchens if the old necromancer's spirit was present. The wind gusted, and the old building creaked. I wondered how strong the building was, or what kind of strain a magic battle might place on it. We were going to find out soon enough.

"Cassidy."

I let out a quiet yip of surprise as Sorren seemed to appear out of nowhere next to our salt circle. "Thompson's definitely been here— and it looks like he means to return. He's got all his ritual artifacts in place, right where the building overhangs the sinkhole. Now, all we've got to do is wait."

"Won't he notice we're here?" I asked in a hushed voice.

Caliel came up from the other side, and this time, I managed not to yelp. "I don't think so," he answered. "I've laid down some spells of misdirection, low level so he shouldn't notice the power or what we're hiding." He pulled a handful of dried bones from a pouch.

"Here. One for each of you. Gave one to Teag already. Black cat bones. An' no, I didn't kill any cats," he said before we could ask. "I found one already dead and took the bones a while ago, savin' them for something important. Keep the bone with you. Makes you hard to see. We'll be able to see each other, since we all have the bones, but Thompson—he won't see us unless he looks straight at us and knows we're there," Caliel said. I noticed that he also wore a gold coin with a sun seal on a strap around his neck, an amulet supposed to hide its wearer in plain sight.

"Now, we wait," Sorren said. "And stay silent. Caliel's charms will make you hard to notice, but if Thompson hears you or looks right at you, he'll know we're here."

We sat in the near-darkness, waiting for a long time. Overhead, the moon made its course, changing where its light filtered down through the grimy skylights. Water dripped and the wind outside caught at a loose piece of plywood over one of the broken windows. I feared there would be rats, but their absence was worse—it was a sign that dark magic was present. Somewhere in the distance, church bells rang eleven times.

Alicia and I sat inside the nearly-closed circle. I tried not to touch much, but the floor tiles themselves held the resonance of disappointment and failure. Alicia wasn't going to attempt to contact Emily until the time was right, but from the dreamy, half-awake look on her face, I wondered if the spirits were already contacting her. Now and then, I caught glimpses out of the corner of my eye, movement that was there and then gone.

The scrape of a door on concrete roused me. I wrapped my hand around the cat bone in my pocket, hoping Caliel's magic worked as promised.

I saw a shadowy figure enter and look around, then as if he were satisfied that the store was empty, the figure began to haul a large, squirming sack and a duffel bag. The person stood up, and immediately I looked away. I couldn't afford to accidentally make eye contact and break the veil of misdirection.

Whatever was in the bag was making a ruckus, and I figured it was a chicken to be sacrificed. Thompson shouldered his burdens and strode toward a place right up against the back wall and directly over where the sinkhole had opened to the depths below. As he busied himself with preparations, I laid a hand on Alicia's arm. It was time. We couldn't afford to let Thompson get too far along. I closed the salt circle and felt the magic activate.

Alicia touched the sewing machine first, and then I laid my hands on its cool, steel form, amplifying the memories and hopefully, Alicia's power. Alicia's head fell back and her eyes closed, but she made no noise. This time, I could manage Emily's powerful memories without being overwhelmed. I couldn't touch her spirit the way Alicia could, but Sorren thought my magic would help create an anchor—and a counterbalance to Thompson's dark magic.

"Who's there?" Thompson called out, straightening suddenly and turning to face the dark expanse of empty store. No one breathed. He stared into the darkness for a minute or two, then swore under his breath and went back to his work.

Thompson picked up the burlap bag with the chicken. It was clawing and fighting, squawking in panic. While Thompson's attention was on the chicken, I saw a blur of motion as Sorren came at the necromancer at full speed. Thompson dropped the chicken and turned with a snarl, raising one hand, palm out, and growling a word of power.

Sorren dodged to the side as a ball of fire flamed past, barely missing him despite his speed. Teag came at Thompson from behind, swinging his staff, pulling one of the knots free to increase his magic. In the background, I heard Caliel begin drumming and chanting, and heard the *skritch-skritch* of his gourd rattle as he called for his Loas to protect us.

Thompson was tall and faster than he looked. He wheeled and caught the staff with one hand, turning its momentum against Teag and throwing him free. I stared in disbelief. Teag was a champion in several martial arts forms. I knew how much power he could put into that staff. Thompson's hand and arm should have been broken to bits, but the necromancer looked no worse for the wear.

"Sorren! Have you come back for another fight?" Thompson's mouth was moving, but the voice didn't seem to belong to him. The voice sounded older, bitter, and far more dangerous than what I would have expected from a guy like Thompson.

"We beat you once, Hitchens. We can do it again." Sorren rose in the shadows and came at Thompson again. This time, I saw an iron sword in Sorren's right hand. Iron grounds magic, and it's anathema to many supernatural beings—and deadly for mortals, too, if enough of it lands on your head.

Thompson/Hitchens shrieked in anger, a cry borne of madness, and it echoed through the huge, empty store. He snatched something from inside his shirt and held up an amulet on a long strap, holding it out like a shield toward Sorren and planting his feet to stand his ground.

Normally, vampire strength and speed not only knocks a mortal across the room, but it breaks some bones doing it. Before Sorren could reach him, a sickly green light arced from the talisman, striking Sorren in the chest. Sorren staggered, fighting the magic, sword raised and ready to strike, moving forward as if against a strong tide. Thompson laughed, enjoying Sorren's struggle, and he pulled a long, thin knife from a sheath at his belt.

Caliel's chanting was louder now. His drumming and the *shoosh-shoosh* of the gourd had grown faster, and I thought I caught a faint whiff of pipe smoke. Alicia had begun to mutter and cry out as the spirits of the dead heard her call and responded. Alicia's body twitched, and her head lolled back and forth, but she stayed upright, hands tight on the sewing machine. I held on too, pouring my magic into the old black and gold steel, and I felt Alicia drawing on that magic to strengthen her own.

Teag was back on his feet, limping as if he had twisted an ankle, but determined to come at Thompson again. This time, he had a rope net in his hands, and I knew his magic was woven into every knot. He threw the net when Thompson's attention was on Sorren, and the tangle of rope and knots settled over the necromancer, who snarled and fought like a wild thing.

The greenish light faltered, and Sorren charged forward once more. Thompson careened to one side, tearing at the net. Just as Sorren swung his sword, the amulet's glow flared again, straining against the fibers in the net. The iron blade cut into Thompson's shoulder, but the necromancer's power burst the net, sending the bits of rope down in a rain of burning bits that forced Sorren back.

Thompson pivoted, and I feared he was going after Teag with the knife in his hand, but instead, he drove the blade down into the flopping, squirming burlap bag with its captive chicken. Blood poured in a black river as the bird gave a final struggle and lay still.

"Did you think I would wait to lay my spells?" Hitchens's voice roared from Thompson's throat. "I will be avenged!" A streak of green light flashed from the necromancer's amulet and struck the fresh, warm blood. A shriek rent the night, coming from everywhere at once, Charleston's restless dead hearing the summons of a mad master.

From beneath the building, in the heart of the sinkhole, I heard the sound of digging. My stomach lurched. Emily and the other lost dead of the old hurricane were being forced from their grave, bound to the will of a bitter, vengeful dabbler who was no less dangerous for his lack of control.

Teag gave a sharp cry and ran for Thompson, this time holding his staff as a lance. One hand gripped his *agimat*, a charm his Filipino martial arts master believed carried protection against evil spirits. A faint golden glow seemed to envelop Teag, radiating from the *agimat*, and he drove his staff into Thompson's gut, running at full speed.

Thompson barely reacted, although the strike should have felled a regular man. He reached up and turned his amulet toward Teag, and the green glow flared blindingly bright. It struck the birch staff and sent it into flames. Teag dropped the burning wood and staggered back, and the sickly green light strove against the golden aura of the *agimat*.

Teag stumbled backwards, and before Sorren could regroup, a coruscating wall of green phosphorescence sprang up, cutting Thompson off from them. Outside, the sounds of digging were louder, along with noises that sounded like bodies heaving their way over obstacles.

"They're coming," Thompson gloated. "My magic raised them. And they're going to make you pay. They're going to make everyone pay. No one's going to push me out again."

Thompson might be a dabbler, but with Hitchens's spirit possessing him, he was a formidable foe. Thompson flung the rear doors of the store open, doors that once had opened into a loading dock and now swung forth over a dark abyss. And as I watched, terrified, I saw bony hands reach up and begin to drag the long-ago forgotten dead to answer Thompson's summons.

Caliel was behind where Alicia and I stood inside the circle, and his chanting had grown fevered. As I watched, a new form began to take shape—inside the circle, which was supposed to be impervious to magic. The figure was of a tall African man in a black and white checkered shirt. He wore a pair of sunglasses with only one lens, and a straw hat. His work pants had one leg rolled up higher than the other, and he stepped up behind Alicia as if to lay his hand on her shoulder.

I moved to intervene, but Caliel's shout stopped me. "Let him be, Cassidy!" he sang in the same cadence as his chant. "Ghede Nibo's here to help. Go now!" He went back to his chanting, but I took his message. Ghede Nibo placed his hands on Alicia's shoulders, and she immediately relaxed against his insubstantial form.

I smudged the circle to let myself out, and at the last minute, I grabbed Danny's award, still holding onto it through the cloth.

Thompson's force shield was keeping Sorren and Teag at bay for the moment, and behind Thompson, a dozen skeletons had climbed from the pit. More followed. I stared at the animated skeletons and as I did, they took on sinew and muscle, then the ragged remnants of old-fashioned clothing. It broke my heart that Emily and her co-workers were being wrested from their grave for this final indignity, and in that grief I found the anger to drive my purpose.

I ran toward the green glow of Thompson's shielding. It had to be taking power and concentration to hold that warding, and I wondered just how long he could hold it and raise the dead as well.

Sorren must have had the same idea. "He can't hold all of us off, and call the spirits," Sorren shouted. "Strike!"

I grabbed a forgotten plastic chair out of the refuse on the floor and ran at the sickly green light. Teag had a plastic pole. Sorren lifted a whole glass display case and threw it against the warding. It bounced back, shattering glass and sending splinters flying. Teag struck just an instant before me, and the field repelled him hard enough to send him sprawling on his back, but it lacked the force Thompson had used before. I hit the shield with my chair, roaring like a deranged lion.

The warding faltered and failed. I went careening toward Thompson just as he turned from his summoned dead. I caught him in the chest with the chair, hard enough to hear bones break. Apparently, with his warding knocked out, he was a little more vulnerable than before. Or maybe, the pale corpses who were thronging through the door were draining off some of his defensive power.

Thompson bared his teeth, and his hand moved toward his amulet. I figured I was a goner, but I was closer than either Sorren or Teag, and someone had to do something. A crazy plan formed in my mind. Jacob

Hitchens's spirit had possessed Thompson to give him his powers. Danny Thompson's mediocre self was epitomized in his pitiful award. Maybe I could drive out the interloper, and force Danny back where he belonged. More desperate than brave, I dropped the cloth that covered the "Best Effort" award and grabbed it as a weapon. As I did so, I channeled all my remaining power into the memories that reverberated in the obelisk, the humiliation, the failure. Screaming at the top of my lungs, I drove the pointed tip of the clear plastic obelisk deep into his chest.

Thompson backhanded me hard enough that I went flying and saw stars. I heard him shouting at the newly-raised dead, and saw the zombies start toward Sorren and Teag. Sorren was strong and fast, and Teag was good in a fight, but the dead never tired and didn't feel pain. The odds weren't good.

I got to my hands and knees, ready to fight to the last. Thompson clutched at the plastic shaft in his chest. Blood covered his shirt and ran down his hands. He fixed me with a hateful glare and struggled to curse me, as blood trickled from the corners of his mouth.

"Kill!" Thompson managed, sagging to his knees. The zombies started forward.

"Stay where you are!" The voice came from Alicia's direction, but the rich baritone was not her voice. I looked over, and the spirit of the man who had joined us in the circle had grown nearly solid. Ghede Nibo, Caliel had called him. He looked formidable, and he was definitely pissed.

Thompson was dying. I knew it, and he knew it, but he wasn't going down without a fight. "I called you," he growled at the pitiful forms behind him. "I command you."

"We will not serve." This voice came from Alicia as well, but it was Emily speaking. One after another, strange voices cried out defiantly, and I saw that the zombies had come to a complete halt.

"Where is your army, little man?" Ghede Nibo spoke again, his deep voice tight with anger. Alicia looked lost in trance, but the cords of her neck strained with the effort. "I am the patron of those lost to disaster, the ghede of the unburied, the unknown dead, and those who drift below the waters. You have no power here, but I have power over you!"

Thompson's whole form began to convulse. Blood frothed at his lips and began to leak from his eyes, nose, and ears. With one final scream of frustrated rage, Thompson's ravaged body fell forward and lay still. And then, as I stared in horror, I saw a gray mist rise from the raw wound where the obelisk's tip had penetrated Thompson's back, and then a second tendril of black smoke.

"I waste no time on you," Ghede Nibo snarled. "Come to me." Powerless, the two wispy souls traveled to where the Ghede stood. "You will be no more." And without another word, Ghede Nibo ate the souls.

Alicia trembled but did not cry out. I was frozen in place, too terrified to move, covered in Thompson's blood. Sorren stayed where he was, and Teag had not moved. All of us watched the ghostly man who spoke through Alicia.

"My children," Ghede Nibo said, addressing the pitiful zombies who stood in the entranceway. "Too long you have been denied your rest. I free you—and I will dig your grave. Be at peace."

The zombies collapsed where they stood, a jumble of bone and rotted cloth. And as they did, all around us, I heard the creaking and ripping of steel and brick.

"Run!" Sorren shouted. He grabbed me and dragged me backward. Teag was limping, but he managed some speed as we ran for the back of the building.

"Go!" Caliel shouted. "Gotta finish what I started!" Ghede Nibo had released Alicia, and Teag hauled her over one shoulder as he limped toward the door where we had entered. Ceiling tiles were falling down around us, and then parts of the roof, crashing into glass display cases and knocking down the battered mannequins.

I cast one last glance behind me before Sorren shoved me out the door. I saw Caliel, still drumming and chanting. Two ghostly men stood with him. One was Ghede Nibo, and the other was a bent old man leaning on a cane, accompanied by a scrawny dog.

We barely made it into the parking lot before the old big box store began to tumble into the sinkhole. When we had reached the cars, we stopped and stared in horror. The big box building was disintegrating, coming apart at the seams as the ground beneath it shuddered, and the sinkhole spread. A roar of smashing brick and screaming steel and the whole thing was gone in a thick cloud of dust.

"Caliel," I murmured, leaning on Sorren for support.

Out of the smoke and darkness, I saw something coming. Caliel walked toward us. His white clothing was still untouched and other than being soaked with sweat from the exertion of calling the Loas, he looked unharmed.

"We had a good night, I think!" Caliel called out to us. "Tonight, we won."

I stared at the billowing cloud where the old store had been and thought about Emily and the other lost girls, and all the unknown flood victims Thompson and Hitchens had tried to enslave. Of how long their restless spirits had sought to escape from their prison. Now, they were at rest. I bet Blair Hunt and the developers would be amazed at how much the plaza's fortunes changed. But right now, all I wanted was to get out of there before the cops found me covered in blood. I would deal with the reality that I had killed a man later. Right now, I was shaking too much to think.

"I've had enough Halloween for one year," Teag said exhaustedly. "Time to call it a night."

RETRIBUTION

I SHOULD HAVE KNOWN WHEN I SAW THE SILVER HIP FLASK, THAT IT was going to be trouble.

"Hey, Cassidy!" Teag Logan called out as we unpacked boxes from our most recent auction adventure. "Take a look. This is a real beauty!"

I glanced up from the box I was unpacking and saw Teag hold up an antique flask. It had the clean lines of an Art Deco piece, and I wondered what long-ago *bon vivant* had tucked it into a coat pocket. "That should sell quickly," I said. "It looks like something out of a Roaring Twenties bootlegger movie. Can you tell if it's more than what it seems?"

For anyone else, a question like that might have referred to a feature that would make the flask more valuable. But not in my world. Teag knew what I really meant was: *Does it have any bad juju that's gonna knock me flat on my butt?*

I'm Cassidy Kincaide, and I own Trifles and Folly, a 350-year-old antique and curio shop in historic, haunted Charleston, South Carolina. The shop has been in my family almost since Charleston was founded back in 1670. And although most people just think of us as a great place to find beautiful and unusual antiques, the truth is a little more complicated. We exist to find dangerous magical and supernatural items and get them off the market before anyone gets hurt. Most of the time, we've been successful. On the rare occasions when we weren't, history chalks the damage up to natural disasters.

I'm a psychometric, someone who can "read" the history of an object just by touching it. That comes in handy for what we do, but it can also make for unpleasant surprises. My gift is the reason Uncle Evan left me the shop and how I inherited the job of getting magically malicious objects out of circulation. Teag is my assistant store manager, and he's got some pretty cool magic of his own. Sorren is my business partner, the store's real founder, and a nearly six-hundred-year-old vampire. Nothing about Trifles and Folly is business as usual.

"I think we might have a 'spooky,'" he replied. "I'm picking up bad vibes, and I'm not nearly as sensitive as you are."

"I'll check it later," I said. "Do we know anything about it?" I stood up and stretched, slipping a piece of my strawberry-blonde hair behind one ear. With blue eyes, freckles, and pale skin, my Scots-Irish ancestry is apparent to anyone who lays eyes on me. Only thanks to the hot Charleston sun and a day spent canvassing yard sales; I was decidedly pink from the sun even though it was autumn.

The boxes had been delivered from the auction at the Legacy Hotel, a long-shuttered landmark that had once been a Prohibition-era speakeasy. "There's nothing unusual, other than the flask, which obviously belonged to one of the Legacy's customers," he remarked.

I looked down at the half-emptied box I was working on. "Put it aside, and I'll have a look once I finish this box."

I turned back to the box and was about to lift out the next bundle when I froze. "Hey Teag, I need your help with this," I called. "I've got another Spooky."

A Spooky is what I call an item that gives off a dark psychic resonance. It may have had a tragedy associated with it, or it might possess dangerous power of its own. Those take special handling, and often, I hand them off to Sorren to get rid of. "Sparklers" have a touch of supernatural power, but aren't usually dangerous. We check them out thoroughly and decide how to handle them on a case-by-case basis. The truly harmless pieces we'll sell to discerning buyers, and anything questionable Sorren takes care of. "Mundanes" are non-magical items, and they go on sale in the front showroom.

"Sure. What do you have?" Teag asked. He eyed the paper-wrapped bundle.

I checked the packing list. "According to this, it's a poker chip set. No idea why it would be 'hot,' but I'd rather deal with it later." I paused, concentrating on what my gift could read even keeping my hand several inches above the item. "It's not active right now, and it's not dangerous to handle, but there's something dark about it."

Teag nodded and bent down to pull out the bundle. He carried it over to the table and unwrapped a beautiful burled birch wooden box that was a smaller version of the kind used to store silver flatware. He sifted through the papers that wrapped the item, and a small card fell out.

"That's odd," Teag mused. "It's a novena card for Our Lady of Lourdes. Not exactly what I'd expect to find packed with a poker set." Teag touched the box and waited a moment, and when nothing happened, he flipped the lid open. The inside of the box was covered with velvet that was in remarkable condition given its age. Vintage poker chips nestled into six rows of shallow depressions in the lining, and a small square area had room for two yellowed decks of cards.

"It's gorgeous," Teag murmured. He reached in and picked up a couple of the poker chips, weighing them in his hand. "Clay chips. They're the right age to be from the speakeasy days."

Teag turned the chips over and held them up for a better look. "Pretty swanky," he said with a grin. "There's a *fleur-de-lis* stamped in the middle of each chip, and it looks like when they were new, those might have been covered with gold leaf. I'm betting this was a custom-made set." He glanced more closely at the chips. "Too bad—a couple of them are missing." He met my gaze. "But the question is—why the bad juju?"

I shrugged. "If the Legacy lived up to its reputation, I can think of about a million reasons," I replied. "Gambling debts, desperate high-stakes players, duels, love affairs gone wrong." I paused and sniffed the air. "Do you smell that?"

Teag shook his head. "I don't smell anything except a little mustiness from all these pieces being closed up in that old hotel for so long."

I sniffed again, but the scent was gone. "It was a floral smell, like an old-fashioned perfume. I can't smell it anymore."

Teag grinned and flicked a strand of lank, dark hair out of his eyes. You'd never know it from his skater-boy looks, but before Teag came onboard at Trifles and Folly, he was a doctoral candidate in History at the university. He's still ABD (All But Dissertation) and likely to stay that way, since I think he's decided that the store's secret mission is his true calling.

"Maybe it's the memory of a spurned lover or a jealous socialite," he joked.

"Actually, that's very possible," I replied. Especially in a place like the Legacy Hotel.

"Once we get everything unpacked, I'll see what I can turn up," Teag said. He made it sound casual, but Teag's got skills at finding data that make the CIA look like beginners. He's not a hacker, he's a "Weaver," with a magic talent for gathering pieces together. When he uses yarn or rope, the pieces he weaves have protection and intention woven into them from his magic. But when he weaves data, Teag can find the truth from strands of information flung far and wide and bring them together to tell a story.

"How's your basket-weaving apprenticeship going?" I thought to ask.

Teag grinned. "You know, the next time I hear someone refer to a simple college class as being 'basket-weaving,' I'm going to set them straight. It's hard to do it well, and my fingers are all cut up from the sweetgrass." He held up his hands, and I could see where many small cuts were newly healing. "Mrs. Teller says I have talent, but I don't think I could ever get as good as it as she is, even if I spent two lifetimes doing it!"

Mrs. Teller was an elderly woman who wove sweetgrass baskets down at the Charleston City Market, the kind of baskets famous throughout the Lowcountry. I also happened to know she was a root worker, which meant she had magical gifts of her own. That's why I was so excited when she agreed to work with Teag and help him better understand his gift.

"You know Mrs. Teller has the Sight," I said. On more than one occasion, Mrs. Teller's premonitions had been eerily accurate. "She didn't happen to say anything about the auction, did she?"

Teag frowned. "Now that you mention it, she told me to keep the women in my life happy, because there was an angry woman who was going to stir up a heap of trouble." He brightened. "Of course, that may cause me fewer problems than she may have realized," he added. "And Anthony's been in a good mood lately." Anthony, a young lawyer from a Battery-row family, was Teag's steady partner.

I chuckled. "Well, I was in a pretty good mood too, until we unearthed two 'spookies' in a row."

It was late on Friday afternoon, and while Teag and I had been out trolling auctions for finds to sell in the store, our stalwart part-time helper Maggie Snyder had been watching the showroom. Maggie's a retired teacher who doesn't look a day over sixty and has the energy of someone in her thirties. With her gray hair cut in a chin-length bob and her fondness for camisoles and broomstick skirts, Maggie looks every bit like the Woodstock-era New Ager that she is.

Today's foot traffic had been light, and I wasn't surprised when Maggie stuck her head in the back room just before five o'clock.

"If it's okay with you, I'll lock up right on the hour," Maggie said. "Things have been slow all afternoon, and there don't seem to be a lot of folks out on the street."

"It's the Garden Show," I sighed. "It always brings a lot of tourists into the city, but they don't get around to doing the shops until they've done all the garden tours. Tomorrow afternoon and Sunday we'll be slammed."

Maggie nodded. "I plan on catching a couple of those tours myself, but if you need a hand, you know where to find me."

I waited until I heard the sound of the sleigh bells as the front door shut behind her, then glanced out to make sure that the door was locked and the sign was turned to "closed" before I looked back at the flask and poker set.

"Are you up to finding out what fine kettle of fish we've gotten ourselves into this time?" I asked, knowing that Teag wouldn't be able to resist the classic movie reference. Old movies were a passion I shared with Teag and Anthony, and the three of us were regulars at the Charleston Film Festival.

Teag chuckled. "I think the flask and poker chips may be more Bonnie and Clyde than Laurel and Hardy, but I'm up for it if you are." He gave me a knowing glance. "After all, it goes harder on you than it does me. You get the visions. I just pick you up off the floor."

"True," I admitted. "So let's do this sitting down. Do you mind carrying the pieces over to the break room table?"

Trifles and Folly was in a charming (in other words, old) storefront on King Street, Charleston's main thoroughfare for serious shopping. We were in one of the oldest buildings on the street, and we were the only shop to have had a continuous lease for the building's entire life. Even so, it wasn't the shop's first location. The occasional "unexplained" fire or explosion had made for a few moves over the store's long life, but that was the price to be paid for trying to keep the world safe from malicious magic.

In this building, where the store had been for the last hundred and fifty years, we had a storefront along the street, a middle room that had long ago been divided in two to create a small office as well as a cozy break room, and a rear room that was largely for storage. Up above was a space that had been my apartment when I first moved back to Charleston and was now used for storage. Below us was an old, hand-dug cellar where Sorren had a day crypt for emergencies. The building had character, and despite all the Sparklers and Spookies, I felt at home here.

Teag obligingly carried the flask and the poker chip set to the break room table and put on water to boil for tea. That was probably wise, because more than once, Teag had needed to revive me after a vision went badly, and a bracing cup of black tea with plenty of sugar or a glass of sweet tea was just the thing for that. I saw that Teag had also brought my laptop out of the office and had it set up on the table as well.

I sat down in one chair, and Teag sat down facing me on the same side of the table. "Ready?" he asked.

I nodded and drew a deep breath, and then I reached for the flask. As soon as my fingers touched the smooth silver, the room seemed to tilt around me, and I was no longer in Trifles and Folly. The first thing I felt was the emotion; very strong fear and anger.

"Good to see you again, Mr. Sanderson!"

"Glad you're back, Mr. Sanderson!"

"Can I get you a drink, Mr. Sanderson?"

I did not recognize the room, or the man everyone else obviously knew as "Mr. Sanderson." I'd had enough of these visions to know that when I was an observer like this, I could do nothing to affect the scene in front of me, and the people I was watching could not see or hear me. That's because I was essentially watching a "replay" of things that had happened long ago, and that history was trapped in the object itself, becoming part of its resonance.

Mr. Sanderson was a wide man with heavy-lidded eyes and ponderous jowls. His watch, the gold rings on his hands, and his clothing all looked very expensive. From the way he moved through the room, favoring those who greeted him with a regal nod, he was accustomed to wealth and notoriety and knew how to use it. Sanderson was wearing an old-fashioned tuxedo, something that looked like it belonged in the Flapper era. Looking around myself, that's exactly where we seemed to be, sometime in the late 1920s, judging by the women's clothing.

"Set me up with a gin and tonic, how about it, Carl?" Sanderson said with a glance toward the dark-haired young man behind the bar.

"You got it, Mr. S." Carl's tone was chipper, but something in the set of his shoulders told me that Sanderson wasn't his favorite customer.

The room was opulent, paneled in dark wood with brass light fixtures and large leather club chairs. The smell of Havana cigars hung heavy in the air, mingling with the scent of bathtub gin. Over to one side, a man in a vest and crisp white shirt poured drinks from unmarked bottles using a tall table as a makeshift bar. I was betting that the panels in the wall behind the bartender opened up to conceal the bottles should the place get raided. *A jazz trio played in the corner.*

On the other side of the room, several equally well-heeled gentlemen were engrossed in a poker game while stylishly thin women dressed in the straight, beaded, and fringed dresses that defined the "Flapper" style stood behind them. An empty table and chairs looked set for a second game. Several of the men who greeted Mr. Sanderson looked as if they were waiting for him to get their own game started.

Sanderson and his crowd drifted over to the empty table. All of the men except Sanderson were accompanied by women who looked tall, thin, and elegant in their fashionable dresses, with their short-cut "bob" hairstyles and headbands and their gin martinis. They seated themselves at the gaming table, and Sanderson raised a hand to signal the lone waitress in the room.

"Hey, Clara! How about another gin and tonic?" Sanderson called. His leer made it obvious that he was as interested in the girl as in the drink. Winks and knowing glances among his friends at the table made that clear as well.

Clara was a pretty girl in her twenties, with short dark hair and a voluptuous figure that was the complete opposite of the straight-up-and-down Flapper ideal. She had a fresh-faced beauty that stood in direct contrast to the jaded, rouged look of the high-rollers' women, and in the instant before she schooled her expression into a forced smile, I could see a glimpse of dislike—and fear—when it came to Sanderson.

"Coming right up, Mr. Sanderson," Clara said and moved over to the bar. Sanderson watched her every move and did not look away until the dealer started shuffling the cards. I was too far away to hear what Clara said to the bartender, but I could read the expression on his face, and it was clear to me—and to Clara—that the bartender noticed and disliked Sanderson's interest. The exchange was brief: Clara put a hand on Carl's

arm, and although I couldn't hear what she said, her expression seemed beseeching. Carl's anger came through clearly, no interpretation needed.

In just a few moments, Clara had the drink and made her way back to the table where Sanderson and his buddies were settling into their game. He took a swig from his hip flask as he waited for Clara to bring him another drink. A ruddy flush spread to his cheeks.

"You're a fine girl, Clara," Sanderson said when she brought the drink, and it had to be obvious to everyone when his hand found its way behind Clara and under her skirt.

"Thank you, Mr. Sanderson," Clara managed, although I could see her cheeks growing red. *She tried to move away casually, but Sanderson landed an unmistakable open-handed slap to her buttocks.* I glanced at the high rollers' girlfriends, wondering if someone would say something, but the women snickered and elbowed each other. Obviously, this was something they had seen before.

Just as the scene began to fade out, I heard Teag calling my name. "Cassidy! Come on back!"

I shook my head to clear it, and the vision vanished. Teag pressed a cup of very sweet, very hot tea into my hands. "Drink some. You look pale—even for you. What did you see?"

I recounted the vision. Teag wrote down the names as I told the story. "I'm afraid it isn't very unique," I said. "That sort of thing happened all the time—and still does. Old rich man likes the look of a young girl and feels entitled to take what he wants." There was a darkness to the flask that went beyond what I had seen in the vision. I needed to spend some more time with the flask, perhaps have Sorren check it out. Until then, I was considering it to be a Spooky.

Teag grimaced. "I'd like to say times have changed, but I have enough friends who wait tables and tend bar to know they haven't changed all that much." He looked at the names on the list. "Not much to go on, but with the approximate date and the location, I'll see what I can find."

He gave me a questioning glance. "Are you up to doing the poker set?"

I took a sip of the tea and felt the sugar begin to revive me. "Sure. Let's get it over with."

Teag moved the old poker set closer to me, setting the silver flask to the side. The poker set was a real beauty. The wooden case was burled maple with brass fittings. Inside, sumptuous red velvet cushioned depressions to cradle the poker chips, plus cards and dice. It was obviously the plaything of a wealthy gentleman. I expected to catch the scent of leather and bay rum cologne, the shadow of a former owner, but instead, I got a whiff of the same very sweet perfume I had smelled earlier.

"Something wrong?" Teag asked.

I shook my head. "No. Just odd. I keep smelling perfume."

Teag looked at me blankly. "I smell tea. That's all."

I shrugged. "Let's see what I get from the poker set."

I reached out to touch the wooden case, and once again, images flooded my mind, and I was bombarded with strong emotion: anger, hatred, and vengeance. I saw what looked like a hotel room, decorated in a style that made me think the vision was still from around the 1920s. But instead of the speakeasy, this was a sleeping room. The poker set lay closed on a desk. Next to it was a silver ice bucket and an open bottle of champagne.

Once again, I was an observer, watching without being seen or heard, unable to participate. I saw a good-looking man with slicked-back dark hair raise a toast to himself in the mirror with a glass of champagne. He was alone in the room, and he had loosened the collar of his shirt, but he still wore the burgundy silk vest that had brought him such luck at the gaming tables.

There was a knock at the door. "Come in," he shouted.

A young woman in a maid's outfit entered, carrying a tray with a steak dinner and another bottle of champagne. "I've brought your dinner, sir," she said. Her accent suggested that she was from the islands, as did the cocoa hue of her skin. Her hair had been straightened and curled into a flapper's bob, the only nod to fashion. Her uniform marked her as a maid, but it could have been issued at any of the city's many hotels. It was utilitarian and nearly sexless, designed to make its wearer invisible.

"And what a good looking dish it is," the young high-roller said, with a tone that made it very clear he was not remarking on the steak. The maid blushed, but said nothing, keeping her eyes averted as she set down the tray.

"Enjoy your meal, Mr. Williams," she said, and turned to head toward the door, but the dark-haired man blocked her path.

"Now what's the hurry?" he asked, his drawl lengthened by the bubbly he had consumed from the nearly-empty bottle by the poker set. "We haven't even gotten acquainted. What's your name, darlin'?"

"Elise," the maid murmured and moved to sidestep the gambler.

"That's a pretty name. Elise." Once again, he blocked her path.

"I'm due down at the front desk," Elise said. I was pretty sure she realized the danger. *"I've got three more orders to deliver, and my boss said to be quick about it."*

"Don't worry about that," the gambler said, moving closer. Elise stepped back, but there was no exit behind her. The gambler raised a hand to touch her cheek. *"I can fix things with the boss. He won't mind if I borrow you for a little while."*

Elise let out a little squeal and dodged, making a break for the door. The gambler's charm darkened into anger, and he grabbed her arm, jerking her back so viciously that she cried out in pain.

"I just won the biggest jackpot the Legacy Hotel has ever posted," the gambler growled. *"And I'll be damned if I'll celebrate alone. Don't fight me, girl, and I won't make it bad for you."*

I came back to myself breathing hard. It was a good thing Teag was trained in capoeira, because he was able to block the punch I threw in his direction and grab my wrists before I could hurt anyone. "Cassidy! It's me. You're safe. You're safe."

I drew a ragged breath, and Teag handed me the cup of tea once more. It took longer before I could tell him what I saw. When I finished, I saw that his disgust mirrored my own. Again, he wrote down the names I had heard.

"So the owner of the flask was a groper, and the poker chip owner was a rapist," Teag said. "No wonder you picked up bad vibes."

The tea steadied me, and I took another deep breath before I spoke. "I think there's more to it," I said. "Unfortunately, neither behavior was that uncommon for that time period and for upper-class men around women with no power to refuse them. I don't think we know the whole story."

Teag made a show of interlacing his fingers in front of him and cracking his knuckles as if he were about to sit down at a concert piano. I knew he did it to make me laugh, and it worked. He pulled the laptop to him. "Watch a master go to work," he said with an exaggerated flourish.

"I didn't give you much to go on," I said, holding on to the cup of tea like a shipwreck survivor with a life preserver. I felt chilled and shaky, and my stomach was still clenched with fear.

"It doesn't have to be much to find a trail," Teag murmured, intent on the screen. I'd watched him research like this before, and it always astounded me. Regular people could find amazing things on the Internet with a little skill and luck. Teag's Weaver magic took that to a whole new level. I wasn't entirely sure how it worked, and neither was Teag, but he told me once that it was as if each piece of data that he found had "threads" visible to his magic that connected it far beyond what could be accounted for by mere hyperlinks. If he followed those threads and watched how they interwove, he could piece a story together to rival the top intelligence agencies.

I watched in silence, happy for the chance to regroup. Teag was utterly absorbed in the data that flashed on his screen. His fingers flew across the keyboard, sending him from page to page. Old newspaper articles appeared, and he scanned down through them quickly, then went on to the next bit of information. Finally, he sat back and stared at the computer, deep in thought.

"Find something?" I asked.

Teag nodded. "I looked up Sanderson first. It was a little easier than I expected. Hansford Quincy Sanderson was a self-made millionaire and cotton baron. He liked rye whiskey, fast horses, and loose women. Not," Teag said, arching an eyebrow, "necessarily in that order. He got mentioned a lot in the news of the day for his penchant for throwing opulent parties, much to the chagrin of the old money types. You know how that goes."

I did. Charleston had a lot of old money, the kind that preferred to be discreet about their wealth, at least in the public eye. Flamboyance, even now, was considered in poor taste and dreadfully *nouveau riche.* "What else?"

"From what I found, Sanderson made a lot of enemies. There was a rumor that he had ties to criminal elements. I suspect there might have been a line of likely suspects when he turned up dead, but the guy they arrested wouldn't have been in it."

"Oh?"

Teag shook his head. "Hansford Sanderson was found dead in the alley behind the Legacy Hotel with a small caliber bullet in his heart. Clara Raintree, the waitress, was found dead nearby with a broken neck. And guess who pulled the trigger?"

"Carl," I said, not sure how I knew, but I was certain. "He and Clara were lovers."

Teag nodded. "Yep. Carl didn't even try to fight the charges. According to the story, he told police, he saw Sanderson manhandle Clara and force her into the alley. Carl heard her scream and went after her, but by the time he got there, he saw Sanderson choking the girl, who was fighting him. Carl says he shot Sanderson with the twenty-two caliber he kept behind the bar in case of robbers, because he was trying to save Clara's life."

"But he was too late," I finished for him. "What happened to him?"

"No one was particularly upset that Sanderson was out of the picture, but the plantation class really couldn't let a bartender get away with killing one of their own, especially for philandering, which was a pretty common pastime," Teag noted drily. "It might have set a bad precedent."

I had a bad feeling about this. "He got convicted?"

"He was hanged. A couple of 'witnesses' turned up who claimed they saw Carl roughing up Clara and that Sanderson tried to intervene, so Carl shot him." Teag made a sour expression. "Funny thing, but the witnesses disappeared after the trial and were never seen again."

"I bet." I paused, almost afraid to see what Teag would come up with on the poker set. "Do you feel up to finding out what happened to Williams? I'm afraid we already know what happened to Elise."

Teag waggled his eyebrows at me, trying to lighten the mood. "Certainly," he replied, turning back to the computer. I sipped the rapidly-cooling tea, glad that the physical repercussions of the visions were fading, but still troubled by the violence of what I had seen.

"Bingo!" Teag said after several minutes of silence, turning to face me once more. "And it's another tie to the Legacy Hotel. Artemis Bennett Williams was our poker player. Where did they dream up those old names?" he wondered aloud.

"And who was Arty, other than a creep?" I asked.

"A wealthy creep," Teag replied. "He was the son of Jefferson Rubel Williams, who made his money in sugar cane and rum down in the islands and returned to Charleston just after the end of the First World War. The Williams family was filthy rich, even by Charleston standards, but there were rumors that they had left St. Croix under a cloud."

"Elise had an islands accent," I interrupted.

Teag nodded. "Artemis Williams had a bad habit of hitting on other men's girlfriends, which got him into some dicey situations with the Country Club set."

"Like what?"

Teag shrugged. "One jealous boyfriend got shot in what was rumored to have been a duel, but Williams got off because the judge was a friend of his father's. In another case, the rival 'suddenly left town.'"

"Or got dumped in the ocean at night," I added. "That is, after all, one way to leave town."

Teag nodded. "My thoughts exactly. Williams was trouble. He was briefly engaged to the daughter of a respectable family, but her father forced them to call off the wedding and sent the girl to Europe."

"Smart man," I replied. "But what happened to Williams? And what about Elise?"

Teag grinned, and I knew he had found something good. "Williams turned up dead in the alley behind the Legacy Hotel—the same alley where Sanderson was shot. Only Williams looked as if he'd been clawed by a wild animal. Official cause of death was heart failure. He was only thirty-five."

"And Elise?"

Teag shrugged. "According to the account in the newspaper at the time, when Williams's body was found, they questioned everyone at the hotel, including a woman named Elise DuPre, but no charges were ever filed."

He gave a dramatic pause. "And get this. The police tried to make a case against Elise because she had been a friend of Clara's and had once spoken sharply about Sanderson to some of the staff for his bothering Clara. They couldn't pin Sanderson's murder on her because Carl was such a convenient patsy, but when Williams died in the same alley, they took a long hard look at Elise, and still came up empty."

"Interesting."

"It gets better," he said with relish. "Over the years, I counted at least fifteen questionable deaths in that back alley behind the Legacy Hotel. All men in their twenties and thirties, and all of them with prior arrests for domestic violence, rape, or assault." He paused. "And at least some of the accounts mention finding a poker chip beside the bodies."

Just then, I got another faint whiff of the sweet perfume, and with it, a pungent odor of tobacco. "Elise is part of this. I don't know how she did it, but I think she arranged for Williams to die… and from what you've found, it sounds like after all these years; her spirit still has an ax to grind."

"Her granddaughter still lives in Charleston," Teag said with a grin. "Do you think she'd talk to us?"

It was tempting, but I couldn't figure out why the woman would open up such a nasty old family secret for two strangers without a good reason. "Hold onto that contact information," I said. "I want to ask

Sorren about this. After all, he's been in Charleston all these years—maybe he knows something about the people or the incidents."

Teag nodded. "Good idea." He paused and gave me a careful look. "How are you? Do you need me to see you home?"

In the time we had worked together, Teag had gone from being my assistant store manager to becoming a friend and a confidant. I was lucky to have him around. My pride made me shake my head. "Thanks, but I'm doing better. And besides, don't you have a dinner date with Anthony?"

"Not tonight," Teag replied with a sigh. "He's working on another big case, and it's my night for basket weaving with Mrs. Teller."

"Then you'd better get going," I said, not wanting to keep him from his lesson. "I'm planning on a quiet night at home with Baxter." Baxter was my little Maltese, who was one of Teag's biggest fans. The admiration was mutual.

Despite my protests, Teag insisted on following me home to make sure I got in safely. I waved from the doorway and heard Baxter yipping himself silly in greeting. When the door was shut and locked, I knelt down and cuddled Bax and took a few deep breaths to let the day —and the visions—slip away.

I fed Baxter and took him for a walk, deep in thought about what I had seen when I touched the flask and the poker set. Two young women who met trouble or tragedy because of men who had been high rollers at the old Legacy Hotel. And the possibility that fifteen men with sketchy backgrounds had gotten what was coming to them in a dark alley behind an abandoned hotel.

When I got home, I raided the fridge for left-over Chinese fried rice and poured a glass of white wine to calm my nerves. Then I called Sorren's cell phone and left a message for him to call me. I don't know how many other six-hundred-year-old vampires have cell phones, but my silent partner is a pretty savvy guy. He told me once that vampires who don't adapt and keep up with the times don't make it very long. He should know.

I decided to do a little Internet research of my own and looked for anything I could find about the Legacy Hotel. There were plenty of pictures and more links than I would have expected for a place that had been out of business for years. As I read through the posts, a picture began to form in my mind.

The Legacy Hotel had been founded in 1897 and at the time, was a very respectable, upscale venue popular with planter-class men who were in Charleston on business. The pictures from the time showed a building at the height of Victorian opulence, praised in its day for having all the modern conveniences. It was the crowning achievement of Rayford 'King' Lanier, who had made his fortune as an hotelier in Europe before coming home to Charleston. But almost from the start, the grand hotel was the site of tragedy.

A newspaper article from the time commented on an unusual number of deaths and injuries during the construction of the hotel, although no reason appeared to be discovered. The grand opening was marred when one of the older guests at the extravagant reception had a heart attack and died. A year later, a woman fell to her death from one of the upper balconies. Then a carriage ran over a child in front of the main doors. In every case, the hotel was absolved of any responsibility.

Baxter had been on my lap, but he got restless, and I put him down on the floor so he could run off. I kept searching, intrigued with the tainted history of the hotel. As the years went on, there was at least one tragic incident a year, none of them apparently related except for the location.

I was beginning to think that the Legacy Hotel itself was a cursed object. The hotel survived the Prohibition years and continued its heyday into the 1960s. But like many grand lodgings of its era, the new chain hotels that sprang up in the 1960s and 1970s were the beginning of the end. The Legacy Hotel staggered on as a dinner theater catering to senior citizen bus tours into the 1980s, when it was sold and turned into condominiums. That lasted for fifteen years, until the developer went bankrupt and the property went into receivership. It closed for good five years ago, and I remembered driving past it and thinking that it was sad that the grand building had fallen on hard times.

It occurred to me that Baxter had been gone and quiet for too long, so I got up, stretched, and went to look for him. I found him in the kitchen, sitting on Sorren's lap at the table. Baxter had a curiously bemused look on his face, which meant that Sorren glamored him to keep him from barking.

"I was in the neighborhood, so I thought I would just stop by," Sorren said, scratching Baxter behind the ears. I sighed and rolled my eyes. This is what comes from inviting your vampire boss into your home. Especially when, five hundred and some odd years ago, he was the best jewel thief in Belgium.

"Have you been here long?" I asked, pulling out a chair to sit down at the table. Sorren looks to be in his late twenties, although the reality is closer to six hundred. With his dark blond hair and sea-blue eyes, there's no mistaking his European background, although, after all this time, his accent is whatever he wants it to be. Sitting in my kitchen dressed in a t-shirt and jeans, he fit right in—unless you noticed that he wasn't breathing.

"Just long enough to say hello to Baxter," Sorren said. "I got your message."

Sorren listened intently as I recounted the visions I had gotten from the flask and the poker set. His eyes narrowed as I told him about what Teag's research had turned up, and what I had discovered on my own. "You've been in Charleston since long before the 1870s," I said as I wrapped up my report. "Have you heard anything about the Legacy Hotel?"

Sorren sat back for a moment and thought. I could imagine that after nearly six hundred years, it might take a while to comb through the memories. Baxter sat on his lap with a goofy look of adoration, his black button eyes slightly glazed.

"Yes, I know of the place," he replied. "And I believe that it's truly haunted. But then again, so are a lot of buildings in Charleston. I can also believe what you've told me about the tragedies that happened there, but again, tragedy is linked to nearly any place in this city that has stood for a length of time. This is a beautiful city, but it was built on the toil and misery of slaves, and it has more than its share of blood-shed in its history."

That was true, much as the tour books tried to downplay it.

Charleston had a fine and proper side, and below that, a darker under-current. What we did at Trifles and Folly often tapped into that darkness. "So you aren't aware of anything special about the Legacy Hotel?"

Sorren shrugged. "I never went there when it was open. It hasn't come to my attention since I've been working with the Alliance, and your Uncle Evan and his predecessors never seemed to find it noteworthy." He frowned. "But I agree that the objects you found and the research certainly point us in that direction now."

Just then, my cell phone rang. I fished it out of my pocket and answered. Teag sounded breathless. "Cassidy—you're not going to believe this. When I was working on the baskets with Mrs. Teller, I happened to mention the Legacy Hotel. After all, she's up in years, and I thought she might have heard something." I could tell that he had hit pay dirt from the excitement in his voice.

"She knows Elise's granddaughter! I should have realized that Mrs. Teller knows everybody in Charleston. She knows the woman we want to talk with, and without me telling her about anything, she said it was about time to put things right at the hotel and lay the spirits to rest." Teag was so excited; I knew Sorren could hear every word even at a distance.

"Not only that, but Mrs. Teller said she would go with us to talk with Elise's granddaughter. She said that between the three of you, you would 'have the skills' to do what needed doing," he added.

I glanced at Sorren, and he nodded. "Okay," I replied, still trying to catch up. "When does she want to introduce us?"

"Tomorrow," he said. "The sooner, the better."

Again, Sorren nodded, so I drew a deep breath and said, "That's fine. If we can get Maggie to close the shop, you and I can go in the early evening."

"I already arranged for Maggie to be there by three," Teag said. "And I told Mrs. Teller, we'd pick her up at six." After another moment's chit-chat about his latest basket lesson, I hung up feeling like I'd been in a whirlwind.

"Mrs. Teller is a root worker," I said. "And she's got the Sight. She may not know straight out what I can do, but she knows I've got a Gift, and I'm pretty certain she can sense Teag's magic, too."

"Ernestine Teller has a powerful magic ability," Sorren confirmed. "I know you think of her as Niella's mother and the old woman who weaves baskets at the marketplace, but she was a force of nature when she was younger, and people came from all around for her cures and conjuring. She's a powerful ally."

"What do you think she meant about the granddaughter and how the three of us would have the 'skills' to handle things?" That made me nervous, even though Teag seemed plenty happy about it.

"I think it suggests that Elise's granddaughter has abilities we'd best learn more about," Sorren replied. "And it may be that those abilities have been passed down from her grandmother. If so, she's the key to the deaths in the alley."

"You think those are somehow connected to Elise?"

Sorren nodded. "At this point, I'm nearly certain of it. Be careful, Cassidy. Whatever's active at the Legacy Hotel has proven it can kill. It may be enjoying its vengeance, and it might not want to stop."

To my surprise, Niella insisted on coming along when Teag and I came by to pick up Mrs. Teller. "Mama told me what y'all are doing," Niella said, in a tone that told me that she didn't fully approve, but that she knew there was no stopping her mother. "I couldn't talk her out of it, so I'm here to ride shotgun." A glance confirmed that there was no actual shotgun, but Niella's purse was big enough to hide other things just as lethal.

"My daughter worries too much," Mrs. Teller said. Niella was thirty, just four years older than me. Mrs. Teller had white hair and an unlined face, and was as spry as people half her age, which I figured must be somewhere in her late sixties, maybe older. I knew Niella was her youngest child, out of eight older siblings.

"You said that the three of us had the right skills to set the problem to rest," I said as Teag drove. "What exactly did you mean?"

Mrs. Teller fixed me with a look like I had suggested she had just fallen off the turnip truck. "Girl, I know you have the Sight. Different from mine, but something special. I can feel it. And you know that I *See* things, things I shouldn't know, but I do know." Niella, always protective, moved to interrupt, but Mrs. Teller laid a hand on her arm.

"Niella, keep your peace. I'm not talking out of school. Cassidy already had me figured. I saw it in her eyes." Mrs. Teller had a tart tongue and had no problem speaking her mind.

"Teag says that you've known Elise's granddaughter for quite a while," I probed.

Mrs. Teller rocked back and forth in her seat as we drove. "I have indeed," she said. "I have known Miss Monette since I was a girl. She must be in her eighties by now." She shook her head and clucked her tongue. "Time sure does fly."

She paused. "Miss Monette has her own skills. We both keep the old ways, but different old ways, if you know what I mean."

"I'm not sure that I do," I said carefully.

Mrs. Teller chuckled. "I do root work. Miss Monette works Voodoo."

I'd gotten the woman's full name from Niella. Monette Lark was the granddaughter of Elise DuPre, the women I'd seen in my vision. And I had some acquaintance with Voodoo from a few of Sorren's friends. Everyone thinks that Voodoo, or as many practitioners today prefer, Voudon, is just in New Orleans, but it traveled anywhere Black slaves went, just like root work did. Some of Charleston's planter aristocrats married off their children to New Orleans high society, and if those couples settled in Charleston, it was likely they brought some of their New Orleans servants with them. Those servants brought their own ways and practiced as they pleased in secret, even here in Charleston.

Teag pulled up to a modest house in a tidy neighborhood. Homes up and down the street looked well cared-for, with neat lawns and carefully tended flower gardens. Teag came around and opened the door for Mrs. Teller, offering her his arm with such gallantry that she laughed out loud.

"Aren't you the gentleman!" she exclaimed, taking his arm like a starlet on the red carpet. Niella looked at me and rolled her eyes, but she was smiling, and I couldn't help chuckling. Once we reached the front steps, Mrs. Teller let go of Teag's arm and paused a moment.

"I gave Miss Monette a call so she would know what we were about," Mrs. Teller said. "And she agreed to see us. I told her that I trust you two and that she can speak her mind." She peered at us like a schoolteacher over her glasses. "She doesn't like to talk about what happened, but this is different. It's about time things got put right."

With that, Mrs. Teller rang the doorbell. We waited for a moment before the door opened an inch on its security chain, long enough for the person inside to make certain who was outside. When the door opened again, Monette Lark stood in the doorway. She was tall and sinewy, with hands that looked as if she had done hard work. Her gray hair was shaved close to her head, and while she looked all of her eighty years, her eyes were clear and sharp.

"Come in," she said, then turned, expecting us to follow without a backward glance. Her living room was comfortable, a mixture of a few older pieces that looked handmade and a sofa that probably came from Sears. Everything was as neat and orderly as the yard had been, but when I went to sit down, I caught a whiff of the same sweet perfume that I had smelled before.

"Ernestine tells me you're asking after my Grandma Elise," Monette said, with a direct gaze. "She said you have a Gift, both of you." She closed her eyes for a moment and hummed a tune I could not catch. Then she opened her eyes and nodded. "That's true enough." Her eyes narrowed. "Why do you care about Grandma Elise?"

I had tried to come up with an explanation in the car that didn't give too much away, but I hadn't been successful. "I can read objects when I touch them," I said, deciding that simpler was better. "I run an antique shop, and I use my gift to make sure that objects that might cause problems don't get resold."

I took a deep breath. "We bought some of the pieces that were auctioned off from the Legacy Hotel. One of them was a poker set, and when I touched it, I had a vision of Elise and a man who caused her pain."

Old anger flashed in Monette's eyes. "Say on."

"I saw what happened to her," I said, seeing no way to back out now. "And I know that Artemis Williams died under suspicious circumstances in the alley behind the Legacy Hotel, and so have fourteen other men." I paused. "I won't say that they didn't get what they deserved," I said. "But I have the feeling that your grandmother called on some kind of power in her distress that turned out to be more than she bargained for."

I could tell from Monette's eyes that I had hit close to the mark. For a moment, I thought she might throw us out. Then Mrs. Teller laid a hand on her arm.

"Miss Monette," Mrs. Teller said quietly. "It's time."

Monette drew a deep breath and then nodded. "What that man did to my grandmother, it wasn't right," she said quietly. "But she had no recourse, 'least not in the usual way. Police wouldn't do anything against someone like him. If she could have found a lawyer to take her case, it would never have gone to court. That's how it was in those days." It seemed to me that Monette's heavy drawl grew deeper as her voice became soft, remembering old stories.

"Grandma Elise came from Haiti," she said. "She had given up the Old Practice when she came to Charleston, 'to be a good Christian,' she said." Her eyes flashed. "They call this the Holy City for its churches, but that man didn't pay heed to anything he learned there. My grandma wasn't the first girl he used that way, I'm sure of it. No one was going to stop him."

"Your grandma did," I said softly. "What did she do?"

"She wrote her problem on a piece of paper and folded it three times, then she stabbed it with a knife and said the words. She called the Loas," Monette replied. "The Voodoo gods. Papa Legba to open the gates, and Erzulie Dantor to bring her vengeance on the man who used her." She stood up. "Come with me."

We followed Monette down the narrow hallway toward the bedrooms. Family photos hung in frames on the wall, along with department store landscapes. She stopped in front of a room and pushed the door open. I smelled sweet perfume and tobacco smoke.

Inside, along one wall, was a shrine. The portrait of a dark-skinned woman holding a baby hung above an altar set in colors of navy, red, and gold. The woman's face was marked with three long scars. A goblet of red wine was set out as an offering, along with filterless cigarettes, several dolls, and a couple of silver coins. Next to the first portrait was another image I recognized from the novena card we had found at the shop. Our Lady of Lourdes. I knew that many Voodoo worshippers used the images of Catholic saints to symbolize their gods and keep their Christian masters unawares.

"I keep smelling the same perfume whenever Elise comes up," I said.

Monette nodded knowingly. "*Reve d'Or*. Erzulie Dantor's favorite." She gestured toward the altar. "Erzulie Dantor protects women and children. She's a fierce Loa, and she avenges her daughters who have been abused."

"Elise opened the gate for the Loa and never closed it, didn't she?" I asked quietly.

Monette nodded. "My mother and I begged her to close it. She said that Erzulie Dantor never punished the innocent and that the men who died wouldn't come to justice any other way." She sighed. "Maybe we didn't push her as hard as we should have because we knew she was right."

"Except that I don't think Elise rests peacefully," I said. It was an unmistakable impression I had gotten from the visions. "I think that because the gate wasn't closed right, your grandma's spirit is still bound up in the tragedy, instead of moving on."

Monette nodded. "I think you're right. That's why I agreed to meet with you. Ernestine has been trying to get me to go to that place and do what needs to be done, but I have been stubborn—or afraid." She met my gaze. "I'll go if the two of you will go with me."

"We'll all go," Niella said in a voice that did not accept argument. "And there's no time like the present."

"I'll need a few things," Monette said. She murmured to herself as she moved around the room, picking up some pieces from the altar and placing them in a bag. Then she said quiet words in front of the painting on the wall and turned to us. She stopped in the kitchen to take several items along with us. "I'm ready," she said.

I wasn't, but we were going anyway.

The sun was setting as we headed toward the Legacy Hotel. I fingered the agate necklace at my throat. Agate is supposed to be a protective gem, and I hoped the stones were ready for a busy night. No one said anything as we navigated Charleston's streets. It was late enough that all but the tourist areas of downtown had emptied out. The Legacy Hotel sat a few blocks off King Street. I don't know what neighboring buildings had been next to it in its heyday, but now it sat, boarded up and forlorn, next to an out-of-business convenience store and a defunct barber shop. We drove around to the back, to the alley that started it all.

Given the number of deaths, I almost expected to see a police cruiser parked behind the Legacy Hotel, but perhaps the cops felt like Elise did, that whatever was killing lowlifes was making their job easier. As we got out of the car, I felt a shiver of dread. Something with power was waiting down that alley. I couldn't imagine why anyone in his right mind would go there.

We went in. Monette went first. The scent of *Reve d'Or* was heavy, underlain with the smell of old tobacco. Monette withdrew a maraca from her bag and began to shake it as she chanted softly. I saw that Mrs. Teller had retrieved a few items from Niella's large purse, including several small bags that smelled of herbs and flowers.

Teag and I came last, unsure of our role. The further into the alley we went, the darker it became, like the street lights couldn't quite penetrate the darkness. Maybe it was because the narrow street lay between two taller buildings, but I didn't think that was the only reason. Nor could I explain the fact that the alley was colder than where we had parked. I desperately did not want to touch anything, because even without my gift, every primal instinct warned me of danger and death.

"Don't be afraid." Sorren's voice nearly scared me witless. He had come up behind us so quietly none of us heard him. Mrs. Teller and Niella nodded their greeting. Monette eyed him for a moment, before returning to chant.

"We stop here," Monette said, stopping midway down the alley, just at the edge of the light from the street behind us. From her bag, she withdrew a piece of blue cloth, a red candle, a silver ring, and several cigarettes. She laid them out next to one of the buildings where the ground was flat, creating her altar. She added a drawing of the *veve* for Erzulie Dantor, a complex drawing of a heart pierced with a sword. Then she laid a small silver dagger next to the *veve*. Next, she pulled out a saucer and several small pieces of pork. She withdrew a flask of what smelled like crème de cacao and poured some of it on the pork. Three times, she let a few drops of the liquor fall to the ground.

Mrs. Teller and Niella quietly passed small mojo bags of dried plants and roots to Teag and me. Sorren had disappeared. It appeared to me that Mrs. Teller was whispering quietly, and I wondered what she was conjuring, and whether it was to strengthen Monette or to protect us or both. I noticed that she and Niella both pulled necklaces from inside their shirts that looked to be silver dimes on a leather strand.

Monette began to dance and sing in a language I did not understand. I caught a few words, enough to know that she was calling to Papa Legba to open the gates to the spirit realm. In the distance, I heard a dog bark, and the scent of pipe smoke wafted out of nowhere. Monette smiled and resumed her dancing, faster than before.

I heard Monette call Erzulie Dantor's name, and saw her throw her head back in ecstasy, dancing harder than I would have believed possible for a woman her age. A sheen of sweat glistened on her skin despite how cold the alley had become, and as I watched, three deep scratches appeared on Monette's cheek though I saw nothing to cause them. She gave a cry of triumph and turned to face us. Blood oozed from the fresh scratches on her face, and a trickle of blood came from a corner of her mouth.

Her eyes were bright red.

Monette opened her mouth, but all that came out was a harsh, stuttering noise. The intent was clear. Whatever spirit had taken over was demanding to know why we had come.

"Tell her, child," Mrs. Teller urged. "We'll open the road for you."

"Elise called to you," I said, mustering up my courage to speak to the spirit who was now in possession of Monette's body. "You took vengeance for her. But that was long ago. Elise is dead, but her spirit can't rest as long as you remain here. Please, we need to close the gate."

"Ke-ke-ke-ke," Monette stuttered. The syllables meant nothing to me, but the voice was threatening.

"It's time to let Elise rest," I begged. "She's had her revenge twice seven-fold. For her to rest, you must go through the gate."

Monette took a step toward me, and instinctively I moved backward. I could hear Teag murmuring something and holding his mojo bag tightly in his hands. I touched the agate necklace around my throat, and it cleared my head enough to realize that Sorren had rejoined us.

"Get the knife from the altar," Sorren commanded. He held the poker set firmly grasped in both hands and set it on the ground. I realized that he had used his supernatural speed to retrieve it from the shop and return to us. I moved toward the altar and bent to take the knife, never letting Monette out of my sight. She watched me take the blade from the sacred space, and this time, there was no mistaking the anger in her voice.

Sorren pulled a piece of paper from his pocket and folded it, then placed it on top of the poker set. "Stab it three times," he ordered. "Don't let anything stop you."

I raised the knife for the first blow, and Monette ran toward me, her stutter now an accusation. "Ke-ke-ke-ke!"

Before she could reach me, Sorren stepped in front, then Mrs. Teller, Niella, and Teag, holding his mojo bag in front of him like a shield. "Do it, Cassidy!" Sorren shouted.

I brought the blade down once, digging its tip deep into the burled wood, pinning the paper to the box. I wiggled the blade free and raised it once again, as Monette's shouts became more vicious and she launched herself at my line of protectors, fighting with a vigor I would not have believed she was capable of.

The knife fell, going deeper into the wood this time. Monette's cries were louder, and I expected the police to show up at any moment. She was bleeding from the mouth, and she spat gobbets of blood at anyone who held her back. It looked like even Sorren, with his enhanced strength, was having difficulty holding her which meant that something supernatural was in possession of her body, using her for its own purposes.

One last time I raised the knife and brought it down hard, splitting the wooden cover of the poker box. As the wood split, a dog howled, nearer now, somewhere in the alley with us. Pipe smoke filled the air, and Monette let out a shriek of rage before collapsing into Sorren's arms, limp.

My hand brushed the top of the poker box, and I saw Elise's spirit, standing behind where Sorren held Monette. She stood with an old man with a cane and his skin-and-bones dog. None of the figures were solid. I blinked, and they were gone.

Teag ran to me as I made my way shakily to my feet. "Are you okay?" he asked, worried. I nodded, breathing heavily, still not sure what exactly had transpired.

Sorren held Monette in his arms. The scratches on her face were gone, and the only trace of blood were a few flecks on her lips.

"She'll be fine once she rests," Sorren said. "The Loa rode her hard. It's the price of speaking for the gods. I'll take her home and make sure she's all right."

"What about the poker box?" I asked, looking down at the broken box at my feet. Niella and Mrs. Teller were gathering up the items from Monette's ritual and putting them into Niella's big purse. She paused when she came to the poker box and looked up at Sorren.

"Whatever resonance it had is gone," Sorren said. "It's just an old broken box." With that, he slipped off into the night.

Niella picked up the box and handed it to Mrs. Teller. "We need to get you home," she fussed.

Mrs. Teller gave Niella a withering look. "I'm just fine. You can see that," Mrs. Teller snapped at Niella's protests of concern. "This is what I *do*, child. You think this is the first time I've seen a Loa come on one of its dancers?"

It was the first time for me, and I was not in a hurry for a repeat performance.

"It's warmer," Teag said, taking my arm to steady me. "Can you feel it? It's no scarier now than any other dark alley in Charleston. The light even seems brighter."

Teag said it in a way to get a smile, but he was right. The feeling in the alley was different. Not quite cleansed, but no longer malevolent. More importantly, I was certain that Elise was finally at rest.

"Let's get out of here," I said. "It's time to go home."

COFFIN BOX

"I don't know why, but I've really got a bad feeling about that house." I sat in the car parked at the curb near the big house on the Battery.

"Bad feeling like they won't pay their bill, or bad feeling like there's a hungry demon inside?" Teag Logan asked.

I shook my head. "Not sure, but if I had to put money on it, I'd go with the demon."

Most people would be kidding. Teag knew I wasn't. I'm Cassidy Kincaide, owner of Trifles and Folly, an antique and curio shop in historic, haunted Charleston, SC. Neither Teag nor I are entirely what we seem, and that holds true for the shop as well.

I'm a psychometric, which means I can often read the history of objects by touching them. Teag has Weaver magic, an ability to weave spells into cloth and to weave data streams—like the Internet—making him an awesome hacker. He's my best friend, sometime bodyguard and assistant store manager. I'm the latest in a very long line of relatives to manage Trifles and Folly in the 350 years the store has existed, but we've all had the same silent partner, a nearly six-hundred-year-old vampire named Sorren, and the same mission: to get dangerous magical items off the market and out of the wrong hands. Most of the time, we succeed. When we fail, people die and really bad things happen.

"How do you want to handle this?" Teag asked.

I drew a deep breath. "We go in, and see what's what. Then we figure it out from there." My magic is touch-psychic, not clairvoyance, so I can't see the future, much as I would sometimes like to.

The house was large, old, and expensive. Most of the homes on the Battery hailed from before the Civil War. Many of the houses are painted in the muted pastels most people associate with places like Bermuda and Nassau. Some of the families who owned these homes had been here since the mansions were built. The houses are beautiful, and tourists flock to see them. But as much as I admire their beauty, I try not to spend a lot of time down at the Battery for the simple reason that it creeps me out.

The Battery is a seawall built in the 1700s to keep back the waters of the Charleston Harbor, where the Ashley and Cooper Rivers merge. Nowadays, the beautiful park on the peninsula is called Whitepoint Gardens, and it's where children play, and couples stroll. But back in the day, it was the place where the gallows stood, and pirates were hanged. Sorren's told me stories about those days, and my magic can still feel the unsettled vibrations of the long-ago deaths. That didn't help my mood. I was jittery as hell.

"Since Anthony got us the referral, we at least need to go in and look around," Teag prodded. Anthony was Teag's romantic partner. They had been together for almost a year, and I hoped they'd make it permanent. They were a cute couple. Anthony came from an old Charleston family, and he looked the part. Blond hair, a wardrobe straight off the pages of *GQ*, and a partnership in the family law firm. Teag, on the other hand, was tall and lanky, with a mop of dark skater boy hair. He had been close to completing his Ph.D. in History when Sorren and I snagged him for a role with the store, given his magic and his love for the past.

"I know, I know." I pushed a lock of strawberry blonde hair back behind my ear. It wasn't even noon yet, but the summer heat was already in the high nineties, and with my pale Scots-Irish coloring, I was red in the face.

I got out of the car, and Teag followed me up the walkway. A dark-haired woman who looked to be in her early forties came to the door. She had a no-fuss chin-length bob haircut, a single strand of pearls around her neck and she was wearing a pale blue twin-set over white slacks with bare feet.

"Marjorie Stedman?" I asked.

She nodded. "You must be Cassidy and Teag, from Trifles and Folly. Please, come in."

Marjorie ushered us into a graceful old house that certainly deserved being called a mansion. The foyer had an original plank floor and a curved stairway with an elaborately carved balustrade. A large yet tasteful crystal chandelier hung from the ceiling, and it looked like it fit right in. I glimpsed a living room big enough to hold a grand piano and not appear cramped, and oil paintings hung on all the walls. I was willing to bet that all of them were Stedman ancestors.

"Thank you so much for coming," Marjorie said. Now that I had a chance to study her features, she looked as if she hadn't been sleeping well. Not surprising, considering that both her parents had died unexpectedly within a day of each other. The deaths had been the talk of the town when they happened a few weeks earlier, but despite the odd timing, police ruled both to be of natural causes. Still, I was certain Marjorie had her hands full settling the estate. Which was why we were there.

"When Mama and Daddy passed on so unexpectedly, they left everything to me." Marjorie's accent was thick as honey, an old-money Charleston accent that was patrician and gracious. Not as stiff-jawed as a Richmond accent, nor as much of a drawl as folks from Georgia, it was a verbal class distinction that was rapidly fading as more people moved in and out of the city.

"I'm an only child, the sole heir, and the executor," she said, brushing a strand of hair out of her eyes. I understood why she looked so harried. Wealth on a Stedman scale would be complicated, and even though I was sure she had a team of expensive advisors, there were a lot of decisions to make and deadlines to meet at an emotionally vulnerable time. My heart went out to her.

"I'm finally getting around to having the antiques appraised," Marjorie said. "I've had someone through already to appraise the run-of-the-mill things, so you don't have to worry about those. But there were some items of daddy's, and some of mama's jewelry, that the first appraiser said needed an expert opinion, so here you are."

"We appreciate being asked to help," I said. Marjorie gave us a quick tour of the rooms as she led us to where the items were she wanted us to appraise. As she talked, I tried to "listen" with my magic, hoping to get a feel for what was making me so jittery. The ominous feeling hadn't gotten any better, and it was strong enough that I was unwilling to chalk it up to my imagination.

"Mama's jewelry is in a case on her dressing table, in that room," Marjorie said, pointing to the double doors to the master bedroom. "Daddy's smoking room is at the far end of the hall, so he could sit on the balcony and not 'stink up the house' as Mama said," she added with a wistful chuckle. "She always did hate his cigars."

"There's a desk in his smoking room that's old, and some antique cigar tools that are silver," Marjorie added. "And a humidor that Mama gave him right before his death. It's old and very unusual, and she got it for him for his last birthday." I remembered from the newscast that Payton Stedman III had died on his sixty-fifth birthday from sudden heart failure.

"Do you know where your mother purchased it?" I asked.

Marjorie shook her head. "No. But I want to get rid of it." She gave me a nervous, embarrassed half-smile, more of a grimace. "I know it's superstitious, but I can't help feeling like that damned thing had some-thing to do with Daddy's death. The sooner it's gone, the better."

I noticed that she wasn't walking us into the rooms. That seemed odd to me, especially given the fact that Marjorie didn't look like she was hysterical with grief. She didn't appear to be the hysterical type. Movie stereotypes aside, Southern women really do have steel beneath the moonlight-and-magnolias exterior, and Marjorie Stedman looked like a very competent woman. But from the way she didn't quite meet my gaze, I wondered what was going on. She acted like she was afraid of something.

"This shouldn't take long," Teag assured her. I knew he was covering for me to give me a chance to see if I could sense magic nearby. I was beginning to think that Marjorie was a savvy woman. I wasn't quite sure what my gift was picking up from inside the smoking room, but it was as if a heavy, dull cloud of something a lot fouler than cigar smoke hung over the area. To my senses, it reeked more of ill-intent and evil than of Cohibas or purloined Cuban smokes.

"You're welcome to stay with us as we work if you like," I offered. Somehow, I knew she would decline.

"That's all right," Marjorie said a little too quickly. "I have things to take care of. Please look over the items on this list, and let me know when you'll be able to give me the official report." She handed me a hand-written list of ten items and then padded down the hallway and out of sight.

I glanced at the list. "There are six pieces of jewelry, and four items in the smoking room," I said. "Let's start with the jewelry." I didn't want to admit to Teag that the vibes I was getting from the room at the end of the hall made me jumpy.

I pushed open the double doors and walked into a sumptuous master suite. The house itself might date from the eighteenth century, but inside, its owners had spared no modern luxury. The room was appointed with exquisite—and expensive—good taste. The antique four-poster bed was covered with luxury linens and a beautiful duvet. The Aubusson carpet on top of the polished wooden floors probably cost more than my car. Oil paintings and a large, gold-framed antique mirror hung on the walls. I noticed that the mirror had been draped with black cloth, an old custom long-forgotten, designed to keep spirits from becoming trapped in the reflection. It made me wonder whether Marjorie's dreams had been dark.

"Very nice," Teag said, an understatement if I ever heard one.

"It's beautiful," I agreed. Yet even before I touched anything, there was an aura of sadness that struck me, and an undercurrent of bitterness. It made me wonder if the domestic tranquility wasn't all it was portrayed to be.

"There's the jewelry," Teag prompted, clearing his throat to let me know I'd been woolgathering again.

I approached the dressing table where six pieces of beautiful jewelry were laid out atop the mirrored vanity top. Before I touched anything, I stood for a moment, eying the pieces and trying to get a sense of which ones might have bad mojo. I'd learned to be cautious the hard way, after nasty items knocked me flat on my butt, more than once.

"Picking up anything?" Teag asked.

I hadn't lost my sense that something about the house was very wrong, but it didn't seem to be coming from these pieces. I shook my head. "I don't think they're dangerous. But there's still something off about them."

Teag pulled out the fancy dressing table chair for me with an exaggerated sweep of his arm. "Your table is ready," he said, sounding like a maître d'.

I chuckled, and sat down, studying the pieces again. There was a sapphire ring rimmed with diamonds that appeared to be from the 1920s and a diamond necklace. I bet both were Harry Winston. The other pieces were from Tiffany & Co., Van Cleef and Arpels, Chopard and Bulgari. Very nice.

But as soon as I touched the first piece, a sleek silver and diamond bracelet, any bling-envy disappeared. The piece was beautiful, and the gemstones top quality, but an unmistakable sense of loneliness and betrayal clung to the bracelet like old perfume. I touched a pair of diamond pendant earrings with double-digit carats and got the same feeling, with a stab of disappointment and humiliation to go with it. The same was true with every lovely piece.

"Cassidy," Teag said quietly. "You're crying."

So I was. I caught my breath and wiped away the tears from my cheeks with the back of my hand. "He cheated on her," I said raggedly. "The pieces… they were all gifts to ingratiate himself after he'd gone off on another fling. I could feel how hurt she was, how betrayed. It happened time and time again."

"Damn," Teag replied. "Do you think Marjorie knows? Maybe she's appraising them to sell them."

I shrugged. "She'd have to do it for taxes anyhow. And if you didn't know the history and couldn't sense the emotions, they're beautiful pieces." Six pieces, six betrayals. Were there more? I wondered. Men who cheated often made a habit of it.

"They're all from famous jewelry houses," I said, feeling heartsick. "We shouldn't have difficulty assigning value. I don't have a doubt about the authenticity. He must have screwed up big time to need these to get out of the dog house."

Funny thing, but as I touched the other pieces, the emotions changed. The disappointment and pain were as bright and clear as the diamonds on the first items. Somewhere along the way, the feelings shifted. Humiliation, self-doubt, and anger crept in as I moved to what were likely newer gifts. The sixth piece was so sharp with bitterness that I recoiled. Caroline Stedman had not been a happy woman, despite her wealth and position.

Teag took pictures of the pieces and wrote down dimensions as I pulled myself together. "I think we've got what we need," he said. "You're right—they've got all the right markings. They're genuine. I don't think Marjorie will have trouble getting rid of them, if she wants to sell them."

"Good idea, but I sure wouldn't want to wear them," I said. People don't realize that objects have as much of an emotional provenance as they do a physical one. It would take a lot to wipe the slate clean with these pieces, so that they wouldn't be a constant drag on the wearer's happiness, with or without magic.

That was one of the reasons I was so picky with the jewelry we sold at Trifles and Folly, especially wedding rings. I'd seen my share of well-to-do young lovers who wanted a unique set of rings, and came looking for estate jewelry. Just in the time I'd managed the store, I'd turned down buying many sets because the emotional resonance wasn't good. No one should start out with a psychic albatross like that in a piece of jewelry that gets worn every day, and on a finger that legend says has a vein that runs straight to the heart.

"Ready to go?" Teag asked.

I nodded, and we headed back to the hallway, then walked toward the doors to Peyton Stedman's smoking room. Cigars were having a resurgence, but among Charleston's upper crust, they had never gone away. During Garden Week, the night air smelled of jasmine, gardenia, and Herreras.

Teag opened the door to the smoking room, and I cried out in alarm. Even before I touched anything, I felt evil and death roil out toward me like the mist off the ocean. I staggered backward, lost my balance, and fell backward. Alarmed, Teag positioned himself between me and the room, but there was no visible threat, no tangible enemy. I was already climbing to my feet when he turned around to help me up, and I could feel my cheeks flaming.

"What was that?" Teag asked, still watching the room with a wary eye.

I shook my head. "I don't know. But there's some definite bad juju in there, and I'm guessing that's why Marjorie didn't want to show us around in person."

I doubted Marjorie had a psychic ability. But some negative energy is so strong that even people without a clairvoyant bone in their bodies know to stay away. It's where talk about curses comes from, and often, the rumors are more right than people realize. Something in that room was either cursed or just plain evil, and it was our job to figure out why.

The room had a decidedly masculine feel to it, with dark paneling, leather chairs and bookshelves filled with antique tomes. A large-screen TV was a nod toward modernity. I saw a mahogany liquor cabinet with Baccarat crystal glasses and Waterford decanters over to one side, and I was betting that nothing in the bar was less than 25-year-old single malt. Peyton Stedman was a man of good taste, but that hadn't been enough to keep him alive.

"What's on the list?" I asked, still scanning the room with my gaze. There was a large teak desk that looked like it had come from Colonial

India, probably a hundred years old. On it sat a beautiful humidor made of wood with a rich, dark grain. Oil paintings hung on the walls: fox hunts, grouse hunts, and the obligatory Victorian nude reclining on a velvet couch. On the wall above the massive desk hung a portrait of Mr. Stedman himself. I guessed he was in his early fifties when he sat for the painting, over ten years ago. He looked confident, even arrogant, like a man who knows he has the world by the tail. Stedman was a good-looking man who had all the mannerisms and trappings of old money. I didn't doubt he had any trouble attracting women, wedding ring or not.

"The humidor," Teag replied, inclining his head toward a wooden box on the top of the desk. "A sterling silver cigar cutter, probably in one of the desk drawers," he continued. "And the desk itself."

I didn't want to get any closer to the dark aura, but I had a job to do. Not only was Marjorie expecting us to do an appraisal; now that we knew there was a dangerous magical object involved, we had a responsibility to Sorren and the Alliance to figure out what was wrong.

"I don't think the problem is with the desk itself," I said finally, letting my hand hover above the hand-rubbed, teak surface. The piece was beautiful, and despite its age, well cared-for. Setting a value on it wouldn't be difficult. "But I'm getting a second-hand disturbance, like something that's in or on the desk is causing the problem. Until we know what it is, I don't want to touch the desk myself."

Teag opened the upper right-hand drawer and found the cigar cutter. He brought it over to me and held it while I passed my hand an inch away, testing the vibes. I shook my head. "Sometimes a cigar cutter is just a cigar cutter," I said. "No mojo."

We both turned to look at the humidor. Good cigars are expensive, and I was betting that Peyton Stedman smoked the best money could buy. Aficionados didn't want their smokes to dry out, so humidors were storage boxes that kept the humidity just-so to preserve those pricy stogies. They could run from a few hundred bucks to tens of thousands, and looking at the one on Stedman's desk, I figured it had come in on the high end of the estimate.

"Brazilian rosewood," Teag murmured, looking closely at the

burled, rich wood. The lid and edges were beautifully inlaid. The hinges were gold-plated. It was a work of art, and as hot as a bookie's ledger.

"Strike one," I replied. "That's a protected wood species—not supposed to be able to cross international borders. She can't legally resell it."

Teag pulled out a pair of white curator linen gloves from a pocket. He put them on, and carefully opened the lid, standing off to the side just in case something unexpected popped out. We both exhaled when nothing happened.

"Strike two," he said quietly. "Cuban cigars." I peered over his shoulder. Nestled next to the Gurkha Black Dragons—the most expensive cigars on the market—were a tidy number of Montecristo grand coronas. Sure, the Montecristos made in the Dominican Republic were legal in the U.S., but I was pretty certain a connoisseur like Stedman would want the real Havanas, and they were still embargoed. Which made the humidor a double problem for Marjorie.

I inched closer and willed myself to stretch out my hand. Teag stood behind me, intent on not letting me fall again. There was no way around this. I had to do it, but I didn't want to.

The instant my fingers touched the rosewood, stone-cold evil curled up my skin. The vision hit me like a train wreck. *I glimpsed a ritual circle, black candles, blood. A voice chanted words I didn't understand, but their malice was clear. The accent was thick as gumbo. Power gathered like a thundercloud, dark and vicious. The chanting voice directed that deadly energy, focusing it with will and ritual, twisting it into a curse. I saw a small black box with broken bits of mirror and a bit of parchment with handwriting on it. And next to that black box was the humidor.*

Coils of dark power undulated from the circle. Some of that power drove the curse into the wood of the humidor. Other darkness drifted and pooled around the black box, caressing it like a homicidal lover. I felt power go into that box, too, killing power. The vision went dark.

I came back to myself sitting in Peyton Stedman's chair, knowing I had blacked out. Teag was watching me with concern. I half expected Marjorie to have called the EMTs, but no ambulance sirens sounded.

"He was cursed," I said. Teag stepped away and brought me a glass of water. He pushed it into my hand, and I drank it, wishing it were something stronger. "Someone Crossed him, but good."

"Hoodoo?" Teag asked.

I nodded. "It would have to be a root worker of real power," I said. "And questionable integrity." Crossing, jinxes, and curses are part of the Hoodoo tradition, a very old practice that came to Charleston from Africa with the thousands of slaves who passed through this port. Some folks call it Conjure. Don't confuse it with Voodoo (or Voudon as practitioners prefer). Hoodoo and Voudon are very different—and both are real and powerful. Teag and I had seen the results up close.

"You think someone Crossed Mrs. Peyton, too?"

I shrugged. "Seems likely—especially since she died the next day."

Teag let out a low whistle. "So that means we're looking for a murderer who can kill with a curse."

"Not only can kill, but has killed—at least twice," I replied.

Just then, I heard Marjorie's footsteps in the corridor. "Is everything all right in there? I thought I heard something." She stayed just outside the door, looking in.

I stood and hoped that I didn't look as pale as I felt. "The cigar cutter and the desk are fine pieces, and I think they'll do well for you at auction. We won't have any trouble setting a value. But there is a problem with the humidor," I added.

"Oh dear. I was afraid you were going to say that."

I frowned. "Have you opened the humidor?"

Marjorie shook her head. "At first, I didn't want to touch anything in case the doctor needed to look at it, and then it just didn't come to mind, what with all that happened."

It frightens her, I thought. "I'm afraid that we can't put the humidor up for sale—no reputable dealer can."

Marjorie looked genuinely confused. "I don't understand."

"The wood is a protected species," I replied. "And there are illegal Cuban cigars inside. Both are enough to create a lot of trouble."

Marjorie's eyes widened with alarm. "Really? Now what?"

Teag gave her a reassuring smile that's so effective; it really should be patented. "Since both the gift giver and the recipient have passed on, it should be easy to resolve. We'll have to go through the proper authorities, including your estate lawyer, but it should be possible to take care of it quietly."

After we lift the curse, to keep it from killing anyone else, I added silently.

"Can you just get it out of here and take care of it for me?" Marjorie asked. "If I never see that damned thing again, it would be too soon."

She might be reacting to the negative energy unconsciously, but I was guessing there was more to it. "Bad memories?" I asked quietly.

Marjorie nodded. "Mama gave that to Daddy for his birthday, and he was so happy. An hour later, he was dead. Then she was gone. I know it's silly to blame the gift, but I can't help feeling like bad things came with it."

She was more right than she would ever know. "Do you happen to know where your mother bought the box?" I asked.

Marjorie shook her head. Sorry, no. Mama was so excited about her big surprise!" She frowned. "Would whoever sold it to her be in trouble?"

Teag shrugged. "Maybe. It would depend on the circumstances. The box is unusual enough; it does open up some questions."

And how. "I know you have a lot on your mind right now," I said gently. "But if you come upon any receipts from purchases your mother made in her last few days, it might help us track this down. Identifying a seller could take the Customs authorities' attention off your mother."

Marjorie gave a quick nod. "I'd like to keep this quiet. There's been enough sensationalism about their deaths, like things weren't bad enough already."

"We can't take possession of the box because of the legalities," I said, and I felt sorry for Marjorie, having to live in the house with that cursed object. "But we'll try to work with the authorities on your behalf as quickly as possible." The authorities I was thinking of belonged to the Alliance. Curses trumped contraband. I figured that once we had a game plan, Sorren could easily get into the house to have a look at the humidor if he wanted to. After all, five hundred years ago, he was the best jewel thief in Antwerp.

I chatted with Marjorie about the jewelry as we walked downstairs, leaving out my knowledge about Peyton Stedman's infidelities. "Once you have the appraisals, the way should be clear for you to sell it, if that's what you want," I added.

"I'm keeping some of mama's older pieces, ones I remember from when I was younger," Marjorie said. "The later pieces don't mean much to me." Or maybe, if she had enough latent sensitivity to recoil from the cursed humidor, she also picked up some of the negative vibes from the newer gifts.

Neither Teag nor I said anything until we were in the car on the way back to the shop. "I think I'll stroll down to the Charleston City Market and clear my head," I said.

He gave me a sidelong look. "You mean, you're going to see if Niella and Mrs. Teller are there, aren't you?"

I chuckled. "Busted. I figure if anyone knows anything about root work in this city, its Ernestine Teller."

Teag leaned back in his seat. "Good idea. I'll work the internet. See what I can find out. I have a suspicion there's more to this, and that's dangerous until we know who sent that curse and why."

OUR PART-TIME SHOP ASSISTANT, Maggie, was helping a customer when we got back to Trifles and Folly. Maggie is semi-retired, and she wears her gray hair short, so it doesn't interfere with her yoga. Her wardrobe is Woodstock-esque, but her brain is Harvard Business School. And when she laughs, everyone wants to be her friend.

Maggie waved to us, her signal that we weren't needed right away up front. Teag headed for the office to start digging on the computer. I returned a few phone calls and emails, and then headed off toward the market. There were some errands I needed to run, too. I had gathered everything into one small plastic bag in an effort to be efficient: a pair of my mother's favorite citrine earrings to go to the jeweler for new posts and my dog's old license tag to remind me to get a new one, plus a list of some spices to buy for dinner.

It was a glorious summer day, and hot even though it was still before lunch. Charleston has beautiful gardens because we also have humidity most people only find in rainforests and hothouses. I had barely stepped outside the shop when I felt sweat bead up on my forehead. By the time I got to the marketplace, I knew my cheeks would be red, and I'd need to stop in the shade. I promised myself a nice tall glass of sweet tea, served up over ice and made the Charleston way, with enough sugar to frost a cake.

There's a reason Charleston is a favorite with tourists. It's a pretty place, with pastel-colored buildings, wrought-iron railings and gates, hidden little secret gardens, and cobblestones everywhere. Down on Market Street is the Charleston City Market, the heart of the historic district. Barring a hurricane, it's open almost every day, and the sides of the big building open up to let in the sun and breeze. Vendors sell everything from jewelry to fresh vegetables to original photography and art. Bakers offer up their Charleston tea cookies and homemade peach jam. Jars of pickled okra and watermelon sit next to bags of fresh, hot boiled peanuts or cans of she-crab soup. It's a shopper's paradise, and there's always something new. I picked up some sage and basil for the pasta I wanted to cook, and couldn't resist a couple of small sample bags of flavored coffee.

"Hello there, Cassidy!" Niella sang out a greeting as soon as she laid eyes on me. Her mother, Mrs. Teller, looked up and flashed a grin that lit up her wrinkled face.

"Good morning!" I enjoyed chatting with Niella and her mother whenever I went to the market, even if I didn't have a cursed object to tame. "You've got some new baskets out."

Niella nodded. "Sure do. Been working on a couple of new handles and shapes. You like?"

"You know I do!" Niella and Mrs. Teller weave sweetgrass baskets.

Mrs. Teller is very proud of her Gullah heritage, and in the Lowcountry, sweetgrass basket-making is a true art form. Baskets like hers sell for hundreds of dollars, with their complicated twists and fine workmanship. Ernestine Teller has been making baskets for most of her seventy-some years, and her hands keep moving even when she looks up. She makes it look easy, but it takes a lifetime for that kind of skill.

"Shadows touched you." Mrs. Teller's voice was quiet, but she gave me an appraising glance. She had the Sight, and I didn't doubt that she could pick up on the evil from the box we had seen today.

"I need your help," I said.

Mrs. Teller nodded. "I know. You've got a heap of trouble. Someone near you been Crossed real good."

Niella glanced around us to make sure no one else heard. She's very protective of her mother. At the same time, Mrs. Teller has skills of her own that I was pretty sure could help her take care of herself when it came to magic.

"I don't know how to ask this without giving offense—" I started.

Mrs. Teller's fingers never stopped their weaving. "You want to know if I know anyone who would put a jinx on someone. Throw a Hoodoo so strong, might even kill somebody."

I nodded. "I'm certainly not saying that you do—"

"'Course I do," Mrs. Teller said, looking back down at her basket. "Can't do what I do for as long as I been doing it in this city without knowing who else has power, good and bad." She paused, and the thin strips of sweetgrass ran through her fingers. I knew how easy it was for a novice to get cut on those sharp strips, but Mrs. Teller never slipped.

"Not many Hoodoo folks could do something like that, thank the Lord," she said. "Most who can know better. You reap what you sow. Bad comes from bad." She shook her head. "Uh huh. But there are some, for sure."

"One person—maybe two—have already died," I said quietly with a quick glance over my shoulder. "I need to know how to lift the curse."

Mrs. Teller shrugged. "If the Crossing is set right, it can't be lifted until it's done, except by the one who put it on the person." She looked up at me again, peering at me with a gaze that seemed to see right through into my soul. "The kind of conjure doctors who would do such a Crossing are dangerous to know."

Despite the heat, I shivered. "That's why I've got to find out who did this. Other people could be in danger."

She had already looked back to her weaving. "High John."

"Excuse me?"

"Doctor High John. Be my bet. He'd do Crossings, jinxes, most anything if you paid enough," she replied, never taking her gaze from her basket as she worked. "Don't go alone. You won't need to tell him I sent you. He'll know I know. That won't keep you safe, but it might make him think twice."

"Where do I find him?"

She named a part of the city that doesn't make it onto the garden tours. It was an older area with modest homes that had been new after World War II, and lately the area had fallen into disrepair. "Blue shotgun house, with dark blue trim," Mrs. Teller said. "You'll know it by the garden in front, full of plants for spell work. He might have a sign out, might not."

She leaned forward. "This is important, child. Don't leave anything of yours behind. Brush out your hair good so you don't leave strands. Don't take anything of his to eat or drink. Try not to touch anything, and sure as the Lord is true, don't step anywhere you'll leave a footprint. You don't want to give High John any way to have power over you."

"Thank you," I said, although I was full of misgivings.

Mrs. Teller made a dismissive gesture with one hand. "You might think otherwise, after you go there. Be careful, you hear?" She paused, then reached down and took a small sweetgrass basket with a lid.

"Take this with you," she said, thrusting it into my hands. "'Til you find out what's what, you keep it with you all the time."

I knew how much her baskets cost, because I had bought one for my mother's birthday. "I couldn't—"

"Oh yes you could," she said, and her dark eyes met mine with a no-nonsense look. "It pleases me for you to have it," she said, lifting her chin. "So. Take it."

Niella rolled her eyes, used to her mother's whims. I thanked Mrs. Teller profusely and then headed back to the shop with the basket on my arm. It was about the size of a small purse, and I decided that was how I would use it, if I had to keep it with me. When I touched the basket, I felt the lingering aura of Mrs. Teller's presence, calm and steady. I put my purchases into the basket along with the small bag of items from my pocket and headed back, figuring I would run errands another day.

The store was busy when I got back, so I put the basket near me behind the counter and joined Teag and Maggie taking care of customers. Summer tourists love the unusual items Trifles and Folly has to offer, and since we keep any of the spooky stuff in the back until we can deal with it, no one's the wiser to what we really do. There must have been bus tours or a convention in town, because we were slammed. It was closing time before I ever got a chance to even talk to Teag.

After we had flipped the sign on the door to "closed" and said goodnight to Maggie, I caught Teag up on what I learned from Mrs. Teller. He glanced at the basket on my lap.

"She's been helping me with my Weaving magic," he said. "You know there's a bit of her magic in everything she makes. That's one reason her baskets attract so many buyers—and such high prices."

I could believe it. I realized that I was unconsciously stroking the smooth twists, taking in the faint, pleasant smell of the sweetgrass. "So what did you find out?" I asked.

"Peyton Stedman had expensive tastes," Teag said. "He liked the good life. The only problem was, he was running out of money."

I looked at Teag as if he might have hit his head. "Hello? Did you see that house?"

He nodded. "Uh huh. I didn't say they were going broke. Yet. But the way he liked to spend cash, between gambling and companions, it went out faster than it came in. Plus, Stedman kept collecting pretty young honeys and buying them pricey presents."

"This doesn't sound good."

"It isn't. Caroline might have given him a luxury humidor for his birthday, but if Peyton hadn't fallen over dead, she was going to serve him with divorce papers a few days later," Teag said. "I hacked their bank records and followed the money. Large payment to one of the nastier high-end divorce lawyers in town."

I frowned as I thought it through. "Do you think Caroline was behind the curse?"

Teag shrugged. "Why bother? She was probably going to take him to the cleaners. Some of the other tidbits I found were emails from a private investigator. She had Peyton dead to rights."

"Why pay a conjure doctor and a lawyer too?"

"Beats me," he replied. "And maybe it wasn't Caroline. A guy like Peyton Stedman is bound to have made plenty of enemies. Bad debts, angry mistresses, business deals that went sour. His wife might have had to stand in line to get a swing at him."

I was going to have to think about what Teag had discovered. In the meantime, we had a Hoodoo man to see. "Let's go. I don't think I want to face Doctor High John after dark."

We drove Teag's old Volvo instead of my Mini Cooper, since his is more forgettable. Just in case, he splashed enough mud on the license plate to make it impossible to read. Teag and I had changed into jeans and t-shirts to fit in better, but I didn't think we were going to fool anyone. High John lived in a rough neighborhood, as Charleston goes. Someday, developers would probably gentrify the area, if there was anything left. The houses managed to be the wrong kind of 'old' in a city that loves old houses. Some of the homes were boarded up. Others had been vandalized, with broken windows and graffiti. People loitered in odd places on a few of the side streets, and I figured they were look-outs. I really didn't want to linger.

We drove past High John's place, and I got a good look. The house was just as Mrs. Teller had described it, only shabbier. It was a one-story 'shotgun' house with a tin roof that was in need of repair. The lawn was overgrown, and some of the grass was as tall as the hand-lettered wooden sign out front. "Conjure Doctor. Consultations. Remedies. Reasonable Rates."

"Doesn't look like anyone's home," I observed. "No lights on."

"I saw an alley around back," Teag said. "I'd rather not have the whole neighborhood wondering what we're up to. Let's park there."

A lot of High John's neighbors were sitting out on porches and stoops trying to catch a cool breeze. They spoke to the few passers-by, and eyed the cars that drove past warily. I didn't think anyone would necessarily call the cops on us, since I had the distinct impression that might be bad for some neighborhood businesses, but I also didn't want to meet the welcoming committee.

I was wearing my agate necklace, for protection, and I had Mrs. Teller's basket on my left arm. Even so, I felt skittish. Teag had learned to store magic in knotted rope, and I saw that he had a couple of charms that looked like macramé knots hanging from his belt, where he could get to them easily. We weren't exactly going in unprotected. Teag's a black belt in a couple of martial arts styles, and I've taken enough classes to put up a good fight. Still, I'd rather not need to use what I'd learned, and I sincerely hoped we were going to have an uneventful evening.

Like that ever happens.

We let ourselves in the back gate, and walked toward the back door, avoiding any patches of bare ground where we might leave a footprint. I guessed that High John might have booby-trapped his place, Hoodoo style, so Teag had brought along a broom and odd as it sounds, swept the back walkway up to the door, just in case there was jinx dust around. To be safe, we each carried an Indian head penny in our pockets and slipped a Mercury silver dime into one shoe. Most people might think that kind of thing was superstitious, but legend often has a basis in fact and charms, amulets, and talismans have more power than modern folks like to believe. We weren't taking any chances.

A strong, unpleasant smell stopped me in my tracks. "Gad. Did someone leave the garbage out in the sun?" I muttered. We moved on, trying not to breathe.

The house was long and narrow, with four rooms each right in front of the other so that you had to go through one to get to the others. That's why the style is called "shotgun," since if all the doors were open, you could shoot a shotgun from the front door out the back without hitting anything. Legend has it that spirits like shotgun-style houses since they can easily pass through them. Maybe that's why High John picked it, or maybe the rent was cheap. High John's back-yard was even more of a mess than the front yard, and I began to wonder if he had picked up and left town. It didn't look like anyone had been around for a while.

Teag rapped at the door. No one answered. He put his hand under the bottom of his t-shirt and used the cloth to try the doorknob. It was old and cheap, and it turned with a snap. He pushed it open, and we both almost lost our lunch. The stench was overwhelming. I had a feeling that High John had bigger problems than his garbage. I was right.

We found his body in the hallway. Charleston heat doesn't do good things for a corpse. It was bloated and covered with flies, and from the maggots I glimpsed, I knew he hadn't died recently. The body was surrounded with ritual paraphernalia. There was a t-shaped, black candle with writing carved into what was left of its half-burned trunk. I saw opened bags of powders and an overturned bottle of something that looked like vinegar. Bits of broken mirror glinted in the dying light. I wanted to throw up, but when I tightened my grip on the sweetgrass basket, it calmed me and helped me to not toss my cookies.

"Watch where you step," I said, remembering Mrs. Teller's warn-ing. Not to mention that we didn't need to leave footprints where there was a dead body.

"Let's get out of here," Teag said, and we backed out. I was expecting to find the police waiting at our car, or at least nosy neigh-bors, but to my relief, no one tried to stop us.

When we were well clear of the area, Teag pulled into a parking lot, and we both sat and shivered for a moment. "Yikes," I said, still queasy from the smell and what we'd seen.

"That doesn't begin to cover it," Teag replied. "Off-hand, I'd say High John could have died not long after the Stedmans."

"That doesn't make any sense," I countered. "If he's dead, and she's dead, and Stedman is dead, who cast the curse?"

"Do you think Marjorie did it?" he asked, putting the car into gear and heading onto the road again.

I grimaced. "I don't want to think so," I replied, thinking back over our meeting. I shook my head. "No. I really don't. Even though she inherits. I don't think she's the one."

Teag glanced my way. "Then who? And why kill the conjure doctor? Unless someone didn't want there to be a witness for murdering the Stedmans."

My head hurt. "We need to pull Sorren in on this. Maybe Mrs. Teller, too. We're no closer to un-cursing the humidor, and there are three dead people. Let's go back to my place, and I'll call Sorren again. I left a message for him earlier, but he hasn't returned my call."

The sun set on our way back from High John's house. As it turned out, Sorren was waiting for us. I own what Charlestonians call a "single house," which has the narrow end facing the street so that the front door comes onto my porch (we call it a "piazza") instead of into the house. The piazza faces a small walled garden. I bought the house at a steep discount from my parents when they moved, or I could never have afforded it. Sorren and Mrs. Teller were sitting on the porch swing, chatting and laughing like old friends.

"How did it go?" Sorren asked, rising as we entered the porch.

I shook my head. "I'll tell you once we're inside and I've poured us all some bourbon."

Baxter, my little Maltese dog, began barking up a storm when I put the key in the lock. But when he saw Sorren, he immediately sat down and stared at us with a befuddled look of goofy admiration.

"You glamored him again, didn't you?" I said drily. Sorren bent over to scratch Baxter behind the ears.

"I keep telling you it won't hurt him," Sorren replied. My boss may be a nearly six-hundred-year-old vampire, but he keeps up with the times. His blond hair was cut in the latest style, and his t-shirt and jeans had a trendy-gothic vibe that was rather ironic on him. He says that vampires who can't change with the times don't survive long. At this rate, he might make it to one thousand.

I flicked on the lights and led us into the living room, where I sloshed some bourbon into two rocks glasses, then turned to see if my guests wanted any. Sorren and Mrs. Teller shook their heads, although I had a feeling Mrs. Teller noticed that my hand was shaking as I poured.

"He's dead," Teag said as he took his glass and sat down. "High John. Been that way for a while. Looked like he died in the middle of doing a spell."

"Tell me exactly what you saw," Mrs. Teller said, leaning forward. "It's important." She listened intently as we told her everything we could remember about the house and grounds. When we were finished, she looked at Sorren and shook her head.

"We got trouble," Mrs. Teller said.

"I know," I replied, trying not to sound testy as I sipped the bourbon and leaned back into the couch, trying to un-see that awful scene. "Three dead people and no idea whodunit."

Mrs. Teller gave a soft, mirthless laugh. "Oh no, child. We know. The problem is, the killing isn't over yet because it wasn't done right."

I didn't like the sound of that. "Meaning what?"

"I did a little asking around, after you left the market house," Mrs. Teller said. "I know people. And they said that High John had let slip he had a big job comin', so he could pay his bills and his poker debts, too. Someone saw him in the dark down near Whitepoint Gardens, talking with a high-class lady. Now, they're all dead." She shook her head. "He got careless."

"I'm totally lost," Teag said.

"When I got Cassidy's voice mail, I put some Alliance resources to work looking into that humidor and the cigars," Sorren said. "The trail leads right to Caroline Stedman. But the humidor was magically neutral. Illegal, yes, but not dangerous. And before you ask, the cigars weren't poisoned—at least not when they left Havana."

He paused. "What's especially damning is the fact that the day before Peyton Stedman's birthday, the day before he received the

Humidor—which was cursed by then—Caroline Stedman made a visit to Magnolia Cemetery."

I arched an eyebrow. "Premonition? Buying a plot for hubby?"

Sorren shook his head. "Neither. She went in, walked to a remote corner of the cemetery, appeared to bury something small, and left."

"How did you know to have someone following Caroline Stedman before there was a murder?" Teag asked.

Sorren chuckled. "I didn't. The Alliance has watchers on all the cemeteries. As it turns out, he didn't contact me about Mrs. Stedman. He wanted to let me know we have a wraith on the loose."

"There have always been stories about Magnolia Cemetery being haunted," I said. "Confederate soldiers and little ghost girls, that sort of thing. What's so special about a wraith?"

"Wraiths aren't just ghosts," Sorren said. "They're malicious spirits that have been brought back for a purpose, bound to the will of someone good with dark magic. They aren't as strong as a demon, but they can cause some real trouble—especially if whoever called them loses control."

"Or dies without banishing them?" Teag asked.

Sorren nodded. "From what you've said, it's likely High John got careless, and the wraith got past his protections. Wraiths don't like being forced to a mortal's will. I'm not surprised that it killed him."

"Now that High John's dead, won't the wraith just go back to where it came from?" I asked.

Mrs. Teller shook her head. "It's not that simple. This wraith was called to do killing, and killing is what it does. Cut loose, it needs energy to continue on in our world, and it gets that energy from death."

"So more killing, unless we stop it," I replied. Something I'd heard didn't quite connect. "Why did Caroline Stedman go to visit a wraith?"

Mrs. Teller laughed. "She didn't. High John, he would have given her a coffin box to bury. That was part of the spell, along with that black cross candle you saw."

"Coffin box?" Teag asked.

"Coffin boxes are conjure tools," Mrs. Teller replied. "Black box with broken mirrors inside and a piece of paper with a curse written on it by the root worker, cursing someone to the grave. Person who wants someone dead takes that box to the cemetery, and buries it, so the spirits take hold and make it so."

"In order to banish the wraith, we've got to get rid of the coffin box, and work some conjure of our own," Sorren said. "Wraiths are stubborn. It's not going to go away without a fight."

"What about all the paraphernalia we saw at High John's house?" Teag asked, taking a sip of his bourbon. "Won't that need to be destroyed, too?"

"Leave that to me," Sorren replied. "I'll have it taken care of."

"What's the plan?" I asked, finding that the bourbon had gone a long way toward steadying my hands and calming my fears. Good thing, because I had the feeling things were going to get worse before they got better.

"I need to gather some supplies," Sorren said, standing. "I'll be back in an hour, and then we'll head over to the cemetery to settle things." He headed out the door.

"I came prepared," Mrs. Teller said. "I brought my hand with me, and things to make you all something for protection, too."

"Hand?" I asked, totally lost.

She chuckled and drew out a small pouch of worn silk from inside the neckline of her shirt. "For one thing, I got my toby, my mojo bag. A hand is a spirit that agrees to keep company with a root worker, help out. Gives me guidance, helps me discern." She patted the bag affectionately and slipped it back into its place. "And I got my demon bowl. We'll need that, going against a wraith strong enough to do what this one's done."

She drew a sweetgrass basket out of her bag. It didn't look like any of the pieces she sold at the market. This basket was more like a shallow bowl with a dark line woven in a spiral from the outer rim to the very center. "Help us hold and trap that thing," she said, noticing my attention.

Mrs. Teller put the basket into her bag and drew out a ball of red yarn, a large needle and a packet of wax. "Before we go out, we're gonna make both of you jack balls." She looked up before we could ask. "Protection. Mojo bags are a commitment; gotta keep that spirit happy forever. Jack balls work different, but good." She glanced at Teag. "With your Weaving, yours will be real strong." Her gaze traveled to me. "Your magic's in your touch, don't deny it. That will make your ball strong, too."

"First, I need a piece of hair from each of you, and some nail clippings." I went to get the clippers from the bathroom. Then she held out the packet of wax. "Take a piece the size of a big marble. Roll it around in your hand until it gets warm and soft, then put your hair and clippings in it, and roll it some more."

Next, she cut us each a long piece of red yarn and a shorter piece. "Now you wrap the ball up good, and leave a tail about a foot long." She watched approvingly as we did as she told us. "Now you take this needle and poke it through the middle of the ball, and out the other side. Then make a pass through the yarn with the short piece, so you have three tails. Then braid them together."

"Like this?" Teag held his up after a few moments, and I was done a minute later.

"Good. Now it's not ready yet," Mrs. Teller said, fixing us with a serious look. "First, hold it up to your mouth and breathe on it. Just like that," she said as I complied. "Then, spit on it, and rub it in. Now make the sign of the cross over it, and then add a drop of that bourbon you're drinking. That'll seal it."

"What do we do with it?" Teag asked.

Mrs. Teller withdrew a blue-yarn jack ball from her pocket. She let it hang from the braided tail. "Twirl it clockwise to attract, counterclockwise to repel. State your intent like a chant as you do it."

"Like 'wraith be gone?'" Teag asked.

Mrs. Teller fixed him with a glare. "This isn't a joke. The stronger your intent, and the better you say it, the better the jack ball works." She eyed our work one more time and nodded approvingly. "Keep those on you, in easy reach. And Cassidy? You keep that basket of mine with you, you hear?"

"Yes, ma'am," Teag replied, chastened. I nodded. I knew humor was his way of handling nervousness. Going after a killer wraith in an old cemetery at night didn't sound like a smart thing to do. Was that going to stop us? Not on your life.

We were done making and activating our jack balls by the time Sorren returned. "Ready?"

We weren't, but we headed out anyway. Mrs. Teller drove with us in Teag's Volvo, and Sorren said he would meet us there. I had a suspicion that with his vampire speed, he was planning to go on ahead and scout the area.

Magnolia Cemetery is a beautiful place in the daytime. Live oak trees, grown tall and gnarled over nearly two hundred years, spread their branches above the tombs, heavy with Spanish moss. The grounds used to be part of a big plantation, and the old house sits on the property. We wound our way around large Victorian monuments and elaborate tombstones. Some I recognized, like the Egyptian pyramid and the reclining figure of "Little Annie," a child from a prominent family who had died very young. Lots of famous people are buried here. Some like it well enough that they don't leave.

Before dark, Magnolia Cemetery was full of tourists, history buffs, and folks out for a stroll. While I knew we weren't entirely alone, I knew we were the only living beings inside the cemetery walls. Inside the gates, it was quieter than it should have been. Summer in Charleston is full of the singing of tree frogs, the buzz of cicadas, and the hoots of owls. Now, all I could hear was the wind rustling in the leaves. I made sure not to touch any of the gravestones. I didn't need to know more tragic stories than the three deaths we were trying to avenge.

"Over there," Sorren said in a low voice, pointing to a corner of the graveyard. I knew that we were being watched, and I was equally certain that the spirits were wondering why we had come. Mrs. Teller had briefed us in the car on the way over, so I knew the plan, but in my experience, plans went out the window as soon as the fighting started. I had the jack ball handy in a pocket, and I was wearing my agate necklace. The basket Mrs. Teller had given me was nestled in my arm, although I would have gladly traded it for one of those ghost-vacuums like in the movies. No such luck. It appeared we were going to do this the hard way.

We followed Sorren to a lonely corner of the grounds. Magnolia Cemetery has been around long enough to be full of monuments and tombstones, but this corner was mostly empty. I saw Mrs. Teller close her eyes and begin to murmur as she let her jack ball swing back and forth like a divination pendant. It seemed to pull her, and she followed it like a dowsing rod until she stood over a place where the ground had been turned up not long ago.

"Here," she said and took out a container of salt from her bag. She walked counter-clockwise around the disturbed dirt, and then placed two black candles and two white candles at the four quarters of the circle. Then she drew out a bottle of Four Thieves vinegar and sprinkled it around within the circle. Finally, she took out a mixture of herbs, roots, and other ingredients she had put together and sifted it over the grass and dirt. She was chanting quietly the whole time, one hand stroking her mojo bag, the other moving her jack ball in slow, counter-clockwise circles. She had her demon bowl ready.

Mrs. Teller swore that her magic could defeat the wraith, if we could keep the wraith from attacking her before she finished. Sorren, Teag, and I took up places on the outside of the salt circle, our backs to Mrs. Teller, facing the dark and quiet cemetery.

We were armed. Sorren had an iron sword—not great against corporeal foes, but a powerful weapon against evil spirits, and something a vampire could wield without harm. He and Teag both had mirrors, good for driving back or trapping certain types of spirits. Aside from that, Sorren had the strength and speed of an immortal, and he was hard to kill. Teag had one of his martial arts staffs, an old birch rod that was almost as tall as he was. It was scarred from battle and covered with protective carvings. Tonight, he wore an obsidian ring and an *agimat*, a Philippine amulet that was a gift from one of his teachers.

Both Teag and I had filled our pockets with salt, and we each had black tourmaline stones with us to keep negative energy at bay. I had an obsidian knife that Sorren had given me, smooth and old and sharp.

Around my left wrist, I wore a bracelet of brass bells, and I had an unbreakable metal mirror on a leather strap around my neck. And I had Mrs. Teller's basket that still jiggled with the things I had put in it on my way back from the market and never took out. It didn't seem like much, out here in the quiet dark.

I felt like I was in one of those stand-offs in the old Westerns, like the shootout at the OK Corral. Sorren had told me that wraiths fed on energy, even the energy of other ghosts, so maybe that explained why the spirits that usually made themselves known were holding back. Crap. We were going up against something that even scared ghosts.

And then I saw it. I was expecting something in a black hooded robe with no face, like in the movies. The real thing is a lot worse. The shape was the same, but it rippled like maggots on roadkill, opaque like thick smoke, an absence of light instead of a solid form. It stank like a corpse left out in the sun. Tendrils descended from a hood-like "head," twitching like ghostly tentacles. I had faced a vampire's ghost, and it drew life energy from the living, but the wraith was like its own life-sucking black hole, withering the grass around it, blotting out the stars behind it, and I swear it made the air harder to breathe.

I gripped the obsidian knife warily and fell into a defensive stance. With my left hand, I took out my jack ball and started twirling it to repel spirits, muttering "stay away" over and over again. Teag was doing the same. I hoped it worked. I wasn't close to Teag's level of martial arts mastery, but I had trained enough to hold my own in a fight —at least with the living. The difference between the wraith and the vampire ghost, Sorren had told us, was that the wraith ate away at the soul, not just life energy. That meant even Sorren had something to worry about.

The wraith stalked us, keeping its distance. Maybe it sensed the jack balls; maybe it didn't like the salt. Or maybe it was just deciding which of us to kill first.

The wraith blinked out of sight, and suddenly reappeared in front of Teag. Teag pivoted and shouted a war cry, stabbing his staff into the wraith. The runes along the wooden rod glowed, and the wraith shrieked and drew back. Again the wraith roiled forward, and Teag reached down with one hand to loosen one of the knot-balls on his belt as he held his staff like a lance. Energy crackled at the tip of the rod, spraying embers like a giant sparkler. Teag was new with his magic, so his control wasn't great, but any weapon is better than nothing.

I wanted to go after the wraith to help Teag, but we had agreed to hold our places unless things got dire. Behind us in the circle, Mrs. Teller was chanting, digging in the recently-disturbed ground to bring up the coffin box. We had to protect her, give her time to dispel the Crossing and lay the wraith to rest, or more people would die—starting with the four of us.

The wraith came at Sorren, and it was a toss-up who was faster. Sorren brought his iron sword down in a diagonal slash that would have split a mortal body in two. The wraith's outline wavered, and it let out an unholy screech that nearly deafened me. If I hadn't been sure the spirits around us had already fled, that scream would have woken them for sure. The wraith's tendrils snapped at Sorren like a whip, leaving red welts where they struck his skin.

I knew it would come for me next. I braced myself, but even so, I wasn't ready for the aura of cold dread that surrounded the wraith. It felt as if the moon and stars had all gone out, as if everyone I loved had died. I fought despair and found anger. The wraith's tendrils flicked toward me, and I tried to evade them, keeping the jack ball twirling. That seemed to keep the wraith's body at a little more than arm's distance, but its tendrils kept moving. One of them caught me on the wrist and thigh. Like dry ice, they burned and froze at the same time, and I slashed at the tendril with the obsidian knife as I raised my wounded arm to shield myself. The brass bells jangled, and the knife stabbed down into the black mist. If the tendrils had been flesh, I would have cut them off.

Once more, the wraith fell back with a god-awful caterwaul, and I staggered back a step, feeling pain sear down my arm and leg. The wraith came at me again, faster than I could blink, and I stabbed and struck at it, channeling my rage as if I were fighting a carjacker for my keys and wallet. I knew it was trying to draw Teag and Sorren off so it could get a better strike at Mrs. Teller, and I wasn't going to let that happen.

I lunged forward, bellowing for all I was worth, bells clattering. I threw a handful of salt from my pocket into the place where a heart should have been, and the wraith froze, just for an instant. Enough for me to dive forward, slash it again, and drop back, getting the jack ball back in motion to keep the wraith from getting any closer.

I thought the wraith would go after me again, but it veered at the last minute and caught Teag by surprise. Three of its tendrils slapped at his skin, and everywhere they touched, a red welt blossomed. Teag screamed, and plunged his staff into the belly of the wraith, but the tendrils caught him again, leaving no chance for Teag to unknot one of his ropes. The jack ball dropped from his hand as he staggered.

Teag tried to hold his stance against the wraith, but I could see him trembling with the strain. "Stay where you are!" Teag shouted before either Sorren or I could move. Teag's left hand went to the *agimat* charm on his necklace, and for just a second, it looked as if his entire body crackled with electricity, throwing the wraith away. Angry, raw, circles marred his face and arms, and he swayed on his feet, but he remained standing. He snatched up the jack ball he had dropped, circling it as he kept a wary gaze on the wraith.

Once more, the wraith surged toward us, flowing like filthy water across the grass. "Mirrors!" Sorren yelled, and the three of us held up our reflecting glass as the wraith drew itself up from the ground to its full height, tendrils swirling like the tattered hem of a shroud.

The wraith hissed its displeasure, then blinked out of sight. A heart-beat later, as Mrs. Teller's chant rose to a keen, the wraith materialized behind me, and its inky tendrils closed around my chest and belly in a freezing, burning grip. The sudden, blinding pain made me gasp for air, and the obsidian knife fell from my hand as my muscles spasmed.

Each welt was a bit of my soul stripped away. How many pieces could be torn from a soul? How long would it take to die like this? And if I lived, soul-wounded, what would I be?

Everything seemed to happen at once. Sorren and Teag came running, weapons at the ready. But I knew that with the wraith pressed close to me; they couldn't attack the wraith without hitting me since the wraith was mere shadow and mist. I fell to my knees, dropping my jack ball and my knife, and my hands gripped the dirt like claws.

There's a reason a psychometric doesn't like to touch things in a graveyard. Things touch back. Magic, fueled by primal fear, seared down my arms, into my hands, into the ground. Terrified almost beyond reason, my conscious mind turned my magic loose, and it shot through the cemetery dirt with a cry for help.

The restless dead answered. I could feel spirits massing beneath where I knelt, adding the weight of their souls to my own, counterbalancing the pull of the wraith, giving me what remained of their tattered strength. I felt their cold hands clasp my own through the dirt, and the meager energy that remained to them, they offered to me against a foe the dead feared as much as I did.

Just as quickly, the spirits left me, but I had new strength to go on despite the pain. Sorren and Teag were striking at the wraith, trying to draw him off. Blood seeped from welts across Teag's arms and chest where the wraith had torn through his shirt. Sorren's shirt was ruined, and blood ran from open wounds on his forearms and face.

The spirits were gone, but anger took their place, cold and pure. It gave me the strength to rise from my knees. With a half-mad cry of rage, I gripped the black tourmaline stone in my right hand, plunging it into the wraith from behind to pull him off Teag, who was staggering like a boxer going down for the count. The wraith gave a banshee wail and turned toward me. In that instant, I shoved the only thing I could reach between us—Mrs. Teller's basket.

A flash of light nearly blinded me, and when my vision cleared, I saw an iridescent barrier between me and the wraith.

The glowing film glimmered like a soap bubble, but it was strong enough to send the wraith screeching back, temporarily out of reach.

"Get behind me!" I shouted, angling to keep the protective, glowing field between us and the wraith, trying to position myself as a barrier to keep the wraith away from Mrs. Teller. Visions filled me from the sweetgrass beneath my palms. Images blurred together, of Mrs. Teller wreathed in candle smoke and lit by firelight, of lowcountry marshes and ancient drumming, of my mother's love and Baxter's protective growls. I could smell the distinctive scent of sage and basil.

I didn't know how long I could maintain the iridescent scrim, but I was prepared to hold it until the white light burned me up, if need be. Anything was better than being lashed by deathly cold, dying one soul-splinter at a time.

Mrs. Teller's chanting reached a crescendo behind us. I heard her shout in a language I did not understand, then heard the crunch of glass and wood.

The wraith froze mid-attack, and its death-cry will haunt my night-mares for the rest of my life. It began to spin, slowly at first then faster and faster until it became a vortex, and then popped out of existence.

I hadn't realized I was holding my breath. My shaking arms fell to my sides, although I still had a death-grip on the basket. Sorren and Teag rushed toward me, amazed that we were all still alive.

Behind us, Mrs. Teller's voice had fallen to a quiet drawl. Even without being able to catch the words, I knew she was thanking the powers that had answered her summons. After a moment, she stood and released the salt circle. On the edges of my raw nerves, I felt a rush of invisible power, called and dismissed.

"That's done," Mrs. Teller said, as matter-of-factly as if she had just put biscuits in the oven instead of dispelling a killer revenant. She looked down at the shattered remains of black wood and splintered mirrors lying atop the demon bowl-basket, all that remained of the coffin box that had summoned the wraith. "I'll gather these up and burn them with sage and rosemary, just in case."

I looked down at the bloody welts that marred my hands and arms. "What did it do to us?"

Mrs. Teller looked the three of us up and down with a practiced gaze. "You all sure do look sorry," she said. "Each place that thing touched you, it took a thread of your soul. You'll feel it. Gonna feel weary, heartsick, hopeless."

"Can it heal?" Teag's voice carried a note of desperation I had never heard before. Even Sorren looked concerned.

Mrs. Teller nodded. "Takes time. You've got to be still, meditate a while. Pray if it suits you. Think on goodness. Go out of your way to do good for someone. Gotta heal from the inside out. There's no potion for it. It's on you to fix."

She gave a sharp nod of her head. "Wraith's gone. Curse is done. Best we be moving on."

～

MAGGIE RAN THE store for us the next day. Teag and I looked like something the cat dragged in. I didn't want to answer questions, and I was anxious to do what I could to speed the healing. On the news, they said that a house had burned to the ground the day before, likely a gas explosion. It was High John's place. I never asked Sorren if he did it, and he never brought it up.

Marjorie called me that evening. She said a man from the government had come by with official paperwork to take the humidor, and she gave it to him with her blessing after he assured her she would not be held responsible. All she could tell me when I asked her to describe him, was that he was tall and blond.

Sorren's skin healed overnight. Vampires regenerate. Teag and I took longer. But soul wounds, Sorren said, take just as long, human or vampire. I had the feeling he knew from experience. Then again, time is on his side. I'm just mortal. So I figured I'd better get working on it. *Tempus fugit.*

WICKED DREAMS

"WHERE DID YOU GET THIS?" MY VOICE SOUNDED SHARP, EVEN TO MY ears. I was looking at a man's ring, made of heavy silver with a raised decorative seal in the middle. And without even touching it, I knew it had drawn blood and caused pain.

"I picked it up at the police auction day before yesterday," my would-be customer replied. "They said it belonged to 'Diamond Dan' Hanahan, the businessman they indicted for racketeering a while back."

My customer didn't have any psychic abilities, I was sure of it. You wouldn't have to be a psychometric—someone like me who can read objects' history by touching them—to feel the malevolence that seemed to be forged into the ring. I was pretty certain that any flavor of clairvoyance would send a big, mental neon warning sign to someone with the faintest trace of a sixth sense. Mine was screaming.

"It's a very nice piece," I said, still refusing to handle it. And I named a price I thought was better than fair.

"Sold," the man said, and waited while I wrote up the paperwork and got him his money. When he left, I sat down in my chair behind the counter and sighed, watching the ring warily.

"We've got a hot one," I called out. "And we need to make sure it stays out of circulation."

I'm Cassidy Kincaide, owner of Trifles and Folly, an antiques and curio shop with more than its share of secrets. We've been in Charleston for over three hundred and fifty years, and in that time, few people outside our inner circle have ever suspected the shop's real purpose: to get dangerous magical items off the market and out of the wrong hands. I'm just the most recent in a long line of my relatives to run the shop, and many of them were psychometrics like me or clairvoyants of some kind. Given what we do, that kind of talent helps.

"Make sure you let Sorren know," Teag said walking over to see what I had. Teag Logan is my assistant store manager, best friend, and occasional bodyguard. He's got his own magic. He's a Weaver, able to weave spells and magic into cloth with the warp and woof of the fabric, and also able to draw threads of data together to find out information that's hidden or secret, making him one hell of a hacker.

"I will. Sorren can get it over to the Alliance to take care of," I replied. Sorren and the Alliance are some of our other secrets. The Alliance is a coalition of mortals and immortals who work together to destroy or secure the dangerous magical items we find. Sorren is one of the Alliance leaders. He's also been the silent business partner behind Trifles and Folly from the beginning, and he's a nearly six-hundred-year-old vampire.

Teag used a set of antique chopsticks to pick up the ring without touching it and drop it into a lead-lined box, which he walked back to put in the office safe. When he came back up to the front of the store, he brought me a hot cup of tea, loaded with sugar.

"Thanks," I said. "I didn't have to touch that thing to get some pretty bad vibes from it. Diamond Dan liked to get his hands dirty. He used that ring when he beat people up, and he enjoyed it." I shivered. If the images were that strong just from being close to the ring, I really didn't want to think about what I would have seen if I had touched it.

"That was in the news when his case went to trial," Teag said. "Real nice guy," he said sarcastically. "If the ring was used in his crimes, why did the police put it up for auction?"

I shrugged. "It wasn't a murder weapon, and it probably wasn't stolen. Just because he was wearing it at the time he did illegal things wouldn't have mattered to the police."

"I hate when they do their auction," Teag said. "We always get a flood of 'spookies' and we end up paying money for things we can't turn around and sell."

"Which means Trifles and Folly is doing its real job," I replied. "Much as it pains the sales figures for the month. That's one more nasty item that won't be out in circulation."

Most people don't realize that even when an object isn't actually magical or haunted it can be so fouled with bad, negative, or just downright evil resonance that it can have an impact on an unsuspecting purchaser. It's not too different from people who move into a house where a murder or an awful crime was committed and then report trouble sleeping, depression, even behavior changes. The unseen world affects us far more than the average person realizes. That's why the Alliance has been doing its best to keep people safe for the last five hundred years or so. When we do it right, no one notices. When we screw up, people die.

"Looks like it's going to be quiet in the shop today," Teag noted, glancing around the empty store. "We must be in between bus tours." Charleston merchants depend on tourists, and we can tell a difference on the days when one group of conventioneers or visitors are moving out, and the new group is moving in. Odds are, we would be slammed tomorrow, as the next batch of sightseers started exploring the city.

"If that's the case, I'm going to seize the moment and head over to Honeysuckle Café to grab a bite for lunch," I said. "Want me to bring something back for you?"

"The usual," Teag said, and I knew that was the rosemary chicken salad on ciabatta with aoili.

"You got it," I said, "and a sweet tea to go?"

"Definitely."

I was more in a latte mood as I walked over to Honeysuckle Café. It's one of Teag's and my favorite lunch spots, and it's popular with the entire King Street merchant group because the food and coffee are so good. I consider Trina, the owner, to be a good friend of mine, and Rick, her best barista, makes the most awesome latte in Charleston. So despite the freaky ring, my mood was pretty high as I headed over for lunch.

The universe has a way of making you pay for that kind of optimism.

I knew something was wrong when the patrons at Honeysuckle Café were talking in a hushed buzz. Usually, it's a caffeine-fueled dull roar. It wouldn't take a psychic to sense the tension in the air, and it was so unusual, I checked the news sites on my phone as I waited in line in case there had been some kind of national tragedy, and I hadn't heard.

"Hey Rick," I said as I got the front of the line. "Skinny vanilla latte please—and what's going on?"

Rick looks like he should be working in the kind of gin joint where world-weary men go to relieve their sorrows. I suspect that he's done more than one tour of duty in such a place, both behind the bar and in front of it. Now, he slings coffee instead of martinis, but he has a "been there, done that" manner that would put Bogart to shame. I'm not the first to make that comparison. There's a sign over the latte bar that reads, *"Rick's Place."*

"Anything for you, sweetheart," he said in his best Bogie voice. He pulled the double shots of espresso like a pro and steamed the milk. "As for the vibe, everyone's talking about the murder."

"Murder?" I echoed. On the whole, Charleston is a pretty safe city, as cities go. Yes, bad things happen as they do everywhere, but not as much as they do elsewhere. I credit the Alliance with some of that since we tend to shut down the worst of the bad things before they get started. Still, one tragedy is too many, and from the look of things, something had hit close to home.

"It's Kristie McMillan, from over at the Charleston City Market," Rick said, and I gasped.

"She was murdered?"

Rick shook his head, and I could see the sorrow in his eyes. "That's the hell of it," he said. "From what the police say, she's the killer."

"There's got to be a mistake," I said.

I'd known Kristie for years. She had a stall down in the Charleston City Market, a wonderful place full of art, jewelry, fresh-made baked goods, and farm-raised produce right in the center of downtown Charleston. Kristie made jewelry, and her stand was always busy with locals and tourists alike. Often, Kristie crafted her jewelry from old items she bought from Trifles and Folly, as well as garage sales and estate auctions. Old silverware became bracelets; gears from broken watches became pendants, pieces of shattered glass got new life set into necklaces and rings.

"I wish there were," Rick said, sliding my latte across the counter to me. "But from what they said on the news, witnesses saw the attack, and they found her with the murder weapon, covered in blood."

"Oh my god," I murmured. "Who did she kill?"

Rick dumped out the coffee grounds and wiped down the milk steamer. "That's just it," he replied. "It doesn't make any sense. News reporter said she got into a fight with her roommate and up and stabbed her."

"Are they talking about drugs? Alcohol? Some kind of sudden mental illness?" I asked. "That really doesn't sound like Kristie."

Rick nodded. "I know, right? That's what's got everyone spooked, I think. Some folks, you see it coming, you know? Like they're a loose cannon, and you wonder who the unlucky guy is who'll be in the wrong place at the wrong time when they finally blow. But Kristie? Just didn't see it in her." He set the machine up for the next customer. "Then again, they say it's the quiet ones you have to watch out for."

I thanked Rick, left my usual generous tip, and took my latte as I moved down the line to order sandwiches. Now that I knew what to listen for, I could catch bits of conversation all around me as people who had known Kristie tried to make sense of the unimaginable.

"Rick told you about Kristie?" Trina, the owner of Honeysuckle Café, was behind the counter taking lunch orders.

I nodded, still in shock. "I'm having a lot of trouble believing it," I said numbly. "Are the police sure?"

Trina nodded. "Unfortunately, it looks like a slam dunk." Her voice dropped. "People saw her do it, Cassidy. There's no getting around that."

My mind spun as I put in my order and Trina made the sandwiches. Kristie was the last person I would expect to kill anyone in a fit of rage, even if the person deserved it. She had always struck me as easygoing, almost the stereotypical artist unconcerned by the ups and downs of the rest of the world.

"Was there something going on no one knew about—a bad breakup, some drug problems, something in the family?" I asked.

Kristie shrugged. "Not that they've said on the news, and not that anyone who thought they were close to her had heard about. You'd think if she was struggling with something, she would have told somebody, wouldn't you? I didn't figure her for the stoic type." She shook her head. "I guess you never know."

The news put a damper on my mood, but I wasn't ready to head back to the shop just yet. I took my coffee and found a seat, but it was more to overhear conversation than because I was in a hurry to drink my latte.

"I just saw her yesterday, and nothing seemed wrong," one woman said, as her companion nodded, wide-eyed.

"Talked to her on Friday, and she was real excited about this whole new line of jewelry she had coming out," another told a friend. "That doesn't sound like someone who's planning to kill somebody."

"She'd shared an apartment with Becca for four years," I heard a man say. "Never any trouble. Everyone thought they were good friends. Now, this."

My mind reeled. I knew both Kristie and Becca, her roommate. Becca was a graphic designer who also sold some of her art at the Market. She was a lively girl, mid-twenties like Kristie, and I remembered thinking that the two of them probably got on well, with so much in common.

I sipped my latte, as the comments around me repeated the same sense of shock and grief. The merchants at the City Market and those of us who have been on King Street for a while are a pretty tight bunch. It's not uncommon for folks to hold baby showers or engagement parties, or to take up a collection and bring casseroles if there's a death in someone's family. Kristie and Becca were two of our own. It was a double loss made all the more tragic because it seemed too random and incomprehensible.

The mood in the cafe was too much to bear, so I grabbed our take-out order and headed back for the shop. But I made a detour on the way, to the Market.

Charleston City Market is the heart of Market Street, and it's a huge draw for tourists and locals alike. Plenty of out-of-towners shop the market for a unique memento of Charleston, and lots of us who live here pick up fresh produce and gifts from the vendors. I'll admit that a stroll through the Market is one of my guilty pleasures, especially on my lunch hour when I need to clear my head. I know most of the regular vendors, either from the Merchant Association or from being a regular customer. And today, I had a certain someone in mind.

"Hello, Cassidy," Niella said. "Mama said we'd see you today."

"I knew you'd come." Mrs. Ernestine Teller and her daughter, Niella, were in their usual spot by the East entrance, where they had a display of their beautiful sweetgrass baskets. Mrs. Teller is descended from the Gullah people, who live in the Lowcountry and have forged a unique culture from their history as freed and escaped African slaves long ago. Among the crafts Gullah folks are known for are their elaborate sweetgrass woven baskets. Collectors and museums prize their baskets, which sell for hundreds and sometimes thousands of dollars.

Mrs. Teller is probably in her seventies. Decades of practice show in the way her fingers fly when they weave the baskets, making something complex look easy. But like us, she's got secrets of her own, and I happened to know one of them. Mrs. Teller is a root worker, someone who can do Conjure and Hoodoo, powerful traditions that blend African and island magic.

"What have you heard about Kristie?" I asked. "I really can't believe she did it."

Mrs. Teller wove a few more strands before she answered me. "She did—and she didn't."

"What do you mean?"

Mrs. Teller never looked up from her weaving. "I mean that Kristie did the deed, but she wasn't herself when it happened."

"Mental illness?" I asked, wondering how I had missed the signs, how Kristie had managed to keep something so serious hidden.

Mrs. Teller shook her head. "That's what they'll call it," she said quietly. "But I think there's something 'other' afoot."

"Other" as in magic, or something supernatural. Mrs. Teller doesn't know about the Alliance—as far as I'm aware—but she does know about my gift, and she's been mentoring Teag with his. She's got some powerful magic of her own, and she's saved my bacon on more than one occasion. I trust her instincts.

"I never picked up any hint that Kristie had the power," I said, keeping my voice low so others wouldn't hear.

"She didn't," Mrs. Teller replied. "I'd have known. All the same, I think something influenced her," she added, and then she looked up and met my gaze. "There's something out there that made that poor girl kill her roommate. Someone needs to do so something about that."

It was pretty clear who Mrs. Teller thought "someone" should be, and it included Teag and me. "Even if I could prove that," I said very quietly, "the police would never believe me."

"No, but Kristie might," Niella said. "I went down to visit her this morning, see if she needed anything, if there was anyone she needed me to call, since she doesn't have family around here. That poor girl is just sick about what happened, and she's afraid she's going crazy."

"Is she?" I asked. "I mean, do you think she just... I don't know, snapped?"

Niella shook her head. "No, I don't. You didn't see how broken up she was about it. They've got her on suicide watch. She's telling anyone who will listen—and even those who won't—that 'something came over her' and made her do it."

"Wow," I said. "Did she say anything else?"

"She sure did. Told me that something had been sending her wicked dreams and that when the murder happened, she thought she was in one of those dreams, then she woke up covered with blood."

My heart went out to Kristie. As much as I grieved for Becca, if there was something supernatural involved that had used Kristie to commit a crime, then she was a victim as well.

"There'll be more killing," Mrs. Teller said without altering the rhythm of her weaving. "Mark my words. There's something bad out there, and it won't stop now that it's started." She looked up at me. "Unless someone puts a stop to it."

"Let me see what I can find out," I said. "If there's any way I can help, I will."

Mrs. Teller gave a curt nod. "Good enough. And if you need my help, you know where to find me. Best you be careful, child."

I thanked her and headed on my way, deep in thought. In the distance, I heard the wail of sirens, and it just sent my mood lower. If it weren't for the chance that the supernatural played a role in the murder, it would be a matter for the police to sort out. But if Mrs. Teller was right and magic or a haunting was involved, then the Alliance had a responsibility to get to the bottom of it, before more people died.

Just then, my cell phone buzzed. I glanced down, expecting a text from Teag wondering why I was taking so long. Instead, the text was from Sorren, just a short sentence letting me know he would come by the store after dark.

Yes, my boss the nearly six-hundred-year-old vampire uses a cell phone—and email, too. He says that vampires that don't adjust with the times don't survive long. I was just glad he was heading our way. I wanted to talk about the murder with him and see what he thought might be behind it.

Teag was preoccupied with something on his phone when I got back to the shop with the sandwiches. "Did you hear about the murder?" he asked.

"Rick told me," I replied. "I can't believe Kristie would ever hurt Becca."

Teag gave me a stunned look. "What are you talking about? What do Kristie and Becca have to do with anything? I meant this—it's all over the local news. Just happened."

Teag turned his phone around so that I could see the website on the screen. "*Local Executive Stabs Boss in Workplace Rampage*," the headline announced. I remembered the sirens I had heard on the way home.

"I know her," I said in a horrified whisper, looking at the picture of the woman in the blood-soaked business suit being led away in handcuffs. "That's Karen Hahn. She's in the Merchant's Association, and I see her all the time downtown and at the Market."

"What were you saying about Kristie and Becca?" Teag asked, frowning with concern. I saw my own worries and questions reflected in his eyes as I told him what I had learned at Honeysuckle Café, and about the warning Mrs. Teller had passed along at the Market.

"This is bad, Cassidy," Teag said. "Two murders within two days, with very unlikely perpetrators. There's got to be something supernatural involved."

"Which makes me really glad Sorren's coming by tonight," I said. "Because we need to get him involved in this."

It was late Fall, and darkness fell early. Most of King Street closed up around six o'clock except for the restaurants and nightspots and a few coffeehouses for the evening crowd. Sometimes Sorren meets us at my house, but he had said he wanted to come by the store, and I figured it was to see a couple of new items with bad vibes we had bought recently and locked up in the back room—including the ring I purchased that morning. So we closed up on time and got take-out Chinese food for dinner, then brought the food back to the store and went into the break room in the back to wait.

"He's late," Teag said when we had finished our dinners and cleaned up. I glanced at my watch. Sorren was punctual, and when he told us to expect him at the store, he meant soon after closing time.

"Should we worry?" I know that sounds silly, worrying about a centuries-old vampire, but Sorren is a good friend. Vampires may be immortal undead, but they can be destroyed, and some of our work on behalf of the Alliance has come closer than I like to remember to killing all of us.

"Can't stop you from worrying," Teag said, "but unless we know where he was coming from, there's no way to go looking for him."

Just then, we heard a loud thump against the back door of the shop.

Teag and I exchanged glances, and he reached for his combat knife and the sturdy martial arts staff he keeps in the office. He's got a black belt in several styles of combat, and while I haven't won tournaments like Teag has, we can both hold our own in a fight.

I peered out the security peephole and recognized Sorren. Even through the distortion of the fish-eye lens, something didn't look right. I signaled for Teag to keep his staff handy, while I opened the door.

Sorren stumbled in, covered in blood, and collapsed on the floor at my feet.

I closed and locked the door, then dropped my knees beside Sorren. Teag did the same. Sorren moaned, looking even paler than usual.

"He's been stabbed—multiple times," Teag said, examining Sorren as I went to get water and cloths from the store's small kitchen to help with cleanup. "If he were mortal, he'd be dead."

Sorren was wearing a sport coat over jeans and a collared shirt. The jeans were soaked with blood, and the coat and shirt had been cut to ribbons with the vicious blows that had gone deep into Sorren's back and side.

"Did he get hit in the heart?" I asked, barely breathing. Vampires can heal grievous wounds, but a strike through the heart or decapitation and their long existence is over.

"No," Teag said, and together we gentled Sorren out of his ruined shirt and blood-stained jacket. "But his back's a mess."

I winced at the jagged cuts down Sorren's back. One of the strikes had taken him below the ribs, and another one went through the ribs but low enough to hit a lung instead of his heart.

I grabbed our First Aid kit from under the counter. It's not meant for life-threatening wounds, but given our penchant for dangerous investigations, the kit does feature a lot more than bandages. I went for all the gauze rolls and pads I could find, hesitated over the antibiotic, not knowing how it would work with vampire body chemistry, and grabbed some butterfly bandages as well, though Sorren's injuries went far beyond a split lip. Already, the slashes were beginning to heal, but I knew that posed a new problem.

"He's going to need to feed, and soon," I said. "Healing himself will use all his energy, with damage that bad."

I glanced at the wound on Sorren's upper back and saw that the bleeding had slowed enough that I covered it with a light layer of gauze. The side wound didn't seem bad from the back, but when we turned him over, I could see a deep tear across Sorren's abdomen.

I layered the gauze and leaned on it, compressing the belly wound, and was distressed to feel the cold blood seeping through the gauze. Vampires don't have body heat of their own except for what they borrow from blood taken in a recent feeding. And while fresh mortal blood is bright red, what circulates in a vampire's system is much darker. Most of the blood staining Sorren's clothing was his own. I'd seen him bloodied from battle before, but mostly with the blood of his opponents.

Teag was already rolling up his shirt sleeve, baring his left arm. "Already thought of that," he said.

"What are you doing?" I asked.

Teag met my gaze. "He's hurt. We can hardly take him to the hospital. He can't—or won't—feed from you because of his bond to your family. So that leaves me." He gave me a wan smile that didn't reach his eyes. "Relax. I've done this before."

I had gotten rid of most of the blood, except from the worst of the slashes that were still trickling thin red streams as they healed from the inside out. Sorren's wounds were healing, but I could still see evidence that he had tried to fight off his attacker, since his knuckles were scraped and bruised and there were gashes on his forearms. He hadn't moved since he had fallen, or tried to speak other than a groan.

"Sorren's a vampire," I said quietly. "He's faster and stronger than mortals, and he's had almost six hundred years of experience outwitting people trying to kill him. How in hell did anything catch him to do this?"

Teag sat back on his heels. "I was wondering the same thing. It has to be a supernatural attacker—but where's the common thread?"

I was wiping off the blood from Sorren's left arm when I realized that his hand was closed in a fist. I tried to pry his fingers open, but even unconscious, he was stronger than I was. I'd have to wait for him to come around.

"The healing is slowing down," Teag said. "The upper wound was open and fresh when he came in, and it's largely closed. The lower wound is still raw—and bleeding."

Sorren's skin was colder than usual, almost corpse-cold, and his color had gone ashen. Blue tinged his lips. I'd never seen him look so dead before.

"I was hoping he'd come around," Teag said, shifting his position to get closer to Sorren's mouth. "I'd like him conscious when we do this, so he knows when to stop. But I'm afraid to wait any longer."

I was afraid for both of them, but I just nodded. "It's got to be your call," I said. "It's dangerous." We both knew that under normal circumstances, Sorren would not hurt either of us. More than once, he had nearly been destroyed trying to protect us. He had told us that he could feed without killing, and preferred to do so except in actual battle. But unconscious and badly injured, there was a chance he might not realize who his "donor" was, might drink too deeply.

"He's not in danger of the final death," I added. "You could wait."

Teag looked down at Sorren. Despite his real age, Sorren looks like he's in his late twenties, because that's how old he was when he was turned. He has blond hair, European features, and eyes the color of the sea before a storm. We were both used to him seeming nearly impervious to danger, and I could tell it shook Teag as much as it did me.

"There's something out there strong enough to do this to Sorren," Teag said quietly. "It's already killed twice, and it tried to kill again. Without my blood, it could take Sorren days or longer to recover. Do you really want to face whatever did this to him on our own?"

I didn't speak, but Teag must have seen my answer in my eyes. He used his knife to cut a shallow groove in his arm and start the blood flowing, then pressed his forearm against Sorren's mouth, gentling Sorren's lips open around the wound.

Reflexively, Sorren's fangs closed onto the skin, and Teag cursed under his breath. Sorren had told me that a vampire could bite gently enough not to leave a bruise, that with enough finesse that the donor felt no pain and lost no extra blood.

That exquisite control wasn't operational given Sorren's current condition. Teag tried not to show it, but I could tell the hard bite hurt, and a little bit of blood trickled from the punctures.

"Bad?" I asked.

"Not fun," Teag said tautly. "Like getting a phlebotomy intern on the first day of class."

He tried to make a joke of it, but I was worried for both of them. I kept pressure on the gut wound, which had torn through skin and muscle, nearly eviscerating Sorren. It had been a savage blow, something more likely on a battlefield than a back-alley mugging. And here we were, just the three of us on the bloodstained floor of the shop's back room, with no one to call for help. I'd never felt so isolated and helpless in my life.

"Whoa there," Teag said. He was looking a little pale. "Slow it down, Sorren."

I leaned forward. "Sorren! It's Cassidy. You're hurt badly. Teag's giving you blood to help you heal, but you've got to take it easy. Take what you need and stop before you hurt him."

I had no idea whether or not Sorren could hear us. Teag looked like he might pass out, but I didn't dare leave up on the pressure I was keeping on the gut wound. Teag managed to shift position to lie down, which was better than falling over.

The flow of blood from Sorren's belly wound had slowed, and it might have been my imagination, but it seemed a little warmer than before. I knew that with fresh blood, Sorren would be all right, but now I was worried about Teag.

"Sorren!" I said again. "You're safe. It's Cassidy and Teag. You've got to feed gently. Please—wake up before you hurt Teag."

A moment later, Sorren's jaw relaxed, releasing Teag's arm. I was ready with the last of the gauze and some ointment, and got Teag's arm bound up quickly, keeping my knee gently over the gut wound to keep up the pressure. By the time I had finished Teag's bandage, Sorren's wound had stopped bleeding. When I removed the gauze, I could see that the deep viscera had already closed.

"We look like we were on the wrong side of a war," I said, glancing down at our bloodstained skin and clothing.

"I... was." Sorren's voice was faint, and he didn't open his eyes, but I was just glad to hear his voice.

"Are you okay, Teag?" I asked.

Teag nodded, looking shaky but determined. "I'll be fine."

"If you're up for it, let's get Sorren into the safe room downstairs, and clean up before the cops come calling," I said. Sorren keeps a windowless locked room in the basement of Trifles and Folly for emergencies. I figured this definitely counted.

"I can walk," Sorren murmured. "But I'll need help." Usually, Sorren doesn't speak with an accent, but when he's under stress or very tired, I've heard a hint of one from his native Belgium. Now, the accent was unmistakable. Before I could try to talk him out of it, he struggled to his feet, swearing under his breath in what sounded like French. Teag and I each got under one shoulder. The narrow stairs to the basement were a challenge, but we got down them.

I opened the hidden door to the safe room and turned on the lights. I'd never been inside before. There was a bed, a chair, and a writing table, without any decoration. We gentled Sorren into the bed, and I checked his bandage, but the gut wound was nearly closed.

"Thank you," he said, his voice a bit stronger. "I'll tell you all about it... later."

"You've got something in your hand," I said. Sorren's fist had never unclenched.

"Too dangerous to give you just now," he replied, sounding like he was on the edge of sleep. "Tomorrow... I'll explain everything."

We left him then, knowing that he would take care of bolting the door from the inside when he felt up to it. Teag helped me clean up the floor, and we changed into the spare outfits we kept in the shop. Our work gets messy. I took the bloody rags and our blood-stained clothing to burn in my garden fire pit.

"Mrs. Teller was right—she said there'd be more blood," I said, washing my hands in the sink.

Teag nodded. "The problem is, it's not over yet."

BY THE NEXT EVENING, Sorren was sitting in my living room, looking remarkably healthy for a dead man. He had gotten a shower and clean clothing, and the attack of the night before seemed like a bad dream. Except we all knew it had been terrifyingly real.

"Nothing mortal should be able to sneak up on me like that," Sorren said. My little Maltese dog, Baxter, sat on his lap. Sorren had glamored the pup to keep him from barking at him, and now Baxter gave Sorren a look of goofy admiration usually seen on star-struck preteen girls at a concert.

"What makes you think it was mortal?" I asked.

"Because when I hit back, the damage was regrettably severe," Sorren replied. "I fought like I had been attacked by another vampire, or a demon minion. It turned out to be a mortal, possessed or influenced by something that increased his strength and speed but not his invulnerability."

"I hacked into the police blotter," Teag added. His color had come back and he was wearing a long-sleeved shirt to hide the bruises and wounds on his arm. "They found a dead man covered in blood with a snapped neck, down by Whiteside Gardens. The report said he had a bloody machete. They're checking hospitals to find the victim."

That victim was sitting on my couch, petting my dog.

"Did they identify who it was?" Sorren asked.

"Steve Alderman, a local real estate agent," Teag said, checking his notes. "No prior record, no history of violence or mental illness—just like the other attacks. Everyone's stunned."

"I think I met him once or twice, at the Merchant's Association," I said. "Not the kind you'd expect to find in a dark alley."

Teag frowned. "That's the third time the Merchant's Association has come up," Teag said. "Think it's significant?"

I shrugged. "Kristie, Becca, Karen Hahn, and her boss, and Steve Alderman all worked downtown, on King or Market Streets. It's not surprising that they would be members." I thought about it for a moment. "I can ask around."

"You asked me what was in my hand last night," Sorren said, and reached into his pocket. "I've got it here, but Cassidy mustn't touch it without preparation. Even without her gift, I'm fairly certain it's got nasty resonance." He withdrew a small piece of cloth and opened it up to reveal a handful of the keypads from a vintage typewriter, then set them out on the coffee table that sat between us.

"I don't get it," Teag said, peering at the keypads. They were made of glass with a letter reverse-stamped in gold on a black background, and rimmed in chrome. I'd seen plenty of Underwood and Smith-Corona typewriters from the early 1900's with keys like that. The old machines were solid workhorses, usually still functional if you could find ribbons for them, and prized by collectors for their film noir look.

"He was wearing a bracelet of them when I grabbed his wrist," Sorren said. "It broke. I knew they might be a clue, so I held onto them." He shook his head ruefully. "I didn't stick around, after I got him to stop stabbing me. As you saw, I wasn't in much shape to even take a look at his body."

A glass of iced sweet tea sat on the coffee table in front of me. Here in Charleston, we like our tea sweeter than honey and strong as a hurricane. Using my psychic gift takes a lot out of me, but I've found that having some sweet tea handy speeds my recovery.

"I helped you two get back on your feet last night," I said with a nervous chuckle. "Don't be surprised if you get to return the favor now." I drew a deep breath, and grabbed one of the keypads, folding it into my fist.

Confusion threatened to overwhelm me. The lights seemed too bright, the noises too loud, all of it crowding into my head, making me feel as if I were drowning in some horrible dream. I was seeing, feeling what the owner of the keypad bracelet had experienced, and it seemed like the verge of madness.

Rage seethed through my blood. I wanted the satisfaction of making someone else pay, making everyone pay. The litany of griev-ances that had led to this point was too large to dwell on, but it had nurtured cold anger and a thirst for vengeance that could only be sated with blood.

He knew that killing would make him feel better. It had before. Watching through the eyes of whoever had possessed the keypads, I knew that he wasn't new to doing murder. He had enjoyed it, refined it, learned to savor the anticipation of a kill and bask in its memory. He had killed in the past, and he would keep on killing, because it felt so good to kill—

"Cassidy!" Teag was calling my name in a tone that told me I hadn't responded. Baxter gave a low growl, like he could see some-thing behind me that he didn't like. Sorren had gently pried open my hand to remove the keypads.

I let out a long breath and collapsed back into the couch cushions, shaking. "He was a killer, a stone-cold killer," I said when I found my voice again. Teag pressed a glass of iced tea into my hand, and I paused to take a long drink.

"Who? Steve Alderman?" Teag asked. "I told you—police database says no priors, no fingerprint matches, no parking tickets."

I shook my head. "I know what I felt. Those keypads belonged to someone who had killed more than once—someone who enjoyed killing."

"Maybe it wasn't Steve's memories you saw," Sorren said. "Maybe it's whoever used to own those keypads, and the typewriter they came from."

As soon as the words were out of Sorren's mouth, I knew the truth of them. "Oh my god," I said. "Kristie loves to make jewelry out of found objects. She's bought a lot of things from the shop over the years and turned bits and pieces into gorgeous stuff. What if she got her hands on a typewriter that had belonged to a psychopath, and made jewelry out of it?"

"And that jewelry carried the bad mojo of the psychopath," Sorren mused. "It would have to be extremely strong to force a normal person to start hacking people down with a knife."

I nodded. "Maybe whatever it is also possessed the psychopath," I speculated. "You said it made Steve Alderman fast enough and strong enough to attack you without warning."

"There was another object you wanted me to see, one that came in yesterday, "Sorren said. "What was it?"

"A ring," I replied. "One that was used quite a lot by a very bad man. The guy who sold it had bought it—"

"At the police auction," Teag finished my sentence. We both looked at each other in stunned silence.

"Can you see what items were sold at the auction?" I asked Teag. "See if there was an old typewriter?" I frowned. "Would the auction site say which person or crime the item was associated with?"

Teag shook his head. "No, although they'd probably make more money that way. There was a post on a blog about it a while back. Said the police didn't want to sensationalize the auction or inspire copycats."

"We have trouble every year with stuff from there," I told Sorren. "Only it's never been this bad before."

Teag got busy typing on his laptop, and in a few minutes, he looked up with a sad smile. "Got it," he said. He turned the screen around so Sorren and I could see.

On the screen was a picture of an old Underwood typewriter, circa 1920. It was a beauty, in good shape with all its original gold paint scrollwork, just the way collectors like. There was a second photo looking down on the keyboard, and I could see that the keypads Sorren had grabbed from his would-be killer matched exactly.

"Who owned it?" Sorren asked. His voice carried a hint of an accent, and I knew he was still feeling the effects of the previous night.

Teag went back to hacking and had an answer in a few minutes. "Oscar Anderson Kenworth," he replied, scanning down through the information he had found online.

My eyes widened. "The Slitter?"

Teag nodded. "Yeah. It fits. He attacked his victims with knives, had a very aggressive style, and seemed to enjoy every minute of it. Serial killer. Psychopath. Shot himself while sitting at the typewriter that he used to type the taunting notes he wrote to his victims and the police."

I eyed the keypads. "The typewriter Kristie bought at auction," I said quietly.

"I thought you said there had been three killings," Sorren broke in. "I can understand the effect the typewriter might have had on Kristie who bought it and worked with the keys, and on Steve Alderman, who was wearing the bracelet. What about the other victim?"

"If there's so much bad mojo associated with the typewriter, why didn't it make the police start killing each other while it was locked away in the evidence room, or wherever they keep stuff like that?" I asked.

Teag dug in again. "Uh-oh. Police report lists the personal property surrendered by Karen Hahn when she was taken into custody. It mentions earrings made from old-fashioned typewriter keys." He searched a little longer. "Kristie was wearing the keypads in a necklace."

He looked up. "As for why it didn't affect the cops while they had it, I'm guessing it's because items that are held for high-profile crimes or long-running cases gets packed up and shipped off to a warehouse in a salt mine somewhere in big crates, like at the end of that Indiana Jones movie. It's not in a place where there are a lot of people around day-to-day."

"And I suspect that, if you were to identify the storage site, you'd find higher-than-average suicides, domestic violence problems, and substance abuse," Sorren said. "That kind of psychic stain lingers, and it taints whatever it touches."

Teag sat back and crossed his arms over his chest. "Do you think the cops have connected Kristie's jewelry with the other deaths? They know about the earrings and the necklace. And if they find any of the links from Steve's bracelet—"

"If the victims were all wearing the same thing, maybe," I said. "But the killers? How likely are the cops to decide that the devil made them do it because of their jewelry?"

"I'm more worried about what will happen if the police seize that typewriter and bring it back into a heavily populated police station," Sorren said. "As I recall, back when The Slitter was on a rampage, there were a lot of unsolved or suspicious deaths around the same time, until the Alliance could shut him down."

"You were involved in that?" Teag asked. Sorren nodded.

"Then maybe it wasn't an accident that you were attacked," I said. "Maybe Oscar's spirit was headed for Trifles and Folly, looking to even old scores. And it found you on the way." I shivered, thinking of how bad it would have been if Teag and I had been caught unawares.

"Possible, although I don't like the sound of that," Sorren admitted. "It means we'll have to be extra careful, since we don't know how many of those keypad-jewelry pieces are already out in the marketplace."

"We can get the answer to that pretty easily," I said. Both men turned to look at me. "Kristie didn't work in her apartment. She had a studio-workshop on the outskirts of town."

"Think the police have already gone there to look for the type-writer?" Teag asked.

"There's only one way to find out," Sorren replied. "But we need to do some preparing before we go. We already know how dangerous this spirit can be."

Two hours later, we had regrouped. Teag had his martial arts staff, and he was wearing a short rope with several macramé knots in it on his belt, a way for a Weaver like him to store magic power to use later. He also wore a vest he had woven himself, incorporating his magic to give it a strong positive resonance. I saw that he was wearing both his *agimat* and hamsa protective charms. I was wearing my agate neck-lace, along with an obsidian ring and a bracelet of small brass spirit bells, all of them good for protection against evil. Just in case, I had an obsidian knife.

All three of us had specially-made faceted mirror pendants, called *hexenspiegel*. It's a type of mirror that can trap a spirit, and we had agreed that whatever was haunting Kristie's typewriter needed to be bottled up as quickly as possible. Sorren also provided a lead-lined chest, something he hoped would shut down the Slitter's ghost until we could destroy the typewriter for good. And as always, Teag and I came prepared with plenty of salt and charcoal for protection.

There was a knock at my door, and I jumped up to answer it, expecting the fourth member of our group. There in the doorway stood a woman dressed all in black, with short auburn hair in a pompadour, understated makeup, and colorful tattoos on her left arm, just beneath her short sleeves. The Reverend Anne Burgett—known to her flock as Father Anne—assistant rector of St. Hildegard's Episcopal Church, was ready for action.

"You've got your kick-ass shoes on," I noted with a glance at the Doc Martens she wore beneath her black jeans.

Father Anne grinned. "Heck, yeah. And Father Conroy's knife, just in case." She patted a scabbard on her belt. We had worked with Father Anne before, the many-times great-granddaughter of a priest who had known Sorren—and supported the Alliance—centuries ago.

Like her ancestor, Father Anne was part of the Expeditus Society, a secret group of Anglican priests who fought demons and supernatural monsters. The colorful, custom tattoo on her arm included the symbols of three obscure saints known for their protection against evil. Father Anne wasn't taking any chances tonight. She also wore a simple cross made of iron on a chain around her neck, and a pair of small agate pierced earrings, as well as an onyx ring.

We drove out to Kristie's workshop and left it up to Sorren to get us in. Before he became a vampire, Sorren had been the best jewel thief in Antwerp. Centuries had past, but he hadn't lost the touch. We found Kristie's studio locked tight and roped off with police tape, and Sorren had the door open before I even noticed he was working the lock. Since Sorren could see in the dark, he made sure the blinds were drawn before we cautiously turned on our flashlights.

"Cute little place," I said, as we entered, looking around. The building had been a small carriage house long ago, when the big home on the other end of a long driveway had been the residence of planta- tion nobility. I remembered Kristie being excited about finding the old building for rent, and while I knew about Kristie's workshop, I'd never been inside before. There was one main room where Kristie had all of her equipment and several worktables. Off to the side was a small closet and a bathroom.

We didn't dare turn on the overhead lights, but enough moonlight filtered through the blinds that with our flashlights we could navigate. The walls were made of thick stone, with a brick floor. Strewn across tables and counters, I saw lots of works-in-progress, jewelry projects that Kristie would probably never return to complete.

One set of jewelry, in particular, caught my eye when it reflected from my light, and my breath caught. I had heard Kristie talking about the project down at the Market. It was a commission, her biggest ever, from someone who had purchased many of her smaller items and came back for a special present.

Designed as a gift for a fiftieth wedding anniversary, the piece was a silver candlestick embellished with custom-made charms that incorporated themes—and even old jewelry—from the couple's life. I stared at the completed piece and felt sad both for Kristie and for the couple who would not get their special present. Even at a distance, I could feel the strong positive energy from the candlestick.

"Look for the typewriter," Sorren instructed. He laid the lead-lined box on the worktable. It was heavy, and I was certain that even with his supernatural strength, he didn't enjoy carrying it. "Just don't touch it with bare hands." He set a pair of insulated gloves next to the box, the kind that could protect against a nasty electrical charge.

We spread out, figuring that such a small room shouldn't be difficult for four people to search. But all of a sudden, a wave of stifling, negative energy washed over me, making it difficult to breathe. I felt as if someone had sucked all of the oxygen from the room, depriving it of life and light. And just behind the first wave of energy came the second: evil, cruel, and hungry for blood.

The door crashed open. I felt a rush of air. Someone screamed, a wild, keening wail. Shadows blurred with motion, and the next thing I knew, a man had grabbed me by the arm and was brandishing a knife. His eyes were wide and not altogether sane. I reacted, bringing my foot down on his instep and my elbow back to his gut. It was enough to break free.

In the dim light, I saw that a second assailant had gone after Teag and Father Anne. Sorren launched himself at the man who had attacked me, and they crashed to the floor, overturning one of the smaller work-tables and sending Kristie's precious jewelry scattering.

"Get the typewriter!" Sorren shouted.

Teag was using his staff to block the second attacker, while Father Anne swung into a graceful high Karate kick that had to have taken years to perfect. Teag was competition-level at mixed martial arts, and his moves should have stopped any normal assailant. Then I remembered that the man who had attacked Sorren had moved with vampire strength and speed, thanks to the spirit possessing him.

Sorren was struggling with the man, and I grabbed the silver candlestick, silently apologizing to Kristie for destroying her handiwork. I remembered what the last person possessed by the Slitter had done to Sorren, even with his vampire defenses, and I intended to stop the spirit from hurting anyone else if I could help it.

"Grab the jewelry if they're wearing it!" I shouted. "If you can pull it free, the spirit might lose power."

I raised the candlestick, hoping for a clear shot at the man's head as he and Sorren wrestled on the floor. But as I gripped the silver with both hands, the memories of the charms and jewelry Kristie had embedded hit me full force, flooding my senses, a clean, pure stream of power like concentrated sunlight.

The blast of light struck the man in the back, not with fire but with a force of energy strong enough to rip him loose from Sorren's hold and send him half-way across the room. Before I could figure out what had happened, Sorren was in motion, tackling the man and ripping open the cuffs of his shirt, popping the cufflinks made from the cursed typewriter of a serial killer. Without the spirit's tokens, the man collapsed in a bruised and battered heap.

The second attacker fought like a wildcat, but as I shakily raised the candlestick toward where Teag and Father Anne battled their assailant, I saw Father Anne grab something from around the person's neck and jerk it free. The attacker dropped like a puppet with cut strings.

With the attack stopped, I turned back to the rest of Kristie's workshop, looking for the typewriter. The Slitter was still here, lurking in the shadows, sullen at having his victory denied. I knew he wasn't going to go down without a fight.

I moved through the half-darkness with every sense on high alert. I wasn't quite sure how I had managed that blast of light from the candlestick, but I kept it raised and ready in my right hand, while I hefted the obsidian knife in my left hand, just in case. I figured I would find the typewriter, and then figure out how to get it into the lead chest. I knew I couldn't carry the chest far, and there was no way in hell I was going to touch that typewriter, or any stray keys.

"I think it's the landlord and his wife," I heard Teag say behind me. "They're going to have nasty headaches when this is all over."

"Any luck, Cassidy?" Father Anne asked.

Normally, when I sense something with vile psychic energy, I run the other way. Now, I was using my gift to help me hone in on the one thing in the room I really didn't want to be near. "I think I'm getting closer," I called back.

One more worktable sat against the back wall, where the shadows were deeper. I could make out the outline of several old typewriters. A shaft of pale light streamed through the windows, and I saw how the vintage machines had been torn apart, keys split off, pried loose from the mechanism that had held them in place. But one typewriter in particular resented its dissection, I knew it just as I knew that the seething spirit that had melded itself with the machine was not going to go down without a fight.

The shadows themselves lurched toward me, sweeping together from the walls, floor, and ceiling into a huge, hulking presence. The Slitter was no stranger to creating terror. Alive, he had been the stranger in the dark parking lot, the shape in the bedroom window, the footsteps in the deserted alleyway. Terror was his foreplay, and blood his release. The people he had possessed had been mere poppets. Whatever the Slitter had done, whoever he had sold his soul to, I knew that the shadow man who loomed over me was the long-dead killer, and he had me in his sights.

Darkness fell. Someone screamed. I felt all hope drain from my soul. And then I got mad. I've never taken well to feeling helpless. It pisses me off, big time. And I came out swinging, bellowing at the top of my lungs to give myself courage, as the ice cold blackness swept toward me.

I slashed with the obsidian knife and felt it tug at the shadows as if they had substance. The next thing I knew, Father Anne was beside me, and she had Father Conroy's demon knife in her hand, a knife that could destroy a vampire's soul. Did it work on serial killers? I didn't know, but together, Father Anne and I stabbed and ripped with our knives, while the darkness did its best to press forward and overtake us.

Sorren and Teag had subdued our mortal attackers, and out of the corner of my eye, I saw Teag playing wingman with his staff as Sorren grabbed the lead-lined chest and headed for the typewriter.

Beside me, Father Anne had begun to chant. "From all evil, deliver us, oh Lord—"

The Slittter surged forward, and I struck again with my knife, struggling to hold back the darkness.

"From sudden and unprovided death, from wrath and the lust to shed blood…" Father Anne continued, not even out of breath, although I was shaking like a leaf with every knife stroke.

Our knives had forced the Slitter back, but he wasn't giving up. He surged forward, and I brought the candlestick down, letting my fear flood through it, meeting the hope, love, and commitment of the trinkets melded into its being. Blindingly white light shot from the end of the candlestick, punching through the darkness.

"From the snares of the devil, from the claws of the Evil One, and the traps of the Fallen—" Father Anne was chanting the rite of exorcism, and fighting the shadow man at the same time. Damn, they grow them tough in seminary. The tattoos on her arm glowed with inner light, patron saints against evil. She and I were standing shoulder to shoulder, forcing the Slitter back toward the wall.

"I command you, unclean spirit, along with all your minions, depart! Be gone from this place, unclean spirit, along with every dark power of the enemy, and all your fell companions," Father Anne chanted, her voice rising and strong. For a moment, I glimpsed the shimmering images of the patron saints from her tattoo, and others, a glowing cloud of witnesses, standing with us, and I saw the long-departed Father Conroy among them.

"Depart, transgressor! Depart, seducer, thief of lives and eater of souls, drinker of the blood of the innocent. I adjure you, depart!" Father Anne's voice had reached a crescendo, and the white light that flared from the candlestick was too blinding to watch, shredding the shadow being's darkness and driving it back.

The Slitter gave a howl of utter rage. The white light flared once more, and this time, Sorren, Teag, and I raised our mirrors, the *hexenspiegel*, to capture the spirit in its faceted reflections. Father Anne's spirit knife had weakened it, and as the light from the candle-stick blazed, and the shadow grew less opaque, shrinking before our eyes, pulled inexorably into the endless reflections of the *hexen-spiegel*.

In the blink of an eye, the shadow of the Slitter vanished and with him, the piercing light from the candlestick. The feeling in the room lightened, as if a deadly thunderstorm had just passed us by. Sorren took the *hexenspiegel* from us, dropped them into the lead-lined chest and then used the insulated gloves to put the typewriter in on top of them. Teag swept up the keys that had been knocked to the floor along with our attackers' discarded jewelry and used a dustpan to put them into the chest without touching the items. Sorren slammed the lid down, and Teag wrapped a knotted cord around it, imbuing the binding with his magic.

Only when Father Anne gently pushed my arm down and pried the candlestick from my fingers did I realize I had been rooted to the spot, shaking from head to toe.

"How—did the candlestick do that?" I asked in a faltering voice.

Sorren gave a tired chuckle. "The candlestick didn't. You did. It must have had very strong positive energy, and your gift was desperate for a weapon. The candlestick itself acted like an athame to focus your power, and you channeled all that Light energy against the darkness."

My knees felt shaky, and I might have fallen if Teag hadn't pushed a chair under me.

"What are we going to do about the mess?" Teag asked, eying the trashed workroom critically. "The cops are going to know they didn't leave it like this, and with all the fighting, we're bound to have left enough DNA for the forensics folks to have a field day."

"One step at a time," Sorren said, running a hand back through his hair. This time, it didn't look as if he had taken any damage, although Teag was sporting a black eye and Father Anne's arm was beginning to bruise where the attacker had struck her.

"As for the landlord and his wife, I can glamor them, change their memories," Sorren said. "If Teag can help me get them outside, they'll remember that they heard noises coming from the workshop, right before the explosion."

Father Anne raised an eyebrow, but said nothing, sheathing her knife.

"Explosion?" I managed.

Sorren shrugged. "Necessary, both to remove any trace of our presence, and to melt down the typewriter. A magical pyre, if you like."

My heart ached for all of Kristie's lost jewelry, but there was no way to know what might have been tainted by the Slitter. I looked down at the candlestick in my hand. "If there's a way to get my prints off it, do you think this could 'survive' the fire?" I asked. "It was a commission for someone's fiftieth wedding anniversary, and the energy I'm getting from some of the trinkets tells me one of the people doesn't have much longer to live."

Sorren nodded. "I think that can be arranged."

Father Anne drove me home. Teag and Sorren stayed to clean up. Late that night, I heard sirens, and saw the news report about the fire. A week later, Trina called to tell me that an anonymous benefactor had created a legal fund for Kristie and Karen, enough to get them both the best lawyers in Charleston, and that it looked as if the court would bargain down to temporary insanity.

I was pretty sure who the "anonymous benefactor" was, and I knew it was the best that could be done. Two people had been murdered, and although the Slitter had possessed Karen and Kristie to do it, there was no getting around the fact that their bodies did the crime. Two people dead, two ruined lives. It was cold comfort that what was left of the Slitter's spirit after Father Anne's demon knife was through with it had been destroyed along with his anchor object.

I went by to see Kristie after the trial, before they transferred her to the penitentiary at Ridgeville. It was heartbreaking to see how resigned she was to her fate, and there wasn't a damned thing I could do about it. I promised to visit her. I will. And I will mourn the future she might have had.

We're the Alliance. We protect people from the bad stuff in the shadows. But we can't protect everyone, all the time. I know that, dammit. But this time, it was personal.

It's over now, but it's going to be a long, long time before I take in another old typewriter at Trifles and Folly.

COLLECTOR

"I'D LIKE TRIFLES AND FOLLY TO HANDLE THE AUCTION FOR MY AUNT Dorothy's estate," the caller said. "I've heard you're very good at specialized collections."

My gut screamed at me to hang up the phone right then. I somehow knew it would save me a world of trouble, death, and new nightmares. But that's what I do.

So, of course I said yes.

"I'll be happy to take a look at your aunt's collections," I replied. "Once I know what we're dealing with, I can give you an estimate for the auction and appraisal services." I wrote down the address as the woman on the phone repeated it.

"How soon can you be here?" Her voice had an odd urgency to it.

I checked my watch. It was the middle of the afternoon, and the store was quiet. My assistant store manager, Teag Logan, could come along since Maggie, our part-time helper, was working today. She'd worked at Trifles and Follies longer than I had. "I can be there in about half an hour."

"And if you agree to handle the auction, how quickly could you have the items out of the house?" the woman pressed. That was definitely unusual.

"I should be able to give you an idea of timing once I see what you have," I replied. "Oh, and you haven't told me your name!" This was definitely one of my stranger phone calls.

"Abby Sondergran," the woman replied. "I'll be watching for you." She hung up, leaving me staring at my phone, perplexed. All my instincts told me that this phone call was the beginning of big problems.

I'm Cassidy Kincaide, owner of Trifles and Folly, an antique and curio shop in beautiful, haunted Charleston, SC. Since the store has been around since the city was founded over 350 years ago, lots of people think of us first for estate sales, antique auctions and selling the family silver. We're good at all those things, but we've also got our secrets. The big one is that we're not what we seem to be. Sure, we sell fancy trinkets, but our real purpose is to get dangerous magical items off the market and out of the wrong hands. When we succeed, life goes on as usual. And when we screw up, the death toll usually gets blamed on a natural disaster.

I'm the second secret. I'm a psychometric—someone who can read the history of objects by touching them. Not every object, or I'd go stark, raving mad. But if there's a lot of emotion connected to an object, or it's just downright evil, haunted, or demon-possessed, I can tell by touching it. My business partner, Sorren, is a nearly six-hundred-year-old vampire who runs the Alliance, an effort by mortals and immortals to get dangerous magical items out of the wrong hands. Needless to say, my vampire boss and our ties to the Alliance are just a few more of our secrets.

Teag walked into the office and tilted his head to one side like a beagle listening for a dog whistle. "Trouble?" he asked.

I sighed. "Probably. Got a call from a lady who is so sure she wants us to handle her 'special collection' that she forgot to ask for a price or give me her name."

Teag chuckled. "Yep, she's got her hands full of haunted, and she wants to dump the whole kit-and-caboodle off on us."

Teag and I are an odd pair. He's my assistant store manager, best friend, and occasional bodyguard. We're both in our mid-twenties, but that's where the resemblance ends. He's tall and slender, whip-cord strong, with a skater-boy mop of dark hair and trendy glasses. I'm tall, slim but curvy, with my Scots-Irish heritage written large in my milk-white skin that burns in the South Carolina sun and my strawberry-blonde hair that frizzes in the Lowcountry humidity. He's an expert at mixed martial arts. I can hold my own in a sparring match, but I'll never win championships like Teag does. Teag's in a serious romantic relationship with Anthony, a lawyer, and Charleston blue-blood. My love life has been on hold for a while, though I'm sure one of these days that will change.

Even our magic is different. I read objects. Teag is a Weaver. He can weave spells into cloth and rope, and he can also bring together threads of information, even when they're hidden or hard to find. That makes him a supernaturally-gifted hacker, and it's saved our bacon more than once, given what we do around here.

"I told Abby I would go over right now," I said. "Want to come with me?"

It was two hours until closing on a rainy afternoon, so the shop had been pretty quiet all day. "Sure," he replied. "Let me make sure Maggie can close up, and I'll ride along. Just in case."

Abby's Aunt Dorothy lived in one of the homes on the Battery facing the seawall and Charleston Harbor. Most of these houses dated from before the Civil War and were solid enough to have survived both war and multiple hurricanes. Like the people whose families handed down the homes generation to generation, the houses were stately on the outside and sturdy on the inside.

"Thank you for coming so quickly." Abby Sondergran greeted Teag and me at the front door. The house was a cheery yellow on the outside, painted in pastel stucco that took its cue from the Caribbean. Bright white paint accentuated shutters, window, and door frames, porch rails, and trim.

This particular house had three wide porches—"piazzas" as we call them in Charleston, one for every floor on the front of the home, and wrought-iron railings for each side window that faced the street. A cupola graced the top of the house. Inside the walled private garden, a profusion of oleander and bougainvillea vied with daylilies and crepe myrtles heavy with blossoms. Along the side, three stately palmetto trees separated the house from the sidewalk. Just beyond the seawall, the Cooper and Ashley rivers flowed into Charleston Harbor, lapping against the bulwark of the old battery fortifications.

"Your aunt's home is beautiful," I said as Abby ushered us inside. Whoever Aunt Dorothy had been, she was an avid traveler and collector. Everywhere I looked, trinkets from around the world filled curio cabinets and competed with leather-bound books for shelf space on tall bookshelves. The walls were filled with paintings, framed photographs, carved masks, hand-hammered sconces, and other treasures. Old Oriental carpets and kilim rugs covered the hardwood floors. The furniture was just as eclectic, with lacquered pieces from Asia, heavy carved mahogany from colonial Africa, elegant birch chairs in the Scandinavian style, and big, brass-bound leather trunks.

Yet underneath the world-traveler appearance, I felt the shift and shadow of something dark and powerful. At the moment, the presence was distant, but when I watched how twitchy and nervous Abby was, I figured I knew at least part of the reason.

"My aunt traveled for business and pleasure," Abby said. "She was married to a diplomat, and she was an author and a cultural anthropologist who spoke a dozen languages." A sad smile came over her face. "When Aunt Dorothy passed away, you wouldn't believe the people who sent condolences! Artists, writers, ambassadors, even heads of state." She shook her head. "Aunt Dorothy was a real pistol."

"Dorothy Lunden was your aunt?" Teag had Googled the address on his phone while we drove over. I recognized the name from the Charleston Social Pages in the local magazines. A brilliant and successful woman who had, at the ripe old age of eighty, inexplicably shot herself while alone in her Battery Park mansion. Her death had made headlines and been the talk of the King Street merchants who congregated at the Honeysuckle Café, my favorite spot for lattes.

Abby nodded, and the preoccupied look returned to her face, making her seem furtive, or maybe just a little scared. "Yes. I'm sure you read the news coverage. It was quite a shock. Not only was Aunt

Dorothy in good health, but she had trips planned and was looking forward to giving several speeches about her travels." She sighed. "I guess it's true. You never think someone is going to commit suicide until they up and do it."

I murmured condolences, but the dark undertow of negative energy in the home tugged at my mind. "Did your aunt live here by herself?" I asked.

"When she wasn't riding a camel across the Sahara or an elephant across India, yes," Abby replied with a chuckle. "Aunt Dorothy didn't sit still much. She said she would spend more time at home once she got old. Meaning a lot older than she was when… well, you know." The humor fled her eyes.

I nodded sympathetically. "Will you be living in the house once the auction is held?" I turned around again, taking in the magnificent architecture. Although Dorothy's souvenirs cluttered the rooms and filled in the spaces, once they were gone the old home would feel spacious.

"Maybe," Abby answered. "I'd love to move back to Charleston, but I haven't decided yet. I don't feel quite… at home here." Her eyes slid to the side, telling me that on some level, Abby probably felt at least a hint of the bad juju that seemed to waft through the house like candle smoke.

"I'd love for you to show us around," I said, raising my voice just a bit to get Teag's attention. He had wandered off to examine the antique rugs and finger the exquisite old linens in the dining room. To others, it might appear to be professional curiosity, but I knew his Weaver magic was busy trying to get a bead on the energy in the house and determine its source.

I intentionally kept my hands clasped behind my back. Something had charged the house with seriously bad vibes, and until I had a better idea of what we were dealing with, I did not want to get a full-blown vision, certainly not in front of a client. My intuition tingled as I passed through the crowded hallways, nearly brushing against mementos from all over the world. Some of the pieces radiated good cheer. Others were flat and neutral. A surprising number of pieces were at least slightly negative in their energy, giving a cumulative effect like walking past a long row of frowning people.

"Your aunt's collection has quite a large scope," I said, eyeing a suit of armor from England, a Samurai helmet from Japan, and a tapestry that I guessed was Medieval Belgian. I wished Sorren could have come with us. Given his vampire immortality, he's lived through so much of history. Though, it makes it difficult sometimes for him to accord antiques and museum pieces proper respect when as he puts it, "they're just like old stuff I used to own."

One wall had entire glass cases of beautiful Native American pieces, including several shelves of Kachina dolls. I glanced back to check on Teag. We'd had a close call the last time we dealt with Native American artifacts… bad enough to trigger Teag's gift and almost put him in the hospital.

Teag caught the glance and gave me a nervous but affirming smile.

Abby seemed more comfortable falling into the role of tour guide. She walked us through the house, pointing out unusual pieces or items that had been gifts from notable people. Throughout it, she peppered her conversation with anecdotes about her aunt, someone she clearly admired.

"Have you given any thought to pieces you might like to keep?" I asked. Even if Abby decided not to stay in the house, just a few of the decorations and furnishings would transform any home into a showplace.

A shadow seemed to fall across Abby's face. "I don't think so," she said, avoiding eye contact again. "I have my memories and photographs of Aunt Dorothy. The things in the house just seem to have so much 'weight' to them, if you know what I mean."

I did know, probably in a clearer sense than Abby could imagine. There's a reason most people find themselves whispering in museums. It's not just the dour docents or the stern tour guides. On some primal level, even people without a clairvoyant bone in their bodies sense the memories stored in items that have been present at pivotal times in history. The things that get collected or put in museums usually witnessed significant events or catastrophes, juicing them up with strong emotions. It's why I do my best to stay out of museums, even though I'm a huge history buff. I like to look at old things, but I don't want to experience what they've seen and done.

As we moved through the big home, the supernatural energy waxed and waned. I was willing to bet that a number of Aunt Dorothy's souvenirs actually packed a magical wallop, while others were resonant with strong emotions. It would be difficult for anyone with even a bit of intuition to be present around this collection day-in and day-out. I wondered if Aunt Dorothy realized that her constant traveling might have been a way to avoid spending too much time with her treasures.

"What a view!" Teag stared out of the cupola window over the harbor. I came to stand beside him, taking in the panoramic vista.

"This was one of Aunt Dorothy's favorite places," Abby said and pointed to a small chair and ottoman. They barely fit in the tiny room, but I could just imagine someone curled up with a book and a cup of tea, looking out over the water.

"It's going to take my team some time to catalog and pack all the items for a sale," I said. "And for a collection like this, we would want to advertise and reach out to some of the collectors and institutions on our list, in order to get you the best price." I named a figure for the appraisal, rounding it up somewhat because I anticipated trouble, as well as the percentage and advance for auction. To my surprise, Abby didn't blink.

"Not unreasonable, given how much stuff there is," she said. "How soon can you get started?"

"Have we seen everything?" I asked. It just slipped out, prompted by an inner voice that suspected there was more to the story.

For an instant, before she covered it, Abby looked scared. Then she composed herself, and her polished manner slipped back into place. "Everything but the cellar," she replied. "More of the same, but much of it still in packing crates, since there just wasn't room for everything."

"Let's go take a quick look," I urged, "just so I know what we're dealing with." I had set a price expecting something like this, so my curiosity lay more with the supernatural flavor of what lay in the basement. I glanced at Teag, and he nodded, so I knew we were on the same wavelength.

On our way downstairs, we passed the glass cabinets full of Native American artifacts again. Beautifully beaded dresses, leggings, and moccasins that filled one display case. Bows and arrows, tomahawks, and war axes, clubs, and knives were presented in another cabinet. The third case held a beautiful array of pottery in the bottom and then four shelves filled with colorful Hopi Kachina dolls. One look told me all of the items were old enough to be quite valuable, without adding the large, loom-woven Navaho blankets that were neatly folded on a nearby set of shelves.

I stopped to take a better look. Something in the case was supernaturally active, but the energy was slippery, as if it did not want me to fix on it. "How did your aunt come to have this collection?" I asked, bending closer without touching anything.

"Kinda creepy, aren't they?" Abby said and stepped back with a shudder. "I like a lot of my aunt's stuff, but those give me the willies. They look like something out of an alien movie."

I didn't know much about Kachinas—yet—but I had to agree. The fanciful carvings were brightly colored, depicting figures that represented the gods upon whom tribes depended for rainfall and good harvests, fertility, and successful hunts. Each figure wore an elaborate headdress, mask, and costume. They were teaching tools, not idols, and the ability to carve them was a prized skill handed down from generation to generation.

Yet as I peered at the figures in the case, I felt a shiver run down my spine. Some of the Kachinas gave off positive energy. Others were neutral, nothing more than carved wood, from a supernatural perspective. A few hummed with pent-up malice. I shied away from those figures, but I forced myself to take note. The Kachinas that raised my hackles were painted in dark hues. Their faces were covered with what looked to me like tentacles, a long, solid fringe that completely shrouded their features. In their hands were knives or whips. Even the posture of the dolls was menacing. Teag gave a nod when I looked his way. He'd be researching this as soon as we got into the car.

"This way," Abby said, although I could hear reluctance in her voice. She led us to a door in the kitchen and opened it wide for us. A basement smell wafted up musty and a little damp, the scent of old cardboard boxes and paint cans due to be discarded.

My psychic senses went on high alert as we descended wooden stairs that trembled under our every step. Whatever remained packed away in the boxes and crates I could glimpse by the naked bulbs in the ceiling fixtures had some powerful juju, and not the good kind. I wondered if Aunt Dorothy had left those treasures boxed because she sensed their energy and decided to keep it at arm's length.

The basement was filled with neat rows of wooden crates and heavy packing boxes, each row stacked on concrete blocks about waist high. I could see packing and postage labels that came from every corner of the globe. I couldn't get a fix on where the bad mojo was coming from, but once we started moving things around it wouldn't be hard to spot.

"Do you know how long the boxes have been stored here?" I asked.

"Not too long," Abby replied. "Most came in a few weeks before Aunt Dorothy died. She had just come back from a trip out West, and her friend shipped back the crates. She tried not to have anything stored in here… in case of flooding. But she ran out of room and had to make do. She had been so excited about her new finds…"

"We can get started in the morning," I told Abby after she had signed our appraisal agreement.

"I'll be here," she said, and something in her voice told me she would rather be elsewhere. "I live in Louisiana, and it's too expensive for me to keep going back and forth while I get things settled. I'll be staying in the house, at least until I've got more of a handle on the estate."

Personally, I wouldn't have wanted to stay in the house with the strange supernatural vibes I was getting. "Great. See you bright and early!" Abby saw us to the door, but she was already looking worried and preoccupied when she gave us a half-hearted wave good-bye.

Neither Teag nor I said anything until we were in the car and headed back to the shop. "I don't think I'd want to spend the night there by myself," Teag ventured.

I shook my head. "Not on a bet. I'm wondering if there's a connection between that last shipment Aunt Dorothy got and her sudden personality change."

"It would be good to get Abby out of the house for a while so you can get a read on which items are dangerous without an audience," Teag added. "Once we've cleared the 'sparklers' and 'spookies,' we can have the auction team in to inventory and photograph the remaining items."

I grimaced. That involved touching pieces and getting visions, and if the item had a sordid or tragic history—or was downright evil—it was no fun. "Yeah. Drea owes me a couple of favors. I thought I'd see if she would invite Abby to join in on some of her carriage tours, see if we can get her busy for a few hours. You doing okay? This is the first time we've run into Native American artifacts since…"

"Yeah. All good. I've actually been working a lot with Native American weaving as part of my training. So in some ways, it feels 'familiar.' I'll see what I can dig up on those spooky dolls," Teag promised as I dropped him off at the shop to pick up his car.

"And I'll leave a voicemail for Sorren and let him know about the new job," I replied. Yes, my vampire boss uses cell phones, as well as text messages and email. He says that vampires who can't adapt don't survive.

"How about if you go straight over to Abby's house, and I'll stop by the shop and make sure Maggie opens okay, then come over to join you?" Teag suggested.

"Sounds like a plan," I agreed.

THE NEXT DAY, I showed up at the house at nine a.m. Abby's car was parked at the curb. I knocked and waited. The house had a large, brass door knocker and the minute I touched it; I felt the world spin out around me.

Faces flashed past me, some famous, some not. All had come with a sense of excitement and anticipation, looking forward to meeting the exceptional woman who lived there. A sense of harmony and satisfaction filled me. Dorothy's house had been a real home at one time, filled with friends and laughter. A very different feeling from the shadowed and uncomfortable atmosphere I had experienced yesterday.

The vision dissipated, leaving me to wonder why Abby hadn't answered my knock. I knocked again, louder this time. No response. I called her cell and got no response, so I called the house phone, and heard it ring inside the house, but no one answered.

I paced the porch, debating what to do. Abby hadn't called me to cancel, and if she had left a message at the shop, Teag would have let me know. The longer I waited on the porch, the more certain I became that Abby was in trouble, although I had no idea why. Reminding myself I had a perfectly legitimate reason to be at the house, I walked slowly around, peering into windows to see if I could spot Abby.

By the time I had circled the house, I was certain something was wrong. I glanced over my shoulder, sizing up how well any of the neighbors could see the front door. Sorren had once been the best jewel thief in Antwerp, and since getting into and out of places was part of handling supernatural threats, he had passed those skills along to Teag and me. I had the door open in just a few seconds, and reeled as the psychic force of the house hit me.

The air smelled like rotting meat, and a gust of winter-cold air blasted me, far too cold for any air conditioner. For a moment, it looked to me as if the entire foyer was layered in shadow, as if the walls and furnishings were darkened by a supernatural soot that turned the vibrant colors to a dull gray. Every instinct I had screamed for me to turn and run the other direction. And if Abby hadn't been inside, I might have. But I had the awful feeling that something about the house had been involved in Dorothy's suicide, and now, I was afraid that it had tried to harm Abby.

I'm not the martial arts expert Teag is, but I have a few tricks up my sleeve when it comes to protecting myself. My hand closed over the agate necklace at my throat, drawing on the protective qualities of the gemstone. I had packets of salt in my pocket, as well as some polished bits of black onyx and tourmaline—good for dispelling malicious energy.

My magic is touch magic, so objects with a strong emotional connection are powerful for me, and they help me channel my magic. That's why I had a worn and dirty dog collar wound around my left wrist, a reminder—and psychic connection—to Bo, the golden retriever who had shared my life for many years. And in my bag, I had an old wooden spoon that had belonged to my grandmother. It didn't look like much, but I had seen what that powerful emotional bond could do to channel my magic when the chips were down.

I shook the dog collar, hearing the faint jingle of the tags, and the ghostly form of a large, beautiful dog appeared to my left. Then I let go of my necklace and reached into my bag for the wooden spoon athame, wondering how on earth I would explain myself if it turned out Abby had been slow coming to the door because she was in the shower.

Bo's ghost headed into the foyer, and the shadows shrank back but did not disappear. "Abby?" I called. No response. The blast of cold air was gone, and I could hear the old house's air conditioning straining against the Charleston heat. I walked toward the kitchen with the definite feeling that the shadows were watching, waiting for a chance to strike.

"Abby?" My voice echoed in the big, empty house. I thought about going back outside to wait for Teag, but my worry for Abby kept me moving. I thought I caught a glimpse of a figure near the display cases in the hallway, but when I looked again, I saw no one.

I could hear Bo's warning growl in my mind. In life, Bo had been a good-natured goofball who didn't even get upset about thunderstorms. But once, when someone tried to attack me, he had gone Rottweiler on the man, winning my eternal gratitude. As a ghost, Bo had saved my hide several times. I took his warning seriously.

Even though I wasn't handling any of Dorothy's objects, my magic was flashing danger signals. I started to run, shouting Abby's name, looking into each room and finding nothing. But at the top of the steps, I found Abby sitting in a chair in the bedroom, unmoving.

"Abby!" I ran to her and searched for a pulse. She was breathing shallowly and unresponsive. "Come on, Abby," I coaxed, trying to get a response.

Bo's ghost was barking frantically in my mind, running toward the door and back again. I had no idea how I was going to get Abby down the stairs. Again I saw a blur of shadows in the hallway, and this time I made out a shape. It looked like a man, but with a huge, bulbous head and it made a swish-clatter noise as it moved, like it was moving through a beaded curtain.

Something tumbled from Abby's hands, and I grabbed it without looking, then felt the psychic wallop like a sledgehammer. I stared down at the Kachina doll in my hands, one of the ones I had seen before in the glass case. It was a hunched figure dressed mostly in a brown tunic and leggings. One hand gripped a bloody knife, and the other held a long, curved wooden crook. The head was out of proportion to the body, covered front and back with long, coarse black hair that fell to mid-chest and mid-back, curling and swinging as if it had a life of its own like Medusa's locks. The figure's face was horrible, wide yellow eyes with black pupils and a toothy maw that stretched ear to ear and a bright red tongue that protruded past the chin. A large reed basket was strapped to the figure's back.

Guilt and self-loathing washed over me like a drowning sea current. Everything I had ever failed to do, every promise not kept, every obligation not met came back to me in crushing force. Every secret unworthy thought, each petty jealousy or word spoken in anger crashed down on me in a torrent of blame. I gasped for breath, feeling my chest constrict. I knew that I had betrayed everyone's trust in me with my mistakes, that I was so flawed and broken that I did not deserve a second chance. Accusing voices howled in my head, unearthing every secret shame. I did not deserve to live. I did not deserve—

Bo's ghost sprang at me and hit with the power of the ninety-pound dog he had been in his life. His eyes were wild and his teeth bared, and I drew back in shock at the attack. Bo lunged forward, mouth open to bite, pinning me to the floor. But before I could react, his teeth closed on the Kachina and flung it across the room and into the hallway.

Abruptly, my thoughts cleared. I could still feel the despair and merciless accusations like a mental stain, but they no longer paralyzed me. I gasped, filling my lungs with air, trying to get my balance, both mentally and physically. The Kachina spirit's attack had been so sudden and unexpected that I had nearly been taken down by it. I was shaking all over, and it took all my willpower not to throw up.

I couldn't afford to wait for Teag. It felt to me like the shadows were closing in on us as more silhouettes joined the first. They were in the hallway, and I could hear the distant hum of voices conferring in language I didn't recognize. Overwhelming sadness and despair rolled over me, smothering and bleak. I closed my hand over my agate neck-lace again, and the dark feelings dissipated. *Was that what drove Dorothy to suicide?* I wondered. *And had the same thing happened to Abby?*

Bo's ghost was standing guard at the bedroom doorway once more, hackles raised and teeth bared. I grabbed one of the salt packets from my pocket and sprinkled it in a circle that enclosed Abby and me. Salt is powerful for protection, and I hoped it would keep the shadows away until I could figure something out.

Shadow figures surged at the doorway, things with bulbous heads and long arms, clicking their teeth and hissing. I leveled my spoon-athame at the shadows, going high as Bo's ghost went low.

White, cold light streamed from the tip of the wooden spoon's handle, hitting the top of the figures while Bo sprang with a growl, going for the legs. I wasn't sure how solid these spirits were to humans, but they were real enough to Bo, and his attack combined with the pure energy that flared from my athame was enough to drive the shadows back, away from the door and out of sight. For now.

I pulled out my cell phone to call for an ambulance, and although we were in downtown Charleston, I could not get a signal. Magic and supernatural energies can play havoc with electronics, and ghosts have been known to jam signals and interfere with reception. I was just about to try to lift Abby onto my shoulder and make our way down the stairs when I heard Teag shouting my name.

"We're in here!" I yelled. "Watch out—there's something in the hallway!"

"I see it," Teag called back, and before I could answer, a cloaked creature swooped into the room. I yelped before I realized that it was Teag with one of the Navajo blankets thrown over his head and shoulders.

"Take this!" he said, tossing one of the folded blankets to me. "The blankets have positive energy; they've been woven with protection. They'll help keep the shadows at bay."

As soon as I touched the woven blanket, the dark magic's hold on me loosened. Not coincidentally, my cell phone got signal again. I put in a call to 911, glad that I had a copy of the paperwork we signed in my purse because there would be questions about how we happened to find Abby.

Teag was careful not to touch anything in the room, but with one of the blankets still around his shoulders like a cape, he took a look around. "Sleeping pills," he said with a nod toward a container on the nightstand. "Want to bet she was having bad dreams, and she either forgot or was misled into taking too many?"

I shuddered, remembering the soul-numbing hopelessness the shadows had inflicted. Magic had helped me drive it back. Abby didn't have that protection. *Maybe it wasn't an accident*, I thought. *Maybe whatever we're up against wanted her to die.*

The ambulance came quickly, and the EMTs loaded up Abby and the bottle of sleeping pills and headed for the hospital, making sure to get our names in case there were questions later. I followed the ambulance since Abby didn't seem to have anyone else in the area. Teag locked up the house and went back to his research, since neither one of us thought being there alone was a good idea.

Several hours later, I dragged into Trifles and Folly. Maggie took one look at me and offered to run out to Honeysuckle Café for a latte, and I was exhausted enough to take her up on it. Teag was with a customer, so I headed for the back office, too wrung out to be much good until I got my second wind.

Teag brought the latte back to me while Maggie took over up front. "How's Abby?" he asked.

I took a sip of the latte and let out a long breath. "She'll be okay. They said it was good we found her when we did. They're keeping her overnight."

"Any trouble?"

I shrugged. "A cop came and took my statement. Wanted to know why we were in the house, how we found her, that sort of thing." I raised an eyebrow. "Good thing we folded up the blankets and put them on the bed before the EMTs came in, or they'd have had a few more questions."

I thought to check my phone, and saw there was a message from Sorren, so I put it on speaker. "Got your call," he said. "I think I know someone who can help. I'll come by your house after sundown, and we can make plans." The message ended.

"I never got to tell you what I found out about those carved dolls," Teag said, sitting down in the chair facing my desk. "They're meant to represent the sacred Hopi spirits. Most of them are helpful, or at least forces of nature. But there are some that get pretty dark."

He grimaced. "That black Kachina doll with the mop-like head, the one that looked like it either had hair or tentacles covering its face?" I shivered and nodded. "It's one of the ogres, maybe even Soyok Wuhti herself."

"Who?"

"Monster Woman. She and the ogres were stories told to frighten children into obeying their elders," Teag recapped. "During certain festivals, people would dress up like Soyok Wuhti and the ogres and reprimand disobedient children. Some of the ogres carry yucca flails— they're the whippers—and they go after adults and children who break the rules."

He raised an eyebrow. "But Monster Woman is hard-core. She has a bloody knife and a long wooden crook, and she carries a basket on her back," he said. "Parents told their children that if they didn't obey, Soyok Wuhti would carry them away in her basket and eat them."

"Yikes," I said, taking another long pull of my latte. "And I thought it was bad that Santa had a naughty-or-nice list."

"Yeah," Teag agreed. "Kinda puts the bogeyman-in-the-woods stories into perspective."

I frowned as I thought about what Teag had discovered. "No one in her right mind would try to attract spirits like those," I replied. "So I'm wondering whether there's some other artifact that's juicing up the doll's mojo, turning pieces with just a bit of sparkle into full-blown spookies." We had run into that before, discovering otherwise mundane objects suddenly taking on a whole new, terrifying magical aspect because someone or something evil and powerful was close enough to power them up.

Teag nodded. "If the Kachina dolls were on display in a cabinet, then Dorothy had probably had them for a while. Maybe they didn't cause any problems, or whatever juju they had was low-level enough not to notice." He paused. "Abby told you that Dorothy got a bunch of boxes not long before she died, things she bought on her last trip, right?"

"Uh huh. Still in the basement," I replied. "And I'm guessing whatever amped up the dolls is in a crate down there." Which meant we needed to go down after it. Damn. Then again, it wasn't in our job description to leave well enough alone.

We waited until closing time, then Teag and I picked up a pizza and headed for my house. I inherited Trifles and Folly from my Uncle Evan, and my parents sold me their house for a pittance when they moved from Charleston to Charlotte. It's what Charlestonians call a "single house," long and narrow with the front door on the side of the house facing the sidewalk, so that visitors enter onto a wide porch or piazza. I love the old house, and I especially love my little Maltese dog, Baxter, who was waiting inside, yipping his fool head off when he heard us park at the curb.

I opened the door, and Baxter pounced. He's six pounds of white, fluffy attitude. Heart of a grizzly bear; body of a guinea pig. I set my purse aside while Teag carried the pizza into the dining room, and bent down to give Baxter the attention he was demanding, then handed him over to greet Teag when he came back to the foyer.

"He wants pepperoni," Teag said, letting Baxter lick his chin. "You know that's what he's after."

I sighed. "Of course—unless there's any other kind of meat, or broccoli." Baxter loves broccoli. Go figure.

I took Baxter for a quick walk in the garden, then got his dinner. Teag and I sat down to chow through one of Jocko's Pizzeria's two-topping masterpieces. We kept the conversation light, knowing there was enough darkness to come. I figured we were both plenty nervous, but there was no point in talking about it.

The sun was barely below the horizon when my doorbell rang. Baxter zipped out from between my feet in a bouncing bundle of terri-torial protectiveness that would have done a Doberman proud. But when I opened the door, Baxter sat down immediately with a slightly glazed look on his face, tongue lolling from one side of his mouth.

"Do you really have to glamor him every time you visit?" I asked Sorren with a sigh of mock exasperation. Secretly, I had often envied Sorren's ability to use a little vampire mind trick on the pup. It would have come in handy whenever Baxter got worked up over deliverymen.

"It spares all of us our hearing," Sorren replied with a half-smile that told me he enjoyed the running joke. Sorren appears to be in his late twenties, with blond hair and eyes the color of the sea after a storm. High cheekbones hint at his Belgian heritage, but I've only heard his accent when he's hurt or badly upset. Dressed in a hoodie, jeans, and sneakers, Sorren looks like a graduate student instead of a powerful, centuries-old vampire.

Sorren stepped inside, and I got my first glimpse of his companion.

The man who followed Sorren into the foyer was probably in his early sixties, with coppery skin lined from the sun, chocolate-colored eyes and white hair tied back in a braid that fell to the middle of his back. He wore a white shirt tucked into faded blue jeans that hung from his spare frame, and he had a canvas rucksack thrown over one shoulder. On his belt was a pouch made of skin and fur. Even from a distance, I caught a frission of power. But the magic felt strange, and something about it reminded me of the energy in the woven blankets that Teag had used to hold the shadow ogres at bay.

"Cassidy, Teag—I'd like you to meet Daniel Mohe Traverner. Daniel, these are my associates with the shop."

Daniel looked Teag and me up and down, then nodded. I got the feeling he wasn't the talkative type. "They'll do," he said. He met my gaze, and his eyes narrowed a bit. "She's Evan's kin, isn't she?"

Sorren chuckled. "The latest in a long line."

I led the way into the living room and got everyone seated, then offered Daniel sweet tea, which he accepted with taciturn politeness. Sorren didn't need regular food or drink, and from the color in his complexion, I figured that he had eaten recently although I did not want to know the details.

Once everyone was settled, Teag and I looked to Sorren to kick off the conversation. "When I heard your voice message about the Kachina dolls, I figured we would need a specialist," Sorren said. "Daniel is a *Didanawisgi*, a Cherokee medicine man." Sorren knew a lot of people in the magical community, from Voudon mambos and houngans to root workers and renegade priests. I was amazed, but not entirely surprised, to see him show up with a Native American shaman.

"But the dolls are Hopi, from out West," I said, glancing from Sorren to Daniel. "Does that matter?"

Daniel chuckled. "We're different tribes, certainly. But let's just say that we talk to many of the same spirits by other names, and those spirits that differ talk to each other."

At Sorren's urging, Teag and I recounted what we had seen and experienced at Dorothy's house, ending with the attack on Abby. "We think something that came in the last shipment of boxes juiced up the Kachina dolls," I finished. "And from the despair those shadow-ogres were able to create, I wonder if they weren't behind Dorothy's suicide and Abby's sleeping pill overdose."

"I fear you're right," Daniel said. "The Nataska—the spirit ogres—are nothing to be taken lightly, and certainly not Soyok Wuhti."

"Have you ever faced them?" I asked. "Do you have something similar in the Cherokee tradition?"

"Frightening as Soyok Wuhti is, I would place my bet on Raven Mocker in a fight," Daniel said. I looked for a glimmer of humor in his eyes, but he was serious. "Raven Mocker is a spirit like your Grim Reaper, only nastier. It attacks the frail and dying, kills them brutally, and steals their remaining lifespan."

"Okay then, I guess that's something to be grateful for," Teag muttered.

"One must take fortune as it comes," Daniel replied. "Or to put it another way, be grateful for small favors."

"I don't get it," Teag replied. "I see Kachina dolls for sale on the Internet. Hell, the gift shop at the Phoenix airport has them. Are they all juiced up?"

Daniel shook his head. "Of course not. Just like the amulets and rabbits' feet in tourist traps don't really bring good luck. The object is only part of the power. To activate an object, something supernatural must happen. A blessing. A curse. Consecration. Use in a ritual. Or contamination. And from what you have told me, I believe that is the source of our problem. Something has contaminated the Kachinas, enabling the spirits they represent to break through into this reality."

"Why didn't it affect the nice spirits?" Teag asked. From his moodiness, I knew that our earlier battle had seriously spooked him.

Daniel shrugged. "Nice spirits—like nice people—have no desire to force themselves onto others." He gave a sad smile. "This is the problem when people consider the sacred items of one culture to be mere art. I don't fault collectors. Items like the Kachinas are beautiful, and our people have made all kinds of crafts for sale outside the tribes. But those pieces—like your airport Kachinas—were never consecrated. It would seem that Abby's aunt managed to purchase relics that were actually used in rituals. Their power might have been latent, but present even so."

"If those dolls become portals for the spirits, why don't they cause problems for the tribe?" I asked.

Daniel met my gaze. "I believe both of you know something of magic. When you make a salt circle, you create a boundary for power. So it is within a tribe. For the Hopi, the Kachina dolls do not exist by themselves. They are part of a web of power and belief woven and renewed every day within a larger context."

"So… take the magical item out of the salt circle, or the ogres out of the culture, and kablooey," Teag summarized.

Daniel's chuckle was deep and low. "Exactly. Kablooey."

"Why would the Nataska prompt Dorothy and Abby to commit suicide?" I asked.

Daniel looked thoughtful. "The ogres and the 'whippers' enforce the tribe's beliefs of right and wrong. They're like a collective conscience, only given physical form. In the legends and ceremonies, they confront people who haven't done what they ought to do and threaten to punish them."

I met his gaze. "But take them out of context, away from the rest of the culture, and they get out of control, like having your worst critic screaming in your ear all the time."

Daniel nodded. "Yes. I believe that is what happened. Dorothy and Abby were unprepared, and the relentless judgment drove them to try to kill themselves."

"Can you get rid of the Nataska and keep Soyok Wuhti from coming back?" I asked. The idea of facing that dark power again made me shiver.

"Something has opened a door," Daniel replied. "We must close it. To do that, we have to find the door."

Teag and I were ready for a fight. Over the time we've been dealing with malicious magic, we've both acquired our own personal arsenal of magic weapons and defenses. Not every item worked for every situation, but it was nice to have a choice.

I had my wooden spoon-athame as well as Bo's collar and my agate necklace. On one wrist, I had an onyx and silver bracelet, and I had refreshed my supply of salt packets. I left the Voudon, Norse, and Conjure amulets in my drawer since I didn't know whether Hopi spirits would heed them, and figured that my fire-spewing magic walking stick would just make things worse.

Teag wore a vest into which he had woven protective spells. Several macramé knots dangled from his belt loops, something he used to store power for later use. He carried his martial arts staff carved with runes and an onyx ring for protection. Around his throat, he wore a Filipino *agimat* talisman.

Sorren was an undead immortal. A lot of magic couldn't touch him, and the kinds that could weren't easily turned aside by amulets. Still, I glimpsed a ring of black tourmaline on his left hand and a mirror set in bronze hanging from a chain around his neck. Although we were going up against shadows and spirits, Sorren wore a sword. Teag and I had knives as well. They didn't do much against specters, but they worked just fine on nasty minions.

Daniel, I was sure, had his own protections. I guessed that the skin and fur bag on his belt was his medicine pouch, sacred and made just for him. I glimpsed talismans of bone and wood on a long chain that ran beneath the neckline of his shirt, and to my senses, the intricate braiding in the leather wristlet shimmered with power. He had a long knife in a leather scabbard on one hip.

Daniel looked at each of us in turn as if he had X-ray vision, and I was sure his shaman-senses saw our protections. "You've chosen well," he said finally. "But I can give you an additional defense, if you will accept it."

"I'm all for anything that saves my skin," Teag replied. I nodded, and so did Sorren.

Daniel withdrew three small paint pots from his rucksack. "Hold out your right arm," he said to me. He daubed a black mixture onto his hand and then pressed it against my skin, leaving a complete hand mark. Beneath the handprint, he drew a symbol in red paint and another in green. As he drew the symbols, he chanted quietly under his breath. Then he made the same marks on Teag and Sorren.

When he was done, he took out an aerosol can and sprayed the symbols. The air smelled of drugstore hairspray. "Ancient tribal secret," Daniel said with a smirk. "Keeps war paint from smearing."

"How do we keep the Nataska out of our heads?" That question had been bothering me all evening.

Daniel looked at each of us in turn. "You are aware, so you can resist. The 'war paint' will help, as will your magic. But you must guard your thoughts. After all, the Nataska have been doing their jobs for millennia."

"What's the game plan?" Teag asked.

"Whatever triggered the problem is likely in the basement, so we start there," Sorren said. "Daniel raises wards to hold off the spirits and asks for the help of the friendly ones. If we're lucky, we find the problem pieces and either destroy or neutralize them. Then we go home."

He made it sound so simple, so straightforward, so clear. I knew from experience that it was not likely to be any of those. We were headed into a storm, and we would be lucky to get out in one piece.

Just another day at the office.

"Let's go," Sorren said. "Tonight's our best shot. Time's a'wasting."

I was afraid that someone might have roped off Dorothy's house with police tape, but there was none in sight when we pulled up. To avoid attracting attention, we parked a couple of blocks away and approached from different directions.

We gathered in the walled garden, and even before we entered the house, I noticed a heavy feeling of despair, the same leaden sense I remembered from being called to the principal's office as a child. A new threat occurred to me. I wondered whether the Nataska had found fertile hunting grounds in the neighbors around the Battery. The thought of primal ogres and whippers stalking the citizens of Charleston made my blood run cold.

Inside the old home, the air felt colder than normal air conditioning. I remembered what Daniel had said about Raven Mocker stealing years of life from its prey. The disquieting energies seemed stronger than they had the day before, making me wonder if the Nataska had taken power from Dorothy's death and Abby's torment. I felt cold anger strengthen me. This had to stop.

"This way," I said, using the moonlight from the windows and our own muted flashlights to lead them toward the basement door. When we came to the case of Kachina dolls, Daniel paused. He reached into his rucksack and drew out a cornmeal cake and an apple, and laid it as an offering in front of the case. Then he began to chant in Cherokee, clapping to keep time, and the mixtures of vowels and consonants were utterly foreign to me, strange and beautiful. He drew out a clay pipe from his sack and lit it. The smell of sweet tobacco and sage filled the air.

After a moment, Daniel turned to us. "I have asked the spirits for their protection, and petitioned Soyok Wuhti and the Nataska to turn away."

"Do you expect Monster Woman and the whippers to listen?" Teag asked. Put that way; it sounded like a bad name for a metal band.

"The spirits may hear what I say. Soyok Wuhti and the Nataska will do as they do, but I have observed courtesies. Now, if we meet aggression, we are blameless in defending ourselves," Daniel replied.

He kept his pipe in his mouth as we headed for the basement door. Then he put down his rucksack and withdrew a turtle shell rattle on a leather wrist strap and a hand drum made of stretched hide over a wooden frame. "My medicine is strong in conjuring," Daniel said. "But not strong enough to overpower Soyok Wuhti. So I must call to the spirits and the ancestors for help, and send a warning to the Nataska that we are not ignorant of the ways of the Old Ones."

"If you don't mind, a little flash-bang-pow never hurts," Teag said. "In case that's in your bag of tricks."

"If the spirits will it. I will not be able to help you fight physically. But I will be with you as I walk the spirit paths."

I knew that Daniel was giving assurance, but I also knew what Teag meant. We had gone up against nasty supernatural beings and vicious ghosts with the help of demon hunters and root workers, mediums, and vampire killers, and so while I wasn't opposed to chants and ceremony, I was hoping Daniel had firepower in his magical arsenal, or we could be in real trouble.

"Cassidy—I'm counting on you to identify the source of the disruption," Sorren said. "Teag and I will back you up. Daniel will gather protective spirits, and use his medicine power to shut down the gateway that's been opened."

Yeah, that's all we had to do. Piece of cake.

Sorren headed down the stairs ahead of me. We turned on the lights, figuring passers-by would be hard-pressed to see. Bare bulbs lit the unfinished basement. It still smelled of damp and disuse, but I could feel magic fairly crackling in the air.

I jangled the dog collar on my left wrist, and Bo's ghost appeared as a translucent shadow of his furry self, padding down weightlessly beside me. My grandmother's spoon was in my right hand, the bowl of it pressed into my palm, handle pointing out with my fist clutched around it. It might not look like something a movie wizard would use, but just holding it tightly connected me with the powerful light energy of my late grandmother's love.

Teag was right behind me. I saw him grab one of the Navajo blankets on the way past the shelf in the other room, but much as I wanted its protection, I knew that I had to risk opening myself to sense the magic in this room in order to find what was bringing the Nataska and Monster Woman through with a vengeance.

"How about you check crates for mojo, and then I open the crates and you hold your hand over them?" Teag said. I saw him pull a small crowbar and a pair of heavy leather gloves from beneath his jacket. Handy to have for a lot of reasons, though I wasn't sure how good the crowbar would be in a fight with shadow-things.

Daniel moved down the stairs slowly, chanting and drumming, and the tobacco-sage scent of his pipe smoke drifted across the basement. Power was stirring all around me, old and strong. As I had seen on my brief visit with Abby, there were more than a dozen crates and boxes in the basement. I wondered how we could ever go through them all. Then I remembered something.

"Abby said the boxes from out West came just a few weeks ago," I said. "That probably means they're in the front and on top."

Sorren circled the room slowly, sword drawn. He was faster and stronger because of his immortality, with heightened senses. I tried not to think about what might be waiting to strike, and concentrated my attention on the stack of boxes where Teag had stopped.

"These all have recent shipping marks," Teag said, pointing to a stack of small crates. "What do you pick up from them?"

I frowned, concentrating, and ran my hands just above the surface of the top box. "There's something of power in there, but I'm not sure what it is." Teag put on the gloves and obligingly pried off the top of the wooden box, and then carefully separated the contents piece by piece. Bracelets, moccasins, necklaces, and pipes, all beautifully made, gave me no shiver of magic at all. Then Teag lifted up a short embellished cedar stick about a foot long, and my senses buzzed.

"Set that aside," I said. "It's not dangerous. Maybe it'll help." I didn't have a deep background in Native American items, but I recognized that piece as a Lakota spirit stick. It was wound with red, white, and black colored twine and a turkey feather was attached to the top. The spirit stick radiated balanced, positive energy. It wouldn't hurt to keep it handy.

Nothing else in that box resonated with me, so we moved on. Sorren moved the box aside as Teag opened the next crate. My senses felt jangly, as if I'd had too much caffeine. So much latent magic hummed around me that trying to sense the key pieces was like listening for whispers after leaving a rock concert: my magical "hearing" was still intact but buzzing and overloaded.

I picked up flashes of magic from a couple of old tomahawks and a parfleche bag, but nothing to account for the attacks. Teag handed the box to Sorren and started on the one below it.

"Take that piece," I said, more on instinct than anything else. It was a round shield made of wood, marked with a handprint like Daniel had placed on us, along with other symbols I did not recognize. I felt a strong protective energy from the shield, and when Teag lifted it, I could tell that its magic spoke to him from the look on his face.

Two more boxes to go. Teag pried off the lid of the next box, and we both fell back a step. Inside was a ceremonial mask in the shape of a bird's head. Dark feathers and paint covered its face, with pitiless black glass eyes above a sharp, vicious beak. Raven Mocker, I knew and shuddered.

"Not what we're looking for," I said. The old mask held power, but to my surprise, it felt ambivalent, as if it had not played a part in the awakening of the Nataska and Soyok Wuhti.

"One box left." Teag gingerly put the crate with the Raven Mocker mask aside and cracked open the lid of the bottom crate.

As soon as the wood splintered, I felt the push of power. It was old, angry, and very strong. Unlike the Monster Woman and her ogres, this power did not feel dark or vengeful, but it was agitated, and to my inner sight, it looked like hurricane clouds, brooding and dangerous.

The temperature in the basement plummeted, and above Daniel's chanting, I heard the swish of yucca whips and the *clack-clack* of teeth gnashing. "It's in there," I said, falling to my knees with Teag as he rummaged through the crate.

"No, no, no," I said as he pushed one thing after another out of the way. Knives, wristbands, shell capes, and bone breastplates filled the box, but none of them were what we were looking for.

"There!" I shouted, although Teag was right next to me. A metal lozenge tin lay at the bottom of the crate. Small as it was, the surge of power coming off of it was tremendous. "That's it!"

Teag wrapped a rag around his gloved hand before reaching for the metal box, and then the storm broke loose.

Soyok Wuhti and her bully boys didn't bother fighting their way past Daniel. They materialized right in the center of the basement, large as life, terrifyingly real. Monster Woman looked just like her Kachina. The two ogres with her had the same heavy fringe covering their features, but one of them had curled horns growing out of the sides of its head, and the other had a headdress with wide, black paddle-shaped pieces fanning out behind his oversized skull.

The nearest ogre brought its yucca flail down hard. Teag shoved me out of the way, taking the blow on his shoulder and I heard him grunt with pain. I flung out my right arm and concentrated my will on the wooden athame in my hand, sending a blast of cold white light at the ogre, driving it back a few steps.

Bo's ghost sprang at the second ogre, going for the throat, and I heard the *snick* of snapping teeth as he hit his target. Sorren's sword glinted in the light of the bare bulbs, slashing down at Soyok Wuhti herself, a powerful strike that cut from shoulder to hip. His blade passed through the specter without effect.

"Don't let them get what's in that tin!" I wasn't sure how I knew it, but I was certain that if Soyok Wuhti and her ogres possessed the tin box, they would be too powerful to stop. The thought of killer night-mares and ghostly whippers stalking the streets of Charleston hardened my resolve.

The Kachina spirits vanished in the blink of an eye, then reap-peared just as quickly a few paces away. Monster Woman wasn't playing fair. The ogre nearest Sorren caught him across the face with his yucca whip, opening bloody stripes and narrowly missing his eyes. Sorren pivoted, striking again with his sword, a slash that should have disemboweled a mortal opponent, but the sword made no mark, passing cleanly through.

Teag sprang from a crouch, slamming into the second ogre with his sparring staff. It had served him well in martial arts tournaments, and Teag had added magic to its strength with the runes he had carved and the spelled braids that twined around its top. The staff thudded against something solid when it struck the ogre, and the shadow creature fell back a pace, surprised.

I sent another blast of white light toward Monster Woman, but this time she dodged with an ear-splitting cry, bringing her crook down on my arm and throwing me off balance as my athame fell from my hand. Her flail hit me hard across the shoulders, cutting through my shirt. I felt warm blood on my back.

The smell of blood sent the ogres into a frenzy. They blinked in and out, pausing just long enough to strike with their flails. Soyok Wuhti lashed out with her crook, hitting Sorren in the head hard enough to fell a mortal, then disappearing before he could strike back. We were getting our butts whupped.

Soyok Wuhti kept after Sorren, while one of the ogres started for me. With one mighty sweep of his flail, he swept Bo's ghost out of the way and came after me.

I hurled a packet of salt at him. He never slowed his pace. His steps were heavy and deliberate, almost like a stomping dance, and he moved with the grace of a predator despite the bulky headdress. I didn't dare take my eyes of him to look for my athame, so I grabbed the next closest thing, the spirit stick.

I could feel the mental assault of the Nataska even as the ogres struck at my physically. Despair threatened to overwhelm me. I focused on the power of the war paint drawings, using the handprint like a psychic stop sign to halt the tide of bleak thoughts from making me lose my will. It was like fighting a two-front war, mentally and physically exhausting, and I knew I couldn't keep it up for long.

Spectral beings were all around us, drawn by Daniel's chanting and the crates we had opened. Some were ghosts, attached to whatever was in the metal tin Teag fought to protect. Others, like Monster Woman and her ogres, were far older. They were beings that had never been human, and whether we thought of them as gods or demons, spirit-guides or something alien and other, they were far more than mere humans, living or dead.

Daniel's chanting and drumming took on a new intensity, and as I opened my senses to it, I felt new spirits join the fray. I recognized them from the Kachina case. These were warriors and seers, spirits of rain, and new life. The spirit stick tingled in my hand, and in a rush, I felt one of the Kachina beings envelop me as if I had dropped a costume over my head.

I was me, and not me. The Kachina seer spirit didn't possess me from the inside, but it overlaid me on the outside, like an exoskeleton, making me stronger, faster, sharper. I felt the spirit stick's magic slide across my body, felt it connect with the handprint and the painted symbols where Daniel had marked me, and felt the power settle in as if taking the marks as acceptance. This time, when I concentrated my will into the spirit stick, a relic from an old and proud native people, the blast of light was a wide cone, and it not only hit the ogre, it drove him back, over a pile of boxes, and into a wall.

"Daniel's spirits are helping us!" I shouted to Teag and Sorren. "Use the relics!"

I was bleeding from several strikes of the ogre's flail. Teag's shirt was sliced open, and I saw blood on the torn cloth and down the deep cuts on his arm. Sorren had gone after Soyok Wuhti one immortal to another, and while the Monster Woman was moving a little more slowly, Sorren was bloodied with deep gashes from her flail and bruised from her staff.

Teag grabbed the nearest relic of power, the round shield. I don't know whether he felt the same transformation I did, but from the outside, I saw a fierce warrior's form overlay Teag's own, one of the brightly-colored Kachina fighters. Teag had his staff in one hand, and he snatched up the Navajo blanket, throwing it across his shoulders so that his Weaver magic could draw from the power invested in its warp and woof. This time when he swung his staff, it connected against the ogre's solid form with much more force, and I saw a slow, triumphant smile spread across Teag's features.

Sorren had taken more damage than a mortal could have withstood. His sword was of no use against Soyok Wuhti, and his vampire teeth, strength, and speed gave him little advantage against such an ancient and powerful being. He fell to his knees under Monster Woman's flail, and as he did, the crate with the Raven Mocker mask tumbled to the floor beside him.

"Put it on!" I shouted as Soyok Wuhti closed with her staff upraised to strike again.

Sorren grabbed the headpiece, put it over his head and rolled to evade the blow. When he got to his feet, Sorren the vampire was gone, overlaid by Raven Mocker in the flesh.

Sorren rose off the basement floor and hurtled into Soyok Wuhti. This time, his sword hit flesh with a sickening thud, and Monster Woman shrieked as the blade bit bone deep across the arm holding the crook. She struck with the flail, but Raven Mocker was faster, and the sword sliced through the stiff reeds, cutting their length by half.

Arm dangling, bone protruding from her flesh, Soyok Wuhti gave a banshee scream, jabbing at Sorren with the spiky remainders of the reeds and swinging her crook like a baseball bat to crush his skull.

I felt like I had a front-row seat at a monster-vs-monster smack-down match. Raven Mocker and Soyok Wuhti seemed pretty evenly matched, but beneath the spirit's overlay, Sorren had the speed and cunning of an ancient vampire going for him as well. He launched himself at Monster Woman, blade angled at her head. The tip slit the black fringe that covered Soyok Wuhti's face, cutting her from eye to chin.

Her crook caught Sorren across the back, and I heard bones break. Sorren sank toward the ground, then sprang up suddenly, ignoring his injuries, driving his blade deep into Monster Woman's belly.

"Yikes!" I yelped, then got in a shot from my spirit stick against the ogre Teag was fighting, while my opponent was still peeling himself off the basement wall. Now that we could do real damage, I grabbed my knife, switching the spirit stick to my left hand, as I saw that my ogre enemy was coming back for a rematch.

Meanwhile, my thoughts spun. Daniel's Kachina spirits had evened the playing field, but they hadn't won the war for us, at least, not yet. I didn't understand spirit politics, and now wasn't the time to try to figure it out, but I hoped their intervention meant that we had some kind of shot at success. Daniel's chants and the steady beat of his drum and rattle echoed from the basement's stone walls, heartbeat and war chant. His pipe smoke sent a haze over the room.

My ogre lumbered toward me, but taking my cue from Sorren, I didn't wait for him to reach me. I used a move I had learned from Teag in martial arts, slamming the Nataska in the chest with a high kick, and swinging around to slice my knife across his chest.

His flail hit me hard, driving me back, opening up new deep cuts with reeds sharp as razors. I countered, lunging forward with my knife, shoving it deep into the ogre's abdomen as I sent most of my remaining will into the spirit stick. The cone-shaped blast of power threw the ogre tumbling into Teag's opponent, then onto the floor.

Teag seized the moment, spinning around and slamming his staff into the head of the ogre he fought. The staff connected with a thick, skull-crushing thud. His shield caught the worst of the ogre's flail, sparing him worse injury as the ogre fell to its knees.

We were scoring points, but could we actually destroy immortal Kachina spirits, beings that native peoples had revered as elemental forces of nature if not outright gods? Were the spirits Daniel called interested in finishing the fight, or just in seeing how valiantly we could pursue a losing cause? I ached in every bone and muscle. Blood was running down my arms and back. I was bruised and battered. If the fight went on much longer like this, odds were good that Teag, Sorren, and I would die of our wounds when the spirits who overlaid us with their power departed.

Teag's ogre was climbing back to its feet, though it was hideously wounded. The back of its skull was crushed, and dark ichor seeped from the wounds. Still, it rose, ready to continue the fight. Despite the spirit that enveloped Teag's form, I could see that Teag was hurt badly. One eye was swelling shut, and the side of his face was already bruising. His shirt hung in bloody shreds, and even his jeans were slashed and wet with blood.

It was harder to see Sorren's injuries beneath Raven Mocker's overlay, but watching the suicidal ferocity with which he and Soyok Wuhti attacked each other; I wondered if either of them would survive the fight.

Teag's ogre landed a series of brutal blows with the flail that sent Teag reeling. The metal box slipped from his pocket, and I dove for it without thinking. Only as my hands closed around it did I realize what I was doing.

Oh shit.

Blinding light flared in my mind as my touch magic connected with the ground zero epicenter of our haunted house disturbance. I saw a vision of a barren stretch of land, something that looked like the Western desert. Dead men lay everywhere I looked, felled in battle. The fighting was done, but the burying had just begun. Images flashed by like a movie set on fast-forward. Bodies were wept over and prepared for their final rest, dressed in beaded finery with weapons befitting their bravery. Something about the beads caught my attention, even as the back of my brain warned that at any minute, the ogre Kachina was going to return for revenge.

The metal tin shook in my hand, and I heard the rattle and slide of a lot of tiny somethings inside. Whatever was in there, it had a hold over the warriors that streamed through my mind, storming forth to do battle one final time.

I had no idea whether the warriors from the vision were real or imagined, but I took a chance that my magic made them tangible. Gathering the last of my strength, I held tightly to the metal tin and ran toward Daniel.

"It's in here!" I shouted. "Pull the plug on this, and it all goes down."

Beaten, battered, bleeding, I stumbled my way toward Daniel. He didn't stop chanting or puffing on his pipe, but he managed to set aside his drum and take the box from my hands. I collapsed at his feet, too exhausted to get back up.

When Daniel's hands closed around the metal box, brilliant white light flared. It limned his entire figure, giving the medicine man an otherworldly appearance. He spoke words of power and words of blessing, and although I could not understand the language, I felt relief and release in the warrior spirits who were bound, somehow, to that small metal tin.

Daniel raised his arms wide in a gesture of benediction. One by one, the warrior spirits walked up to Daniel's luminous figure, stepped through his body and into the light—and vanished.

Daniel was holding open a portal to the afterlife, shimmering and shining with the cold moon glow. Most of the warrior spirits had passed through the portal, and I felt the balance of magic shift. The pent-up energy of the trapped warrior spirits had been the catalyst to bring Monster Woman and her bully boys into the mortal realm. As those ancient warriors went to their eternal rest, the long-denied anger and vengeance that fueled their rage and fed Soyok Wuhti's power dissipated.

Soyok Wuhti gave a banshee screech, hurling herself in a desperate attack at Sorren, but the Raven Mocker spirit countered by driving

Sorren's blade into the Monster Woman's chest with one hand while the other hand thrust itself inside the shattered rib cage to yank free the blackened, shriveled heart. She gave one final shriek, and disappeared.

Teag was fighting off both ogres, but their movements had become sluggish and slow. He smashed the butt of his staff into one ogre's face, slamming him to the ground, then hit the other ogre hard with his shield. He straightened for the next blow, and the ogres were gone.

As the last few warrior ghosts passed through Daniel's portal, I felt the Kachina spirits that had overlain Teag, Sorren, and me with their power begin to flicker and wane. Another heartbeat and they vanished, leaving me merely mortal once more, bleeding and spent on the cold stone floor.

Daniel murmured a few words of gratitude and lowered his arms. Only then, as the otherworldly light of the nimbus faded did I see the cost of the evening's fight in his face. Though he had taken no physical damage that I could see, Daniel looked worn out and on the verge of collapse.

"Some fight," I said, feeling like breath was more effort than it was worth.

"That," Daniel said with exhausted pride, "was one for the legends."

Later, back at my house, after Sorren's private physician left, Teag, Sorren, and I were all stitched and bandaged. We sat in my living room and looked at each other with sheer amazement that we had survived.

"What was in the box?" I took a sip of the bourbon I had poured for Teag, Daniel, and myself.

"Grave beads," Daniel answered. Teag and I must have looked puzzled. "Our ancestors buried their dead all across these lands. Out West, where the dry climate preserves the dead longer, it's common for huge ant hills to rise in the desert," Daniel explained.

"The ants dig tunnels far underground, and often, they run through the graves of the long-dead," he continued. "To the ants, the remains are in the way, and they carry what they can to the surface to clear a path. Find one of those anthills, sift through what they've brought topside, and you're likely to find old beads that were originally part of clothing worn by the dead."

"Is that legal?" I asked, staring at the little metal box that had caused one death and nearly four more.

Daniel shrugged. "So long as the graves themselves aren't disturbed, what the ants bring to the surface has been fair game for collectors for a long time. For some reason, the beads that Abby's aunt purchased came with some supernatural baggage. Those dead warriors weren't able to go to their rest on their own, and there was enough energy trapped in the beads that it made it possible for the dormant Kachina spirits to awaken."

I shivered. "You're sure the passageway to the other side is closed now?"

"It's closed. I don't think Soyok Wuhti and her ogres will be back this way again," Daniel reassured me. He glanced at Sorren. "And I'll be just as glad if Raven Mocker stays away as well."

Sorren actually looked a little shaken by the fight. Teag and I had compared notes about the Kachina spirits that had overshadowed us, but Sorren had been unusually quiet. "I will be grateful as well," he said. His wounds were nearly healed, but something in his eyes made me think that the price of being overtaken by Raven Mocker's spirit had left their own, invisible scars.

"So it's over?" I asked, sipping my bourbon and relishing the burn of the liquor that reminded me I was still alive, and so were my friends.

"The Kachina spirits are quiet. The monsters are gone. All those boxes of artifacts are just interesting souvenirs, supernaturally speaking," Daniel said. "Abby should be able to go back without danger." He tossed off the rest of his bourbon. "Yeah. It's over."

Teag and I would take a while to heal, even with Daniel's medicine magic to speed our recovery and assure that our wounds were cleansed of any magical residue. I was pretty sure that the memory of the fight would be part of my dreams—and nightmares—for a long time. And we still had a big job ahead of us, finishing the appraisal and auctioning off the collections.

But sitting in my house, with Baxter curled up on my lap, surrounded by friends, I was willing to deal with the work and the dreams. That was the price to be paid for fighting monsters in the dark. We deal with the nightmares, so everyone else can rest easy, never knowing how close they came to a terrible fate.

We know. And that's enough.

BAD MEMORIES

I recognized Kell Winston's voice on the phone, but the tone sent a shiver down my back. Because I figured that anything Kell needed my help on was going to be trouble.

"What's going on?" I asked. I played with a pencil, trying to contain the nervousness I felt.

"We got called in because there was a situation over at the new World War I exhibit near the Navy Yard," Kell said. "And we've documented the sighting, but we can't figure out the anchor."

Oh, joy. Two sentences spelled a heap of problems. Kell was a professional ghost hunter, and unlike some of the folks you see on TV, he was the real thing. He and his team didn't just go looking for spirits; they were pretty good at laying bothersome ghosts to rest. So if he was calling me, that meant a couple of things, neither of them good.

First, that someone had been bothered by a haunting enough to get over their skepticism about the supernatural world and hire a ghost hunter and second, that Kell's folks hadn't been able to handle the problem, so he thought I could help.

Like I said, trouble.

I'm Cassidy Kincaide, owner of Trifles and Folly, an antique and curio shop in historic, haunted, Charleston, SC. The store has been around for three hundred and fifty years, always run by someone in my family and our silent business partner. We're a great place to sell off grandma's silver tea set or buy a few pieces with vintage charm. But the store's real business is getting dangerous magical and supernatural items off the market and out of the wrong hands. When we succeed, no one notices. And on the rare occasions we slip up, lots of people die.

Most people don't know about my magic. I'm a psychometric, someone who can read the history of objects by touch. Not every object, thank goodness, but pieces that have been touched by magic or strong emotion. I work with Teag Logan, my assistant store manager, who has Weaver magic. That's the ability to weave supernatural power into fabric as well as to weave data strands together to find hidden information, meaning he's a hell of a good hacker. Our silent partner is Sorren, a nearly six-hundred-year-old vampire. We don't advertise the 'special' side to our business, but a few people have figured out my abilities, and Kell is one of them.

"What do you need?" I asked. I had picked up the call while I was up front in the store, and Teag was giving me a curious look, hearing only one side of the conversation.

"Can you come over and take a look for yourself?" Kell asked. I had been afraid of that, but Kell sounded really worried, and he'd helped us out before, so I wanted to return the favor.

"Sure," I said, trying not to let him hear me sigh. "When?"

"Five o'clock?" Kell asked, and he sounded relieved that I had agreed. "That way, you can be in position to see what's been going on. Things start to get interesting between six and seven."

"All right," I said, although the old Navy Yard is definitely not one of my favorite places, especially at night. It's had a bloody history, and I've personally had some bad experiences out there. But I owed Kell, and he sounded pretty freaked out, which wasn't like him. "Where?"

Kell gave me an address, and I wrote it down. "Mind if I bring Teag with me?" I asked.

"Sure," Kell replied. "The more, the merrier."

When I was off the phone, Teag raised an eyebrow, his question unspoken. "Kell's got a 'situation' out at the old Navy Yard, and he wants me to see if I can pinpoint the source."

"Sounds like fun," Teag said, with a tone that made clear it wouldn't be. "I figured it was something like that. I've already checked, and Maggie can close up for us."

Maggie is our wonderful part-time helper, a retired teacher with a great smile. She dresses like Woodstock and thinks like Wall Street, and she often covers for us when Teag and I have to go save the world.

"Think we should tell Sorren?" Teag asked.

I shook my head. "We don't even know what we're dealing with yet," I replied. "Let's see what's going on, and then we can figure out whether it's a matter for the Alliance."

Sorren is part of the Alliance, a coalition of mortals and immortals who work together to neutralize or destroy dangerous supernatural objects. If we can't handle a situation on our own, Sorren's got a network of colleagues with a variety of powerful—and lethal—magical talents he can call for backup. I really hoped we wouldn't need the Alliance's help. That usually meant really big trouble.

"Whatever you say," Teag replied skeptically. "Are we going in armed?"

Teag didn't mean guns. He meant magical protections. "Damn straight," I replied. "If something scares Kell, we already know we've got a problem."

FIVE O'CLOCK ROLLS around a lot sooner when the evening isn't likely to be fun than it does when you're looking forward to a night on the town. Teag and I drove over to the old Navy Yard in my blue Mini Cooper, and I felt like someone had dropped an ice cube down my back as soon as we passed the defunct guard booth at the gate.

"Not too late to change your mind," Teag said with a nervous grin. But we both knew it was. Kell was counting on us.

"Have I mentioned how much I don't like this place?" I asked. Teag and Sorren and I had nearly gotten killed by some seriously evil magic out here a little while ago. That's not the kind of thing you forget.

The old Navy Yard had been many things over the centuries. Pirates had claimed it as their safe haven. Smugglers and sleazy businessmen had taken up where they left off. The grounds had housed a Confederate hospital and holding area for captured soldiers during the Civil War, and plenty of war equipment had moved through here for several conflicts when the Navy owned the land. Since the area was decommissioned, it had fallen into disrepair. The effort to renovate the place and make it into a business park was just getting started, more of a dream than a reality, although a few start-ups were making a valiant effort.

Abandoned buildings hulked all around us, boarded up and falling into ruin. Lots of bad things had happened on this land, and the blood seemed to have soaked into the ground itself, giving it some bad mojo that probably contributed to the faltering efforts to revitalize the area. It set my magic on edge, warning me to get out while I could.

I should listen better when my instincts tell me to turn around and go home. But it's our business to get rid of dangerous stuff, so it doesn't hurt anyone, which means rushing in where sane people fear to go.

"This is it," Teag said as we drove up to an old three-story brick building. The new museum was in one of the blocks where the renovated businesses were located. I pulled into a spot near the other cars in the lot and took a moment to look the place over.

From the brick, I'd guess the building was more than century old. It had been built with solid walls and stone under the windows and around the door. Outside, banks of red poppies swayed in the breeze, the symbol of the First World War. An inscription over the entrance made my heart sink.

"Base Hospital," I read with a groan. Next to the door, a much newer sign proclaimed "Charleston and the Great War—a World War I Retrospective."

"Just your kind of place," Teag joked. I sighed. Military hospitals had a higher than average death toll, which probably explained why

Kell and his people had been brought in for the ghost issue. More dead people meant more ghosts, usually. And a museum display of items associated with war was likely to set off my abilities in uncomfortable ways. Exhibits from a World War were unlikely to have a happy history. But we had made a promise to Kell.

"Let's try to make this quick," I replied, although I doubted it was going to work that way.

Kell was waiting for us at the door. "Thank you for coming on short notice," he said, looking so relieved I felt a little guilty for not being more enthusiastic.

Kell was tall, with light-brown hair, blue eyes, and a boater's tan. He wore a trendy tweed jacket over a dark t-shirt and jeans, professional but functional for setting up cameras and microphones to catch the ghosts in action. Kell was the founder of SPOOK—the Southern Paranormal Observation and Outreach Klub. What began as a hobby had turned into a full-time paying business, with talk of a TV show. More importantly, Kell was a friend of Teag's long-time romantic partner, Anthony, so we were doubly obligated to try to help Kell out of a jam.

"So, what's in the bag?" Kell asked, looking at the beat-up canvas backpack Teag had slung over one shoulder.

"Just some tools of the trade," I said off-handedly. Actually, they were weapons of the supernatural sort. The bag held Teag's blades, salt, and his weaving cords as well as a walking stick that I used to channel my magic defensively. And depending on what kind of big nasty we were going up against, Teag and I had collected a variety of magical odds and ends that might not look like much but could pack a supernatural wallop. On top of that, Teag was a championship martial arts kind of guy, and while I hadn't won trophies like Teag, I could hold my own pretty well.

"Have you seen the exhibit yet?" Kell asked. "It hasn't opened to the public, but you know Alistair over at the Lowcountry Museum pretty well. I figured he might have given you an early pass."

I shook my head. "No, but I heard that the exhibit was in the works," I replied. Kell led us through the partially-completed displays.

I saw glass cases with soldiers' uniforms from the First World War, military gear and weapons, and medical equipment that would have been used when the building was a hospital. In other displays, I glimpsed letters, official documents, photos, and journals, and off to one side in an alcove was a small movie screen for video.

Near the entrance, a large plaque held the text of a famous poem about the war's casualties lying beneath fields of poppies. And in every room, artists had brought their own interpretation to the theme, with paintings, sculpture, and textiles of red poppies.

It looked like a great exhibit, except for the warning prickle that raised the hair on the back of my neck. I glanced at Teag, and he gave a nod, showing that he felt the power, too.

"There have always been rumors about the old hospital being haunted," Kell said, comfortable in his role as tour guide. Elsewhere in the building, I could hear carpenters and the sound of power tools as the workmen finished up for the evening. A few museum employees locked up the display cases they had been working on and gathered their things.

"I'll close up," Kell said as the construction workers came downstairs. They nodded and headed out, and suddenly the old building seemed too quiet.

"As I was saying," Kell began, and just then, we heard someone coming down the stairs from the second floor. Teag and I turned, expecting another workman, but no one emerged from the stairwell. When we turned back, Kell gave us a knowing smile.

"Spooky, huh?" he said. "This kind of thing has been going on since the museum decided to renovate the building for the exhibit. Footsteps. Cold spots. Glowing orbs. Lights that turn on and off by themselves, and doors that open and close. Oh, and at least two different ghosts that look real enough people have tried to talk to them," Kell added.

"Was that why they called you in?" Teag asked.

Kell shook his head. "Nope. Museum folks are used to a fair amount of ghost stuff. Comes with the territory. But then, things escalated."

I peered up the empty stairwell when we passed, but no one was in sight, and I repressed a shiver. My right hand went to the agate necklace I wore, grounding myself by touching the protective gemstone. Around my left wrist, I wore a stained and worn old dog collar, wrapped a couple of times and buckled. It belonged to Bo, a golden retriever of mine who passed beyond the veil a couple of years ago, but whose spirit remained close as a loyal protector.

Kell led us into one of the small rooms toward the back of the building. It had exposed brick walls that still showed the wear of more than a century. On one side, a World War I-era metal hospital bed had been set up with a mannequin dressed like a wounded soldier lying beneath a military-issue blanket and sheet.

In the middle of one wall hung a display of old-time photos, and when I looked more closely, I saw that they were all doctors who had served at the Navy hospital. A similar photo display showcased the nurses assigned to the hospital during the First World War. And on the far wall, a somber document listed the names of all the soldiers known to have died in the hospital during World War I.

A glass case stood over to one side, shattered as if someone had given it a good kick.

"Your ghost did that?" I asked.

Kell nodded. "My folks are pretty sure it's a different spirit than people have reported before. There've been sightings of a woman in an old-fashioned nurse's uniform walking down the hall. She disappears halfway down the corridor, always in the same place. Then there's an older man in a long jacket who walks from room to room. We think he's a doctor, still making his rounds. Those two have never hurt anyone or bothered the exhibits."

"What about the patients?" Teag asked. "Did any of them... stay behind?"

As if on cue, we heard the clatter of a metal pan hitting the wooden floor. A moan sounded from somewhere upstairs.

"Yeah," Kell said. "A few of them hang around. They don't seem to do more than make noise. Sometimes, you'll get a whiff of rubbing alcohol or smell cigarette smoke when no one's around. So the whole building is a hot spot, but the rest all seem pretty harmless."

"Are they ghosts, or stone tapes?" I asked. "Stone tape" was the phrase ghost hunters used to mean memories that were impressed upon a physical location, replaying themselves in an endless loop, like an old-fashioned cassette tape.

"Some of both," Kell replied. "Then the new one showed up and started turning things upside down."

I noticed there were remote cameras trained on the four sides of the room and an odd sensor with an array of blinking lights that were aimed at the far corner. A couple of tiny microphones dangled from the ceiling. Kell had the room under surveillance.

He led us into another room, where two of his ghost hunting team watched a bank of computer monitors. One was a girl in her mid-twenties with goth-black hair and a gray hoodie over black jeans. The other was a guy about the same age sporting a brown ponytail and a t-shirt with one of Shakespeare's bawdier quotes on it. "Kendra and Tom," Kell introduced, and the ghost hunters acknowledged us with a nod.

"We've been recording since the first night," Kell said. "I was afraid it would be hard to narrow in on just this one ghost's manifesta-tion, since there's a lot going on here, but whoever is kicking up a fuss in the next room pegs the meters. The energy is really strong, and he's pissed off about something."

"And the damage only started when people began working in that room?" I asked.

Kell nodded. "Yeah. I did a little digging. Before the museum bought the building, a couple of different owners tried to use it for other things. One company leased out office space. Nobody would stay because of the ghosts, so that didn't work. A pest exterminator company bought it next and only used the bottom floor, but they had so many problems with their electrical equipment that it wasn't worth it, plus their receptionists kept quitting because of the ghosts."

"Are the exhibits going to be on all four floors?" I asked.

Kell shook his head. "No. The museum didn't need that much

room, and the upper floors haven't been modernized. They're blocked off and locked up."

"What kind of readings have you gotten?" I asked, looking at all of Kell's equipment. It looked he had enough stuff to launch a mission to Mars.

Kell typed on one of the keyboards, and a graph came onscreen. "The flat areas are where there's no ghostly activity in the back room," Kell said, pointing. "Then you can see, the readings go way up here," he said, noting the spike, "and here."

"What kind of activity caused the spike?" Teag asked.

Kell shook his head. "You name it, it happened. The motion sensors went off, but no one was around. The electromagnetic frequency recorder triggered with strange sounds, but there was no one in the room. The temperature dropped."

"Okay, that's definitely strange," I said, leaning in to get a better look at the screen. "Is it the same set of occurrences each time there's a spike?"

"Not necessarily," Kell said. "A few people say they've seen a shadow by that back wall, but there's no one to cast it. When furniture has been placed up against the wall, it's been moved by morning, with no one around. And listen to this," he said, pivoting to grab a hand-held recorder from one of the tables.

Kell thumbed a button, and the recorder blinked on. We heard a lot of white noise, hissing, and popping, turned up to high volume. Then out of the background hum, what sounded like a man's voice, and two syllables: "Sa-rah."

I looked up. "A woman's name? Sarah?"

Kell played the recording again, and we listened closely. The ghostly voice was low and muffled, but to my ears, it sounded like "Sarah." Teag nodded in agreement.

"So, who's the ghost? And who is Sarah?" I asked.

Kell put the recorder back on the table and turned to me. "I was hoping you could help us figure that out."

In the distance, I heard the bells from one of Charleston's many churches ring six times. "Things tend to happen back here between six and seven," Kell said. I followed him back to the corner, and it seemed to grow colder the closer I got.

"I'm still not sure how I can help," I said, looking around. "I'm not a medium. I don't talk to ghosts. I read objects."

"And I think I know which object may have triggered this new haunting," Kell replied. He went to the display with the cracked glass and carefully withdrew a worn and stained bundle of canvas.

"This was a soldier's shaving kit," Kell said. "The museum had it in their storage area for quite a while, and it never seemed to have caused any trouble. When they sent it over to us for the display, all hell started to break loose."

He turned the small bundle over in his hands. "It looks as if someone inked a name on here," he said, tracing a dark, smudged area. "But part of the cloth is torn, and after a lot of use, the marking isn't readable."

Kell held out the bundle to me. "I was hoping that maybe you could find out who this belonged to, and why he's raising a fuss after all this time."

"All right," I replied. "But I'd like to sit down," I said, knowing from experience that sitting was better than falling. "And since the ghost likes that corner, let's put the chair over there."

Teag moved the chair, and Kell carried the shaving kit. I sat down in the chair, took a deep breath, and held out my hands. Kell placed the old kit across my palms, and I closed my eyes.

Cold, dark clouds hung over the blue-gray ocean. From the deck of the ship, I saw a rocky coastline far in the distance. Smoke filled the sky, and the sound of gunfire carried across the water, even this far out from shore.

The wind was laced with salt-spray, and I felt chilled to the bone, though it was only autumn.

Our look-out shouted a warning. I could just make out a strange object in the waves before the men on deck scrambled for combat positions. The big guns fired, then fired again. The shells hit the ocean, sending a wall of water skyward. There was a muted thud, then bubbles and oil percolated to the top. A cheer went up. We'd hit a sub.

The cheering died as another shout came. Torpedo sighted—oh God. I felt the ship turn hard, but the torpedo caught it midships with a sickening thud. Metal squealed, and the ship jerked, sending men flying.

Seeing the action through the eyes of the man who had owned the shaving kit, I felt his terror, saw him thrown off his feet and into a bulkhead. *The whole ship shook, and smoke rose, making it hard to see and harder to breathe. The ship listed, and I glimpsed something large and heavy coming straight at me…*

The scene shifted. I lay in a bed, staring at a hospital ceiling, drifting in and out of consciousness. I looked over at the brick wall, eyeing the place I had stored my treasure, knowing it was still safe. Fever and chills wracked my body, and a never-ending thirst. I could taste blood on my lips. Not much longer—

"Cassidy!" Teag was calling my name, kneeling next to my chair. He took the shaving kit out of my hands, and Kell held out a glass of cold water for me. My hands were nearly shaking too badly to accept it, but I managed to take a drink without spilling too much.

"He was on a warship. It got hit by a torpedo," I said when I found my voice. "He was hurt. They probably sent him home to recover." I paused. "Except—I think he got worse here. He was very sick, dying. Fever."

Kell sat back on his haunches, studying the shaving kit thoughtfully. "That might explain some things," he said.

I sipped my water. The visions I see when I handle potent objects really send me for a loop. As reactions go, this wasn't the worst I'd had. Still, it would take me a while to be back to my old self.

"Explain what?" Teag asked.

Kell stood. "Charleston had a big military base here for a long time. Back in World War I, a lot of fellows were just getting ready to ship out when the Spanish Flu came through town. Some of them never left port. Others, sent here to recuperate, ended up dying from the epidemic."

He nodded in the direction of the old hospital's back parking lot. "The museum just found the site plan for the building and grounds as it was back then. It had been misplaced for a long time. There was a graveyard behind the hospital—pretty common back in the day, but people had forgotten all about it. I bet this poor fellow never made it home."

Something about the vision stayed in my mind. I stood, and Teag followed me over to the corner, where I got down on my knees and stared at the wall.

"What are you doing, Cassidy?" Teag asked.

"In the vision, the man kept looking at the wall, as if he were checking on something," I said, beginning to let my hands slide over the rough bricks, testing them as I moved down the wall. "What if—"

I found two loose bricks and jiggled them out of their place. Inside was a small hollow, and in it, a small, round object lay wrapped in a stained kerchief.

"I'll get it," Teag said before I could reach for the cloth. He reached into the hiding place and withdrew the bundle. Carefully, Teag peeled back the covering to reveal a tarnished pocket watch.

Everything happened at once. The lights went out, and the temperature dropped like a miniature blast of winter. Something shoved Teag, hard. Footsteps sounded nearby, though none of us were moving. The door to the hallway slammed shut.

"Hey!" Teag yelled at the darkness, protesting the shove.

Kell, Teag, and I stood with our backs to each other. I heard Kell snapping the switch on his flashlight, to no avail. Teag held up the light on his phone. It shone for a moment before the light died away. Ghosts are hell on electrical objects and batteries.

Nearby, glass shattered. We heard pounding on the hallway door and shouts from Kell's worried team, but the door stayed closed.

"Sa-rah." The voice was muffled and distant, but there was no mistaking what it said.

As abruptly as the lights went out, they struggled back on. The hallway door burst open, spilling Kell's team members into the room with the sudden release. Kell's flashlight and Teag's phone gleamed brightly.

The glass case holding the shaving kit was completely smashed.

"What happened?" Tom asked.

Kendra focused on the broken glass. "Damn! The museum isn't going to charge us for that case, are they?"

Teag moved forward, holding the watch out for them to see. "There's an inscription—JCS," he said, pointing to the back of the case. He pressed the release gently, and the two sides swung out.

"Look," Kell said. "Want to bet that's Sarah?" Inside the watch cover was a picture of a dark-haired young woman.

Kendra had already gone over to the roster of names showing the servicemen who died during the First World War. "JCS," she mused, scanning the columns. "Geez, there are a lot of names here."

"Odds are, this is what the ghost was trying to protect," I said. "I know a medium who's pretty good at convincing spirits to pass over. If you'd like, we can bring her out tomorrow night," I offered.

Kell nodded. "That would be great. If the ghost has hung around here since 1918, he's overdue for his eternal rest, and once he's at peace, we can get on with the rest of the exhibit."

"James Carl Sturdevant." We all turned toward Kendra, who was pointing to a name on the list. "He's the only one with those initials— assuming all of the dead made it onto the list." She glanced nervously at her phone.

"Don't you think we should get out of here?" she asked, looking from Kell to Tom. "You know... before?"

"Before what?" I asked.

I couldn't read the expression on Kell's face. He might have been annoyed at Kendra, or he might have been worried. He seemed to be trying not to show whatever emotion he was feeling at the minute, but he was definitely uncomfortable.

"I should have told you," he said. "We've had some problems in the parking lot. No one's harmed the cars, but someone's out there, watching when we leave the building."

"Or something," Kendra muttered. "It's freaky. Tom and I have both caught a glimpse of something moving, but when you look, it's gone. We all go out to the cars together, and we park together." She paused. "It's worse the later in the evening it gets."

"Have you called the cops?" Teag asked.

Kell sighed. "The museum doesn't want any bad publicity—it will be enough of a stretch to get people to come out to the old Navy Yard to see the exhibit in daylight. It's probably just some vagrants."

I knew from experience that vagrants were the least of the dangers to be worried about in the sprawling old Navy Yard. Bad things and dark magic gravitate to abandoned and decaying places, especially when those places have a bloody history. Teag, Sorren, and I had seen some really scary stuff go down out here, so Kendra's concern worried me.

"Well, here's another item for the exhibit," I said as Teag handed over the watch. "I'd like to come back in daylight and try to get a reading on the watch, if you're interested," I said. "James and Sarah might give the museum a nice human interest story."

Kell nodded. "If you're up for it, I would love to record their story, although we may have to fudge the source a little unless we want to explain things to the museum."

"Did you show them the thing in the wall?" Tom's expression was somewhere between worried and defiant. "You said she might know what it was."

Teag and I looked at Kell. "Was there something else?" I asked.

Kell looked uncomfortable but nodded. "Yeah, but we're not sure what to make of it." He placed the pocket watch in a drawer for safe-keeping and gestured for us to follow him from the room and down the hallway.

"The museum isn't doing a huge renovation, but it's got to make some updates for wiring, air conditioning, and modern plumbing," Kell said as we walked. "So they've had to bust open some walls, take down some plaster, that sort of thing. And yesterday, when they opened up a wall, they found something kind of strange inside."

"Something hidden in the wall?" I asked.

Kell shook his head. "No. More like something actually embedded into the wall—cemented in with mortar." He flicked on the lights and led us into a large, plain room. Crates and cases were stored against the inside wall, some covered with moving blankets or sheets to keep out dust.

On the far side of the room, looking out over the back parking lot, were a bank of large windows. I could see where the old asphalt in the lot had been torn up, waiting for a fresh base and resurfacing before the museum opened. Beneath the windows, the old plaster had been torn away in a long stretch to allow for new lines to be run. Right in the center, a larger square had been cleared, and set into the bricks was an odd-shaped hole. Sitting on a nearby desk was a black stone carving of a menacing-looking figure.

"Wow," I said, moving a little closer for a good look. Even from here, I knew I didn't want to touch that thing without some serious preparation. It was magical—and it radiated a prickly energy I didn't like.

"What is it?" Kell asked, leaning over my shoulder on one side as Teag crowded in on for a better view on the other side.

"I'm not sure," I said carefully. "But can we make sure no one touches it until we do some research? I don't know why it's there—but even from here, I know it's got a lot of mojo."

Kell sighed. "We're just the ghostbusters. We don't have any clout with the construction guys, but I can put in a word with the foreman, maybe make it sound antique and valuable..."

"Sounds like a plan," I replied, snapping a photo with my phone and texting it to Sorren. "I'll get back to you with something tomorrow."

TEAG AND I hadn't eaten yet, so we picked up a pizza and headed to my house. I have what locals call a "Charleston single house," meaning that the narrow side of the house faces the street while the front porch looks into a walled garden. My front door leads onto the wide, covered porch, not into the house itself.

It probably says something about my life that I was not in the least surprised to find a vampire sitting on my porch swing.

"Hi, Sorren." Yes, my nearly six-hundred-year-old vampire business partner texts and emails. Then again, he looks like he's still in grad school, forever in his late twenties, and tonight in a black t-shirt and jeans with sneakers, he might have even been able to pass for younger.

"I got your text," Sorren said as we crossed the porch. "Figured I might as well meet you here."

I put my key in the lock, and my little Maltese, Baxter, went ballistic, yipping and prancing like a maniac. He took one look at Sorren and sat down with a goofy, adoring look on his face.

"You glamored him again, didn't you?"

Sorren grinned and leaned down to pet Baxter. "Who, me? Maybe he just wants your pizza."

Sorren had fed recently. I could tell because he wasn't as pale as when he's hungry. I didn't want to know the details, but he had assured me he had learned long ago to feed from donors without needing to kill. And he had sworn an oath more than three hundred years ago to protect my family and those who worked with us, so I had never had cause for fear. Still, I felt a little guilty sitting down to eat the pizza without offering him some.

"Go ahead," he replied, shaking his head. "Fill me in on what you saw at the museum exhibit."

Teag and I took turns munching on pizza and talking with our mouths full. When we were finished, Sorren was quiet, his eyes pensive.

"The flu was bad that year," he said softly. "So many died. I hadn't seen death on that scale since smallpox, back in Belgium. The cemeteries were full. That's when they started to take the dead outside of town, to potters' fields, anywhere to bury them." His voice was distant, remembering.

"We buried some of them in the land where part of the old Navy Yard sits," he continued, finally looking up. "Quite a few were buried behind the military hospital."

"Kell said there's a parking lot over that land now," I replied. "And Kendra thinks something scary is out there in the shadows."

"Kendra's right," Sorren said. "Did you have any trouble getting out to your cars?"

I shook my head. "No. But we all went together, the cars were parked close to each other at the front, and we stayed under a street light. I wouldn't have wanted to be out there by myself—even with some of the weapons we've collected."

"I have a suspicion, but we need to go over there to test it out," Sorren said.

"What about a medium, to help set the ghosts at rest?" I asked.

"If I'm right," Sorren replied, pulling out his cell phone. "What we really need is a witch." He paused. "Finish up your food—we're heading back to the museum."

Half an hour later, a woman in her early forties rang my doorbell. She wore a cute twinset over dark jeans and boat shoes, and her blond hair was smoothed back in a high ponytail with a headband. She was carrying a designer handbag that was large enough to be a shopping tote. *Just what I don't need—a real estate agent.*

"Sorry, I'm not interested in selling the house," I said impatiently. "Just leave me your card, and I'll let you know if I change my mind."

She tugged on a silver chain around her neck and pulled out a pentacle. "Not a real estate agent. Not Avon calling. Not trying to convert you. I'm Liz Mitchell. Is Sorren here?"

"Oh, you're the witch!" I said with a sigh of relief, then realized just how strange that sounded. Her laugh let me know she did not take it the wrong way.

"Yeah, I get that a lot," she said. "And before you ask, no, I'm not related to the housewife witch in the old TV show, although people say there's a resemblance."

Bewitched, bothered and bewildered... "Come on in," I said.

But before we could get farther than the front hall, Sorren and Teag were coming toward us. "I don't think we should wait," Sorren said. "If I'm right, we've got a big problem." He nodded in greeting.

"We'll fill you in on the way," Sorren said. We piled into Teag's old Volvo since it was a more comfortable ride for four than my little Mini Cooper. As we drove, Teag and I caught up on Liz what we knew.

"Old graveyard full of war dead and plague victims that's been sealed under a parking lot for a long time, and now everything's being ripped up," she summarized.

"Yep," Sorren replied.

"All right then," Liz said matter-of-factly. "Ghouls."

"Ghouls?" Teag echoed.

Sorren nodded. "Unless good wardings have been put down and refreshed frequently, old cemeteries draw ghouls like roadkill draws flies. One or two at first, then more if the feeding is good."

He looked at me. "That's probably what the ghost hunters saw lurking in the shadows. When there aren't many of them, they'll hold off on attacking the living unless they can get an easy kill. Once there are enough to swarm, all bets are off."

I shivered, despite myself. "All right," I said. "Go ahead and hand me the duffle bag. I don't think we want to fight those guys bare-handed."

I was already wearing plenty of magically protective gear. Besides my agate necklace, I had an onyx ring and tourmaline earrings, all good protective stones. In one pocket of my jeans, I had a very old stone disk with a hole in the middle; a protective charm Sorren had given me that had some serious mojo. Packets of salt were stuffed into my other pockets, and I was wearing the dog collar wrapped around my left wrist. In the duffle bag, I had a walking stick that had belonged to Sorren's maker, something I used like an athame to channel my touch magic into defensive energy. I learned the hard way that I could tap into the strength of a memory and sometimes into the magic of an object's former owner, and use both for a power boost. Since ghouls were physical as well as magical, I also had a long knife in a sheath I could clip to my belt.

Teag wore a vest beneath his hoodie into which he had woven protective magic, and he stored extra energy in some knotted rope that hung from his belt. He also had his share of salt packets. Teag wore an *agimat* charm and a hamsa on a chain around his neck, and he had a wicked looking knife with a blade even longer than mine. Teag's fighting staff was in the back, along with Sorren's sword.

Sorren didn't need much beyond the supernatural speed and strength that came with being a vampire. But he did have a sword, and I'd seen him fight with it. A couple of hundred years of practice makes perfect. I had no idea what Liz had in that huge designer bag of hers, but I now suspected it was more than lipstick.

"What about the ghosts?" I asked. "Don't we need a medium to get them to rest?"

Liz shook her head. "I'm pretty good with ghosts, so I can handle that if we can't resolve things any other way, but I don't think that's our problem. The construction people disturbed the graves when they tore up the parking lot. That stirred up the ghosts, and the ghost activity was like an 'Eat at Joe's' sign for the ghouls."

"And ghouls put the ghosts into a frenzy," Sorren finished. "So, let's take things in order. Ghouls first."

"And the strange carving? The thing that was in the wall?" Teag asked, keeping his eyes on the road.

Liz studied the photo on my phone. "Once we deal with the ghouls, I'll take a look at it. My bet is, there's been a ghoul problem before, and that totem was how the last witch smoothed things over."

The last witch. Before I had inherited Trifles and Folly, I had no idea what a supernatural hotbed Charleston was. Now, it seemed like the city was teeming with all kinds of magic, good and bad. And we were always right in the middle of it.

The old Navy Yard was deserted when we drove up. Teag shut off the lights when we were a block away, and we relied on the streetlights overhead. I knew from experience that even the cops didn't like to spend a lot of time in the abandoned military campus, although they made an effort to patrol the sections where new businesses had moved in. Even the police stayed well clear of the boarded-up old buildings. That was okay because, for the most part, criminals didn't like this place, either.

We coasted to a stop in front of the hospital/museum. A few security lights glowed dimly through the windows. Staring up at the light, I thought I saw a shadow or two take shape and then disappear.

"Oh yeah, you've got ghosts all right," Liz murmured. "We'll take care of them later."

Teag pulled into the old hospital's driveway, moving slowly so we could see what we were up against as he pulled around and parked the car facing the temporary fence. Most of what had been the back parking lot had been scraped down to the bare, sandy soil. I guessed that work had halted when the construction teams discovered what was underneath the asphalt. A temporary plastic mesh fence sagged on its supports, cordoning off the area.

I couldn't see the ghouls, but I could feel them watching us. Many of the streetlights in the area no longer functioned, so it was darker than usual. Teag switched the headlights back on since none of us wanted to take on the ghouls in the dark. The flash of light caught a half dozen hunched, disfigured shapes loping into the shadows. *Game on.*

We opened our car doors together, and no one wasted time getting out. Weapons drawn, we moved carefully along what remained of the asphalt around the lot's edges. Now and then, I caught a whisp-like shape floating above the torn-up ground, only to have it vanish when I turned to look.

"The ghouls have been digging." Teag pointed toward the sandy soil. The entire area was marred by deep pits that looked like they had been dug by hyperactive dogs. In a few places, I glimpsed a yellowed bone or a bit of old cloth. "They're feeding on the corpses."

Liz bent down and chalked a circle around herself, chanting as she drew the line that would help her summon and control her power. She added candles and lit them, then sprinkled salt and bits of broken mirror between the candles.

"I'll handle the ghosts," Liz said. "And I'll work up some energy to help you with the ghouls. But that will take time. For the first while, the fight's all yours. Don't worry about me—the circle will keep them out."

Liz closed the circle and stood, murmuring an incantation as she turned to face each direction in turn. Sorren, Teag and I advanced warily, weapons in hand.

I knew the ghouls were out there, and they still scared the hell out of me when they attacked.

Ghouls are every bit as ugly as the stories say. Their bodies are twisted and emaciated, like dried-up corpses that won't stay dead. Long-fingered hands with nails broken back to the quick. Lantern jaws filled with sharp, blackened teeth. Naked, sexless bodies and oversized feet with claws where toes should be.

And they're fast.

One minute, the parking lot was empty. The next, a dozen ghouls were coming at us, teeth bared and hands outstretched to tear us apart.

People think ghouls only eat the dead. They prefer an easy meal, but if they can get fresh meat, they're just as happy.

Ghouls are fast, but vampires are faster. Sorren moved in a blur, setting about himself with his sword. He hacked down two or three of the monsters before they realized what was happening. More ghouls emerged from the shadows, and the closest ones went after Teag and me.

I had my knife in one hand, and the walking stick in the other, held out like a sword. I gave the dog collar on my left wrist a shake, and the ghostly form of a solidly built Golden Retriever materialized beside me. Goldens have a reputation for being mellow, but when one of their family is in danger, they can turn into ninety pounds of snarly fury.

Two of the ghouls launched themselves at me, while three more went after Teag. Sorren had his hands busy with at least four of the things, and more of them were emerging from the shadows every minute.

My ghost dog Bo lunged, and his spectral canine teeth worked just fine on the ghoul he knocked to the ground. Bo snapped and snarled, seizing onto the ghoul's forearm and worrying it back and forth, tearing the arm from the shoulder.

I sliced at the other ghoul with the knife, getting in a hit that slashed across its face. The ghoul hissed, trying to reach me with its sharp claws, but I brought up the walking stick and focused my magic.

A streak of fire burst from the tip of the walking stick, hitting the ghoul square in the chest. The monster screeched as the flames caught its straggly hair and parchment-dry skin, flapping and shrieking as it went up like a torch.

Out of the corner of my eye, I saw Teag bash in the skull of one of the ghouls with his staff, then slam the end of the staff into the belly of the other ghoul, knocking it off balance and right into his waiting blade. On the other side, Sorren was spattered with black blood, setting to with his sword with single-minded focus. Three of the ghouls were out of the fight, dismembered on the ground in a pool of ichor. The fourth ghoul lunged at Sorren with crazed frenzy until Sorren thrust his sword through the ghoul's chest where the heart should have been.

Before I could celebrate, two more ghouls came at me, and half a dozen more followed, intent on Teag and Sorren. I forced the two closest ghouls back with a fiery blast from my walking stick. Bo's ghost sailed through the air, tackling a ghoul that tried to circle around behind me, pinning the squealing, thrashing creature to the ground as Teag swung his staff and smashed the ghoul's head.

The body parts strewn around the blood-spattered lot didn't deter the ghouls; in fact, it put them into a frenzy. Some stopped to eat the carcasses of their fallen comrades, while others were focused on fresh meat—us.

"Any time now, Liz!" I shouted.

Liz had raised an iridescent cylinder of power along the chalk circle of her warding. Five or six ghouls hunched along the outside, taking care to stay well clear of the scintillating curtain of energy, stalking the woman inside. Meanwhile, we were getting our butts whipped.

Liz shouted a command and flung the wall of energy outward. The stalker-ghouls were the first to fry, going up like dry tinder. Sorren hurled his attacker into the consuming power and got out of the way. Teag and I followed his lead, but we were too far into the center of the lot to get out of the way of the roiling wave of light.

Wondering what kind of ally sends out a blast to cook the rest of the team, I braced myself for flames—and felt the power sweep right over me like a warm wind, leaving me untouched. Teag looked up at me in astonishment a few seconds later, even as the power incinerated most of the ghouls.

We were still alive—for now. There were more ghouls headed our way.

"Where the hell did these things come from?" I muttered, sending a few more to oblivion with a stream of fire as I concentrated my will on the walking stick-athame. No one answered me, but I figured "hell" was as good a reply as I was going to get.

I glanced back at Liz, to see if she had another fiery curtain coming our way. No such luck. She was still inside her protective circle, but now she had her hands raised and spread wide, palms open and outward, and her eyes were fixed on the torn up parking lot behind us. Liz's lips were moving, but her eyes looked glazed as if her attention was fixed on something I couldn't see.

Another ghoul came at me, and I brought my knife down across his forearms, cutting bone deep. Then I gave a martial arts kick that sent him flying. Bo's ghost tackled a second ghoul. A third monster almost got me from the other side, raking my shoulder with its claws, but before I could bring up my walking stick, Sorren had the ghoul by the neck, which he snapped with a flick of his wrist.

The torn up parking lot was covered with ghoul corpses, and still, they came. Sorren might have immortal strength, and Liz was protected in her circle for as long as her power held out, but I knew that Teag and I had mortal limits, and we were tiring quickly.

"Cassidy—the ghosts!" Teag shouted from where he still battled two of the ghouls.

I glanced over to the area of the old graveyard and saw dozens of ghosts hovering over the dug-up parking lot. They were fully-formed, wearing clothing that spanned a century or more, hollow-eyed and gaunt. They were dead—and angry.

A cold wind swept toward the ghouls from the old cemetery. Once again, it passed over Teag and me without damage, and this time, Sorren did not stop fighting to get out of its way. We didn't need to be afraid. The ghosts weren't after us.

Behind us, I could hear the ghosts in the old hospital going berserk, rattling the glass and pounding on the doors. The graveyard ghosts were focused with lethal intensity on the ghouls, and whatever magic Liz had worked to power up the ghosts, they were making the most of it.

Some of the ghosts hurled fist-sized rocks and clumps of asphalt, energized into murderous poltergeists. Others slipped their icy forms through the ghouls—and stayed inside the ghouls until the monsters began to spasm and shudder, freezing from the inside out. The strongest spirits tore at the ghouls ferociously, ripping away strips of skin, clawing at hair and eyes, a foe that was everywhere and nowhere, impossible to fight.

Sorren, Teag, and I waded into the fray, although the ghosts left few ghouls for us to handle. Between the fire and the ghosts and some good old-fashioned smiting, we seemed to have run out of ghouls. Good thing. I was covered in ghoul-guts, dripping with sweat, heaving for breath, and aching everywhere. Teag looked just as tired, and even Sorren was moving more slowly. Bo's ghost gave me a wag and disappeared.

Liz hadn't dropped her circle of light yet. She brought her hands in close to her body and clasped them in front of her chest with a slight bow of thanks to the ghosts. Then she spoke words I couldn't quite catch, and one by one, the ghosts dissipated, some wafting away on the night breeze and others slipping back beneath the sandy ground to their resting places. That's when I realized that the racket from the ghosts inside the museum had quieted, and when I turned, the faces in the windows were gone.

"What a mess." Teag looked out over the spread of ghoul-parts and black blood. "How the hell are we going to clean this up before the cops see it?"

Liz lowered the iridescent curtain of light and smudged her circle open. "Allow me," she said as she approached us. We stepped back, and she sent a wave of blue, cold energy in a horizontal sheet across the asphalt, turning the ghoul corpses to ash. A gust of perfectly-timed wind scattered the cinders into the next parking lot.

"What about the totem in the building?" Teag asked.

"I drew on its power, there at the end," Liz said.

I turned to look up at the hulking form of the old military hospital. "Was it the construction that triggered everything? Or removing the totem?"

"Probably a mixture of both," Liz said with a sigh. Her twinset and hair were still perfectly in place, but I could see exhaustion around her eyes and in the set of her mouth. "Disturbing the building would have riled the ghosts inside, and digging up the parking lot would have troubled the ghosts from the cemetery. And I suspect that when the totem was moved and the ghouls showed up, that upset both groups of ghosts further."

"So what now?" I asked. "Won't the ghouls just come back?"

Liz chuckled. "Not for a while. They prefer food that doesn't fight back." She looked up at the old hospital. "I would suggest finding a place in the new construction where the totem can be sealed away where no one will bother it for another hundred years."

"I'll take care of it," Sorren said, and he and Teag headed off toward the building. Less than an hour later, they were back.

"We found a place inside the basement walls," Teag said as he and Sorren dusted themselves off. "Doesn't look like anyone will have a reason to renovate there, so with luck, it can just go on doing its job for a long, long time."

"Let's get out of there," Sorren said, listening to the night sounds. "We've overstayed our welcome."

THE NEXT EVENING, I got a phone call from Kell. "Hey Cassidy—guess what? We figured out whose picture was in the old watch. Name was Sarah Cooper. Kendra found her listed among the flu casualties." He sounded surprised. "Maybe she was even buried in the lot behind the hospital where her boyfriend died."

Two ghosts, trapped within sight of each other, held apart for over a century by what anchored their spirits to this world. And if we were right about the ghouls, then James's worry over the monsters desecrating his beloved's body fueled the poltergeist's rage.

"Oh, and I thought you'd want to know," Kell went on. "The Lowcountry Museum is going to work with the city to relocate the graves underneath the parking lot. Turns out the paperwork on those graves had been lost for a long time, which is why they weren't moved before this. So maybe those folks will finally get to rest in peace."

"Kell, can you do me a favor?" I asked, reaching down to scratch Baxter on the head as I sat on my porch and sipped a tall glass of sweet tea.

"Sure," he agreed. "Whatever you did, the ghosts have stopped acting up, and the museum can go on with its renovation, so the exhibit will open on time. I'll put a check in the mail for your consulting fee. What did you need?"

"That pocket watch—can you ask the museum to bury it with Sarah Cooper's remains? After all this time, Sarah and James deserve to be together, and it might keep their spirits quiet."

"I think I've got enough pull to make that happen," he said, and I could hear him smiling. "You're a hopeless romantic; you know that?"

I chuckled. "Not usually, but I'll make an exception in this case. Thanks."

Kell paused. "Something else we documented, but I didn't tell the people at the museum. This morning, when we went out there, we found something strange. One fresh red poppy, lying in the middle of the dug-out parking lot. Weird, huh?"

A chill went down my spine, and I hugged Baxter a little tighter. I had the feeling that when the graves were exhumed, Sarah Cooper would be right under where that poppy lay.

"Yeah," I said, hoping my tone sounded convincing. "Weird."

SHADOW GARDEN

"Why is your garden gnome in a cage?" I frowned as a plump middle-aged woman deposited a stone statue locked in what looked like a large "live trap" steel mesh box.

"Because this thing ate my cat," the woman declared. "And I want rid of it before it goes after the dog, too."

We see all kinds of things at Trifles and Folly, but even for us, this was a first.

"Are you sure about the cat?" I asked, warily eyeing the gnome. It looked much older than the brightly-painted resin figures on sale at the big national-chain garden supply stores. The statue was weathered, with some bits of lichen stuck to its body, and I wondered if it had been custom-made. Now that she mentioned it, the gnome did look a little creepy. The features looked sly instead of welcoming, and the set of the mouth seemed to hide sharp teeth behind the carved stone lips.

"I'm sure," the woman said, slapping her palm against the wooden counter. "Fuddles never did like the statue. Always hissed at it when he walked by it. I should have taken that as a sign."

"Where did it come from?" I asked, looking away from the creepy gnome and returning my attention to the lady who had brought in the caged decoration.

"My mother said she bought it from one of those architectural salvage places," the woman replied.

"Have you had other problems with it, before the… um… cat incident?" I'm sure she was embarrassed and believed I was secretly laughing at her, but I had seen much stranger things.

I'm Cassidy Kincaide, and I own Trifles and Folly, an antique and curio shop in historic, haunted Charleston, SC that is a lot more than it seems. The store has been in my family for over three hundred years, and we've got a secret. While we're a great place to find beautiful old heirlooms and estate jewelry, our real job is getting dangerous magical and supernatural items off the market and keeping them out of the wrong hands. That means we see more than our share of cursed, unlucky, or possessed objects, so I was taking my hapless customer's tale seriously. Her murderous gnome sounded exactly like the kind of problem we deal with every day.

She pushed a lock of bottle-blonde hair off of her perspiring forehead. "When it started moving around, I should have known. I wish I'd have gotten rid of it sooner."

I raised an eyebrow. "The garden gnome moved by itself?"

The woman hesitated, then nodded. "I thought someone was funnin' with me, at first," she said. Her bright pink lipstick made the rush of blood to her cheeks all the more noticeable. "And it's not as if it moves across the yard. Just a bit, but it doesn't stay put, and the man who does the yard says he hasn't touched it." She glared at the statue. "In fact, I don't think he even likes to go near it. It doesn't look like he weeds or trims close to the statue, now that I think about it."

"Do you know if your mother ever witnessed anything unusual about the statue?" I asked, taking a closer look, though I kept well back from the cage itself. I was glad it came with a handle on the top. There was no way I would stick my fingers through that wire mesh.

The blonde belle shook her head. "No. Mama never said a word about it, and she used to spend a lot of time out in the garden. Always loved to watch the birds and the squirrels, but now that I think about it, I haven't seen any of them in the yard since I came back to settle up her house."

"Your mother passed away?" I asked gently.

She swallowed hard, blinked back tears, and nodded. "Yes. A month ago. So I came back from Richmond to see that everything was closed up properly, and start taking care of her estate." She extended her hand. "I'm sorry. I haven't introduced myself. I'm Beverly Callahan, but my friends call me Binky."

I recognized the last name. Binky's parents had been movers and shakers in Charleston society until their deaths. I was pretty sure their names were on every museum and historical association's donor lists, plus the patron listings for the hospitals, the Junior League, and the university. That made it doubly odd that someone like Binky would risk ridicule with a story like this if the gnome hadn't seriously weirded her out. And to my eye, Binky looked scared right out of her Lilly Pulitzer pink pants.

"Mrs. Callahan—"

"Please, Binky."

I nodded. "Binky. Of course we're happy to buy the statue from you. But out of curiosity, is there anything else you can tell me about the gnome's… behavior? Was there anything that seemed to trigger it becoming dangerous?"

Binky looked at me as if she was trying to decide whether or not I was mocking her, then finally realized I was taking her seriously. She reached out and grabbed my hand. "Oh, thank heavens. You believe me, don't you? I have been scared out of my ever-lovin' wits since Fuddles disappeared. I mean, if it can eat a cat, who knows whether or not it could get into the house when I'm sleeping?"

Across the store, Teag Logan, my assistant store manager, was keeping his head down, studiously polishing the estate silverware for the front case. I knew he would take Binky's dilemma seriously, but I also knew her delivery, which was dead-on Paula Deen-esque, was making it hard for him to keep a straight face. "I can completely understand your concern," I replied.

Binky smoothed her hair. "Thank you," she said, lifting her chin as she regained her composure. "As for what mama saw, I'm not sure.

She said some strange things near the end, but I chalked it all up to the Alzheimer's. Now, I wonder."

"So the gnome was a relatively recent addition to the garden?" I probed. I kept an eye on the caged statue. It gave me the willies. And since my gift is psychometry—the ability to read the history or emotional memories or magic—of an object by touch, I decided someone else could take the cage into the back room. That's where we keep the potentially dangerous acquisitions until my business partner, Sorren, figures out how to dispose of them.

Binky shook her head. "That's just it. He'd been there for a little while, I'm sure of it. Mama was always picking up odds and ends from one of those restoration places, or antique stores, or yard sales—you get the idea." I did. Many older people filled their time shopping for cast-off treasures, and when they passed on, their harried children often brought those impulse purchases by the truckload to shops like ours.

"And there wasn't anything that might have happened—anything at all—that might have 'activated' the gnome?" I pressed. There was just no way to ask Binky if her mother had suddenly taken up practicing black magic or had someone put a root on her.

Again a shake of the head. "No. Mama spent most of her time going on garden tours and helping out at the Historical Archive or the Shady Ladies' Garden Club. She knew every garden in this city, and all about the old gardens that aren't around anymore, too."

It was pretty clear that Binky couldn't tell me more about the cat-eating gnome, so I paid her a fair price for the "acquisition" and waited until she glanced around our front showroom and departed before I looked to Teag.

"If you're wondering, it's a 'hell no' about me carrying this to the back," I said drily.

He chuckled. "I figured as much. And I already sent Sorren a text that we had something potentially dangerous. He said he'd be back in town tomorrow." Teag walked over and peered through the wire cage. "Do you think she was telling the truth?"

I shrugged. "I think she believed what she told us was the truth," I replied. "And I'm getting creeped out just standing next to that thing.

So whether or not it ate her cat, I suspect that the gnome has some kind of bad mojo."

Teag gingerly carried the caged gnome back to the office. The bell over the door rang, and I looked up, wondering if Binky had returned, to see a svelte gray-haired woman in a St. John suit wave a cheery greeting.

"Cassidy! I'm so glad I caught you. I was on my way back from lunch, and I wanted to remind you about the Archive fundraiser. You know, to restore the Bethany Plantation? I can count on you and Teag to attend and help us out, can't I?"

Mrs. Benjamin Morrissey was a true doyenne of Charleston society and the Director of the Historical Archive. She had the trifecta of wealth, family history, and social connections to be a rainmaker for the Archive's preservation projects, and she was often a big help to Teag and me when we were researching local history. She had been a good friend of my Uncle Evan, who ran Trifles and Folly before I inherited it, so I was never quite sure how much she knew about the family magic or about the store's real purpose. I suspected it was more than she let on, just as I wondered whether or not she and my late uncle had at one time been an "item" after her husband died.

I grinned, in spite of the spooky gnome problem. "It's always good to see you," I said, and meant it. I enjoy Mrs. Morrissey's wit, and although she's in her seventies, her energy usually leaves me feeling like a slacker. "And yes, I'm planning to attend."

"Count me in!" Teag called from the back.

"I've heard stories about the Bethany place for a long time," I said. "I think it's wonderful the Archive is taking on the restoration project."

Mrs. Morrissey adjusted the pearl necklace at her throat. "I agree," she said. "It's something I've been advocating for years, and I'm so thrilled that we're finally making progress. In fact, the initial donations have been enough to have the house and grounds professionally appraised, hire an architecture firm that specializes in old homes, and remove some of the trash from the site." She wrinkled her nose. "We also identified pieces that just weren't up to the quality of the original plantation, and sold them off to raise more money."

Preservation was the lifeblood of a city like Charleston, and at any given moment, there seemed to be dozens of worthy causes raising funds to rebuild, renovate, repair or safeguard pieces of the city's past. I couldn't support every one, but I had a soft spot for Mrs. Morrissey, so her pet causes usually got priority.

"I can't stay," Mrs. Morrissey said. "Just poked my head in to say hello. Give my best to Teag. Ta-ta!" And with that, she was gone.

My cell phone rang, and when I answered it, Kell Winston, our favorite ghost-hunter, was on the line. "Hi, Cassidy! Are you and Teag doing anything tomorrow night?"

I hesitated, and Kell barreled on ahead. "SPOOK is going out to look at a house you might find interesting," he said. "No one said it was haunted until the place was renovated, and now they seem to be having a lot of problems." SPOOK stood for "Southern Paranormal Observation and Outreach Klub." Kell was the leader of the group, which had started to make a name for itself in ghost-hunting circles.

"I can ask Teag," I said. "You need an antiques consult?" Kell knows a little bit about my ability to read objects, but he doesn't know about Trifles and Folly's secret mission, or about other things best kept under wraps, like Teag's magic and the fact that our patron, Sorren, is a six-hundred-year-old vampire. Family secrets aren't for sharing.

"Got it in one," he said with a laugh. "It's the old Hoffman house, south of Broad. Know the place?"

For obvious reasons, Teag and I were pretty well connected to Charleston's historical renovation circles. Teag's partner, Anthony, did pro bono legal work for several preservation societies. And since I'm a history buff on top of what we do at the shop, I've been on house tours of nearly every old house that opens its doors to the public, and a few that don't. But I couldn't place the Hoffman house. "Remind me. Which one is that?"

Kell chuckled. "I know—there are so many old houses in Charleston, right? It's the one with the wrought iron gate, the pineapple finials and the double stairway to the front door."

"Yeah, that really narrows it down," I remarked. He had just described more than half of the historic homes in the city.

"The plum-colored mansion that isn't on the Battery."

"Gotcha." I frowned, thinking. "I remember going through it a couple of years ago when the Preservation Society first purchased it to fix up. They were trying to raise the money for the renovation. I don't recall hearing anything about ghosts then." I also didn't remember getting bad vibes, which is something I never forget.

"That's what makes it interesting," Kell said. "Apparently, the ghosts came with the renovation—or something they brought in to do the remodel," he added. "We haven't been inside yet, but even the garden pegged our meters—and that was from the other side of the wall."

Now he had my attention. I wondered if the Hoffman house had any cat-eating gnomes. "Sure," I said. "I can go. I have to check on Teag's calendar."

"Tell him I'm going," Teag said as he walked out from the back. "If you're ghost-hunting, someone needs to be along to watch your back." Actually, Teag and I watch each other's backs pretty well, but I appreciated the sentiment. My touch magic can be pretty intense, and when I'm wrapped up in a vision from a supernaturally-charged object, I'm vulnerable if something spooky and nasty attacks. Teag makes a great wing-man.

Kell gave me the details, and we agreed to meet up after dinner. Teag was watching me as I ended the call. "Okay," he said. "Give."

I leaned against the display case. "Two places with haunted gardens that didn't used to be haunted. Seems like more than a coincidence. Especially since Binky's mother liked to buy from architectural salvage shops and I'll bet anything the preservation people who fixed up Hoffman House also bought from those stores."

Teag nodded. "Seems like a reasonable guess. But this is Charleston. Architectural salvage shops are almost as common as antique stores, and that's not counting the swap meets, estate sales, and other places you can buy old stuff."

"There's got to be a reason the gnome suddenly turned dangerous, and the Hoffman ghosts got riled up," I said. "Want to bet they won't be the only places that start having problems?"

Teag sighed. "You're probably right. So the sooner we figure out what triggered the reaction, the faster we can shut down other problems."

"That's the plan," I replied. But I should have remembered that plans change.

~

THE NEXT EVENING, Teag and I stood with Kell and the rest of his SPOOK group outside the gate to the Hoffman house. In some ways, the old mansion was just like its more sedate neighbors—including being haunted. An old, custom-designed wrought-iron gate guarded the entrance. Dual staircases curled toward the wide front porch with its pillars, dating from a time when women and men entered by separate stairs to avoid an unseemly glimpse of ankle. Carved wooden pineapples, a symbol of welcome from the days of sailing ships, adorned the gateposts. But beyond the fence, the Hoffman house was painted a deep plum color, unlike its more discreet white clapboard or brick neighbors. On the Battery, with its rainbow of houses reminiscent of the Caribbean, a plum-colored house might not be unique. But in this neighborhood, it had always made the Hoffman residence a one-of-a-kind treasure.

"We've got the key," Kell said, holding it up. "The Preservation Society actually called us, if you can believe it. They started running into situations they couldn't explain, and it got strange enough they figured we could take a stab at figuring it out."

That alone spoke volumes. While Charlestonians believe in haunts, it's one thing to quietly co-exist with the ghost of an ancestor, and it's another to call in the ghost-hunters. "What kind of things have been happening?" I asked. I preferred to get my briefing now, on the outside of the wall, rather than later when we might be running for our lives.

"The Hoffman family trust sold the house to the Preservation Society last year, when the last of the Hoffmans died," Kell said. "Until that point, the only ghost stories involved sightings of an old man on the stairs and a lady in a rocking chair—standard stuff, very quiet, no danger to anyone. So the Society bought the house and raised funds to renovate, and did their best to make sure everything they used was period-authentic." Charlestonians are sticklers for their history. They prefer real old stuff to reproductions, even if the real stuff isn't original to the house.

"The remodeling went well at first," Kell went on. "Then in the last few months, there started to be problems. Voices. Footsteps. Sounds of things sliding around on the floor or chairs rocking—that kind of stuff. Out in the garden, a couple of the gardeners had a bad enough experience with something—they wouldn't say what—that they walked away and didn't even come back for their paycheck."

"Did the problems stop the renovation?" I asked.

Kell shook his head. "No. They managed to finish. But there have been enough problems—escalating incidents—that the Society is privately afraid to hold an Open House. And of course, they don't want to tell all their donors it's because of ghosts."

While Kell briefed us, his team spread out along the wall. Calista, who always rocked a goth vibe, already had her tablet computer out and was recording from a variety of sensors. Drew, tall and dark-haired like a skinny raven, was getting readings on an EMF monitor. Pete, the sound guy, had a small action cam like extreme sports athletes wear attached to his hat, and he was gathering audio readings down toward the end of the fence.

"From what I've been told, the ghosts got worse little by little, probably as new items were brought into the house. But when the contractors finished up the landscaping, things got bad," Kell said. "The ghosts had been noisy before or mischievous—hiding objects, moving things—but at the end, they were more aggressive."

We had been out with Kell and his team on some pretty wild situations, so Teag and I could picture too well just what Kell was talking about. "All right," I said. "Let's get started."

Teag and I did not come unprepared. My touch magic enables me to pull from the memories and emotions associated with an object in order to defend myself. I had an old dog collar on my left wrist, which connected me to the protective spirit of my beloved golden retriever,

Bo. As a ghost, Bo was one hell of a watchdog. I also carried an old wooden spoon that had been my grandmother's. When I connected to its emotional resonance, I could send out a cold blast of energy that could knock most things right on their asses. I have other weapons, too, but they tended to be a bit extreme for tonight's situation.

Teag has Weaver magic, which means he can weave spells and magical protections into cloth, and he can also weave data streams, making him one hell of a hacker. Tonight, Teag and I both wore vests beneath our clothing into which he had woven protective spells. Teag is also a champion martial arts competitor, and he's been making sure I do enough training to protect myself. He carries a tall wooden staff, which is both a weapon and a way to channel his magic. I suspected he had some other weapons hidden in his bag as well, and both of us wore an assortment of protective charms and amulets. We were ready for trouble.

Kell unlocked the gate. The lights in the house were already on, likely a security measure. We stuck together, walking in pairs, heading up the stairs to the wide front porch. Kell brought out a second key and unlocked the gate, then disarmed the security system.

The house had a huge foyer with parquet floors, a large circular table with an empty vase that was ready for a big bouquet of fresh flowers, and a tasteful, tiered brass chandelier. A huge mirror in a gilt frame hung against one wall, above a Hepplewhite table. The house was cold, a rarity in Charleston except in mid-winter. I doubted the chill could be attributed to the air conditioning.

A thump upstairs made us all jump. "Readings are off the meter," Drew said, watching as the needles jumped on his EMF instruments.

"Picking up some audio," Pete said. "Nothing I can make out—like voices in the distance."

"Damn, they're starting up early," Calista observed, watching the graphs jump on her tablet. "Cold spots all over the place. I'm live-streaming the video from Pete's hat. Picking up a couple of orbs at ten o'clock," she indicated. We looked up, and sure enough, two silvery orbs drifted like soap bubbles near the chandelier, only to wink out an instant later.

"After what happened last time, I'm going to advise that we stay downstairs," Kell said.

"What happened?" Teag asked.

"I was pushed," Calista muttered, and her hand went to a newly-healed scar above one eyebrow.

"I think you'll get the idea from what happens down here and in the garden," Kell said.

As hauntings go, this was one that should have been on reality TV. I glimpsed a bluish, transparent figure in the parlor that wasn't there when I looked again. Teag pointed to a shadow that had taken the shape of a person on the upstairs landing; only no one was around to have cast the image. The crystal in the chandelier began to rattle as if there was an earthquake, but the floor beneath our feet remained still. Upstairs, we heard doors slam, one after another.

"You're certain no one's here," Teag said. "Someone could be pranking us."

Kell shook his head. "No. The Society is really worried. You can imagine the idea of bringing donors into this—"

From up ahead of us, we heard the sound of shattering glass, as if someone had overturned an entire cabinet of tableware. At the same time, I saw a reflection in the mirror of a woman in a long, gray dress. She seemed far away, but as I watched, she grew ever-closer.

No one in our group was wearing gray.

"I think we'd better keep moving," I said, with a glance toward the mirror. Kell followed my gaze and paled, then nodded curtly and led us forward.

The Hoffman house's renovation had been beautifully done. I knew antiques, and I was impressed that the Society had spent a pretty penny to furnish the house with pieces appropriate to its time-period. Where there had been nods to modern life, like with electric lights, the fixtures were old pieces that had been retrofitted. Even the hardware for the doorknobs and latches was old.

The thud of footsteps overhead reminded me that the house's ghostly inhabitants were unimpressed by the remodeling efforts.

I staggered into Kell, shoved off-balance by an invisible force.

Teag reached for me, but I shook my head. I was all right, but someone —something—had made its displeasure clear. A moment later, a small bit of gravel pinged me in the forehead. I heard the gravel fall on the hardwood floor as more pieces pelted us. Calista protected her tablet and cursed the ghosts. Pete protected his eyes with one arm even as he turned face-forward so that his action cam could record the assault.

"The voices are louder," Drew reported, deflecting the hail of gravel with his arm while he studied his read-outs. He turned the audio on so we could all hear what he was listening to on his headset. The low babble sounded like what you'd expect from a party held in the apartment next door, except the tone made me think the ghosts weren't having a good time.

"Anything?" Teag asked me quietly. I shook my head. We hadn't lingered long enough for me to zero in on any single object that called to my magic.

"Nothing in particular," I murmured. "We've passed several things that had a resonance, but nothing that screamed at me. I don't think any of the pieces we've seen are causing this."

The pebbles stopped as quickly as they started. I heard heavy foot-steps coming down the steps in the foyer, and hoped Kell meant to take us out the back door. The lights flickered, but we all had heavy-duty flashlights, just in case. It was cold enough that gooseflesh rose on my arms, and I almost expected to see my breath mist.

"Keep moving," Kell said quietly. "I think you see the problem."

I winced as another crash sounded overhead like a huge plate glass window shattering. "What about the damage?" I asked.

Kell shook his head. "This happened before. They'll come back in daylight, and nothing's broken, doors that 'slammed' are open, no evidence of anything—maybe a few bits of gravel. This is all supernat-ural phenomena."

He sounded pretty calm about it. I was jumpy as hell.

I took a deep breath and tried to shut out the house's attempt to frighten us. Hoffman House was beautiful and had been lovingly redone. Ghosts often dislike being disturbed by remodeling, but I remembered how distressed the house had looked in the declining days of its last owner, and to see it restored to its glory was truly amazing. I couldn't imagine what its ghosts might dislike, other than the unexpected buzz of activity, and the constant parade of strangers. Ghosts are funny like that.

I concentrated on what I felt from our surroundings. I wasn't a medium or a clairvoyant, but when a location has this much pent-up mojo, it comes through the walls and the floor, too much to overlook. I could feel the Hoffman house's age. Blurred images like a movie on fast-forward crossed my mind's eye. So much life had filled this home over generations, love and loss and hope and pain. I felt the resonance of the Hoffmans' lives in the walls and floorboards, but while it was bittersweet it was... very normal. No deep secrets or dark tragedies loomed in the house's memories.

But something was wrong. I picked up a jarring buzz, and whatever its source, it upset the longstanding equilibrium. The house had adapted to the rhythm of its residents' lives, and that rhythm had been disturbed. That was not surprising, since the last Hoffman had died, the house was sold to strangers, and a parade of newcomers invaded its hallways. And yet... the more I tuned into the house's resonance, the more clearly I sensed points of turbulence within its walls. I struggled and failed to hone in on those points, but I came away with the distinct impression that items new to the house had brought the supernatural unrest with them, and that the house itself was as much of victim of the bad mojo as the people who bore the brunt of the negative psychic energy.

"Let's keep moving." Teag's voice made me look behind us. The shadows had grown dark in the foyer, and they were stretching in our direction. I don't like to tempt fate. Maybe they would just be shadows if they reached us—but maybe they wouldn't.

"Yeah," Kell said, glancing toward the foyer. "This way."

We all picked up the pace, though no one had said to hurry. "Still pegging the meter," Drew reported.

"I hope this all records," Calista said, watching her tablet as she walked.

"I'm making out words now," Drew said, and I noticed that he had paled. "They're not friendly. They keep saying 'get out' and 'go away.'"

All of a sudden, the lights went out.

Something cold touched my arm. A cold wind blew from the foyer to the back of the house with enough force to nearly knock me off my feet. Pebbles pelted like hail, larger and thrown with more force. Calista screamed, and Drew gave a yelp of pain and surprise. A crunch sounded as something hit the floor, hard.

Kell's people had flashlights at the ready, flooding our little circle with light. Calista's cracked tablet lay on the floor. Drew cradled his left arm. His sleeve had been shredded as if a clawed hand had taken a swipe at him. Pete cried out and ripped his earbud away as his instruments screeched.

"Keep going," Teag urged. Kell hurried his crew on down the hall, while Teag and I turned to face what was coming from the foyer. Shadows stretched toward us in way that weren't explained by the light of our flashlights, and a gray female form had stepped out of the mirror and was heading our direction. Neither Teag nor I were looking for a fight; we just wanted to give the SPOOK people enough time to make it to the kitchen exit.

I shook the dog collar on my left wrist, and the glowing ghostly form of a large, really angry dog manifested by my side. Bo's ghost gave a low-throated growl and advanced a step in the direction of whatever had grabbed at me. Teag's staff glowed at the top from a dozen woven rope strands into which he had poured stored power. I let my wooden spoon athame fall drop into my right hand.

The gray woman swept toward us, arms outstretched, hands formed into claws, mouth unnaturally wide and toothsome. The too-dark shadows were right behind her. Teag and I moved in unison. I leveled my athame at the gray lady and let out a wide fan of cold-white force, and Teag muttered words of power, pointed his staff toward the shadows, releasing a wave of energy. The gray lady's image stopped as if frozen, and then dissipated, while the shadows were forced back. Bo's ghost snapped and snarled, driving the shadows even further toward the foyer.

"Let's get out of here," Teag murmured. Neither of us were about to turn our backs on where the apparitions had been, but we managed to catch up to where Kell and the others waited in the kitchen, with Bo's ghost fading as we rejoined the group.

"We're almost out," Kell said, but I could hear in his voice that the supernatural show had rattled him. Teag and Pete turned their flashlights behind us. Drew and Calista sent their beams ahead. "We've just got to get through the garden."

He unlocked the back door and sent the rest of us through, then paused long enough to lock up behind us. Tiny walkway lights illuminated the small garden, which had been groomed and landscaped to make the most of the small walled area. Boxwood hedges, crepe myrtles and a riot of perennial blooms would make for a beautiful setting in daylight. Now, they looked gray and ominous.

"Something bad is out here," I murmured. "Can you feel it?"

Kell and Teag nodded. Calista was still swearing at her broken tablet, trying to coax it to turn on, while Pete and Drew were dealing with equipment that continued to register readings in the red zone. "Yeah," Kell said. "Maybe we need to come back during the daytime."

We moved together in a close knot toward the gate. I kept my athame in hand, hidden by my sleeve, and Teag made sure his staff was ready if we were attacked. Although I was careful not to touch anything in the garden, the bad vibes were unmistakable. I felt as if we were moving through enemy territory, or maybe a jungle full of hungry, dangerous predators staying the shadows and ready to pounce.

As we headed through the center of the garden, the feeling of being watched grew stronger. I focused my gift, trying to get some sense of where the danger was located. Two areas of the garden seemed to light up in my mind, and I got the image of a large cat and a winged fairy.

"Hey!" Pete yelled and began beating at the air around him. "Something just bit me!"

From my left, I heard the growl of a cat.

"Get out now!" Teag shouted, and while the others were focused on opening the gate, Teag leveled his staff again and sent out a warning blast of energy. The cat yowled in protest. Something buzzed past me, and Bo's ghost leaped into the air, snapping its ghostly teeth at the apparition, which moved in a blur.

A moment later we were all outside the gate, breathing hard and shaken by what we had seen. Kell locked the entrance, and in the glow of the streetlight, I could see that he was pale. "Now do you see why the Preservation Society is worried about doing tours?"

"Oh my god. I'm bleeding," Pete said. He withdrew his hand from his neck, and I could see a bloody wound that looked a lot like the scrape of small, sharp teeth.

"I've got a first aid kit," Teag said, and pulled a few items from his messenger bag. "I never leave home without it," he said, forcing a smile. I knew that the ointment he put on the wound was a poultice from a friendly root worker, and that the bit of cloth gauze he placed on the wound beneath the Band-Aid was enhanced by his magic.

"This is going to sound really strange, but are there sculptures in the garden?" I asked as we all tried to get our breath back.

Kell gave me a sidelong look. "Yes, several. Brought in from various sources, and one or two original to the site."

"What are the new ones?" I asked.

"There's a fountain, which was part of the Hoffmans' garden but needed to be repaired. Then there is a stone bench purchased new by the family trust in honor of the family. And then there's a stalking leopard and a pixie, which were old pieces from elsewhere. Why?"

I didn't have the heart to tell Pete he had been bitten by a pixie, and I was glad we hadn't had to tangle with the leopard. "I don't know what your meters show, but my… sensitivity… cued in on the pixie and the leopard," I said. "Can you ask your contacts at the Society where they got those?"

Kell nodded. "Sure. They're pretty desperate to get things to settle down. Do you think those pieces are what's haunting the place?"

I had a theory, but no proof. "I think it's more than just those items," I said slowly, "but I do believe they're involved. It might not be a bad idea to see if any of the materials used to remodel the house were also purchased from whatever source supplied the two statues," I added. "It might be that the salvage store got a bad batch from a place that's got a malicious haunting, and the pieces carried the taint with them."

"I've heard about that kind of thing," Calista said. "But more with furniture and knick-knacks."

"I'll let you know what I find out as soon as I can," Kell promised. "If you two can help un-haunt the Hoffman house, the Society would be really grateful."

"We'll do everything we can," I said. Just then, Teag's phone rang. He stepped away to answer, and returned looking grim.

"That was from Alistair McKinnon," Teag said. That got my attention right away. Alistair runs the Lowcountry Museum. It was very unusual to get a personal call from him, especially this late in the evening. "Mrs. Morrissey is in the hospital. She was attacked out at the Bethany Plantation."

Teag and I went straight to the hospital. Alistair met us in the lobby. "Thank you for coming," he said. He looked haggard. "Betsy—Mrs. Morrison—was adamant about needing to talk to you, even though I assured her I would handle the Committee and any fundraiser issues while she recovers."

"What happened?" Teag asked as we walked with Alistair to the elevator.

"The Bethany restoration is a pet project of Betsy's. She's been talking about it for years. So she's been more hands-on than usual," Alistair said. "She stopped in this afternoon to meet with one of the contractors, and he left her walking the garden while he went to get something from his truck. When he came back, she was on the ground." He frowned, and I could see the worry in his eyes. Alistair and Mrs. Morrissey had been friends as well as colleagues for a long time, and moved in the same circles.

"The contractor called me, and I notified the Archive and came here to meet the ambulance," he continued as the elevator arrived and we stepped out. "She's conscious, seems to be doing well, and is increasingly impatient with all the tests the doctors want to run." He sighed. "I'll let her tell you the rest."

"It's after visiting hours," I said. "Will the staff let us in?"

Alistair gave a snort. "Who is going to say 'no' to Mrs. Benjamin Morrissey—at the hospital that is home to the Morrissey Outpatient Center?

"Cassidy! Teag! Thank you for coming." Mrs. Morrissey was sitting up in bed. She looked drawn, and there was an angry red bump on her forehead, but her hair was perfect, and she was as dignified as if we were holding the meeting at her office.

"How are you feeling?" I asked, genuinely worried.

Mrs. Morrissey reached out a thin, veined hand to take mine and gave a squeeze. "I'm tougher than I look," she whispered. "As the Board of Directors well knows!" She gestured for us to sit down.

"Now before that pesky doctor comes back, I need you to do something for me," she said, directing Alistair to watch the door with a nod of her head. "I need the two of you to figure out what's going on at the Bethany Plantation. Because what attacked me out on the grounds wasn't natural," she added. She leaned closer and dropped her voice. "It was supernatural."

I started to protest, and she fixed me with a gimlet glare. "Don't even try to deny it, Cassidy. You have a gift. And a responsibility," she added with a knowing look. "I was a very good friend of your Uncle Evan. He trusted me with his secrets."

"What happened?" Teag asked.

Mrs. Morrissey clasped her hands together in her lap. "The landscape architect went to get the plans for the lawn layout from his truck," she said. "The house and grounds have been neglected for so long, that the beautiful formal gardens and lawns have all gotten badly overgrown, and the house is a wreck."

She sighed. "I've loved that old ruin for a long time. Always thought it was so romantic, hidden behind trees and vines, like something out of a novel. The reality is less glamorous. The project has had unexpected problems and hold-ups from the beginning, and higher expenses. That's why a few months ago, when we did the initial cleanup, we tried to sell off anything that wasn't historically important to raise some extra money."

"Let me guess—that's when the spooky problems started," Teag said.

Mrs. Morrissey nodded. "Yes. Just little things at first, and to be honest, there isn't a renovation project in Charleston that doesn't chalk up some strange things to ghosts. But the more the work progressed, the bigger the problems, to the point where the crew chief today told me some of the equipment was sabotaged. And then, this happened," she said, spreading her hands to indicate her situation.

"The Bethany place had some scandals associated with it, didn't it?" I asked, searching my memories. Scandals were nearly as common as ghosts when it came to old homes.

"Plenty," Mrs. Morrissey said. "That added to the glamor." She reached up to rub her forehead with a rueful expression. "Now I'm beginning to think the scandals were more than rumor."

"Out of curiosity," Teag said, "Did the Archive keep a list of who purchased the items that were sold off?"

"I can tell you that without a list," Mrs. Morrissey said. "Henderson Architectural Salvage."

Teag and I exchanged a glance. I was pretty sure we were on the same wavelength. Mrs. Morrissey didn't seem to notice. "I think all the construction stirred something up that was resting uneasily," she continued. "And if there's a way to set it right, I'd like to see that happen so that no one else gets hurt."

I managed a smile. "I'll see what we can do," I said, unsure of what that would be. "Now we need to let you rest so you can get better."

Mrs. Morrissey waved her hand dismissively. "Don't worry about me. I'll be fine with a good night's sleep."

My phone went off as we walked to the car. "That's Sorren," I said, after a glance. "He's waiting for us at the store—and he brought in some backup on the gnome problem."

SORREN WAS WAITING for us when we drove back to Trifles and Folly.

He looks like he's in his mid-twenties, though he's really centuries older than that. Before he was turned, he was the best jewel thief in Belgium. For the last several hundred years, he's been part of the Alliance, a coalition of mortals and immortals that get dangerous magical items off the market and out of the wrong hands. Trifles and Folly is just one of his locations around the world, which is why he's often out of town.

"I'm glad you messaged me about the gnome. This kind of magic is nothing to fool with," Sorren said. I realized he wasn't alone. Father Anne—Reverend Anne Burgett—was with him. She was wearing her usual black shirt with clerical collar, black jeans, and Doc Martens boots. The short-sleeved shirt revealed the elaborate color tattoo on her left arm of the patron saints of the St. Expeditus Society, a group of Anglican and Episcopalian priests dedicated to fighting malicious magic and supernatural threats.

The vicious garden gnome was still in its cage, which sat on the break room table. There were several new dents and bulges in the steel wire as if the gnome had lunged against its restraints. Some of the wires were dark with what looked like blood. But when I looked more closely, the statue's appearance had changed. Its gray stone had lost its internal luster, and the expression was petulant, no longer scheming.

"We found an old rite that warded off Fey," Father Anne said, and the liquid in the glass she held looked more like bourbon than sweet tea. "The gnome statue imprisoned a Redcap, and whatever magic is afoot let the Redcap bring the gnome to life." She shook her head. "That's over now."

"I just got an email back from Kell," Teag said. "The two problem garden pieces were purchased from Henderson Architectural Salvage, and so were a lot of other pieces in the Hoffman House."

I grimaced. "Want to bet at least some of those pieces were purchased from the Bethany Plantation sale?" We caught Sorren and Father Anne up on what had happened on our tour with of the Hoffman House with Kell, and our visit to Mrs. Morrissey. Sorren's expression darkened as we spoke.

"The Bethany Plantation has had a history of trouble since the early days of Charleston," he said. He would know, since he was present shortly after the city was founded, and started Trifles and Folly with my ancestor. "Rumor had it that either Charles Bethany or his wife, Matilda, were witches but they were wealthy and powerful enough no one dared move against them, even back then," Sorren added.

"If the gnome statue came from the plantation's garden, then someone had considerable magic to do what was done," Father Anne observed. "Redcaps are notoriously tough to beat."

"If the Bethanys were so bad, how did they avoid the Alliance all these years?" I asked.

Sorren sat forward and clasped his hands in front of him on the table. "The Alliance doesn't go looking for fights," he said. "There's too much evil in the world for us to take it all on. We go after the big threats, the most imminent danger, the situations likely to hurt the greatest number of people." He looked down at his hands. "We can't save them all, and we can't stop all the dark magic," he added softly, and I could hear in his voice the admission came at a price.

"Charles Bethany and his descendants were smarter than most dark witches," Sorren continued after a moment. "They didn't get greedy. They never had grandiose dreams of taking over the city or destroying the world. They used their power to enrich and protect themselves and kept the death and destruction to a minimum. We had bigger fish and more dire situations to deal with."

"What now?" Teag asked.

Sorren raised his head and looked up at us. I could see the steel come into his sea-blue eyes. "Now, we go lay to rest whatever evil Charles Bethany raised."

Teag and I added a few more magical weapons to the large duffle bag we carried for times like these. Father Anne had a black motorcycle jacket reinforced with Kevlar and blessed with prayer and Holy Water. Sorren had his supernatural speed and strength. He made a call to Lucinda, a Voudon mambo, and she agreed to go with us. We headed out, just after midnight, and I could have sworn the caged gnome watched us leave with a malicious look in his eyes, as if he knew something we didn't.

Bethany Plantation had been deserted for decades. I had seen pictures of the old place, a huge brick mansion that looked like something out of a Civil War movie, long past its glory days, overgrown with kudzu and vegetation. The wooden pillars of its front porch were cracked and streaked with dirt, and its roof sagged in places from neglect. No one seemed to know why the place had been abandoned or where the last Bethanys went, but the years went by, and no one returned to take possession of the old property. People gave it a wide berth and said the place was evil. Even vandals left the old plantation alone, or never emerged from their attempt to deface it.

The long driveway had once been shadowed by an allée of live oak trees, but many of those had fallen to storms over the years. I could see tracks where the construction trucks had been through recently.

"If the family trust decided to sell the plantation, do you think it means the last of the Bethanys are really dead?" I asked, breaking the silence as we approached.

"Maybe," Sorren replied. "Or perhaps they finally chose to move on to somewhere else. There were rumors of a family curse. I never heard details."

Lucinda raised her face to the wind, as if she could smell magic, and maybe she could. "What's been worked here still has power," she said. "Old, strong spells linger. People may have left this place, but the magic is still here, and it's bad stuff."

Once we got closer, it was clear that the restoration project had begun clearing away brush and refuse. The old mansion was still standing, built to last from red brick though its porch sagged and looked like it would collapse at any moment. Still, the trees, vines, and bushes that had overgrown it were gone, and as we carefully circled the grounds in the moonlight, we could see that the rear garden area had also been cleared.

"There were stories about the Bethanys burying their slaves in sight of the house, so Mistress Matilda could control their spirits with her magic," Father Anne observed.

"I wouldn't be surprised," Sorren said. "I was told on good authority that she sacrificed and buried a slave at each of the four corners of the garden, to protect the house and give more power to the plants she grew for her spells."

Teag glared at them. "Aren't you two both little rays of sunshine," he grumbled. "I vote we keep a sharp eye out for trouble. I tapped into the police database before we drove over. This area's had more than its share of disappearances over the years. So maybe Matilda's descendants kept her garden—or its occupants—well fed." I thought about the garden gnome in its cage and shivered.

Teag had his staff in one hand, and a fighting net made of magically-woven, silver-infused fibers in the other. I had my athame ready in my right hand and an old walking stick that had belonged to Sorren's mentor, Alard, in my left. I could reach through the walking stick's memories to channel old power, and that made it a formidable weapon. Bo's ghost materialized next to me when we got out of the car. People don't think of golden retrievers as guard dogs, but Bo was ninety-five pounds of muscle when he was alive, and fiercely protective. We also each wore charms and protective amulets, to help dispel harmful power. I had the feeling we were going to need all the help we could get.

Sorren wore two swords, and Father Anne had a couple of deadly, blessed silver-plated knives as well as plenty of other weapons that packed a religious whammy. Lucinda always carried powders and items she needed to call to the Loa, the Voudon gods. We were as ready as we were going to get. I just hoped it was enough.

"House or garden?" Teag murmured.

I concentrated, opening myself to my magic. Tonight, I had worn shoes whose heavy rubber tread blunted my power's connection to the ground. I wanted to control that link myself. So I bent down when we neared the tumbled remains of the garden wall, and sank my fingers into the dirt, ready for what the visions showed me.

Screams echoed in my mind. Images forced themselves through my defenses, of flame and blood and pain. Sacrifices had been made here, human and animal. Restless spirits remained bound to the sullied ground. Dark intent tainted the foundations of the great house, the mortar in the walls, the plants that thrived in the blood-soaked earth.

And over it all were faintly glowing lines of old power, sparking and crackling like a bad electrical connection, but still full of enough juice for a deadly jolt. Most of all, there was something present, something that sensed my power and turned its attention on me with a malicious force of will. In my mind, I saw what I searched for, glowing points of light that showed me where the dark magic was anchored in the garden.

I must have cried out from the intensity of the vision, because Teag and Sorren pulled my hands away from the dirt, breaking the connection, and Father Anne was chanting a litany as they helped me stand. After a moment, the hellish images receded, and I caught my breath.

"It knows we're here," I said breathlessly. "And it's not afraid of us."

"What did you see?" Teag asked as I stopped shaking.

"The magic is anchored at each corner, like we thought," I said. "There's a section toward the back that feels jumpy and restless. Maybe the slave cemetery. They're not resting quietly. And there are five other points of power inside the garden. I'm betting they're statuary."

"And I'd bet the five anchors are points of a pentacle," Teag added.

"Well, that gives us something to go on," Father Anne said. "I'm in the mood to be disagreeable. Let's get started."

The closer we got to the brick garden wall, the more my magic prickled a warning. "Do you feel that?" Teag asked quietly. I nodded. Father Anne was still chanting under her breath. Sorren had the stubborn set to his jaw he gets when there's bad business to be seen to its conclusion. I suspect he figured this reckoning was long overdue.

The garden wall was little more than rubble, reduced to mounds of broken bricks after years of storms. Lucinda walked a circle counterclockwise around the wall, chanting and singing and sprinkling a generous amount of salt in a large, protective ring around the area. At each corner, she pushed a piece of a broken mirror into the ground and sprinkled more salt.

Father Anne walked the same circle clockwise, with her own chants and prayers, reinforcing Lucinda's warding with a mixture of rosemary, garlic, and juniper that she had blessed. She stood back and looked at the garden, which seemed to have grown darker. "Somewhere in the garden is a focus for the spells Charles and Matilda set long ago. It could be anything, anywhere. Find it, and we find their weak point."

We crossed over the protective barrier, being careful not to smudge the line of salt and protective powder. I felt a ripple of energy as I did so, but the power was clean and pure. A few steps later, we climbed over the broken bricks of the wall, and a new wave of energy hit me full force. It felt foul, unclean and although the night air outside had smelled of gardenia and green grass, in here, the sluggish wind carried the tang of an abattoir. I had no idea how workmen had ever stood the negative energy long enough to clear away overgrowth, and decided they must have been psychically blind and deaf not to have noticed.

A quick glance around the flower beds at the plants that had grown untended showed me nightshade, monkshood, Jimson weed, oleander, and angel's trumpet, all deadly poisons. Elder trees and weeping willows loomed over the garden, along with a variety of thorned bushes. Down the slope from the garden was a cypress swamp, with dark trees and black water. Over our heads, the branches of the trees rattled like dry bones, although there was no wind.

Statues and stone decorations dotted the old garden. Angels, animal figures, fountains, and decorative shapes occupied each of the flower beds and hunched in the shadows beneath the trees. They looked old and weathered, but even at a distance, the objects raised my hackles. I saw a few empty pedestals and wondered if one had once held a garden gnome or a pixie statue. One look at the arrangement of the paths told me Teag's guess has been right. The Bethany garden was a large pentacle inside a warded brick-walled area. Charles, Matilda, and their descendants might be gone, but the dark power anchored here was as strong as ever, and it didn't like us being here.

The garden hit us with everything it had.

Strands of bougainvillea curled toward me, moving fast as a snake across the ground, covered with inch-long thorns thirsty for blood. Bo's ghost lunged and snapped at the tendrils, then dove out of the way as I leveled Alard's walking stick and tapped into his memories and the magic of the stick's maker. Fire burst from the tip, and the thorny tendrils shrieked as they drew back, their leaves singed, blooms cindered.

A manchineel tree, better known as a "death apple," shook loose its poisonous fruits, and where they hit us, the caustic sap raised red, blistering welts. Sharp-edged tall grasses swept like scythes, whipping out into the walkways on the still air, slicing at us and opening bloody cuts on unprotected skin. The weeping willows lashed their thin, flexible branches like flails, trying to drive us off the pathway.

I focused on the image my gift had shown me of the key points on the pentacle. The four corners were likely the graves of the unfortunate slaves. I turned in a slow circle, trying to match what I saw with my eyes to what I had "seen" with my magic. One was a little girl, but this child was holding the body of a headless rabbit, and smiling a nasty smile. Another statue, farther away, looked like a large, crouching lizard. I saw a third monument and thought it was an angel before I realized it was a winged skeleton. The fourth statue was the Grim Reaper, a faceless robed figure with a scythe. And the fifth monument I couldn't quite make out, since it was in the shadow of the manchineel tree.

"There," I shouted, pointing out the important anchor statues. "Destroy those, and we break the focus of the power."

Lucinda was already chanting, laying down a circle of salt to surround her as she focused her Voudon magic on the sacrificed victims buried at the four corners. That left the rest of us to take on the malicious monuments, and fight off the plants that stirred and rustled, looking for a chance to slash with their sharp edges and tear at us with their thorns. The manchineel tree flung its poisoned apples harder, pelting us, causing more burns.

"That's enough of that." Teag brought his staff down in the dirt and channeled his power. He's a Weaver, and I realized immediately that he was reaching for the mat of roots beneath the ground, tangled and woven together over the years. He sent his magic down into the ground, and after a moment, I watched as he began to shiver. His lips turned blue, and his breath misted although the night was warm.

The plants around us darkened and turned brown as a killing frost chilled their roots. Teag was panting with the effort, and a thin skin of ice formed on his wooden staff. The trees and grasses stopped moving, shrinking back on themselves away from the deadly cold. With a start, Teag broke out of his trance and looked at me. "Did it work?"

All around Teag in a ten-foot circle, the plants and trees were blackened, frozen, and dead. "Yeah," I said. "That worked." He grinned, and I reached out to him. His skin was ice cold.

The sound of stone grating on stone jarred me to attention. The statues had begun to move. The lizard shuddered, as if waking from a long sleep, and then took one, lumbering step toward us. I heard a giggle and realized the murderous child had jumped down from her pedestal, still smiling her serial-killer smile. The wings on the skeleton trembled, and the skeleton turned to fix its hollow gaze on us, as the Grim Reaper swept forward, moving fluidly as if he had wheels beneath his concrete robes. Bo's ghost growled and barked, hackles raised, staring down the enemy.

"Take them down!" Sorren yelled.

Sorren ran at the Reaper, our fastest-moving foe. Teag gripped his staff in both hands and squared off with the lizard and the skeleton. That left the killer kid for me and Father Anne.

Teag swung his staff with his full strength, cracking the skeleton statue across the wings, its most fragile feature. The thud of wood on stone reverberated in the night air, along with the crack of old concrete snapping away as part of one wing crumbled. A hiss sounded, and the lizard struggled forward, as the skeleton turned, grasping at Teag with one bony hand that caught at his jacket.

Plenty of martial arts competitions had taught Teag how to take on multiple opponents. He slammed the butt of his staff into the lizard's snout and gave a grim smile as the concrete broke. Then he wheeled, ramming the other end of his staff into the skeleton, knocking its carved arm off at the elbow, and shaking off the hand and forearm that still clung to his jacket.

The Reaper moved more quickly than the other statues, but not as fast as a vampire. Sorren tackled the statue from behind, staying well away from its scythe, and gave the hooded head one vicious, powerful twist, breaking it from the body.

From where Lucinda danced in her salt circle, I could hear her chants growing louder, and the air stirred, heavy with magic. Blue-green lights, like foxfire, shimmered at the corners of the broken brick walls, and I thought I glimpsed figures in the lights, moving toward us from far away.

A creepy giggle brought my attention back to the killer child's statue. She still gripped the headless rabbit in one hand, but I saw a stone knife now in one hand, and murderous intent in her sightless eyes. I pointed my athame at her, reached into the well of power created by the emotions and memories I associated with the old wooden spoon, and blasted her with a cone of cold force. I hit her point-blank, right in the chest, and the statue blew apart, sending rock shrapnel into the air. Immediately, I felt one of the five anchors of power wink out.

"Destroy the statues!" I shouted. "It breaks some of the garden's power."

Teag was already swinging his staff at the skeleton, taking off chunks with every blow. Father Anne had grabbed a piece of rebar from where the construction crew had piled their materials, and she swung the heavy iron rod with both hands like a major league batter, crunching it down through the lizard's thick stone body while making sure to stay well back from the creature's long, clawed feet. Sorren used his supernatural strength to lift the headless Reaper statue. I saw the carved figure writhe in Sorren's grasp, and then he hurled it against the brick wall, breaking the statue into pieces and bringing down a hail of bricks on top of it.

Four statues attacked, but there was a fifth, somewhere. I steeled myself, picked up a piece of the child's statue, and felt old malice like the smell of spoiled meat. I forced the fading remnants of the statue's trapped spirit away and felt for the other anchor points I had sensed before. Four of their lights vanished in my mind as I stretched out with my gift. That meant one more anchor point we hadn't found, one that was keeping itself hidden. It still glowed brightly as I pulled impressions from the concrete in my hand, stone that was crumbling as I held it. But not before I heard one final, evil laugh from whatever had animated the child's statue, the promise of worse to come.

A moment later, the ground beneath our feet began to tremble. All across the garden, the dirt split open, and things began to wriggle up from the depths. Toward the rear of the garden, I saw corpses drag themselves out of the ground. Some looked very old, the Bethany's slaves, pressed once more into service against their will. Others wore the remnants of more modern clothing, and I figured they were the people who had gone missing near the plantation grounds over the years. At least a dozen of the zombies had already crawled from their graves, and more were struggling up through the ground.

Sorren brushed the concrete dust from his hands and drew both swords. Father Anne was chanting the Episcopalian burial rite, but she had a long silvery blade in one hand and a blessed boline knife in the other. I knew from prior experience that knife could vanquish even a vampire's ghost. Teag still gripped his staff, but he held his *daga*, a martial arts fighting dagger, in his left hand. I still had my athame and Alard's walking stick, and I was pissed off.

"Watch out!" I shouted, and channeled my frustration and fear into the old cane, tapping into its power and memories. Fire shot from the cane's tip, incinerating the front row of zombies that lumbered toward us. I knew it wasn't their fault, that they were being misused in death as they had been abused in life, but I also knew that the curse controlling them would not be gentle with us if they reached us. So I poured my magic through the cane, amplifying it with the power its long-ago maker had infused into the wood, until the torrent of fire had forced the animated corpses back a pace, stumbling over the charred bodies of the front line.

Sorren waded into the fray now that the fire was gone, moving at superhuman speed, swords glinting in the moonlight in a blur as he cut through the dead figures. Father Anne was right beside him, knives flashing as she stabbed and slashed, murmuring prayers for the dead as she sent the corpses back to their eternal unrest. Bo's ghost lunged at the zombies, teeth snapping, and from the damage he inflicted, his spectral defense was real enough against them to make a difference. I plunged my hand once more into the disturbed ground of the garden bed, and I knew what I needed to do.

"Teag!" I shouted. "This way!"

Lucinda's chanting and dancing had reached a fever pitch. I could feel strong power in the air, her magic and the power of the Bethany curse, fighting an unseen battle. The curse had sent out its foot soldiers against us: plants, statues, and zombies. But the real power anchoring the curse lay at the four corners, where Lucinda was gathering her magic, and in the fifth and most important anchor statue, the one hidden in the shadow of the poison acid tree.

I knew a little about manchineel trees, enough to know that I couldn't just barge in beneath its canopy to find the fifth statue, even if this particular tree wasn't animated by malicious magic. The manchineel's leaves, sap, bark, and fruit weren't just poisonous to eat; touching them was enough to burn skin. Setting fire to the tree was out of the question because its smoke could blind. But the tree was native to the islands, used to the heat of the tropics. And that gave me an idea.

"Can you do that deep freeze thing again?" I asked. Teag grinned and nodded. I could see where the skin on one side of his face was blistered from an apple the tree had thrown. It was payback time.

Teag thrust his wooden staff into the ground among the manchineel's spreading roots and closed his eyes. Even the air around him grew colder as he focused his magic. I kept my eyes wide open, and my athame leveled at the tree. It rustled in the still air, sensing an attack, and as it drew back to hurl more of its poisoned fruit and lash us with its acid-tipped limbs, I let loose with a blast of white, cold power, trained on the trunk of the tree.

The old tree groaned, or maybe that was a roar of anger. Teag was shaking, his lips tinted blue, as a heavy white frost gathered on the ground, spreading rapidly along the tree's roots, freezing into the heartwood. The manchineel shuddered and drew back, and that's when I saw the fifth statue, the key to the Bethany curse. It was a tarnished metallic ball on a pedestal, protected by the hateful tree that had grown around it, and it glowed with a sickly, greenish light.

I hit the tree with another blast of cold force, and Teag sent a push of magic through the roots, so that a thin, sparkling coating of ice covered the trunk and the lowest branches. Then he sheathed the knife he held in his left hand, and in one fluid movement pulled the silvery rope net from his pack and swung it so that the net draped over the glowing ball.

A piercing scream rose from the garden itself. The ball pulsed wildly, trapped inside a magically-woven net threaded with strands of silver, soaked with colloidal silver and holy water. The ball blinked like a strobe light, and behind us, I could hear the battle with the zombies reaching a fever pitch as Lucinda's chant rose to its climax.

I sent all of my remaining magic channeled through the athame as Teag dove forward, holding his staff like a lance. My magic hit the ball at the same time as the butt of his lance, and the cursed sphere shattered into pieces with an unholy shriek.

Everything went suddenly still. The air fairly vibrated with old power, and when I looked up, four figures stood at the corners of the garden. One was a tall man, skeletally thin, wearing a tuxedo, a top hat, and sunglasses missing the lens over one eye. Another was a flamboyantly dressed young man with the ashen skin of a corpse, who was wearing a black riding coat and smoking a cigar. The third was the wizened figure of a short old man who carried a cane and wore an old-fashioned black hat. And the fourth was a rakish young man in a black tie and tails, taking a swig from a bottle of rum. I inclined my head in respect to Baron Samedi, Ghede Linto, Ghede Nibo, and Baron Cimitere, powerful Voudon spirits, protectors of the dead.

The four sacrificial victims whose deaths had helped set the garden's curse and anchor its power now stood in spirit above their graves, one with each of the *ghedes*. The two Barons and the *ghedes* lifted their arms, spreading their hands wide, then brought their palms together in a clap like thunder.

The victims' ghosts vanished. The curse fell away, unraveling as its final anchors lost their power. Lucinda gave a deep bow to the otherworldly figures in the four corners, and they each raised a hand in greeting, then faded into darkness.

The Bethany plantation garden, scene of so much death and pain and horror over the years, was just a ruined lawn covered with chunks of broken statuary and scarred by burned or frost-bitten plants. It was as dead as its owners now, no longer able to hurt anyone.

Behind me, I saw Father Anne standing over the fallen bodies of the zombies, hands raised in blessing, chanting prayers of her own. For an instant, I thought I saw the glowing figure of a man with a head of thick white hair and a full white beard wrapped in a cloak covered with purple crosses. I blinked my eyes, and the vision was gone. Father Anne lowered her hands and turned toward me. She was covered with concrete dust and splattered with zombie ichor, but she managed a faint smile.

"Saint Cyprian," she said, answering my unspoken question. "He has been known to help out on occasion, with the restless dead."

Lucinda released the warded circle and walked toward us. She looked tired, but her eyes were bright from the power of the working she had raised. "The Barons and the *ghedes* take a dim view of imprisoning the dead," she said as she rejoined us. "They'll see the spirits get where they're going."

Sorren was the last to rejoin us. His skin was already healing where the manchineel had burned him with its fruit and sap. His clothing was torn from the fight with the statues and the zombies, but the wounds were closing quickly. "Nice work," he said.

"What about the gnome and the other pieces that were sold off from here?" I asked.

Sorren nodded at the devastated garden around us. "They lost their power when the curse was broken. They're just ugly old stone statues that can't hurt anyone anymore."

I still repressed a shudder. Maybe so, but I wouldn't want one of them in my yard. After this, I was going to take a dim view of any garden statues, for a long, long time.

"I'll come back tomorrow and leave an offering for the Barons and the *ghedes*," Lucinda said.

"And I'll talk with Mrs. Morrissey about having a proper grave marker installed to honor the slaves who were buried here," Father Anne added.

I looked across the ruined garden, then up at the bright, full moon. The wronged dead had been avenged. The Bethany's dark magic was banished. And the restoration project could move on, without endangering anyone, although no one would ever know what we had really done here. Although I was happy we had lifted the curse, I felt the exhaustion of the fight hit me. "Let's head out," I said. "It's way past bedtime."

Maybe so, but I tired as I was, I didn't count on sweet dreams. Not tonight. Maybe never again.

SPOOK HOUSE

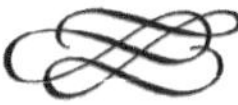

"WHAT DO YOU MAKE OF IT?" KELL WINSTON GESTURED TO THE partially furnished bedroom. The four-poster bed was swagged with tattered cloth curtains, and the formerly white linens were splashed and soaked with crimson. A partially dismembered body lay among the tangled bedclothes, and every five minutes, the "corpse" sat up and screamed.

"I'd be able to tell you better if you can get that thing to shut up," I replied.

Kell grinned and flicked a hidden switch on the side of the bed. The screaming corpse flopped back onto the pillows.

"Tell me again - why, when Charleston is bursting with real haunted houses, someone needs to create a fake one?" I looked over to Kell. He was tall and lean, with light brown hair and blue eyes, and a perpetual tan that made me think he spent all his spare time out on a boat.

"Because most of those real haunted houses are historic mansions, and they don't take kindly to having a few thousand screaming teenagers tramping over their carpets and past their antiques," he replied. He shot me a grin. "Not to mention what they'd say if we tried to spread some fake blood and plastic body parts around, just for atmosphere."

The house was an old two-story white clapboard from before World War II. The neighborhood around the house was now commercial, and it didn't look like anyone had lived in the place for a long time. Maybe that was part of its spooky charm. A big sign out in front read, *"Are you ready for... The Evil Neighbors? Coming this Halloween. A Thrill Night Production."* The lettering was designed to look like it had been painted in blood.

"So what makes you think there's something here that requires... my attention?" I asked. I had been scanning the house since the moment we parked in the driveway, trying to sense any hint of a supernatural threat. I had spotted plenty of theatrical menaces, from looming monster figures to ghosts that dropped from trap doors in the ceiling, but so far I hadn't picked up any strong indication that real magic or dark energies were in play.

I made a slow circle of the room. Kell had brought me right upstairs, past the rooms that were decked out with terrifying tableaus on the first floor, so I figured there was a reason he wanted me to focus here.

"I don't want to prejudice you," he replied. "But we've had some creepy situations, and I immediately thought of you."

Some people might take that the wrong way, but I knew what Kell meant. I'm Cassidy Kincaide, and I own Trifles and Folly, an antique and curio shop in historic, haunted Charleston, SC. Sure, Trifles and Folly is a great place to pick up the perfect one-of-a-kind item to decorate your home or a unique piece of estate jewelry for a gift, but we have some big secrets. I'm a psychometric—I can read the history, emotions, and sometimes, magic—of an item by touching it. Teag Logan, my assistant store manager, has Weaver magic, meaning he can weave power into fabric and weave data strands together—making him one hell of a hacker.

My business partner, Sorren, is the biggest secret. He's a nearly six-hundred-year-old vampire, and for over three hundred years, he and my family have watched over Charleston—and the world—getting dangerous magical items off the market and out of the wrong hands. When we succeed, no one notices. When we miss something, it gets chalked up as a "natural disaster." Kell knows a little bit about my magic, but nothing about the store, Teag's magic, or Sorren.

"The problems have all been here on the second floor," Kell said. "Several of the crew have reported seeing shadows or hearing noises they couldn't trace back to our equipment. These folks have been doing haunted attractions for years, so they didn't just let their imaginations get the best of them."

I glanced around at the fake blood, realistic-looking plastic body parts, and the wires that I could see with the lights on, but that would be invisible in the dark. "Someone playing a prank?" I asked. "I mean, there are so many props and gadgets someone could rig up the mother of all pranks."

Kell shook his head. "Rennie—the guy who owns Thrill Night—doesn't think so. You're right about them having all the cool toys. But these folks are professionals, and the equipment is expensive. Putting on a rubber mask and jumping out of a closet? Yes. Rigging some elaborate gadget and cutting into productivity?" He shook his head. "I don't think so. The people who work on these attractions like what they do. That kind of thing could get someone hurt and get the perpetrator fired."

"How did you get involved?" I asked. "You usually have enough to do, dealing with the real thing." Kell was the head of Southern Paranormal Observation and Outreach Klub (SPOOK), a well-equipped group of ghost hunters who specialized in Charleston-area hauntings. There were enough of those to keep them busy for a lifetime. Teag and I have helped out a few times when Kell's group ran into something really strange, and I think he's figuring out there's more to both of us than meets the eye. That didn't stop him from asking me out, and so we're seeing each other, but taking things slow.

"The guy running the haunted house, Rennie Montague, is an old college friend of mine," Kell replied. The last name struck a bell. If he was part of *those* Montagues, they were an old, wealthy, and influential Charleston family. "So when he asked for some 'technical assistance,' I said yes." He raised an eyebrow. "And when he offered to donate a portion of the house's proceeds to SPOOK, I was totally in."

"Did anyone get hurt—or anything get damaged—when the strange things happened?" As I walked, I held my right hand a few inches over the bed, side table, and armoire. There wasn't much furniture in the room, but then again, it wasn't a real bedroom, just a set for the live-action spook show. I was careful not to touch anything until I knew more about what I was getting into.

"No—at least, not yet," Kell said.

I paused as I came to a dressing table. It was the kind I'd seen in old movies, with a three-part mirror where a lady could do her make-up. I thought I caught a glimpse of motion in the mirror, but when I looked back, there was nothing unusual. "Do you know anything about this piece?" I asked. Although it was old and had some wear, it looked like it was originally expensive.

Kell nodded. "Just another one of Rennie's finds. His crew is donating their time, and the other charity that gets part of the proceeds has sponsors for a lot of the equipment. I'd heard Rennie got a local estate auctioneer to donate some of the furniture from inventory that didn't sell."

I wasn't ready to touch anything yet, mostly because Kell didn't know how to back me up if I ran into something truly nasty. The dressing table set off my internal warnings, but I couldn't figure out why. When I ran my hand just above the surface of the mirror's frame, I had the oddest feeling that the "memories" of the piece had somehow been erased.

"I can't say for certain this piece is causing the trouble," I said. "But it feels... strange. I'm not picking up actual danger, but there's something about it that makes me uneasy."

"It was close to where we picked up a few readings when we brought our crew in and ran our usual tests." I knew Kell's folks. They were good at what they did, and they had good equipment. If there were temperature fluctuations, strange sounds, and the EMF changes that tend to accompany ghostly activity, his group would find them. "We didn't find anything conclusive, either."

"So you picked up something—just not much?" I asked because I was getting the same kind of "readings" from my psychometry. The pieces of furniture gave off a jumble of impressions, probably from multiple owners and hard use. Not all of the energy was happy, but nothing seemed dangerous or dark. The dressing table was the only thing that felt odd. I kept looking back at it, but nothing strange appeared in the mirror. Just in case, I snapped a photo with my phone.

"Yeah," Kell said. "We picked up snippets of conversations, a few temperature changes, a couple of EMF flutters, but nothing to indicate a ghost—or ghosts—with enough power to manifest in a way that would send seasoned people running like scared kids." Kell paused and watched as I completed my circuit. "How about you?"

"This isn't a new house. I figure it's about a hundred years old, give or take," I said. "It would be unusual in a house that age if someone hadn't died here of old age or illness, or left some kind of psychic impression. I'm not getting a happy vibe off the stuff that's here, but it's more weary than bad." I paused. "Was any of this furniture original to the house?"

He shook his head. "Sometimes there's a piece or two left behind in a house, but Rennie told me they mostly buy from yard sales, get stuff cheap since they're going to beat it up."

The four-poster bed was not only splashed with fake blood, but someone had cut into the posts to make it look like they had been hacked with the machete that was sticking out of the sit-up corpse. I could see why they wouldn't want real antiques.

"Let's see what else is up here," I said. "Maybe it's something in one of the other rooms."

I followed Kell out into the hallway. Down on the first floor, workers bustled like backstage on opening night, which it sorta was, since Halloween was coming up soon. Carpenters, electricians, and painters moved around each other carrying lumber, tools, ladders, and cans of paint. Other people had bolts of fabric, naked mannequins, and plastic body parts; decorations to turn a tired old home into a house of horrors.

"This is the nursery," Kell said, leading me into the next room. "It's not as far along. Rennie's waiting for a new shipment for this room and a couple of the others." An old-fashioned bassinette had been rigged up with a motor underneath so that the monster baby inside could pop up. Wind-up toys on the dresser and bookshelves had wires coming out of the bottom so they would turn on and off by themselves. I could see the switch that made a rocking chair move on its own.

"The bassinette has some negative energy attached to it," I said. "Sadness. Loss. I'm betting there was a real death connected to it."

"Dangerous?" he asked.

I shook my head. "No. Just sad. If you were sensitive and you spent much time in here, I think it would rub off on you." I picked up on enough of the emotion without touching the bassinette. I had no desire to be plunged into a long-ago tragedy.

"Do you know anything about the history of the house?"

"Rennie didn't seem to think it was anything out of the ordinary. Just a good house in a good location."

I figured I'd get Teag to do research when I got back to the shop, and ask Sorren some questions too. Between the two of them, we'd be able to figure out the house's secrets. Then we walked into the next room, and I stopped at the doorway so sharply that Kell almost ran into me.

"What?" he asked.

"Someone died in this room," I said. "There's a deep sadness and darkness. I'm guessing the person committed suicide."

"You can tell all that without stepping into the room?"

I gave him a look. "That's why I'm *not* stepping into the room." I searched my feelings and stretched out my magic. "It was a young person, consumed by problems that seemed too big to handle. Now, there's regret." Unfortunately, people find out too late that some decisions can't be undone.

We headed back downstairs just as another man was coming up. He brightened when he saw us. "Kell! Thanks for coming. Is this Cassidy?" A man I assumed was Rennie bounded up to shake hands. He was in his mid-twenties, with reddish blond hair and green eyes that were not too different from my own Scots-Irish coloring. Rennie was dressed in a t-shirt and jeans and looked like he was working right alongside his crew.

"Rennie, meet Cassidy Kincaide. Cassidy, this is my old friend, Rennie," Kell said.

"We've got some all-new thrills and chills for this year that we've never done before," Rennie said. I had to give him credit for enthusiasm. He sounded like a kid on Christmas. "It's a really competitive industry," he continued, "even for charity houses like this one. The guests don't want to see the same thing they saw last year. So we're always trying to dream up new scares and tread that fine line between really cool and totally tasteless."

Kell gave him a good-natured punch in the arm. "You crossed that line years ago, bro."

A woman snickered behind me. "He's got you dead to rights on that, Rennie," she laughed. I turned to see a slim, brown-eyed woman with her dark hair caught up in a ponytail. She was wearing a t-shirt that read "*I'm your Evil Neighbor*," advertising for the spook house.

Rennie grinned and rolled his eyes. "Thanks, Briana," he replied. She headed over to the lighting crew. "That's Briana Foster, who heads up our special effects. This would be a pretty dull place without all the high tech stuff she and her crew make happen."

Rennie turned to me. "We make most of our own props, just like a theater company. Many of the people who work for me are theater majors—plus a bunch of computer geeks, electrical and robotic engineers, and some lighting and special effects folks who are probably going to leave me behind and go make it big in Hollywood."

I was taking in the half-finished tableaus in each of the downstairs rooms. "You like these?" Rennie said. "Let me give you the tour." He pointed toward the kitchen. "On this side, you have a typical dinner scene—if your family were psychotic cannibals." By daylight, the scene looked overly dramatic. A mannequin of a screaming man lay partially dismembered on the kitchen table. "Steam" rose from stewpots on the kitchen stove with disquietingly realistic arms and legs partially protruding. On another table, a cook dressed like a mortician was "stuffing" a corpse on an autopsy table. Except for all the blood and body parts, the kitchen looked like a set from a 1960s sitcom.

"What do you think?" Rennie asked, clearly bursting with pride.

"I'm not sure whether to be fascinated or sick to my stomach," I replied honestly.

Rennie clapped his hands. "Eureka! Just the reaction we're working to get." He led us across the hall. "And here's the dining room."

A dozen ghouls and unbalanced-looking figures sat around a table heaped with platters that held arms, legs, fingers, and hands in various sauces or as ingredients in familiar holiday dishes. Some of the fingers were wiggling, and the figures were realistic enough that in dim light, they would have looked scarily real. I noticed there were two empty seats at the table. "Are those for the actors?"

Rennie nodded. "We mix our people in with the figures and change it up every night, so even if you come back two or three times, it's never the same." We walked back into the hallway, and I glanced to the side and saw extra alcoves had been added, like small closets.

"And those?"

Rennie grinned. "We call them 'scare pockets.' Our people can jump out and seem to appear from nowhere."

We passed rooms with names like the *"Den of Despair"* and the *"Library of Lucifer."* I couldn't resist looking into the *"Bathroom of Beelzebub."* A bloody shower splashed gore on the white tile and tub, and the "body" of a man lay on the floor. Blood bubbled up from a toilet, and a message was written in blood on the mirror over the sink. A crazy looking old woman with a butcher knife wheeled to face me and raised the knife as if to strike. Even though I knew it was fake, I gasped and jumped back.

"Pretty good, huh?" Rennie asked. "We call her 'Bathroom Bertha.' Some of the nights, that old lady will be one of our actors. I guarantee that'll get a lot of screams."

With the lights on, the rooms looked like something out of a gory wax museum or the backstage of a theater. But with the lights out, good special effects and creepy background music, Rennie's guests were going to get their money's worth of scares.

We thanked Rennie for the tour and Kell offered to drive me back to the store. "Can I bribe you with dinner?"

"I'm hungry, and the company is good, so I'm pretty bribe-able," I joked. "Want to pick me up after we close the store?"

"Sure thing."

It was a beautiful day to drive anywhere, for any reason, one of those gorgeous Fall afternoons that draws so many tourists to Charleston. The sun was shining, the sky was blue, and the leaves hadn't really started to turn yet. Still, the temperatures had cooled off, and there was a hint of autumn in the air.

Secretly, I was relieved that we hadn't found anything significant at the house. Kell hadn't seen me do much with tainted objects. Things could go really wrong really quickly, especially if there was dark magic involved or very strong negative emotions. More than once, a tainted supernatural object had knocked me flat on my ass. Teag was used to that and had a lot of experience helping me recover, or protecting me if things got bad.

It was early October, so Halloween was still a couple of weeks away. That meant the haunted house people still had time to set up their attraction. My problem was that I'd seen too much of the real thing to consider any funhouse amusing.

But I couldn't tell Kell that. "How did Rennie get into the haunted house business?" I asked.

"Rennie was the kind of kid who started a lawn service in seventh grade and ended up running an afterschool business that paid for his college education," Kell replied. "He's got a knack for making money. One fall, a friend of a friend asked him to help out on a haunted attraction." He shrugged. "That was it. Rennie was hooked."

"Really? I would have thought a guy like him would have headed for Wall Street," I replied.

"Cassidy, Rennie says haunted attractions are a five-hundred million dollar a year business," Kell said, awe coloring his tone. "Rennie started out doing funhouses for charities—like this one—and eventually figured out a winning pattern and started his own company."

Kell dropped me off, and I headed into Trifles and Folly. Teag was working with a customer, but he waved as I came in. Maggie, our part-time assistant, gave me a big grin.

"Hi, Boss! How was the spook house?" Maggie is a retired teacher who decided that bus tours and yoga just weren't keeping her busy enough, so she decided to get a job doing something completely differ-ent. Except, of course, she's a history fiend who manages to teach customers more than they ever expected about a piece while making it all sound like juicy gossip. Her fashion sense is more hippy than hipster and Teag and I both utterly love her.

"It's pretty interesting seeing the inside with the lights on," I admit-ted, putting my purse in the office and grabbing a cup of coffee on the way back. "I know this particular site isn't as big or elaborate as some of the haunted houses, but they sure go all out."

"They're popular on date night," Maggie replied. "Nothing like a good scare to make you grab your sweetie tight!"

We were busy in the store for a fall afternoon, which was great for the month's bottom line but didn't make it easy for me to tell Teag what I had seen at the haunted house. Right before we were ready to close, it finally got quiet enough for Maggie to cover the front on her own while Teag and I went back to the office for a quick consultation.

"I can look up the history on the house," Teag said after I filled him in. "And see if I can find any matches on the furniture pictures you texted me. Sometimes, estate auctions post photos of items for sale."

"I'm not sure anything Rennie would buy would be valuable enough for that kind of thing," I said.

Teag shrugged. "You never know. Sometimes 'valuable' furnish-ings don't sell because they've fallen out of style. It won't hurt to check." That meant Teag was on the hunt. He took it as a personal challenge to find details that no one should be able to find, even if that meant a little magical hacking.

"Do you and Anthony have plans for dinner?" I asked. Teag and Anthony had been seeing each other for more than a year and had finally moved in together. "Kell's picking me up to grab a bite after the store closes. He could tell you more about the spook house then." Anthony had a little more knowledge about what Teag and I really did at the store, but even he didn't know everything. Kell and Anthony had been friends for a long time, so it would be a fun group even if Teag and I couldn't say everything on our minds.

"Wouldn't you rather have some alone-time with Kell?" Teag asked, raising an eyebrow.

"Sure, but it won't be tonight," I replied. "After dinner, he's going back to help Rennie on the spook house." I paused. "Have you heard anything from Sorren? I wanted to see if he knew anything about the house, too. I texted him, but I haven't heard back. Come to think of it; I'm not even sure he's in town."

Yes, my business partner is a vampire who texts and uses both a cell phone and email. He says that immortals who don't keep up with the times don't survive. He must be planning to live forever, because he's very up on everything, from technology to clothing styles.

"I knew he was going up to the new Boston location for some-thing," Teag said. "And he mentioned Chicago and Philadelphia, but I don't know any details."

Sorren has partnered with my family for over three hundred years with Trifles and Folly, but we're not the only store he has like this. There are other locations and other long-time mortal partners. Sorren doesn't give us a lot of details because it's a dangerous business. He's been working with the Alliance—a group of mortals and immortals who protect the world from dangerous magical objects—since the Middle Ages. Unfortunately, there are some bad guys who have been working the other side of the street for just as long, and they play rough. That means that Sorren comes and goes without telling us a lot about where he's heading or when he'll be back. It might be for our own protection, but sometimes it's inconvenient as hell, and after some bad stuff happened not long ago, he'd been traveling more than ever.

"I texted him a picture of the house and the address, just in case," I said with a sigh. "He's been in Charleston long enough; he might remember something about the original builders—if there's anything worth remembering."

Dinner was fun and relaxing. We went to Forbidden City, our favorite Chinese restaurant. Teag and Anthony and I eat there often enough the staff knows our usual orders. Kell seemed happy not to talk much about the spook house, so we chatted about other things and the time passed quickly.

Around nine, Kell's phone buzzed. "Oops," he said, glancing at the screen. "That's Rennie, asking if I'm coming back to work tonight." He sighed. "I promised him I'd help out."

"Go ahead," I encouraged him. "Halloween isn't too far off, and there's a lot more left to do." I caught his gaze. "But let me know if anything else strange happens, okay?"

Kell gave me a peck on the cheek. "Will do."

Anthony finished off his sweet tea and exchanged a glance with Teag. "Unfortunately, I have to head home early, too," he said. "I've got to argue a big case tomorrow, and I need to prepare my notes." Anthony's a lawyer with his family's firm, and he's done well for himself. He looks the part of a Charleston scion—blond, tall, and well-dressed even when he's casual. Teag, on the other hand, is more likely to be in a t-shirt and jeans. His dark hair usually hangs in his eyes with his skater-boy cut. He and Anthony make a great pair, but they look like complete opposites.

Teag volunteered to drop me off back at the shop, where I had left my car. We headed to my house from there. I was disappointed that Sorren had not responded to my text, but sometimes we don't hear from him for days at a time. Teag parked and followed me in through the piazza. I could already hear Baxter, my little Maltese, barking up a storm.

I opened the door, and Teag was ready to scoop Baxter up in his hands. Bax is six pounds of pure attitude, doomed to not be reckoned a great watch dog because he resembles a marshmallow. Baxter settled down quickly as soon as we properly greeted him, which involved nuzzling and treats. I put kibble in his dish for dinner, and Teag went to get the laptop from my office so we could do a little more research on the spook house.

"You were right about the suicide," Teag said after a little while. He turned the screen and showed me the scan of an old newspaper article. "Susan Mayfair, the daughter of one of the house's owners, killed herself back in 1955. No one ever seemed to figure out why."

"That's sad. I hate when I'm right about things like that," I said. "Anything else?"

"If you were hoping for old burying grounds beneath the cellar or an owner who was a serial killer, you're out of luck," Teag said. "At least, I haven't found anything like that. And I figure if it the house had a really bad history, you'd have picked up on it right away."

I had poured us some wine, and I took a sip, then nodded. "Most of the time, yes. Except for that uneasiness I felt upstairs and knowing a death happened in that poor girl's room, I didn't feel much at all from the house—certainly nothing evil." I paused. "Except—"

Teag raised an eyebrow. "Yes?"

"I wouldn't have said the dressing table was 'evil' exactly, but I didn't like the way it made me feel. Go ahead, pull up the photo—let's see if we can find anything out about it."

Teag brought up the photo of the dressing table and mirror. I gasped. We both just stared.

There was a very clear image of a woman staring back at us—a woman who hadn't been in the room when Kell and I took the picture.

"Wow," I said after a moment. "What is *that*?"

"That," Teag said, "is probably what was making you feel uncomfortable." He glanced at me. "You didn't actually touch the mirror or table, did you?"

I shook my head. "I didn't touch anything. Kell wouldn't know what to do if I had a full-blown reaction to one of the pieces. I figured that if I picked up bad vibes, you and I could go back out tomorrow and poke around, and let Maggie mind the store."

"I think that might be a good idea," Teag said. "Because whoever she is, she doesn't look very friendly."

Teag and I searched for more information for another hour or so, but found nothing more about the house. We hadn't given up looking for details about the dressing table, but we seemed to strike out on that, too. Teag headed home, and I took Baxter out to the walled garden in my backyard for a little walk. My mind kept replaying what I had seen in the spook house, feeling as if I had missed something and not knowing what. Baxter was his insufferably cute self, and cuddling him always makes me feel better, but tonight even that only partly lifted my mood.

By the time I went to bed that night, I still hadn't heard from Sorren, although I'd left him a voice message to catch him up on what was going on. Technically, he might not consider it to be Trifles and Folly business, since none of the objects had come through the store. But the Alliance was usually on the lookout for magically dangerous items no matter what the source, and I figured he would want to know.

My dreams were dark. *I was in a shadowy hallway that was lined with mirrors. Reflections flitted in the mirrors ahead of me, just enough for me to notice they were present, but gone by the time I reached them. It felt like a game of cat and mouse, and I was definitely the mouse. In my dreams, I didn't know exactly what I was running from or what would happen if I got caught, only that it wouldn't be good to find out.*

I ran down the hallway, and it seemed to stretch on forever. The doors to other rooms slammed shut as I passed them. I could hear foot-steps behind me, and they were getting closer. My imagination showed me the spook house as it might have looked when someone lived in it— maybe something my magic had picked up without me realizing it. But it was an odd mish-mash of real life and the gory theatrical scenes.

Some rooms were normal, others filled with monsters—but in my dream, the monsters were real.

I rounded a corner and found myself in the suicide bedroom. All the furniture was covered with sheets, and the windowsills and mantle were thick with dust. But there was one piece of furniture left uncovered, and oddly enough, it didn't seem to have any dust on it at all. It was a large oval mirror on a stand. I was drawn to it, just like in the movies, when Sleeping Beauty can't seem to wake from the trance that pulls her toward the poisoned spinning wheel.

My dream self didn't stop until I was in front of the mirror. Two faces looked back at me; neither was my own. One was the dead girl. I recognized her from her obituary. The other was a thin old woman I had seen in my cell phone photo. Her gaze was piercing and malicious. She had one hand around the throat of the dead girl. And the other bony hand reached out, protruding from the mirror's surface, reaching for me—

I woke up, shaking. It took a few deep breaths to calm down and realize that I was safe at home. Baxter was at the foot of the bed, looking at me quizzically. I got out of bed and picked up Baxter, then went to make myself a cup of hot chocolate. It was just after six in the morning. Earlier than I usually ate breakfast, but I knew I wouldn't get back to sleep after those dreams.

Bax pranced and bounced as if he could read my mood and was trying to cheer me up. I fed him breakfast, then settled him into my lap as I drank a cup of coffee. On impulse, I reached for my computer.

Teag had gotten me a software program that worked like a police sketch artist, to help me draw the faces I saw when I read objects. Since I'm not much of an artist, my attempts to show Teag and others what I saw was frustrating, because everything had come out looking like Charlie Brown. With the software, I could easily play with features, face shape, and details until I got something close to being right.

I fiddled with the program settings, taking time every few minutes to sit back and sip my coffee. I made the face a little thinner, a little longer. The eyes more deep set. She had good bone structure, high cheekbones. Probably a stunner when she was young. I wondered if she looked so haggard from an illness, or if she had just gotten mean in her old age. The choices we make catch up to us as we get older, and so does our world view. Believe the worst about everyone and everything, and that's what you'll find—and it'll make you bitter and angry. I saw some of that in the mirror lady and wondered what her story was.

When the image gave me the creeps, I knew I had it right. I didn't want to look at it anymore, but I couldn't seem to look away. Except this time, I didn't feel compelled like I did in the dream. I was curious—and worried. The ghost of the dead girl—or at least, her energy—made sense to be in the house. But why was the old lady in the mirror? Who put her there? And maybe more importantly—could she get out?

I was on my second cup of coffee and had a biscuit with jam to go with it when my cell phone went off. I glanced at the time and frowned. It was barely seven—much too early for a social call. It wasn't Sorren, since he sleeps during the day—unless he was in a different time zone. Then I realized the number belonged to Kell.

"Cassidy? Did I wake you?" Kell sounded a little freaked out.

"No," I assured him. "I was up. What's wrong?"

"A bunch of us worked all night over at the spook house," Kell said. "It was fun—like a work-party. Most of the people were Rennie's core crew, plus me and a couple of others. After midnight, we finished cleaning up our materials outside and came in, so we didn't bother the neighbors. Rennie insisted we lock the doors. No one was supposed to go back out. But sometime between midnight and six, Briana disappeared."

A chill went down my spine. "What do you mean, 'disappeared?'" I asked carefully. "Maybe she left without telling anyone—perhaps because Rennie didn't want anyone to go?" It's always best to start with the most normal possibilities and then get progressively weirder than to immediately assume something supernatural.

Kell really sounded upset. "No one saw her, and we were all up and moving around. There were people downstairs, going back and forth—it would be hard to slip out with all that going on."

"Is her car missing?"

"No one remembers whether she drove or not. We haven't been able to get her to answer her cell phone, although I thought I heard it ring—she has a really unique ringtone—but it seemed very far away. Then I couldn't hear it anymore."

I took another sip of my coffee and wracked my brain for normal explanations. "Did she have a fight with anyone? Maybe a disagreement with Rennie? Could she have had a personal problem that came up and she didn't want anyone to know?" I told myself there could be a hundred different, perfectly normal, reasons Briana might have quietly let herself out the back door without wanting anyone to see her go.

"No—at least, not that anyone is saying. Rennie swears they didn't argue. No one overheard her on the phone, so if she got an emergency call, she didn't tell anyone."

"Did you check the accident reports? Maybe she was out of cigarettes and desperate for a smoke and figured she could get to the all-night drugstore and back again before anyone noticed." It was a slim chance, but possible.

"Briana doesn't smoke," Kell said. "And even though Rennie seems pretty easy-going, none of his crew would go against his direct order for something stupid like cigarettes. He runs a tight ship, and he expects people to do as he says."

"Did you call the police?"

"How can I call the police when we aren't even sure she's really missing?" Kell sounded like he was pacing. "Everyone's worried, and they'll be pissed if it turns out she just went AWOL. Rennie won't be thrilled, either. That's just it—I don't think she'd risk her job to go off without a really, really good reason."

"Did anything else change since I was there?" I had finished my coffee, but I toyed with the empty cup as I spoke.

"No. Well, one thing but I can't imagine how it would be related."

"What?" I asked.

"We got another shipment of furniture from Rennie's supplier. Some of it's kind of weird stuff—not so surprising. But there were also two more pieces to that mirrored vanity table you said gave you the creeps. I was going to show you the next time you came over."

"I don't know how—or if—it has anything to do with Briana's disappearance," I said. "But I'd like to bring Teag and come over as soon as I can get Maggie in to cover the store."

"I was hoping you'd say that," Kell said, sounding relieved. "See you soon."

Maggie agreed to open the store, so Teag and I met Kell at the spook house by nine. He looked haggard. Part of that, I chalked up to working all night. But Kell was definitely worried, and something that was very unusual for him—he was scared.

"Thanks so much for coming," he said when we parked. I noticed he had been waiting for us by the driveway, not inside the house.

"Where is everyone?" I asked. I assumed people would still be around since they spent the night working.

"Rennie sent everyone home," Kell said, and ran a hand back through his hair. I had thought to bring him a travel mug of fresh coffee and a donut. He accepted both gratefully.

"What about Briana?" I asked.

"No one's seen her," Kell replied. "Her car is at her apartment. Turns out she rode over here with a friend—who hasn't seen her since then. No one else took her home. She isn't picking up on her cell phone. It's not like her."

"Let's go through the house, and see if we can pick up on anything," I said, with a glance back at Teag, who nodded. I knew he had my back, but heading into the spook house still made me nervous, even though the lights were on and it was broad daylight.

I could tell the team had gotten a lot done overnight. Outside, the house was done up like something out of a monster movie—the perfect abandoned, ramshackle haunted house. The team had added a lot of decorations in the yard like tombstones and zombies that looked like they were clawing their way out of the lawn. I saw speakers in the eaves to serenade the people waiting in the queue with creepy music. In fact, the path for the line wound through a corn maze where guests could get a head start on being scared to death by actors jumping around dark corners.

Not much seemed to have changed on the first floor, but those decorations had been well-along when I had visited the first time. Heading upstairs, I could see more evidence of how hard Rennie's team had worked to get ready for the crowds. Ghoulish paintings hung on the wall. Lots of fake spider webs stretched artfully from the balustrade to the chandelier and between furnishings. I almost leaped out of my skin when I stepped on the carpet, and the sound of a chainsaw roared to life right beside my ear.

"Pretty cool, huh?" Kell said, and I knew that despite his worry for Briana, he was still in love with the haunted house. I hoped nothing we found spoiled that fun for him.

"Yeah," I replied, slightly less enthusiastically. "Cool. That was just the word I was looking for," I added, trying to get the hearing back in my right ear.

This time, we started at the "suicide" room. "This was where Briana was working right before she disappeared," Kell said.

I willed myself to walk into the room. The impressions I had picked up of the unfortunate former occupant were not so strong this time, perhaps because it was daylight. Teag moved around the room slowly, paying special attention to the draperies and bedclothes. His magic is different from mine, but he can pick up if fabrics have any supernatural power. He touched the curtains and recoiled as if he had burned his hand.

"These are original to the room, aren't they?" he asked, looking at the draperies warily.

Kell nodded. "We think so."

"They were here when Susan killed herself," Teag said quietly. "She used the drapery rod and one of the curtain tie-backs to hang herself. That kind of thing leaves an imprint—a magical mark."

"What does that mean?" Kell asked. He looked a little surprised at Teag's comment, and I knew that at some point, I'd have to figure out how to explain at least part of it to Kell, especially if I wanted to keep going out with him.

"It's not dangerous," Teag explained. "But it stained the energy of the room, and since the curtains were here—and a part of what happened—they hold that stained energy more than the room itself did. That's what's amplifying the negative energy."

Kell nodded. "All right. We can see about replacing them. I want people to have fake scares that are fun, not real scares that aren't." He paused. "Anything about Briana?"

Neither Teag nor I are psychics. We can't tell the future or read minds. But doing appraisals at the shop has given both of us a good eye for detail, and so we made a slow walk around Susan Mayfair's bedroom, looking for any sign of Briana that Kell and the others might have missed.

"Was the house remodeled?" I asked, eyeing the uneven wallpaper and a closet in the corner of the room, near the hallway wall, that seemed to be in an awkward location.

Kell nodded. "Yeah. Probably several times. It's not in the historic district, so people made modifications whenever they needed more space. We never got the original blueprints, but we think the original owners used this as a maid's bedroom."

Nothing else in the suicide bedroom made us pause, so we worked our way back to the nursery. I stopped in the doorway so fast that Teag ran into me.

"Whoa!" I said. "Where did *they* come from?"

At least two dozen old-fashioned dolls sat or stood at various places throughout the nursery. Many of the dolls were broken, which added to the creepiness. Some of the porcelain faces were cracked. Others were missing an eye or a limb. The dolls' hair was original, and many had bald spots or places where the hair had been cut lopsidedly. Their clothing was stained and torn, faded and discolored. Most were missing one or both shoes.

"Rennie got them from a junk dealer who said they'd been in a box in his basement for years," Kell replied. "The guy thought his father might have bought them cheap from the thrift store since they were damaged." And the thrift store would have taken the broken dolls in with donations, cast-offs from people who didn't want them anymore.

"No one's actually going into that room, right?" I asked.

Kell looked at me oddly. "Why?"

Even without touching the dolls, I felt an overpowering sense of loneliness and abandonment—and anger. The dolls held onto the strong childhood emotions of the ones who had given them up. They were not a cheery, welcoming crowd. "Anyone with even a low-level psychic sensitivity is going to be weirded out by them," I replied. Then again, I suspected that people who had some level of sensitivity avoided spook houses, whether or not they knew exactly why.

The last room was the master bedroom. It still had the four-poster bed with the dead mannequin in it, but I was prepared this time when the "body" sat up and screamed. Even so, I flinched away and found myself staring into the mirror.

For just a heartbeat, Briana stared back at me, then vanished.

"There! Did you see her?" I pointed at the vanity table mirror, heart thudding.

Teag and Kell shook their heads. "I saw Briana in the mirror—just for a second," I said.

Teag met my gaze. "Are you certain?" I knew Teag didn't doubt me. What he was really trying to figure out, without discussing magic in front of Kell, was how that was possible.

"I'm sure it was Briana," I said. "But she looked different from the way the old lady seemed that I saw before."

"In what way?" Kell asked. It encouraged me that he was intrigued instead of frightened. That boded well for the future.

I thought, trying to put my thoughts into words. "The old lady I saw seemed to be inside the mirror. With Briana, I felt like I was looking through a window to somewhere else." I sighed. "I know that doesn't make any sense, but it's the best I can do."

Kell took a piece of paper out of his pocket and unfolded it to show me a sketch of a woman's face. "One of the lighting techs drew this. He says he saw this woman looking back at him from the mirror. He won't come in the room, after that."

Teag looked over my shoulder. "That's Susan Mayfair, the one who hanged herself. I saw her obituary in an online database. It had a picture."

I glanced down at the dressing table, mostly to keep from staring in that damned mirror. That's when I noticed the two new mirrors. One was a tray, made to hold a fancy brush and comb set, and the other was a hand mirror. The three pieces had matching frames, so it was clear they were a set. "That's new," I said, pointing.

Kell nodded. "Yeah. They were in the same shipment as the dolls. Rennie said the three pieces went together, so we put them together."

Teag and I exchanged a glance. I was certain he was thinking what I was thinking. "Do you have Briana's phone number?" I asked.

Kell pulled out his phone and dialed it. "Yeah. I've been trying it on and off. No answer." Yet I could hear distant music—a song I recognized from the Rocky Horror Picture Show.

"Did you hear that?" Teag asked. I motioned for him to be quiet, and closed my eyes, moving toward the sound. It was faint, and just as I thought I had gotten a lock on it, the sound stopped. I opened my eyes and found myself up against the dressing table.

"I swear it was louder near the mirror," I said, and dared to stare at the silver surface, but I saw just my own reflection.

"Are you saying that... something... took Briana and Susan Mayfair inside a mirror?" Kell asked incredulously.

Actually, I had wondered about that, but I hadn't said it out loud. "I've heard of spirits being trapped in a mirror," I said carefully. "There are particular circumstances that apply. I think we need to do more research."

"Kell," I said, "are the crews going to be working on the house tonight?"

He shook his head. "No. Rennie thought we had gotten enough done; everyone needed a break. I think he's hoping we find Briana and then we can all get our heads back in the game."

"Do you think he would allow us to come back tonight to see if we can deal with whatever's in the mirror before it hurts someone—and see if we can get Briana back?"

Kell frowned. "Why do you have to come back at night? Can't you do whatever it is you need to do now?"

I paused. Kell had trusted us enough to ask for our help. Now I needed to trust him with a little more of the truth. Briana's life might depend on it. "I think that the old woman whose face I saw the first time in the mirror was a witch."

"Wiccan?"

I shook my head. "No. I mean someone who seeks out supernatural power in order to hurt or control other people."

Kell raised an eyebrow. "Those are real?"

Teag and I both nodded. "Yeah. And we need some people with special skills to deal with it."

I could see Kell struggling. "All right," he said. "But I want to come with you." He had a stubborn set to his jaw. "Either I come, or it's no deal. For one thing, Rennie trusts me with access to the house, so I have a responsibility to manage that. And secondly, Briana is a friend. If we can get her back, I want to help." He met my gaze. "Do I need to remind you that I have all kinds of special equipment that might help?" That was true. SPOOK was pretty well outfitted with ghost hunting gadgets. "So what do you say?"

I glanced at Teag. He shrugged, telling me it was my call. "Okay," I said. "But follow our lead. We run into this kind of thing more than you'd think."

Kell didn't look like he liked the terms, but he finally nodded. "All right. Anything to get Briana back and keep anyone else from getting hurt."

We agreed to meet back at the spook house after eleven that night. Teag turned to look at me when we drove away. "I don't know how Sorren is going to feel about having Kell along."

"I'll text him, while you do some more research," I replied. "He hasn't been here, so he doesn't get to decide. Kell's got a point about being responsible to Rennie. I don't want to put him in a bad spot."

"And if it gets too wild, Sorren can always glamor him and make him forget?"

That really wasn't a path I wanted to go down with Kell, especially if we were going to think about being a couple. It wasn't fair to erase his memories, and it wasn't honest. But sometimes, it couldn't be helped. "Hopefully not," I replied. "He's a ghost hunter. We can explain a lot of strange things to him that other people don't understand."

"What else?"

"I'm going to call Father Anne as soon as we get to my place," I replied. "And leave a voice mail for Sorren to bring him up to speed. Let's just hope Father Anne is free for some exorcising tonight."

Back at my house, I fed Baxter while Teag pulled his laptop out of his messenger bag and set up on my dining room table. "Hexenspiegel," he said, after a few minutes.

"Witch mirrors," I replied. I had run into them before and wondered if Teag had followed the same train of thought I had when we saw the faces in the reflections.

Teag nodded. "Yeah. It's a way to trap an evil witch in a mirror like one of those fun houses that have so many reflections; you can't find your way out."

I pulled up the sketch program I had used to draw the face from my dreams. "Can you do anything from this?" I asked.

While Teag searched the deepest recesses of the internet, I paced, checking my cell phone every few minutes for phone calls even though the ringer was on high. When it did ring, I jumped.

"What's up?" Father Anne asked, getting right down to business. She's not what most people picture as an Episcopalian priest, with spiky short black hair, tattoos of several saints on her arms, and a penchant for wearing Doc Martens when we need to go ghost whupping. She's also a member of the St. Expeditus Society, a secret group of priests who help out with setting supernatural threats to rest. We've worked with Father Anne on several occasions, and she's good in a fight. I hoped it wouldn't come to that.

Father Anne listened as I explained what was going on, and what we suspected about the witch mirror. "Sounds like my kind of fun," she said when I finished. "Give me the address of the spook house. I'll meet you there."

"Well, that's something," I said as I put my phone back in my pocket. I called Sorren again, left an updated voice mail, and tried not to grind my teeth in frustration.

"I think I've found a couple things that might be useful," Teag said. "Quit pacing and come over to look."

I pulled up a chair where I could see his screen. "First off, what do you think—is this the woman from your dream, the one you saw in the mirror?" He brought up an old photograph. The woman's hair was slightly different, and she looked a little younger, but the hard set to her jaw and the cold eyes were unmistakable.

"That's her."

"Her name was Wilomena Patten," Teag said. "The photo is from her obituary, so it's of her when she was younger. At one time, she lived in the spook house. That was about five years ago. Wilomena died without any heirs, and the property was foreclosed for back taxes."

"So whatever magic she had didn't make her wealthy," I observed.

Teag shrugged. "A lot of people aren't into magic for money—they want control. Reading between the lines, I don't get the impression very many people liked Wilomena. Maybe that's why."

"What else?" I glanced at my phone again. Sorren hadn't called, so I checked the time instead.

"I found this," Teag said, and another photo came up on the screen. I recognized the vanity table and mirror sets immediately. "Where did you find that?" I asked.

He grinned and waggled his fingers. "My Google-fu is strong," he intoned. "Actually, it was at the public auction on the house. And from what I can see, the three pieces didn't sell. Someone bid on them, but they backed out at the last minute. So the best I can figure out is that the auctioneer has had them in a back room all this time."

That would figure, especially if the pieces had bad juju. Pretty as they were—and maybe even valuable—buyers would shy away. I wondered why the auctioneer hadn't just junked the pieces. Maybe Wilomena was still able to exert some control from beyond the grave.

"You're sure it's the same auctioneer Rennie used to source the pieces for the spook house?"

Teag nodded. "Yeah. I wonder if the auctioneer has noticed a difference with the mirrors gone. Like his health improving or more money coming in. I wouldn't be surprised."

I went to the fridge and poured glasses of iced tea for both of us. There isn't much in life that can't be made better by a glass of ice-cold tea with enough sugar to make you vibrate. "They'd had the vanity table for a little while at the spook house. It just caused some minor paranormal activity. What made it suddenly get so dangerous?"

Teag brought up another photo. "I think the mirror pieces were separated for a while," he said. "Look—in this auction photo, it's just the table with the larger mirror in back and the hand mirror. No tray. But all three pieces are in the spook house—the house that Wilomena used to own until she died and outsiders 'stole' it from her."

"So the tray went missing for a while," I speculated. "Maybe it got mixed in with other stuff from the house, off in another crate some-where. They auctioneer finds it and just so happens to get a call from Rennie for props—for the house that Wilomena used to live in." I'll chalk one or two things up to coincidence, but not this many. It sounded to me like Wilomena was using her power to orchestrate the situation.

"But what does she want with Susan Mayfair's ghost—and Briana?" I asked.

Teag leaned back in his chair and sipped his tea. "We don't know whether Wilomena was forced into the mirror by someone else, or chose to send her spirit in there because she knew she was dying," he said. "If it was the second situation, perhaps she was growing weaker. If she needed an energy boost, she might have been able to get one from trapping Susan's spirit in with her."

"And Briana?" I asked, feeling a shiver go down my spine.

"I'm not sure she's dead," Teag replied. "But I don't know where she is. And I think that whatever occurred, Wilomena made it happen."

I drained my glass and poured myself another one. I couldn't be more jumpy with caffeine and sugar than I already was. "I wish Sorren was here."

"Maybe he'll get your message," Teag said. "Stranger things have happened."

~

Eleven o'clock rolled around faster than I expected, and Teag and I found ourselves back at the spook house with Father Anne and Kell. Father Anne was wearing a clerical collar over a black t-shirt, black jeans, and her Doc Martens. Teag and I brought some of the magical items we use to protect ourselves and fend off supernatural bad nasties. Kell had enough ghost hunter gear that it made me want to start humming the theme to Ghostbusters.

By night, the spook house looked much more intimidating than in the daytime. Rennie and his special effects crew knew what they were doing. I'd been in plenty of genuinely scary abandoned houses, most of which did a good job of hiding just how dangerous they were until you were inside.

This house had been designed to prey on every Hollywood horror trope, from the boarded up windows to the shutters that were rigged to "flap" against the siding, to the creepy, lit-from-below lighting that gave me the shivers.

"Just remember, it's all fake, except for the mirror and the ghost," Kell said from behind me.

"It's the 'except' part that might be the sticking point," Teag replied. He and I had come with plenty of gear to take on paranormal threats. I still hadn't figured out how I would explain that part to Kell yet. I knew that Teag had a net made of knotted rope soaked in colloidal silver, and another fine metal net with a powdered silver coating. He also had his fighting staff, carved with runes and juiced up with rope knots that stored magic power, which made him a formidable opponent. Just for luck, he wore a hamsa charm and an *agimat*, both talismans to ward against evil.

I had an old dog collar on my left wrist that could summon a ghostly dog protector, my wooden athame up my right sleeve, and an old Norse spindle whorl in my pocket to amp up my magic. For protection, I wore an agate necklace and had rings and bracelets made of onyx and tourmaline.

Father Anne had her faith, a potent weapon in itself, and in case that wasn't enough, an old boline knife from a long-dead priest that had its own potent magic. If Sorren got here in time, we'd have his vampire strength and speed, always an advantage. I checked my phone, but there were no new texts. I swore under my breath, then sighed and squared my shoulders. We'd have to handle this without him.

Kell had his ghost hunter equipment—EMF readers and audio recorders and temperature detectors. None of that would protect him. Those gadgets were all about proving the existence of ghosts. If the spirit in the mirror was really behind Briana's disappearance, I was afraid that our problem wouldn't be getting a ghost to manifest—it would be making the ghost disappear. Then I noticed Kell had also brought a Louisville Slugger. Maybe he was going to be all right after all.

"Everybody ready?" Kell asked as we stood on the sidewalk.

"I really think you should let us handle this and stay here, on watch," I said.

Kell shook his head. "That wouldn't be right. Rennie trusts me with access. I'm responsible if anything goes wrong—or if anyone gets hurt. I should be there." I couldn't argue with him. Based on what he knew, we were all a bunch of amateurs doing our best to find Briana. And knowing how stubborn Kell was, he might not agree to back off even if we did tell him that Teag and I had the supernatural vigilante gig down to a science.

"Let's go," I said, and Teag gave a curt nod.

I tuned in to my gift, listening hard with all of my senses. When a place is deeply haunted, sometimes I can't help picking up on the resonance just by walking across the ground. I hadn't sensed such a strong, malicious presence either of the times I had visited before, but now, my sixth sense was screaming for me to get out of there. I kept on walking, forcing myself to pay attention to what my ability was telling me. Out here, the images were distant but still disturbing. I sensed Susan Mayfair's distress, and the dislocation her spirit felt after her suicide, along with a new and panicked desperation. I sensed another, darker entity, and knew that it was the ghost of the woman I had seen in the mirror. What I couldn't pick up was any sign of Briana. I took that as a good sign—maybe she was still alive.

"She knows we're here," I murmured.

Teag glanced at me. "Dangerous?"

I nodded. "Until proven otherwise."

"I just want to find Briana—alive," Kell said. He looked pale and nervous, but I knew from the set of his jaw that he was going to see this thing through.

My sense of foreboding grew stronger as we walked up to the house. I wish psychic gifts came with an on/off switch, but they don't. Kell unlocked the door and switched on the lights.

"Wow." Teag and Father Anne spoke at the same instant. The downstairs tableaus were as I remembered them from my previous visit, garish and theatrical in the electric light. Still, they were done well enough to send a chill down my spine. Not real, but real enough to evoke a level of primal fear.

"This is fake. The real work is upstairs," I said.

Teag led the way. Kell insisted on going next. Father Anne was third, which put me in the rear. I turned back frequently to make certain nothing was following us, but the stairs were empty. The feeling of dread grew stronger as we climbed, and I wondered if the others felt any of the psychic energy that was the equivalent of a "no trespassing" sign in neon.

Every step felt leaden. I wondered what the others were feeling. They looked scared and nervous. But beneath it all, I felt something else. Wilomena's ghost knew we were coming. So did Susan. We were too far away for me to gather much from the resonance. But I did pick up that one ghost was hoping for rescue, and the other was bent on vengeance.

Just before we reached the landing, Teag paused. "Did you hear that?" he whispered.

"I heard something," Kell replied. "Just not sure what." Teag slipped up the last few steps, his staff raised to strike, and Kell was right behind him. Kell had his EMF monitor in one hand and his baseball bat in the other. He flipped the switch for the hallway lights, but they didn't work.

"Damn," Kell muttered. We had come prepared with flashlights, but I didn't like the fact that something was tampering with the electrical system. Wilomena was getting stronger, and that meant trouble.

"Listen!" I hissed. A distant banging sounded through the old house. I couldn't place where it was coming from. "What's that?"

"Pretty sure we're going to find out," Father Anne muttered. She had an iron cross in one hand and her blessed boline knife in the other. Both were formidable weapons.

One by one, we emerged onto the second floor. Our lights drove back the shadows, but could not dispel them completely. Wan moonlight filtered from the bedrooms into the hallway. We dared to step toward the master bedroom, where Wilomena's mirrors were located. That's when we saw them.

The dolls were waiting for us. They emerged from the shadows with shambling steps, their wooden and porcelain feet thumping against the floorboards. Their faces were expressionless, but their arms were outstretched in unmistakable threat. How they had managed to get from the nursery to where they stood, blocking the hall, I did not want to know, but I could guess. Wilomena had gotten strong enough to make them move, and she was using them to defend herself.

Teag went first, swinging his staff to clear a path. Kell followed with his baseball bat, knocking the wooden bodies out of the way and sending them tumbling down the hallway. The dolls slammed against the walls and crashed into the shadows, but they came crawling back, dragging their damaged bodies along the floor, intent on stopping us.

Father Anne muttered a prayer against evil as she landed a martial arts kick that threw four of the dolls out of the way. I let the old dog collar on my left arm jangle down around my wrist, and the glowing, ghostly figure of a large dog materialized beside me, my old Golden Retriever, Bo. Bo's head was down, and his teeth were bared. He leaped and took down five of the dolls. They flailed at him but could not do him any damage.

Father Anne dodged to the right, and I dove left, letting the wooden athame beneath my right sleeve fall down into my hand. I drew on the strong emotions and memories invested in that old wooden spoon and sent a blast of cold, white power down the hallway that swept a dozen of the dolls out of our way.

My cell phone buzzed in my pocket with a text message, but there was no time to look at it now. The thumping was louder, though I still couldn't figure out where it was coming from. The dolls weren't giving us time to think. Bo's ghost swung his blocky head, knocking the dolls out of the way, but they got back up and kept on coming. My athame's blast sent the dolls reeling but didn't destroy them.

Kell was swearing under his breath as he used his bat like a croquet hammer, knocking dolls this way and that. Teag was fighting off a dozen dolls that were grabbing at his legs and clinging to his staff with their arms and legs. I didn't want to ruin Rennie's decorations, but I drew the line on handling them with care when they attacked.

Even without touching the dolls or the walls of the house, I could sense dark energy all around us. That creepy feeling the mirror had given me when I first visited was now much, much stronger, and every primal instinct warned me to run. Something had juiced up Wilomena's energy, and now that she had a taste of power, she wanted more.

I heard something on the steps behind us, and turned, hoping Sorren had been able to join us. Instead, I saw the glint of light on a knife blade just in time to dodge out of the way as the mannequin from the bathroom tableau lurched toward me. Bathroom Bertha's face was a maniacal grimace, and her jointed body moved stiffly. I yelped and dove out of the way, bringing my heavy metal flashlight down hard enough to shatter the mannequin's plastic cheek. It only made her more horrific as she kept on going, unharmed. I leveled my athame and sent a blast toward her, knocking her down the stairs, but I was certain she would be back—unless we could stop Wilomena.

"Kell and I will hold the hallway," Teag said. He and Kell stood shoulder to shoulder, blocking the dolls from getting closer to the entrance of the master bedroom. "Cassidy, Father Anne—get to that mirror!"

I managed to avoid stepping on the hidden button that would make the corpse on the bed shriek and move, but it sat up anyhow with a bloodcurdling scream that made both Father Anne and me jump. "Over there!" I said, pointing toward the vanity table, while I held the light on the bed to make sure the figure wasn't going to come after us. The pounding had grown louder, and it seemed to come from everywhere at once. I watched the door, having no desire for Bathroom Bertha to sneak up on us. A scrabbling noise from the direction of the stairs made me suspect she was already dragging her way back for a rematch.

"I see them!" Father Anne said, and I spared a glance toward the mirrors. Poor, doomed Susan Mayfair's ghost was pressed against the mirror, screaming soundlessly as she tried to escape. Wilomena tore her away from the glass, and as Father Anne moved closer, Wilomena's ghostly arm stretched beyond the mirrored surface, and grabbed at Father Anne's shirt, pulling her off balance.

I dove to help Father Anne, grabbing her with my left hand and pulling her back from the mirror while with my right hand, I sent a blast of cold white power from my athame down the connection from me to Father Anne and through Wilomena's grasp beyond the surface of the mirror.

Wilomena shrieked with rage. Father Anne wrested her arm free of Wilomena's grasp. Outside in the hallway, I heard Teag and Kell slamming wooden dolls out of the way like a demented bowling tournament. The pounding continued, rattling through the whole house. My phone kept buzzing in my pocket. Behind me, I caught a glimpse of Bathroom Bertha with her prop knife clearing the stairs and lurching through the doorway.

Bo's ghost gave a deep, dangerous growl and leaped at the homicidal mannequin, hitting Bathroom Bertha at chest level and taking them both to the ground. The mannequin's prop knife looked sharp enough to be a hazard, but it couldn't hurt Bo. His spirit, empowered by my magic, was strong enough to make him solid enough to do some damage. He bit at the figure's mechanical arm, grabbing the wrist between his strong jaws and refusing to let go as Bathroom Bertha flopped from side to side trying to shake him off.

Father Anne raised the boline knife to shatter the mirrors. "Wait!" I yelled. "If you do that, we'll never free Susan's spirit!"

I knew what I had to do, even though I didn't like it. "Anchor me!" I shouted to Father Anne. Then I dove toward the mirror and felt my arm sink through the glass as if it were water instead of solid.

"Susan!" I shouted. Susan Mayfair's ghost grabbed for my hand as Wilomena surged forward. I closed my grip on Susan's cold hand, solid here behind the mirror. I hurled her past me, toward the mirror's surface, out of this place between life and death that had imprisoned her. Father Anne had a hold of me by the waist, anchoring me in the world of the living.

Susan's ghost fled the mirror-world through my body, and I shivered uncontrollably. Wilomena screamed in fury and grabbed my shoulders with her bony hands.

"She was nearly used up," Wilomena's voice grated as she pulled me toward her. "You'll do nicely instead."

Bo was barking in a frenzy, but he couldn't get through the mirror to help me. I had slipped my athame back up my sleeve to grab Susan, and now I let it slide back and drew on the stored memories of the old wooden spoon, as my fear and anger juiced up my power. The blast caught Wilomena square in the chest, but the old witch hung on, trying to grab my athame away from me.

Father Anne pulled hard. I felt like I might be torn in two. Suddenly, the cold metal mesh of Teag's net fell over my head and shoulders, enveloping me and the vanity table's mirror in its silver knots. Wilomena's grasp faltered, and Father Anne jerked me back out of the mirror. I stumbled backward, but my head came up just in time to see Father Anne bring her boline knife down into the hand mirror.

Wilomena screamed, throwing herself at the mirror to grab Father Anne and drag her into the shadow world, but the silver net kept her back. The knife hit the small mirror and shattered the glass an instant before Teag slammed his staff into the mirrored tray and then pivoted to splinter the larger vanity table mirror. Father Anne had been chanting all along, and as I got to my feet, I realized it was the Rite of Exorcism which she finished in one final shout as the mirrors cracked.

Wilomena's apparition was gone. I was breathing hard, and so were Teag and Father Anne. But before I could say anything, Father Anne turned toward the far corner of the room where Susan Mayfair's sad ghost hovered in the shadows.

"Would you be free?" Father Anne asked gently. Susan nodded. Father Anne spoke in Latin, a phrase I had heard her use before—a blessing to speed the dead safely on their way. Susan's spirit faded as if she had been waiting all these years for permission to move on. I blinked my eyes, and she was gone.

That's when I realized someone was missing. "Where's Kell?"

"Out here," Kell said, poking his head into the bedroom. "Whatever you did took the juice right out of the dolls," he said. "Did it work?"

I glanced at the ruined, shattered mirrors and shuddered. "Yeah," I replied. "It worked." Just then, the pounding started again.

"Wilomena's spirit is gone," Father Anne said. "She can't be doing that."

In the moment that Wilomena had grabbed me on the other side of the mirror, my touch magic took in a lot of information, but since I was fighting for my life, I didn't have time to think about it just then. Now, a few of the pieces fell into place.

"I think I know what's going on," I said, trying hard to make sense of the jumble of impressions I had gained. The others followed me warily past the limp, motionless bodies of the dolls that littered the hallway, back to the suicide room, Susan's room. The pounding grew louder and more desperate.

I walked toward the far wall and began knocking. Immediately, the pounding stopped. Someone on the other side of the wall echoed the pattern of my knocks. "Here," I said, pointing. In the dim light, it was just possible to make out something I'd missed before—a thin line where a door was hidden by the pattern in the wallpaper. I slid my hands down the wall until I found a clasp and pushed. The door clicked and sprang open.

Briana staggered out. "Oh thank god!" she said, looking frazzled and wild-eyed. "I didn't think anyone was ever going to find me."

Kell looked at me. "How did you know?"

I hesitated. Kell is a good friend, and maybe more, but he still didn't know much about my magic, and I wasn't quite ready to let him in on all the secrets, at least not just yet. "Wilomena's ghost trapped Susan's spirit to feed off her energy," I explained. "I had a feeling that Wilomena might have found a way to imprison Briana to draw from her, too."

Briana looked shaken and wan. "I don't know anyone named Wilomena," she said. "But I found that hidden door and went inside to see what was what. It's an old servants' staircase, but the bottom exit has been covered over. The door slammed, and I couldn't get out. Then I fell down the stairs and must have got knocked out for a while." She shivered, and I could see the bruise on her forehead. "Let me tell you, being trapped in this spook house is going to give me nightmares for the rest of my life." She glared at Kell. "Rennie owes me a bonus."

"I'll drive her home," Father Anne offered. "I think my job here is done." I thanked her, while Teag and Kell walked out to the hall and found that the lights now worked fine.

"Rennie's going to be glad we found Briana, but he's not going to like the mess," Kell said, taking in the broken dolls and Bathroom Bertha's mangled form. He sighed. "It could have been worse. I'll get my team to come out tomorrow and help me put things right."

Teag recovered his net from the vanity table. I watched the shattered mirrors closely, but no sign of Wilomena remained. "Thank you," Kell said, glancing from Teag to me. "I'm not exactly sure how you did some of the things I thought I saw you do, but I don't need to know," he said. "At least, not right now," he added with a smile intended for me. I smiled back.

Kell walked us back to Teag's car. "I've got a call into Rennie," he said. "I'd better wait here for him. He said he'd be over to see the damage." He managed a wan grin. "I owe you both a good dinner. Let me get Halloween and the spook house over with, and we'll go celebrate."

I got in Teag's car, and my phone buzzed again. I pulled it out of my pocket and saw a message from Sorren. "Got caught up with some bad business in Philadelphia that's going to take more time," I read aloud. "Can you handle the problem on your own?"

Teag and I both laughed. "What are you going to tell him?" Teag asked.

I was already busy texting a reply. "Problem handled," I read aloud. "All in a night's work."

BONUS

VANITIES

I WAS DEAD WHEN I FIRST SAW ANTWERP.

The year was 1565. I had only been dead for about one hundred years.

"Isn't it beautiful?" Alard was my traveling companion and the vampire who made me. It was nighttime, and we came up to the deck of the ship to see the city as we came into port.

"I didn't realize the city was quite so… big." Alard had been telling me about the city for years. But even so, the sight would have taken my breath away, if I still had breath to take. Ships filled the port. Buildings towered over the shoreline and the lights of the torches and candles glittered in the River Scheldt. Above it all were the spires of the Cathedral of our Lady, not yet one hundred years old, one of the newest of Antwerp's wonders. Behind the cathedral, brooding and old, hunkered the fortified castle of Het Steen, still watching over the city and the river from the empty, darkened eye sockets of its deep-set windows.

"Big and full of diamonds," Alard said with a grin that showed his elongated eye teeth plainly.

Before Alard turned me, I had been a petty thief in Bruges. A very good thief, meaning, I was good at what I did, although my marks

285

might not have thought me a good person. I ate regularly, had a warm place to live, and eluded the Watch, which is to say, I was at the top of my game. Until I died.

I'd got myself into the home of a well-heeled nobleman, and managed to work all twenty of the mechanical locks on his infernal strongbox. That was my specialty, lockboxes. I had the touch for the gears and an ear for the way they fit together. The job had been worth the risk. The box was full of gold and jewels. I'd even thought that I might quit thieving and open a respectable pub if the take was large enough. Oh, I had plenty of dreams, until things went sour.

That night, I was spotted by the Watch when I was almost over the wall. I might have outrun them, except that I landed badly when I jumped from the top of the wall and turned my ankle. I ran blindly and took shelter in an abandoned warehouse. Alard found me before the guards did. I knew what the Watch would do if they caught me. First, they'd cut off my hands for thieving, and then my head.

I can still remember what Alard said to me. *Do you want to be the best thief in the world?* Since the choice was between truly dead and dead with benefits, I took him up on his offer.

And now, here we were sailing into Antwerp for the biggest theft of our, um, lives. For the first time in a long while I missed the way my heart used to beat faster before a job, the way my breath came short and quick, and the feel of a light sheen of sweat on my brow. But now I was stronger, faster, and immortal, and I could levitate, a little. I still thought I'd made a good trade.

"Sorren, are you listening to me at all?" There was exasperation in Alard's voice, but beneath it, joviality. On the whole, he was a very good-natured dead man, not at all the way I'd pictured a vampire back when I thought such things were only in children's tales.

"When was the last time you were in Antwerp?" I hurried to bring my focus back to our conversation.

Alard thought for a moment. "I was here quite a bit during the textile 'wars.' And before that, I made most of my fortune in the silver exchange with the Spaniards. But the first time I saw Antwerp, none of this was here." He swept his arm to encompass the waterfront crowded full of buildings and wharves. "The Het Steen was newly built, and I always thought it glowered over the river." I could guess where his thoughts went after that. He'd been the youngest son of a noble family, thrown into the Het Steen's prison as security for his father's debts. There he had languished until a visitor came one evening and offered him a different sort of freedom. By my reckoning, that made Alard over three hundred years old. But to everyone else, with his blond hair, crisp blue eyes and slightly crooked nose in an otherwise perfect face, he looked like the young aristocrat he had once been, just over the cusp of thirty and certainly in his prime.

I wasn't convinced, that despite the care Alard devoted to teaching me to choose a wardrobe befitting my new station in life, I'd ever look the part of a noble with as much grace as he did. I'd been in my late twenties when he'd turned me. My hair was a dark, unremarkable blond and I was wiry and thin-built. Great for slipping through windows, but not so good for impressing women with my physique. Alard told me once that I had good enough looks to not stand out, and not quite perfect enough looks to be remembered. I wasn't sure whether or not that was a compliment, but being easily forgettable is good for a thief. In fact, the only feature anyone had ever really remarked on was my eyes. They're blue-gray, and my mother said they were the color of the sea when a storm's coming. I worried, a bit, that being dead might change them. It didn't.

"We've got a busy schedule ahead," Alard said, with a note of resignation as if he realized I'd been woolgathering again. "Let's get below and take our bags. We'll wait until the rest of the passengers are off the ship. The less notice we attract, the better."

We'd taken a night passage ship for obvious reasons. There were few other passengers, and the inside cabins were ridiculously cheap. The ship had seen better days, and its captain was happy for the coin. Even so, I had the feeling that Alard knew the man. Alard knew everyone. Now, with a big job in front of us, that could be both a blessing and a curse.

Alard left me with the bags. "I thought we were supposed to be two gentlemen on holiday," I grumbled. I wasn't surprised to find Alard's bag was heavier than mine.

"Who told you that?" Alard's tone was flat, but a smile quirked around the corners of his mouth.

"Forget it." While I would have found the bags heavy as a mortal, their weight wasn't what bothered me. They were bulky and awkward, and I wasn't happy being the valet.

"Two gentlemen might be remembered. As a collector of fine art and artifacts, I might even be remembered. No one will take a second look at my valet."

"Thanks a lot."

I followed Alard through the winding, cobblestone streets, taking every opportunity to twist my neck to see the buildings around me. I hadn't existed for enough centuries to become jaded yet, and part of me hoped I never would. Even Alard, as old as he was, still managed to have a spark of curiosity about him. He'd told me once that the vampires who survived the changing times were the ones who never stopped being curious. Then he told me that by that measure, I'd outlive them all. I'm still not sure whether that was meant to be a good thing or not. I took it as a plus. So far, being dead (perhaps "undead" was a better word) had been good to me.

Alard stopped in front of a small shop several streets behind the waterfront. A sign said "*Vanities*," and, from the window, I could see that it was one of the antiques and curio shops that Alard favored.

"In here. Be quick about it." Alard motioned for me to maneuver our bags through the narrow door. The shop looked closed. I was about to protest that breaking into a shop might attract the attention we were trying to escape, when a lamp flared behind us, its glow shaded to avoid making it too easy for passers-by to see.

"Alard. Come in."

I put the bags where Alard bid and followed as Alard and our host continued, more than began, a lively conversation. Two things stood out to me: they were obviously old friends, and our host was clearly mortal.

"Drink this." Alard must have known that after the voyage my hunger might endanger our host. I usually had good control, but it wasn't wise to be in close quarters with such fresh, delicious blood when I hadn't eaten. He handed me a goblet of blood, goat blood by the smell, and while not my favorite, I was hungry enough not to quibble.

"I thought you might be hungry, so there's a flagon for each of you." For the first time, I got a good look at our host. He was an older man, perhaps in his late sixties. Spry but beginning to show his age. He had a bald head with wisps of white hair that refused to lie flat. He squinted like a scholar, and he wore a jacket that looked worn at the elbows. "I'm Carel. Welcome to Antwerp. You must be Sorren."

Carel motioned for us both to take a seat. We were in a fairly large sitting room. Everywhere I looked there were manuscripts: old, leather-bound illuminated manuscripts, and such a multitude of trifles and treasures that I hardly knew where to look first. The books alone would have been worth a small fortune. Alard had been expanding my thiefly education to recognize value that the commoner might overlook.

"What do you see, Sorren?" Alard downplayed my guesses that he could, as my maker, at least partly read my thoughts. But there were too damn many coincidences for me to doubt. I'd learned to keep my mouth shut when I was mortal. Now, I'd learned to keep unflattering comments in the back of my head, where they hadn't quite taken form as words. I was grumbling a bit to myself like that now, and if Alard read it, he didn't respond.

"I see pottery, probably Greek, definitely ancient. The gold jewelry on the desk: Egyptian. I'd have to be up close to know the dynasty. The brooches on the shelf are ancient Celtic. Nice work, too. From the number of manuscripts, I'd guess someone ransacked a monastery. The inlaid box is a miracle, but I've no idea where it comes from."

"India," Carel replied offhandedly. "Not surprised you couldn't place that."

"You're a collector?"

Carel gave a smile that didn't quite reach his eyes. "Of sorts. It was dark in the shop when you came in, and we hurried you through, so you probably didn't get much of a look around. I deal in treasures and antiquities, most legal; some not so much."

"You're our fence."

Carel chuckled. "Really, Alard. You can take the thief out of the alley, but have you taken the alley out of the thief? I prefer 'merchant,' thank you."

Before we could quibble more over wording, the door opened. Alard moved before the handle turned, and I was just a blink behind him. Without a word, we'd both flattened ourselves against the ceiling. Mortals rarely look up when they're indoors.

"You're at the shop late, aren't you?" A young man walked into the room, and from his manner and the resemblance, I knew he had to be Carel's son. To my surprise, he glanced upwards. "Hello, Alard. You need to change your hiding place."

Alard grinned and drifted down to the floor. I followed him. "No one but you ever looks up in here, Dietger."

I took another look at Dietger. He was about my age, or at least the age I appeared. He had light brown hair, and his eyes were a cold blue, like mine. His jacket was newer and less worn than his father's, and I noticed that someone had replaced its buttons with old Roman coins. A chain with an amulet hung around his neck. When he shifted his stance, it disappeared into his shirt, but I'd seen enough to know that it was Etruscan and magic.

"I guess father didn't tell you that I think he ought to cut down on the side deals," Dietger said, directing his comments to Alard. "He's getting too old for this kind of thing. It's dangerous."

Alard chuckled. "From my perspective, he's still a young pup."

Dietger rolled his eyes. "Easy for you to say. But it's too dangerous. You and..." He looked at me and realized we hadn't been introduced.

"Sorren," I supplied.

"... Sorren can get yourselves out of a jam if a deal goes bad. You're not what you appear to be. But father doesn't have your defenses. I thought we'd covered this last time you came."

"We did."

"But you're back."

Alard shrugged. "It was too good of an opportunity to miss."

"I don't want to know."

"We're going after the Black Dragon," Carel spoke. Alard raised an eyebrow. I probably looked surprised. No one had told me anything except that the job would be big, dangerous, and worth it. Dietger's eyes widened.

"No. Tell me you're not."

"It's the best chance we've had in a century," Alard said, and his voice had gone serious. He wasn't trying to use his vampire powers to sway Dietger's mind, so I figured he actually liked the young man. He was trying to persuade him. Obviously, we were going to do this the hard way.

"Seventy men have died trying to destroy the Black Dragon," Dietger said. His tone had grown resolute. "I don't want father to be the seventy-first."

"Who said we were going to destroy him? The Black Dragon can't be destroyed. He can be bound. He can be weakened. His alliances with mortals can be subverted." Alard clucked his tongue. "My dear boy, I haven't survived all these centuries picking fights I can't win."

"It only takes one." Dietger was going to be stubborn.

"This might be a good time to tell the thief what he's stealing." Everyone had forgotten about me, but I knew that when it came down to the wire, I'd be the one doing the real work.

"Now's as good a time as any." Alard withdrew a folded piece of parchment from his vest pocket and laid it out carefully on the cluttered desk. Carel and I clustered around it. Dietger gave a sigh and joined us after a moment. I took a good look at the drawing. It was of a necklace with a pendant made from what appeared to be a cluster of small gemstones set in an unusual pattern. Rather garish, but no one asked my opinion.

"That's the Verheen Brooch," Carel said in a low voice. "No one's seen it in over a hundred years. I thought it was lost."

"Not lost. Purposely hidden. We made a deal with the Verhoeveren family to be the guardians of the brooch once Edmund finally tracked the thing down the last time it got away." I heard a note of anger creeping into Alard's voice that made me look up. "The fools were supposed to keep it inside the magical wards and out of sight."

"What happened?" Carel asked. He looked worried, too. Even Dietger appeared concerned. I was obviously the only one who hadn't been in on the story.

"Their dim-witted granddaughter, Anique, found it after her parents died in that carriage accident a few months ago. I'd brokered the arrangement myself with the grandfather, and come back for good measure when he died to make my point to his eldest son. They understood how dangerous the brooch was. Obviously," Alard said, disdain clear in his voice, "the girl's parents never took her into their confidence. So we've got a debutante planning to wear the Verheen Brooch out in public at Lady Evelien's ball."

"The only thing more dangerous than wearing that... thing... is trying to sell it. Are you trying to get us all killed?" Dietger was angry now. I could smell his anger. Underneath it lay fear.

"I'm not going to sell the brooch," Carel replied calmly. "Alard and I are just going to make sure it gets into the hands of a responsible guardian."

"If the brooch is so dangerous, why not just destroy it?" As soon as I'd spoken, I felt like I must have sprouted a second head. Everyone stared at me. It was my turn to feel righteously annoyed. "How come the mortals here know all about this, and I don't—even though I'm the one stealing it? You said this was a 'big' job. You didn't tell me there was a dragon involved."

Carel sighed and exchanged glances with Alard. "Perhaps we should all sit down. This could take a while. I'll fetch more tea and blood."

"I'll get those, father." Dietger looked happy to leave the room. I suspected he would have been even happier if Alard and I had been the ones leaving.

"The Black Dragon isn't a dragon," Alard said. "He's a very old spirit, one that finds a new body to possess every lifetime or so. I don't think he ever was completely human. Someone imprisoned him long ago in the New World, but the damned Spaniards set him free in their quest for gold and silver, and brought him over with their loot. That idiot, Pizarro, never even wondered why the people he conquered had so many relics hidden and locked away. All he saw was treasure. Never occurred to him that it could be anything else."

"What was it, if not treasure?" Mention gold, and my fingertips get itchy. I can't help that. Thieving is in my blood.

"Oh, some of the pieces were decoys. But several of those beautiful breastplates and necklaces of gold, silver, and gemstones were magical. They were objects of power, and strong magic users had charged them with spells to keep what was bound beneath those towers bound forever."

"And it's taken us several lifetimes to find those pieces again and get them back into the hands of people trained to use them as intended," Carel said tartly as Dietger returned with the drinks and a hunk of bread and cheese with ale for himself.

"So this Verheen Brooch is an object of power?" I sipped the blood. That kept me from watching the pulse beat in Dietger's neck.

"And if the granddaughter is wearing it, that means the brooch has been taken out of the vault where it was sealing in something that really shouldn't get out," Carel finished.

"Antwerp is built on a very old, very large, mound of earth. There are stories from the city's beginning about strange creatures exacting a terrible price for crossing the river," Dietger said, and I guessed he'd been an unwilling pupil of his father's. "Legend says that the city was made possible when a hero battled a giant and cut off his hand. Hundreds of years ago, those dark creatures were imprisoned in the mound beneath the city, and in the deepest caves. Objects of power guard the entrances to that prison. In this case, the home of our debutante lies directly over one of the main shafts into the caves where the spirits are imprisoned. That's why we felt the need to ward it with the brooch. Now that the warding is compromised..." Alard let his voice drift.

"The Black Dragon may be able to escape." It was Dietger who spoke.

"Who, exactly, did the imprisoning? Who's the 'we' you mention?" I didn't like what I was hearing, and I liked less that Alard had obviously had just this kind of thing in mind when he turned me.

"*We* are a loose alliance of vampires, shifters, magic users, and mortals who would prefer to keep the dark things buried," Alard replied. "A similar coalition imprisoned the Black Dragon and spirits like him. This sort of thing has been going on since long before I was turned. I'm one of the elders now, and, unfortunately, these kind of responsibilities fall to me."

"What happens if they get out, these spirits?"

Alard's eyes grew dark. "Imagine beings whose hunger for blood is never sated. Things that are unwilling to slake their thirst from goats and deer. The Black Dragon and his kin feed off blood, but they also feed from life itself. They can drain a man's life without opening a vein. Can you picture what that would be like, loosed across the kingdoms? Even the Black Death would pale in comparison to the horror."

"So my job is to steal the brooch—and then what?"

Alard turned away. I had a bad feeling that this job even made him nervous. "We steal the brooch. Carel helps us get it into the hands of a trusted guardian. The Black Dragon stays buried."

"But what about the passages under the granddaughter's house? Won't they be unguarded?"

"It seems that Anique wants to travel. She'll be leaving Antwerp for Paris right after the ball and isn't expected home for more than a year. If she finds a nice young man, perhaps never."

"And while she's gone, someone puts the brooch back, but in a secret hiding place?"

"Exactly."

~

TWO NIGHTS LATER, Alard was dressed for a reception at the Verhoeveren house. Anique's home. Even I was impressed. He wore a black doublet with slashed sleeves that showed glimpses of his red silk shirt. A wide, stiff ruff around his neck and cuffs seemed to decrease the contrast between Alard's pale skin and the stark black velvet of his coat. Alard was trim enough to look good in the heavy hose tights, and soft leather boots came up above his knees. I knew that, under his ruff, Alard wore several charms and amulets against dark magic. A short cape set off the outfit nicely.

"You expect to hide in that?" I was put out more over my outfit than his. I was in solid, form-fitting black from head to toe, the epitome of a well-dressed valet. A waist-length jacket covered a black shirt with full sleeves. The jacket held thieves' tools and the spelled dagger Alard insisted on giving me. I had a variety of lock picks and other items of dubious legality hidden about my person, though since I'd become a vampire, I'd relied more on enhanced hearing, sight, and touch than on gadgets.

"I expect to hide in plain sight." Alard picked at the stiff fabric at his ruffs and jerked his head to move his chin out of range of the abrasive ruff. "I'm the guest of one of Carel's friends, a professor at the university. That will get me invited over the threshold, and once I'm inside, I can invite you."

"Does your patron know you're dead?"

Alard smiled. I looked again and saw that there was a tinge of pink in his cheeks and lips, and that his hands had lost their pallor. "You've fed. On whom?" Again, I was jealous. I got goat blood. Alard had dined on a human. Nothing but human blood works as well to warm us and revive our color. Alard was no more pale than a scholar who spent his days indoors.

"The wharves have more than their share of cutpurses and murderers. Let's say that my dining companion won't be missed by anyone except the Watch."

"I used to be one of those cutpurses," I muttered.

"You didn't make a habit of slitting your mark's throat for the sheer joy of watching them bleed."

I couldn't argue with that. I'd found my thrill in liberating heavily guarded objects. Hurting people had never been something I'd enjoyed, and I'd managed to do most of my thieving without causing physical harm to anyone.

"You have the knife?" Something in Alard's voice was tighter than usual. This was the third time he'd asked me. Maybe he really was nervous.

"I have it, although why is beyond me. I've never stabbed anything except a side of beef."

"You've got the knife for the same reason I had Carel give you the amulets. The charms should get you past the wardings on the vault. The knife is just in case anything's got loose."

"Got loose? Now, wait a second!" Alard had begun to walk away from me. I started to follow and came to an abrupt halt. "Hold on. If I need charms to get into the vault because it's protected, how did Anique get the brooch in the first place?"

"Because her charm is in her blood." Alard turned to look at me. "The Verhoeveren family has a long history of magic. In generations past, they also chose one of their most talented sons to take the Dark Gift. That certainly didn't hurt the family fortunes." He grimaced. "Unfortunately, the recent generations have moved away from those practices. And magic, as well as common sense, certainly seem to have skipped the granddaughter."

Alard hailed a rented carriage several streets over from Vanities, not wanting anything to tie us to Carel's shop should we be noticed. For the same reason, we had agreed to travel separately. Alard got the fine carriage. I was on foot, sticking to the back alleys where I could use my supernatural speed without attracting the attention of anyone except the gutter drunks and the doorway strumpets.

The Verhoeveren home was as impressive as I'd expected. A grand home rising four floors high, the house was a step-gabled masterpiece of Gothic style. The home stood shoulder to shoulder against other homes, each equally luxurious. Tonight, the house glittered with candles and lanterns. I watched from a safe distance, hidden in the shadows, as Alard met his new friend and they went in together, already busily talking. If all went well, Alard would have a wonderful evening chatting about art and antiquities with a professor while I did all the heavy lifting.

In the old days, when I was still alive, I would have taken a couple of deep breaths to get myself in the mood to work. Now, I made do with rubbing my hands together. Oh, I could make myself breathe if I really wanted to, make my chest rise and fall the same way I'd raise and lower my left foot, but the breathing would stop if I stopped thinking about it, and since I didn't need the air, the process felt strange. I rubbed my hands together and found that even dead, my nerves could still feel jangled.

In the dark, I slipped easily around to the back. The servants' door was ajar. I approached carefully, and heard Alard whisper, "Come in." There it was, my invitation across the threshold. I was in.

Alard was gone by the time I opened the door. In the distance, I could hear the clatter of pots and dishes. I might be dead, but I was newly crossed enough that the smell of food woke a hunger in me for more than blood. I'd learned the hard way not to give in to that hunger. My body no longer tolerated anything but blood, and so what else I ate had to come back out the way it went in. Once was enough. But the memory of how food tastes still haunted me. That was one of only two things I missed about being mortal. Getting drunk was the other one.

I had work to do. I slipped past the kitchen and down the back stairs. I thought I'd moved silently before I'd been turned. Now, I moved like a ghost. I didn't have the same skill Alard had at clouding mortal minds so that they didn't see me, but I hardly ever had the need. Not being seen was my one of my specialties.

The wooden stairs creaked for the servants who passed me in the shadows without noticing. I moved on silently, levitating just a bit with each step to avoid putting stress on the old wooden stair treads. Carel had got his hands on the original plans to the house. I didn't ask how. Alard knew where the modifications had been made for the vault. I'd memorized the plans, and now I moved through the darkened cellar as surely as if I'd lived there all my life.

A servant laden with wine bottles came down the corridor singing to himself. I stepped into the shadows and disappeared. A few more steps and I was in front of a door. When I'd been mortal, I'd relied on my gut feeling as much as any lock picking equipment. Now, my gut told me that the door led to somewhere I didn't want to go. Alard had said that my intuition was a type of magic, a form of second sight. I wasn't sure I believed that, but my second sight sure didn't want to see what was behind that door.

I set my jaw and stepped up to the door. While I wasn't certain about intuition being magic, I didn't doubt that what I was about to do qualified. I'd learned quite young that with enough concentration I could work a lock just by touching the wood. Gradually, I got good enough to work locks through metal, even thick iron. It was almost as if my fingers could "see" right through the door and turn the tumblers.

Right off, I knew this door would be a challenge. Alard had warned me it had layers of locks. I closed my eyes, trusting in my vampire hearing to alert me before any passer-by came close enough to see me. I needed my eyes closed to work the locks. I made myself relax and pressed my fingers to the first lock. Alard told me that the locks began simple and became increasingly complex—and dangerous. The first challenge was a padlock, intricately forged to look like the head of a dragon in black iron. Subtle. I had a master key infused with a bit of magic that could sense the shape of the mechanism inside and adapt. The key had been expensive to make, pricy enough to keep such a useful tool out of the hands of the average thief. Alard had given me the master key as a present on the first anniversary of my turning.

The key hesitated in the lock for a moment, and then turned smoothly. I reclaimed the key and left the lock hanging. I'd need to be able to put everything back as I found it, or Anique would suspect. Next came a door secured with an elaborately knotted rope. I knew before I touched it that the deceptively silken cord was infused with magic. I withdrew one of the amulets from beneath my tunic and held it up. The cord glowed a faint blue, and then went dark, and the tingle that warned of magic vanished in my mind. I was good at knots, and without its magical enhancement, the cord gave way to me within a minute.

The next door had a lock like a chest lid, with a complicated series of bolts and gears. The gears turned when I "felt" the lock, moving my fingers to align the bolts and pins. The bolts slid back, and I smiled.

In the distance, I could hear the sounds of the party. My goal was to be through the locks and gone with the brooch before the guests moved on to their third course. The final door had a set of pin tumblers. Again, I'd use my ear and my fingers to feel my way into the vault. I touched the lock and frowned. The first attempt to turn the lock felt wrong. At the same time, one of the charms around my neck had grown suddenly warm, then hot. Irritated, I pulled the thing out from beneath my shirt, and it glowed. I was about to stash it beneath my jacket when I glanced at the lock in the amulet's glow. The sequence of figures on the lock that I saw in the light of the amulet was completely different from the way the sequence appeared without the talisman. Just to make sure, I shielded the amulet's light and looked again. It hadn't been a trick of my eyes. Leaving the amulet out, I worked in its dim glow. The lock turned smoothly for me now, and I had the satisfaction of feeling the tumblers drop into place.

Lock by lock, I made my way into the vault. Alard had warned me that the last trap was on the floor. Unless Verhoeveren blood flowed in my veins to counter the charm, I'd need to cross a span too wide for a man to jump without touching down on the floor between here and there. The tiles, Alard warned, were actually carefully balanced, and they would set off a series of alarm bells if disturbed. Difficult to impossible for a mortal, but not for a vampire. I couldn't fly properly yet, not like Alard and the old ones could, but I could float. Floating was all I needed.

I made a small sound of triumph as the last door opened. Inside lay the spelled chest that held the Verheen Brooch. Alard had assured me that the words he made me memorize would open the chest, although they sounded like nonsense to me. He'd drilled me on how to pronounce them correctly until I heard them in my sleep.

"*Nonnes javar viciat, alrum valonas fideras.*"

I could hear the magical locks working, hear the bolts sliding and the gears turning, hear the pins falling into place. It was a joyous sound. I rubbed my hands together in anticipation and floated over to claim my prize.

The chest was empty.

Empty! If I'd had a heartbeat, it would have been racing. All this work, all this time, and no brooch. Alard hadn't said anything about it being charmed, or invisible. I felt around the velvet-lined bottom of the chest. Nothing. I tapped at the bottom of the chest, inside and out, listening for a false bottom. I examined the sides of the chest for hidden openings. I even searched the inside of the chest lid and sized up the chest to see if the dimensions inside compared to the outside suggested a secret compartment I'd missed. I came up empty, as empty as the chest. Panicked, I looked around the vault. It was empty, too, except for the chest.

Think. Where would the brooch be if not in the vault? And then it hit me. The answer would have been obvious if Alard and I hadn't been men. It would have been doubly obvious if we'd been thinking of the brooch as a piece of jewelry instead of a priceless magical object.

The granddaughter thinks it's just a nice, shiny necklace. Valuable, but no more so than the other sparklies she's got. It's in her goddamn room, probably lying right out on her dressing table. Damn, damn, damn.

Angry and resigned, I worked my way back out of the vault. I'd just wasted precious time, and used up some of my luck. It was a rule I'd thieved by all my life, and breaking it had got me dead. Only pull one job in a house at a time. Get in, get the goods and get out. Sure, there could be silver in the dining room, diamonds in the lady's jewelry case and gold coins in the master's desk, but roaming from room to room looking for treasure increased the odds of getting caught. Greed catches more thieves than the Watch. I'd forgotten that just one time, and I died because of it. Now, I was going to have to break that rule again. And whilst I was already dead, Alard had impressed upon me that getting caught would create problems that made death look simple. I didn't want to find out.

Someone was coming. I got the last lock latched and plastered myself against the ceiling just in time. It was a vaulted barrel chamber, and the bricks were uncomfortable at my back, but I stayed hidden until the servants passed. The one saving grace in having to look for the brooch in Anique's room was that she was likely to be down among the guests tonight. Alard thought she was saving the brooch to make a big splash at Lady Evelien's ball tomorrow. Now that I thought about it, a silly young woman would want to keep a treasure like the brooch handy where she could try it on with her dress and admire herself in the mirror. Did the brooch's magic speak to her blood? Could she feel the power of the brooch, or was it just a pretty, shiny, dead thing?

Working my way up the stairs to the living quarters was harder than slipping into the basement. As I moved through the house, I caught a glimpse of the party. Banks of candles and huge candelabra laden with dozens of candles lit the room, which was walled with mirrors.

I found the back stairs, the servants' passageway, and I grabbed a tea tray from near the kitchen to carry, hoping no one looked closely at my face. I got up the stairs without a challenge and set the tray aside. As a vampire, I could usually sense where mortals were. I could hear their heartbeats, smell their blood. As I listened to my senses, I did not feel any mortals nearby. I'd got lucky.

I slipped down the hallway, trying the doorknobs. None of the rooms looked as if they belonged to a spoiled young rich girl. I came to the last door and turned the knob. The room was decorated with delicately-sized, feminine furnishings, and swathed in luxurious fabrics and sumptuous pillows. Mirrors reflected candlelight, making the whole room glitter. The tables and chests were littered with extravagant trinkets of silver and crystal, playthings that cost more than a workingman might make in years. A dressing table sat against the wall with a large mirror and a pink velvet-cushioned chair. The top was cluttered with exquisite bottles of perfume, silver-handled combs, and a variety of cosmetics.

A small chest, covered with ornate inlay, sat amid the clutter. It was a lady's jewelry chest, and I went straight to it, digging carefully through the strands of pearls, gemstones, and diamonds. In the old days, I'd have just grabbed the chest and run. Alard had taught me patience. But despite my thorough search, the Verheen Brooch was not in the box.

"Looking for this?"

I spun around. A blonde young woman stood just inside the doorway. She was dressed for a dinner party, her long hair braided up. She was dressed in a black gown, as was the fashion, but the jewels in her earrings and bracelets dispelled any thought that somber colors meant simplicity. Pinned to her gown, just above the swell of her breasts lay the prize, the Verheen Brooch.

I should have heard her approach. I would have heard her approach, if she'd been mortal.

"What are you?" My heightened senses were practically screaming an alarm. The body was young, but around it, inside it, enveloping it was an ancient evil.

"I'm just a silly, spoiled rich girl with a fondness for pretty things." The voice was mocking, but the eyes were dead serious. No, the eyes were just dead. Whatever was looking out through them had never been a silly, spoiled girl.

"You don't know what you've got."

Her laugh chilled me. Hard to scare a dead man, but she managed. "Oh, yes. I know." Her fingers fondled the brooch like it was a lover. "I've got something that will make everyone take me very seriously."

They say that the devil whispers in everyone's ear the thing he or she wants most. For some, it's money, for others, social status, power, beauty. She was born with all those things, and Alard told me she was already courted by the most desirable men in the city.

"You thought I was nothing but a stupid girl."

She was right. Alard and I made the same mistake everyone else made. But the Black Dragon didn't. And he'd whispered the one prize she couldn't buy when he'd seduced her. Not just power. Respect.

"What did it offer you?" I asked. I kept my eyes on hers. What looked out at me through her eyes wasn't human, and it certainly wasn't a vapid socialite. What glinted in those blue eyes was cold, calculating, and ancient.

She laughed, and I shuddered. Something in that sound felt as if her long nails had raked down my spine. "My father thought I was too stupid for him to trust me with the family secret. He forgot that Verhoeveren blood doesn't play favorites. I've heard the voices since I was just a little girl. Everyone else ordered me about or spoke to me like a child. Not the voices. They saw my true potential."

Your true potential to be a pawn, I thought, but didn't say. I didn't know how much of Anique was still inside, and how much was the Black Dragon. "When did you take the brooch out of the vault?"

"Just before my dear, dear parents had their tragic accident."

Alard and Carel had been expecting the girl to be an innocent. The Black Dragon had recognized her as an ally, willing to do anything to get what she craved most.

"What did he promise you?"

Anique smiled. Although she was a beautiful girl, her smile bared her teeth in a way that said she shared a hunger for blood. "He promised me that I'd be free from an arranged marriage. Free from my father. Free from the lawyers that tried to steal my money after father died. I want what would have been mine if I'd been a son instead of a daughter."

"All it needed was your blood."

Her face twitched a little when I said that. I wondered if the Black Dragon was whispering to her while she spoke to me.

"The brooch didn't lock him inside the vault, you know," she said smugly. "The brooch is the vault. They bound his spirit inside the brooch to contain it, just like father's stupid rules tried to keep me locked in a box. But together, we got out of the box."

"Now what?" I wanted to keep her talking while I thought of something brilliant. I was a thief, not a fighter. I'd made my way robbing empty homes where I never had to encounter the prize's owner. I hadn't counted on having to do more than grab the necklace and run.

"Now you die, permanently."

Anique moved with the speed of a vampire. She came at me and, as I threw myself out of the way, it was almost as if there were two images, not just one, when I looked at her. I saw Anique, beautiful, greedy, and deadly, coming at me with her teeth bared and her hands raised like claws. But the image was blurred as if a painter had tried to paint a second portrait over the top of an existing one. In that blurred image, I saw a black shadow with real claws and real fangs, and I didn't want to find out whose jaws I'd feel if they clamped down on me.

Something else stirred in the room, and before I'd truly had time to process what I'd seen, Alard had tackled Anique from behind. He'd come in prepared to fight, and I was certain that the telepathy he'd always refused to confirm played a big part in his perfect timing.

Anique shrieked, but the band downstairs had begun to play a loud tune, covering the noise. The black shadow seemed to fill her, leeching the color out of her skin until she was a dull grey, the color of a corpse. Filled with the Black Dragon's power, she tore free from Alard's grip, something a mortal could never do. Alard stumbled backward, and Anique came at me again, matching my speed and reflexes in a game of cat and mouse.

I'll hold her. Use your dagger. It was Alard's voice sounding clear in my mind. I guess he'd decided to stop pretending. Alard told me that the dagger was spelled. That had made me feel pretty good, until I got a look at the Black Dragon. Now, it seemed like a puny weapon against a monster.

Too late for second thoughts. Alard was already launching himself at Anique, and I was moving too, trying to get a clear strike at her heart. Taking a vampire's heart destroyed the vampire. I was going to have to hope that putting a knife through Anique's heart would at least slow down the Black Dragon long enough for me to get my hands on that damn brooch.

Alard grabbed Anique from behind, locking his arms around her waist in a grip that should have crushed a mortal woman. I threw myself towards her, expecting Anique to struggle, or to buck and kick. Instead, the darkness around her shape grew more solid, and she arched, reaching back with both hands to grasp Alard's head.

My knife plunged into her chest, and for good measure, my fangs sank into the artery that pulsed at the base of that beautiful white neck. Suddenly, I was covered by a fountain of blood. Warm blood, spurting from the gaping wound in Anique's chest and the bright red liquid that filled my mouth from her throat. And cold blood, dark blood. Anique's arms came back down holding their prize. In her hands, she held Alard's head, torn from his body with the Black Dragon's inhuman strength. The whole house seemed to shake as if the earth suddenly moved beneath it, and from the lower levels of the house, I heard the revelers scream.

Anique crumpled, and I stumbled backward. Alard's voice was suddenly silent, and I knew then that I'd accepted his presence as a constant background hum in all the years since I'd been turned without thinking about it. Now that it was gone, I reeled, as if blinded. Anique had killed my maker, my source. I'd taken her heart with my knife, but she'd wounded me far worse. The middle of a battle is the wrong time to learn how to deal with the death of your maker. I fell to my knees as Anique's body dropped to the ground, my dagger still sticking out of her blood-soaked bodice.

Then I realized that the shadow was shifting. A dark mist coalesced above Anique's body. The Black Dragon was taking its true shape, and in that dark mist, I saw every nightmare I'd ever dreamed.

The shape grew taller and darker, a giant that stretched to the ceiling. Its arms were too long for its body, and the hands ended with talons. Faceless, eyeless, it still found me. I had to get that brooch. The Black Dragon swung clawed hands at me, but I dodged, barely. I felt hot slashes open down my back. It dived at me, and again I scrambled out of the way as long teeth snapped just a breath away from my leg.

I threw myself at Anique, trying not to see Alard's headless corpse behind her. She was still breathing, which meant my knife had missed its mark, or whatever spell it held didn't work as Alard had planned. I wrapped my fingers around that damned brooch and pulled, but the clasp held.

The dark mist swirled back around me, and as I watched in horror, it streamed back into Anique's body, entering through her eyes, her nose, her mouth, her ears. I jerked my spelled blade out of Anique's chest and stumbled backward. Anique's body began to tremble, as if the power that filled her was too much for her dying form to handle. But the Black Dragon brought Anique to her knees, and then to her feet. The disdainful sneer that twisted her finely drawn lips was all Anique, regardless of the power that animated her.

Anique came at me again, even as I heard something in the hallway. The distraction slowed me down just enough for Anique to nearly close the distance. A loud blast came from the doorway, sending flame and smoke into the room. Anique's head exploded in a shower of blood and gore, and I dove aside as a musket ball tore through bone and flesh, taking off her head the way she had torn Alard's from his body.

As she fell, I grabbed for the brooch. The edge of the brooch tore a gash in my palm from the strength I used to jerk it clear. The brooch was slick with blood: Anique's, Alard's, and my own.

Dietger stood in the doorway with a matchlock.

Everything happened at once. The black shadow shed Anique's dead body and came after me. And in that instant, I had a plan. I held up the brooch.

"Come and get it."

The Black Dragon streaked toward me and stopped, and I began to laugh, a high-pitched sound born more of nerves and fear than my normal chuckle.

"You can't touch me." I had Verhoeveren blood in my veins. Anique's blood, which I'd drunk from the punctures in her neck. Verhoeveren blood not only ran in my veins, but now, it covered my clothes in bloody gobbets, and it ran down my arm where I held the brooch that was sticky with her blood.

I held the brooch in my left hand. In my right was the spelled dagger. Now, I knew why Alard had insisted that I bring it.

It wasn't meant for Anique.

Antwerp has its own way of dealing with monsters.

Brandishing the Verheen Brooch like a weapon, I charged at the Black Dragon. With a war cry, I brought down the spelled dagger not in its chest, but across its right arm at the wrist. The dagger cut through the cold, dark mist and met resistance, but I brought all my vampire strength to bear, knowing that my existence, and Dietger's, depended on it.

An inhuman wail tore from the Black Dragon. I had no free hand to clap to my ears, and the sound seemed to tear at every fiber in my body. Dietger fell to his knees, dropping the gun and covering his ears in pain. I was shaking all over, but I forced myself to move forward, still brandishing the brooch.

"Verhoeveren blood runs in my veins. You must obey the blood. Return to the brooch."

This time, when the Black Dragon came at me, I thought I was ready. Some say that the dead don't feel fear. They're wrong. Terror filled me as that black mist swirled towards me, no longer bothering to take shape. The air around me became freezing cold, and I braced myself with all my immortal strength to hold up the brooch as the mist entered it, and the dome of the brooch began to glow. In a moment, it was over, but I stood, trembling, unable to speak.

Only then did I realize that smoke was seeping into the room from the hallway behind Dietger.

Dietger seemed to come back to himself. He grabbed up his gun and gave a pained glance to where Alard's body had collapsed into dust. "Great job with the brooch, but I'm afraid there's no way out. The house is on fire."

"How's that?" I heard him, but I wasn't processing the information. I still felt as if I were making my way through molasses; everything seemed to take enormous effort.

"Something rocked the house while I was on the way up here. Damn near knocked me down the steps. It must have knocked over the candles."

All those candles, and the tinderbox of fine, billowing skirts and kindling-dry wigs. The smoke was thicker now.

I looked to Dietger. Either we took our only chance, or we burned with the brooch. "On my count, we run for the windows."

"We're four stories in the air."

"Trust me."

Dietger gave me a look that told me clearly that self-preservation had more to do with it than any kind of trust, but on my count, we ran for the window and burst through the glass. The brooch was clasped tightly in my left hand. I flung out my right arm, letting the dagger fall, and caught Dietger around the waist as we fell.

"You can fly?"

"No."

We plummeted. Beneath us, I could see flames shooting from the lower windows of the once-grand home, and chaos in the street. No one looked up to see us fall. Mortals never look up. They didn't see us until we were almost on them, and they scrambled out of the way, expecting us to hit the ground in a spatter of blood. To Dietger's credit, he did not scream, but I could hear him reciting a prayer. I didn't pray. Instead, I focused all my will on what I could do.

I couldn't fly, but I could float.

We fell like a cast stone. Then, when we were only about the length of a man's arm above the unyielding pavement, we slowed with a jerk that must have sent Dietger's heart into his throat. We hovered for a moment, and then touched down gently. But before the crowd around us could react, I ran, carrying Dietger with me, still clutching the brooch. To the mortals in the street, we must have disappeared in a blur. I hoped that they would take it as a trick of the smoke, but I had more important things to worry about.

Dietger whispered directions, taking me through the winding streets. We made enough switchbacks and turns to deter even the more dogged pursuer. I came to a stop in front of Vanities and put him down.

Dietger looked pale as one of the undead. He swallowed and straightened his waistcoat. The door to the shop opened, although the front of the shop was dark.

"Come in. Hurry."

We didn't need light. Dietger and Carel knew the shop's crowded layout by heart. I could see in the dark. We followed Carel to the same parlor where he had greeted Alard and me just a night before. Only then did I feel the magnitude of my loss.

Alard was gone.

I collapsed into the chair where Alard had sat and put my head in my hands. The Dark Gift denied me the release of tears, but my whole body shook with grief. More than grief. Alard had brought me across. For the first hundred years of my undead existence, it had been his power that sustained me. I was only just at the threshold when fledglings could leave their maker and survive. Now that the battle with the Black Dragon was over, I felt Alard's destruction in every sinew of my body. For the first time since my turning, I felt like a dead thing.

I can give you what you crave.

For a moment, I didn't know where the voice was coming from. And then, I knew. It was the Verheen Brooch. I had jammed it into my vest pocket during the escape. Now, it called to the same Verhoeveren blood that had enabled me to imprison it, and I understood why Anique's family had kept this thing locked away, buried beneath stone and iron.

I can make you rich. Powerful. Respected.

With a cry, I tore the damned brooch from my pocket and hurled it across the room.

Dietger and Carel looked up from where they were huddled in conversation, respecting my need to grieve. I saw that Carel had tears running down his cheeks. He, too, mourned my maker, his friend.

"It speaks to him," Carel said to Dietger, with a nod toward where I'd thrown the brooch.

Dietger went to retrieve the brooch, and held it warily, dangling it from the chain Anique had used to hang it around her neck. "Alard was right. Once he had Verhoeveren blood in his veins, the Black Dragon had to obey."

A bitter smile touched the edges of Carel's mouth. "Fortunately, that will pass."

I nodded. It took about twelve hours for a feeding to spend itself. I would not carry Verhoeveren blood in me forever, and when it passed, the Verheen Brooch would be a dead thing to me.

Carel brought me a goblet of blood and pressed it into my hand. "Eat. You've been through a lot." The thick strip of linen wrapped around his arm told me whose blood it was. I looked at him, questioning.

"Alard and I were friends for a long time," Carel said quietly. "Over the years, I gained immunity to his powers, and he used his Gift to extend my life. Many a time, I gave him human blood when nothing else would suffice. This is one of those times when naught but human blood will sustain you. Drink."

The blood cleared my head and steadied me. Only then did Carel's words sink in. I turned to him. "Alard extended your life?"

Carel nodded, and I could see the answer to my next question in his face. Just since our first meeting, it looked as if he had aged decades. His eyes were sunken, and his skin had grown paper-thin. "There's not much time left," he said. He looked from me to Dietger and motioned for Dietger to join us. Dietger knelt next to his father, watching with a mixture of horror and grief as the managed in front of our eyes.

"Swear to me, both of you, that you will carry on the work."

"What work?" I looked from Carel to Dietger.

"The Alliance Alard and I created has kept the Black Dragon and things like it from returning to the world. Dietger knows everything you need, even if he's never put the pieces together to realize it. What is bound must remain bound." Carel's voice had grown wavering, and he began to cough. "This store, Vanities, is much more than it appears. For decades, Alard and the Alliance brought me found objects, objects of power, and I moved them to places of safekeeping. Sometimes, other people brought me things they thought to be cursed or haunted, and I made them disappear."

Talking had become difficult, but determination flashed in his eyes. "You must take over for me," Carel said, reaching out a bony hand to clutch Dietger's arm. "You must take over the work."

Dietger bowed his head. I could see his struggle. He had only grudgingly acknowledged this part of his father's life, and now the full responsibility was about to fall on his shoulders. "I swear to."

Carel turned toward me. Cataracts now covered both of his eyes, but he stared at me as if he could still see. "Swear to me, Sorren. Swear that you'll take Alard's place. Swear it, and he won't have died in vain."

I didn't want to do this. Like Dietger, I wanted to be leagues away from this place. Then I thought of Alard, and how his dust by now was mingled with the ash of the Verhoeveren home. I swallowed hard. A million objections screamed in my mind, and they were my own objections, not the voice of the damned brooch. I didn't know how to reach the Alliance. I didn't know how to find the objects, or what to do with them. I didn't know anything, anything except that I owed a great debt to Alard, one I might spend my immortality repaying.

"I'll do it."

The light seemed to fade from Carel's eyes. "Good," he said in a raspy whisper. "Good." He began to sway, and Dietger reached out to grab his shoulders, but I knew that life left him before he slumped to the floor.

I looked at Dietger over his father's body. "Now what?"

Dietger took a deep breath to steady himself. I knew the grief he was feeling. Tonight, we had both lost our fathers. "Now, we bury our dead." He closed his eyes and seemed to give himself a shake to clear his head. When he looked at me, his blue eyes were clear, filled with the same determination I'd seen in Carel's eyes.

"Tomorrow, we carry on the work."

I thought about everything that had happened since my ship anchored in Antwerp. I'd crossed a vale as final as when Alard had brought me across, long ago. Then, my death gave me a new existence as an immortal. Now, Alard's death gave me a mission. I held out my hand to Dietger. A hand covered with soot and blood, which he shook.

When Alard turned me, I learned that death wasn't the end. Now, in the oath I'd given to Carel, I learned that my immortality could have purpose. I wasn't the same man who'd landed in Antwerp two days ago. "Let's see about burying your father," I said. "And then, I want rid of that damned brooch."

THE WILD HUNT

"I FEAR THE BONES ARE HAUNTED." THE OLD WOMAN FINGERED HER rosary and looked down. "I hope I've done the right thing coming here, but I don't know where else to go."

My partner, Dietger, reached over to pat her hand and smiled reassuringly. "We'll do whatever we can to help," he replied. "Go ahead and drink your tea; it'll take away the chill."

April in Antwerp could be cold, at least if you were mortal. I'd been dead for a hundred years—undead—and I still hadn't gotten used to the lack of body heat. It was one of the things I missed the most about being mortal, other than the taste of food, and being able to go out into the sunlight without catching on fire.

"Isn't that true, Sorren?" Dietger said, with a tone that let me know he'd caught me woolgathering. "I was just reassuring Mevr. Geerts that she made the right decision to trust us with her concern over the odd relic that traveling monk brought to the city."

Ah, the traveling monk, I thought, grateful that Dietger had framed the question in a way to help me recover. "Absolutely," I said. "You'd be surprised how many times we encounter old objects that have a darker past than the present owner realizes."

That was putting it mildly. Vanities, the antique and curio shop

Dietger inherited from his father, was much more than it appeared, part of an underground alliance to remove dangerous magical and supernatural items from circulation. And it sounded like this relic was going to turn into a job for us.

"If Father Verhelst found out that I'd come here, I might lose my position," she said, shifting in her chair. She was a plump woman in her sixth decade, and a lifetime of hard work showed in her calloused hands and careworn face. I'd overheard her tell Dietger that she was the housekeeper at St. Walpurgis Church's rectory, which explained her concern over seeking us out. While Vanities' role in keeping Antwerp safe from dark magic wasn't exactly well-known outside select company, I doubted the Church would look fondly on our activities, or on my existence, for that matter.

"I assure you, we'll handle this discreetly," Dietger promised. He was in his mid-twenties, and I guessed he looked just as his late father, Carel, would have looked when he was that age. Light brown hair, cold blue eyes, and a pleasantly earnest manner befitting a respectable young shopkeeper.

The old woman drew her shawl around her. "Maybe it's just my imagination, but I've heard the bones rattle in the reliquary that strange monk brought, and once when I was passing by, I heard a voice laughing. It was a nasty kind of laugh, and it made my blood run cold."

"Tell me more about the traveling monk," Dietger prodded gently and held out the tray of shortbread to Mevr. Geerts. Dietger and our guest were nearest the fireplace in the cramped little office behind the store. I purposely sat further back, partly in shadow, the better to avoid questions on my pallor, and my cold, cold skin.

"He arrived at the beginning of March," she replied. "We hadn't received any letters to arrange the visit; he just showed up one day, along with that box." Mevr. Geerts hadn't sworn, but I was quite sure from her tone that she really meant "that damned box."

"Is that unusual?" Dietger was listening attentively, and I knew he was leaving it to me to assess our "client" with my sharper-than-mortal vampire senses.

"Unexpected visits?" She chuckled. "Not entirely. St. Walpurgis is an old church, with a long history. We get the occasional scholar, the pilgrims who come to ask our saint for healing, that sort of thing. But to have someone show up with a relic and claim to have bones from our saint's body, that's very unusual." She shivered and sipped her tea. "Suspicious, even."

I could hear the old woman's heart beating faster than usual, smell the scent of fear, and could see the sheen of sweat on her forehead. Her hands shook a bit, I was willing to bet, more from emotion than palsy. She was afraid, and I was certain it went well beyond being discovered chatting with the owner of an antique shop.

"Do you have other relics from St. Walpurga?" Dietger asked, with that charming smile that made every woman over a certain age treat him like their beloved son. Even when I was alive, I never evoked that response, not even from my own mother. I'd been in my late twenties when I'd been turned, so I would always appear young, though I was now a centenarian. Dark blond hair, wiry build, and average-looking features made me forgettable, not a bad thing back when I was a jewel thief. My eyes were the only thing remarkable about me, blue-gray eyes the color of the sea when a storm is coming. I turned my gaze back to Mevr. Geerts in time to see her shake her head vigorously.

"No, and that was the first thing that made me suspicious of Friar Jansen," she said. She looked up and met my gaze. If she had any suspicions that I was more than I appeared, she wasn't frightened of me, yet a traveling monk made her nervous? I was increasingly curious.

"Why?" Dietger probed.

Mevr. Geerts looked surprised. "Our saint's bones are supposed to be in Eichstatt," she responded. "Surely you've heard the story, how her body was buried on a rock ledge, and the stones weep a healing oil?"

I'd never been very religious even before I was turned, and even so, I thought I'd heard the legend somewhere. Dietger, too, nodded although I'd have bet that he was indulging the woman.

"I've never heard tell that the saint's bones were scattered," Mevr. Geerts went on with a scandalized tone. "Such a thing has happened, of course, to other saints, but not to Saint Walpurga. So I wondered right away just whose bones were in the reliquary, and why Friar Jansen happened to have them."

A good question, I thought. The rectory's housekeeper had obviously paid attention to her catechism. And I wondered why the same questions hadn't occurred to Father Verhelst.

"Did Father Verhelst seem to think anything was strange, either about the monk showing up or about the relic?" Dietger asked.

Mevr. Geerts sighed. "No, but then again, he wouldn't. Father Verhelst is a very good priest, but he accepts things at face value. I've been at the rectory for ten years, and I've never seen him question anything, whether it's the bill from the butcher or the price of a load of firewood. He's not a curious man."

Not a curious man. I suspected that what Mevr. Geerts really meant was that our good Father Verhelst was likely to have received his position based more from family connections than because of his theological intellect. Personally, I found that people devoid of curiosity made my job easier. Back when I was a thief, non-curious people tended to see no reason to remember my face—all the better for me. Now, when my work involved stealing back things that had been stolen in the first place, in order to return them to their proper location, I traded on the public's indifference and lack of curiosity to hide in plain sight.

"Did you tell Father Verhelst your concerns?"

Mevr. Geerts looked down. "It's not my place to say such a thing, directly. When the monk first came, I did ask a few questions, as if I were interested in the saint and the relic, figuring that Father couldn't fault me for questions about the faith."

"And?"

She sighed. "Father seemed completely distracted, like he couldn't imagine what I was talking about. Later, when I asked more questions, he got quite angry." She looked up, meeting Dietger's gaze with a desperate expression.

"That's what worries me the most. Since that awful monk and his box of bones came, Father Verhelst has changed." She paused, and I worried that she might not continue, but then she got up her courage to go on.

"Father might never be bishop, but he is a good parish priest," she said loyally. "He cared about the parish, and he worried over the people and their troubles. I never heard him lose his temper, even when some of our parishioners vexed him sorely."

She let out a long breath. "I see that Father has a hot meal three times a day, and we used to chat while he ate, and I cleaned up the kitchen. I enjoyed those chats, especially when he would repeat a joke he'd heard from someone in the town." Mevr. Geerts shook her head. "But once the monk came, Father Verhelst seemed to pull away from everyone—everybody except that monk. He gave instructions for me to leave food in the kitchen for them, but that my presence was not required."

I could see the obvious hurt on her face. "But it's not just that," she went on. "He's gotten snappish with the parishioners, and he barely gives a homily at mass. Then when the alms-basket went missing, and I told him about it, he got so angry I thought he might cuff me, and shouted for me to keep to the kitchen and not bother him."

Dietger and I exchanged glances. *A stranger comes to town unannounced, bearing a questionable relic, and things begin to go topsyturvy. Not a good sign*, I thought. From the look on Dietger's face, the same thoughts had occurred to him.

"Has anything else strange happened since the monk came, anything at all?" he asked.

Mevr. Geerts thought for a moment. "It's been a bad two months," she said. "Until you asked, I was ready to say we'd just had a run of hard luck, which happens sometimes. But it seems as if Father's had a funeral to do several times a week. Not just the very young and the very old, either. Freak accidents, some of them were, like men getting eaten by dogs or falling into the grist mill. Horrible things."

If I'd been suspicious of Friar Jansen before, a slew of dead bodies sealed it. I was just about to say something when Mevr. Geerts went on.

"Then there's the relic box itself," she said. "It bleeds."

Dietger frowned. We'd both heard stories about statues or icons that bled. Tales like that had been part of the lore of the saints for a long time. But somehow, I suspected that this was different.

"When did it bleed?" Dietger pressed. "And did you see it yourself?"

Mevr. Geerts nodded. "I saw it, more than once. And each time, right after someone in the parish died."

"How can we get a look at this reliquary, without making either Father Verhelst or Friar Jansen suspicious?" Dietger asked. A new look had come into his eyes, like a dog on a hunt. I suspected the same was true for me.

Buoyed by our acceptance of her fantastical tale, Mevr. Geerts seemed to regain a little starch in her spine. "The saint's day is coming up, and Father Verhelst is saying a special mass each evening leading up to it. Friar Jansen should be at mass, with his reliquary."

"We'll take a look—and we'll make sure no one can link us to you," Dietger reassured her. "How can we contact you safely if we need more information?"

Mevr. Geerts thought for a moment. "I walk to the dairy every morning at eighth bells for a fresh bottle of milk. The road is usually empty on that stretch, if you happened to be passing that way at that time," she said with a crafty smile. "And Friday evenings, after supper, I visit my husband's grave. It's in the back corner of the churchyard by a stand of trees, behind the charnel house, so the grave can't be seen from the rectory." I decided right then that Mevr. Geerts was nobody's fool.

"We'll find you if we discover anything," Dietger promised. "And we'll do whatever we can to help Father Verhelst and the parish be rid of the monk and his bone box."

Mevr. Geerts let out a long breath. "Thank you. You're good boys, both of you. Now I'd best be going, before anyone misses me."

She turned down Dietger's offer to walk her part of the way back to the church, and slipped out of the back door to the shop, glancing both ways to make sure she would not be seen before heading down the alley. Dietger locked the door behind her. He poured a glass of wine for himself and returned to his chair by the fire, motioning for me to join him.

"Unless Mevr. Geerts has a very active imagination, I think we've got another dangerous item that's gotten loose," Dietger sighed. "Now what do we do?"

"Damned if I know," I replied. "Your father and Alard were the brains of the operation." Alard was my maker, my father in the Dark Gift. It was Alard who had recruited Dietger's father, Carel, into the business of scouting out dangerous objects. Alard and Carel were killed during our last mission, and before he died, Carel made both Dietger and me swear to continue their work. Unfortunately, neither of us had been privy to the business long enough to know what exactly that meant.

"What did your father tell you about his work with Alard?" I asked.

Dietger shook his head and took a sip of wine. "Not much. I was off at university, and I'm sad to say I didn't pay a lot of attention to the shop. I had met Alard on occasion, but I discovered he was a vampire quite by accident, when I got nosy about the strange marks on father's arm."

"Did you know Alard was extending your father's life?"

Dietger sighed. "No, although I thought it was remarkable that father was so spry for his age. He was longer-lived than the rest of the family, and I was happy to put it down to cautiousness and clean living," he added with a deprecating smile.

"How about you? Do you know how Alard disposed of the items?"

It was my turn to look chagrinned. "If you mean, do I have a ready list of his contacts, no. For the first while, after I'd been turned, Alard just told me what I needed to do for the job. I was in the business of stealing, and I figured Alard used the things I stole to maintain our rather comfortable lifestyle."

If I had needed to breathe, I would have let out a long sigh. "As time went by, and Alard learned to trust me, I began to get a glimpse behind the curtain. Some of the items we destroyed. Some we had to return to the place they'd been taken from, because they were part of a binding spell or curse. Then there were the few that Alard 'took care of.'"

"Do you know *how* he took care of them?" Dietger asked, taking another swallow of wine.

I grimaced. "Not really. Sometimes, Alard would go out with the object, and come back without it. Once or twice, he met someone, exchanged a few words, and the stranger took the package. No introductions were made."

"So you have no idea who he contacted or how he set up the meetings," Dietger summarized, "or how he decided which items to handle himself and which to hand off?"

"Not precisely," I admitted. "As the years went on, I started to ask more questions. Alard always answered me, but now I see that his answers left a good bit unsaid." I paused. "Although I may have overlooked something."

Dietger raised an eyebrow. "Oh?"

I looked away. "A number of years ago, after one of our 'jobs' got a bit dicey and Alard and I nearly didn't survive, Alard gave me a key to a flat outside of Antwerp and told me that I must only use the key if he had been destroyed." I wondered now if Alard had a premonition about the mission that killed him. In a hundred years, Alard had never brought me to Antwerp, though we traveled all over Europe together.

"What did you find?" Dietger asked, in a tone that let me know he had repeated the question more than once to jolt me out of my thoughts.

"Nothing. I mean, I haven't gone yet." Alard's passing was so recent, and my grief so fresh, that I had put off going, as if procrastination could make his death less final.

"Father told me that, if anything happened to him, I should go to the Crooked Gate, an inn on the outskirts of town, and ask for a box they were keeping for 'de Heer Oldman.'"

"Oldman," I chuckled. "An interesting *nom de guerre*. And did you go?"

Dietger nodded and drained the rest of his wine. He stood and crossed to a large desk, which he unlocked, withdrawing a small iron box that was also locked. I watched as he withdrew the key from a chain around his neck, and opened the box. Inside was a yellowed piece of parchment, which he handed to me.

I read down through the cramped handwriting and looked up. "It's the deed to a burial vault in Groenplaats," I said.

"With a note that I'm to 'pay my respects' to the vault in the event something were to happen to father," Dietger remarked. "The wording is very specific. It says nothing about burying father there. Just a mandate for me to visit." He paused. "And no, before you ask, I haven't gone yet, either. It's only been a few weeks… I just wasn't ready."

"Sounds like we've both got tasks to do—once we take care of Mevr. Geerts' little relic problem."

"She said Father Verhelst was holding special masses this week," Dietger said. "Let's go have ourselves a look at that box of bones."

"I DON'T KNOW why you think I needed to come along," I muttered as we approached St. Walpurgis Church. The old stone church was not as elaborate as the city's newer cathedrals, but what it lacked in architectural ornamentation, it made up for in a sense of permanence, as if it sprang from the bedrock of the land beneath it.

"I want to get your impression of our good traveling monk," Dietger replied. He paused and looked at me. "Unless there's a reason you can't enter?"

I knew what he meant. It was a common misunderstanding that vampires could not enter a church or stand in the presence of holy relics. Alard had explained these rumors, one of the few times his voice had grown bitter. Those of us with the Dark Gift were not cursed by God, as churchmen assured the masses. Nor were we abominations, Alard said, no more so than any other predators on the face of the Earth, including mortals, the deadliest of all nature's killers. Vampires avoided churches for a single reason: we were certain most of the church-goers would happily murder us if we were revealed.

True, silver burned our skin, but that was so whether the silver was part of a crucifix or a lady's bracelet, a matter of alchemy. Holy items often were made of silver or painted with silver, making them uncomfortable for us to handle, and silver objects tainted anything contained in them, hence the fables about holy water being dangerous for our kind. Hearing mass would not cause me to burst into flames, as some alleged, nor would I be unable to speak God's name from my undead lips.

No, only one thing was denied to us, and the irony of it was not lost on me. I could not receive Eucharist, because the miracle—or magic—that caused wine to become the blood of our Lord warred with the magic of the Dark Gift. Vampires were God's bastard children, Alard had said, forever denied the feast and absolution, exiled to wander in hunger and darkness.

"I can enter," I replied quietly. "But I dare not take the cup. We'd best sit in the back."

Still, I felt nervous as we crossed the cathedral's threshold. I was not afraid of the hand of God. I had not been overly religious before I was turned, something which probably contributed to my thiefly vocation. Undead, I did my best to hew to the code of honor to which Alard subscribed, killing only when necessary, drinking from animals or miscreants whenever possible, stealing only from those who would hardly miss the baubles. In my observation, Alard's code constrained my actions far more circumspectly than did the faith of many church-goers, but I might have been a tad biased in that regard.

No, my nervousness stemmed from the crush of mortals in which I found myself, many of whom I had no doubt would consider burning me would be the height of moral rectitude. I had made sure to feed well before we came, so that my skin was as flushed and warm as it would ever be, and to avoid feeling peckish among so many beating hearts.

A glint of gold caught my eye, and I elbowed Dietger. An icon of St. Walpurga hung on the wall, resplendent in gold leaf, and beneath it was a granite chalice on a shelf. Many of the faithful stopped to ask a blessing of the saint, and more than one dipped a finger into the empty chalice and touched it to somewhere on their body of that of a child or cripple who accompanied them.

"It would seem that the saint's icon may also weep healing oil," Dietger murmured. "Interesting."

What interested me was why a long-established church would fall so quickly under the sway of a fraudulent monk, especially when it had its own, presumably bona fide, miraculous relic. I scanned the crowd, looking for a likely candidate to be Friar Jansen. We settled into the back of the church, and I selected a shadowed place from which I could have a broad view and yet not attract attention.

A small choir began an *a cappella* chant, and the crucifer began the walk down the center aisle. I scanned the procession. Father Verhelst was easy to spot in his vestments. To my surprise, Friar Jansen, clad in a plain cassock, followed the priest in the processional, taking a seat of honor to the side. I looked more closely at the two clerics. Father Verhelst was a man of in his middle years with a broad, plain face. I remembered Mevr. Geerts' comment about the good father's lack of curiosity, and saw nothing in the priest's eyes or manner to contradict the observation.

There was, however, something my heightened senses discerned as the priest swept past me. A certain stiffness in his movements, a constant flickering of his eyes, and the set of his jaw gave me to think that Father Verhelst was under pressure, or perhaps, I thought, eyeing the traveling monk, compulsion.

For all that Father Verhelst was a blank slate, Friar Jansen was another matter. The monk was a thin, stooped man whose cassock hung on his skeletal frame like a shroud. Jansen's pallor nearly equaled my own, and for an instant, I wondered if he were also undead. No, I corrected myself as he passed by, I could hear a heartbeat, smell his blood. Mortal, and yet not quite right, though I could not put my finger on what was wrong.

As I watched the procession, Friar Jansen slowly turned as if he felt my stare. For a second, our gazes locked, and I felt a ripple of fear at the cold depths of those eyes. *What*, I wondered, *did he make of me?*

Could whatever had altered him also alert him to the presence of the undead among the faithful?

Jansen's attention turned away from me, and I stifled a sigh of relief. Then I noticed the reliquary in his hands. It was an ornate box of elaborately carved dark wood, roughly the size of a lantern, a rectangular shape with a peaked top. I extended my senses toward the reliquary and instinctively recoiled. What I touched was ancient and evil, and I marveled that none of the mortals could sense its ominous presence. Then again, I corrected myself; perhaps they did on some unconscious level. As Friar Jansen made his way toward the chancel, the worshippers on the ends of each row fidgeted away from the aisle, shrinking from something they could not name.

The rood screen of this church had been removed, and so we had a clear view of Father Verhelst going about his priestly duties. I was surprised that after all this time, my long-ago catechism stood me in good stead, and I managed to make my way through the Mass without fumbling. Alard had taught me Latin, and so I was able to follow the Mass, something that had eluded me in my mortal days. *How many of these people have given any thought to the reality of the "eternal life" they pray for?* I wondered, knowing that my own relative immortality had enlightened me to the dark side of deathlessness. *You know what they say, be careful what you wish for.*

Had my heart been able to beat, it would have pounded nervously as the time came for the Eucharist. I watched Father Verhelst remove the host from its tabernacle and pour out the wine, saying the words of institution. *"Hoc est enim Corpus meum* [this is my body]" The consecration of the host, which Catholics believed to be the miracle of transubstantiation, turning bread and wine into the literal body and blood of Christ. *"Hic est enim calix Sanguinis* [this is the cup of my blood]." Unexpectedly, I felt a pang of sadness as I eyed the silver chalice, knowing that if such a miracle had, indeed, taken place, then Father Verhelst held the one blood from which I was forbidden.

To steer my thoughts in another direction, I eyed the large stone altar, and my gaze fell to the altar cavity, marked by an elaborate carved bas relief of St. Walpurga. Echoes of my long-ago catechism came back to me, and I felt a tingle of excitement as one particular memory surfaced. The altar cavity held a saint's relics, preferably those of a martyr, by requirement, a piece of the saint's body. Relics that were to be encased in a lead reliquary. My gaze flickered to Father Jansen and his damnable box, one that a devout woman swore she had heard laugh and seen bleed.

If Saint Walpurga's bones weren't scattered, then whose bones are in the altar? I wondered. And if the church already has one set of relics, why get more? One other question occurred to me, and I felt a sudden chill. *Friar Jansen's relics aren't encased in lead. Lead traps and concentrates power. Whatever's in that damned box, that little wooden filigree isn't going to keep it contained, not if it really wants to get out.*

To my relief, I was apparently not the only one to go unshriven and therefore not file to the front to receive the host. I kept my head down as I knelt, hoping that I looked as if I were praying intently, all the while trying to put the pieces of the puzzle together as the Latin droned on. Finally, the Mass ended, and the processional made its way to the nave. I noticed that the chalice remained on the altar, and remembered what Mevr. Geerts had said about Father Verhelst being remiss in properly disposing of the consecrated wine. That seemed a major oversight, and I wondered again just what was on the good father's mind to make him so derelict in his duty.

Dietger and I did not speak until we were safely back at Vanities. A quick comparison of our observations brought us back to three relics: the weeping icon, the mysterious altar items, and whatever unholy thing resided in Friar Jansen's reliquary.

"Alard maintained a correspondence with a man in Antwerp who used to be a professor of history at the University at Leuven," I said, a plan forming as I spoke. "I remember his address since I often posted Alard's letters for him. I think it would be wise to pay him a call and see what he knows about St. Walpurgis Church," I said.

Dietger nodded. "And tomorrow, I thought I would take a stroll in the morning along the lane where Mevr. Geerts gets her milk, and see if she can tell us anything about the icon, as well as the altar relics. I can't help thinking that there's a reason Friar Jansen traveled to this specific church with his relic at this particular time. I think the answer to the riddle is right under our noses—if we can figure it out."

The Mass took place just after sunset, so the evening was still young when I left Dietger at Vanities and headed in search of Alard's friend. I remembered a name, Simon Cuvelier, and an address that was on the edge of town. I paid a man with a wagon to drive me to Cuvelier's house, not wanting to make an appearance too late in the evening, as I was arriving unexpected and uninvited.

"I hope you've got a place to spend the night," the driver said, breaking his silence as we rode out of the thickly settled areas and down a road where the houses were few, and the open spaces between them were dark.

"Why's that?" I asked, curious.

He gave me a sidelong glance as if I were an idiot. "Surely you know that the saint's night is coming? Saturday is the first of May, and that means the night before is the feast of St. Walpurga. 'Tis a bad time to be about at night. The dead leave their graves, and spirits wander the empty places." He shivered. "They say the dark spirits of the Wild Hunt sweep across the hills, collecting the souls of people foolish enough to be abroad." He flicked the reins, and the horses picked up their pace.

"After I drop you off, I'm headed back home to stay until morning," he added. "And to be honest, if you hadn't offered me silver to bring you, I probably wouldn't have agreed to it." He glanced from side to side nervously, and it was clear that he was regretting the arrangement the more he thought of making the trip home alone.

"I'll be fine," I assured him. I might not have been as confident had I been mortal, but with the speed, strength, and sensory advantages of being a vampire, my chances were good against most things that went bump in the night.

"If you say so," he replied, warily watching the shadows at the edge of the roadway. Personally, I doubted that Professor Cuvelier would welcome me as an overnight guest. I intended to return to Vanities that night and counted on my enhanced speed to get me there safely. Such bursts of energy were limited, however, which was one of the reasons I had chosen to hire a ride. The driver's nervousness was beginning to affect me, and although I didn't sense danger in the shadows, I suspected that I would be looking over my shoulder the entire way home. The wind had picked up, cold and sharp. I didn't flinch from it the way the driver did, but then again, I was always cold.

At the gate to the professor's house, I gave the driver an extra coin for his trouble. He urged his horse to a fast trot, and I wondered if he would ride at full gallop as soon as he was out of my sight. Something about what he had said prickled in the back of my mind, but the thought eluded me. I looked toward the windows of the small house, heartened that there was a glow within. I would have hated to journey all this way to find the professor was not at home.

I knocked at the door, then stood back a pace so that Professor Cuvelier would be able to see me from the window. Whether or not he would open his door was another matter. The cold wind whipped my hair and tore at my cloak. The curtains twitched, and I had a glimpse of a thin, dark-haired man with a pinched face. I smiled, careful not to show my long eye teeth. Cautiously, the window opened a crack.

"Do I know you?" the professor called through the opening.

"I'm Alard's apprentice, Sorren," I replied, doing my best to look non-threatening. "I'm sorry to bother you, but I need your help on a most urgent matter."

I wouldn't have faulted him if he had closed the windows and drawn the curtains, leaving me out in the cold. To my surprise, a moment later I heard the bolt slide back, and the door opened. "Come in, quickly," he said, giving a glance to each side.

I stepped into a modest cottage redolent with the smell of beef stew. A tall shelf packed with scrolls and a few leather-bound manuscripts sat opposite the fireplace, and from the quill and parchment on the table, it was clear I had interrupted the professor's work.

Cuvelier gave me a head to toe glance as if appraising Alard's choice of apprentices. "Where's Alard?" he asked.

"Alard was killed in an accident two weeks ago," I replied. "He's left the business, so to speak, to me."

"I see." Again, Cuvelier raked me with an evaluating gaze, and then nodded and stepped to one side. "Please, sit down."

Two worn but comfortable chairs were near the fire, and Cuvelier motioned for me to take one as he sat in the other. Outside, I could hear the wind howling, but the cottage was pleasant and warm. "Now tell me, Sorren, what brings you out to a stranger's house on such a night?"

"I'm looking into a matter for a friend," I began, uncertain of just how far to take Cuvelier into my confidence. "The matter concerns St. Walpurgis Church. I remembered that Alard said your specialty was history, and I was hoping that you could tell me a little more about the Church's origins."

Cuvelier seemed to consider my question for a moment, then rose and went to a shelf, taking down a yellowed piece of parchment. He spread it out on the table, and I could see that it was a map of Antwerp, but quite old. "St. Walpurgis Church was built in the early 1100s," he said. "It was named for one of the patronesses of Antwerp, Saint Walpurga, protectress against dark magic."

My eyebrows lifted at his last comment. "Why would Antwerp feel a need for protection from that particular saint?"

Cuvelier smiled. "Surely you've heard the legends about the city's founding? The tale of the giant?"

I nodded. "Of course."

"Antwerp was built on an ancient mound, a place legends say many dark creatures were bound deep in the caverns below," Cuvelier went on. "Those caverns extend beneath St. Walpurgis Church. There's a very deep cave beneath the church with a pool of water some say is bottomless. There were rumors, when the church was founded, that putting a holy site over that deep well might contain the spirits that were believed to escape from the caverns and cause mayhem. The city's fathers may have felt it prudent to invoke the help of a saint such as Walpurga, who was said to have prevailed against the hounds of Hell herself." He gave me a look as if he were testing my credulity.

After what the wagon driver had said, Cuvelier's comments did not seem as outlandish to me as they might have just a few candlemarks before. "The hounds of Hell," I repeated. "Does that include the Wild Hunt?"

A smile spread across Cuvelier's thin lips, and he brushed back a stray lock of brown hair from his eyes. "Ah, you've heard the stories?"

"The man who drove me out here seemed to think there was a very real risk of running into the Hunt on the way home," I ventured, and it was my turn to watch for his reaction.

Cuvelier met my gaze. "Alard trained you well," he said. "Perhaps your mission will best be accomplished if we stop dancing around each other." He straightened. "I don't claim to know all of your master's business, but I did know something of his efforts to remove dangerous objects from circulation, and I both knew and accepted what he was," he added with a meaningful look.

"What do you know about the relics in the altar at St. Walpurgis Church?"

Cuvelier put his map away and sat on the edge of the table. "St. Walpurgis isn't the largest or the wealthiest church in Antwerp, but for some reason, it's drawn more than its share of attention over the years," he said.

"There's talk that a famous painter may do a mural for the church, and several wealthy patrons have left generous bequests over the years," the professor continued. "But there is a darker legacy as well. Several of the church's first priests died under mysterious circumstances, and there were disappearances near the church—and some gruesome corpses found—for over a hundred years after its founding." He pursed his lips as he thought.

"What made the problems stop?"

Cuvelier gave me a knowing smile. "A new altar was given to the church by a nameless benefactor, with the bones of St. Elionette enclosed in the reliquary inside the altar."

"St. Elionette?"

Cuvelier's smile grew broader. "St. Elionette's legend is not as widely known as the stories of many of the saints. She was a Breton girl who resisted the attentions of a powerful man in her city. He punished her by sealing her up in a cave without food or water for seven days. When the cave was opened, the legend claims, she had been torn limb from limb, and her blood drained, though there was no other opening in the cave." Cuvelier shrugged. "She became the patron saint of the victims of monsters."

Dark magic and monsters. I thought back to the spate of recent unexplained deaths Mevr. Geerts had told us about, deaths that coincided with Friar Jansen's sudden appearance. *Could whatever is in the box cancel out the relics in the altar?*

"Were there any other relics in the church?" I asked.

Cuvelier stared into the fire for a moment, thinking. "Legend has it that when the church was first built, the townspeople took two of the bones of the giant as well as the bones of murderers and dropped them into the cave and the well, hoping that the church would seal their evil." He shrugged. "For a while, the deaths in the town stopped. When they began again, the new altar seemed to end them."

Until Friar Jansen appeared with his box of bones. "If something broke the warding from the new altar," I said hesitantly, "how could it be put right?"

The wind swept past the cottage with such violence that I could hear shutters being torn from their moorings. The fire sparked, and embers swirled in the fireplace. With a crash, one of the front windows shattered, and the blast of cold air put out the lanterns. There was a thud, and something moved in the shadows that had not been there moments before. I heard a sound like the rattling of chains.

Cuvelier was on his feet in an instant. "Who's there?"

I moved to stand between Cuvelier and the shadow, but something knocked me to the floor with enough force to slam me into the floorboards. Cuvelier screamed, and I heard the snarl of a wild beast and the snick of teeth before I could regain my footing.

A huge black dog stood over Cuvelier, its fur matted, its eyes glowing yellow, and its sharp-toothed maw red with fresh blood. Alard had warned me about the *kludde*, but I had never seen one before. The hellish dog stood larger than a mastiff, with a rusted chain for a collar. I lunged for the *kludde*, trying to pull it away from Cuvelier's body, fearing I was already too late. My strength should have moved it easily, even if it were the size and weight of a draft horse, but the *kludde* barely budged. I bared my own fangs and roared at it, something that was enough to send any wild animal I had ever encountered running. This time, I succeeded in getting it to turn its ugly head toward me and felt the cold glow of its eyes fix on mine.

The hellhound sprang at me, fast enough that my reflexes could not get me completely out of its way as it attacked, snarling through sharp teeth that bested mine, its clawed feet outstretched. I evaded the jaws but felt the claws tear through my sleeve and gouge into my arm, leaving a deep gash. I managed to put myself between the *kludde* and Cuvelier, unsure whether or not the professor still lived, and equally unsure that I would be able to hold the beast at bay. Desperate, my choices were few. I could perhaps save my own skin by levitating myself to the ceiling or using my speed with the hope of outrunning the hound, but that would leave Cuvelier unprotected. Instead, I grabbed the iron fire poker and swung it with all my vampire strength, a blow that should have felled anything made of flesh and bone.

The massive black dog snarled and sprang again, crushing me to the floor under its weight, which seemed far too heavy for its size. It took all my might to keep the snapping jaws away from my throat. *Anything short of beheading or a stake to the heart I can survive*, I thought, though Alard had always been a bit vague on that topic.

The *kludde's* teeth tore into my shoulder, and I gasped with pain, bucking and twisting to throw it off of me. Its claws raked across my chest, slicing to the bone. I sank my fangs into its front leg with enough strength to break bone. It flinched, and I twisted my head sharply, taking dark satisfaction in being able to inflict a wound on my attacker.

The black dog drew back as I released its leg from my jaws, giving me the opening I sought. I leveraged my feet beneath the belly of the beast and shoved with all my strength. It snapped at me, and its claws tore across me, so that I gained my freedom but lost more of my skin in the process. My waistcoat was shredded and covered with the ichor that was my undead blood.

Cuvelier's moans had grown quieter, and I feared for him.

Looking into the jaws of the hellhound, I feared for myself. I knew from Alard's death that while I might be immortal, I was not indestructible. Outside, the wind rose in a furious howl, billowing the curtains through the broken windows and whipping sparks from the fire into the air. The sparks lodged on the curtains, catching them afire.

A desperate plan began to form. Excruciating pain flared through my injured shoulder as I bent down, never taking my eyes from the hellhound, and grabbed a fistful of Cuvelier's waistcoat, hefting him off the floor. With my good arm, I snatched up one of the darkened oil lamps and threw it at the *kludde*. My aim was good. The lamp smashed against the hell hound's solid frame, dousing it with oil. Just as the monster poised to spring, I muttered a curse under my breath and dove through the opening between the flaming curtains, doing my best to shelter Cuvelier with my body.

Flames caught at my clothing and hair. We landed hard outside the window, and I began to roll, still clinging to Cuvelier, attempting to douse the fire before it could engulf me. The grass, wet with evening dew, snuffed the flames though not before I felt my skin blister and peel in a dozen places.

The *kludde* followed as I had hoped it would. Flames licked at the oil that coated the huge black dog's matted coat, wreathing it in fire. For a moment, it seemed to hang in the air, its eyes the color of the fire, teeth bared. It gave an ear-splitting shriek, and disappeared.

I lay stunned on the lawn amid the broken stalks of Cuvelier's garden, his body still clasped in my arms. Where I had not been gouged by the hell hound I had been burned, and every motion was agonizing. Knowing that I would heal quickly did nothing to quell the pain. I willed myself to release my death grip on Cuvelier, afraid of what I would find. Gently, I set the professor down on the lawn. The cottage was afire, and it wouldn't take long before there would be onlookers. I did not dare be caught nearby, but my concern for Cuvelier overrode my fears for myself.

Cuvelier's color was gray, and his breath was shallow. The bites and gashes had gone deep, and the black dog's claws likely carried poison for mortals. In that, at least, I was spared. I could hear Cuvelier's heart struggling to beat, and I knew he was dying.

The professor's fingers closed around my wrist, and he worked to form words as he drew me down to hear his whisper. *"De profundis..."* he rasped. A spasm seized him, tearing a gasp from his throat and his fingers dug into my cold flesh. A breath later, and he fell back, dead.

In the distance, I could hear footsteps growing closer. I regretted leaving Cuvelier lie, but self-preservation took over and I ran, biting back my screams, willing myself to ignore the pain. I kept to the shadows, making for a stand of oak trees that ran along the roadway. Far away, I could hear the howling of dogs as the wind picked up once more, tearing through the branches overhead. Through the bare branches, I thought I caught a glimpse of black shapes against the stars, and wondered what sighting the Wild Hunt would do to one already dead.

Several candlemarks later, I let myself into Vanities through the back door.

"What the hell happened to you?" Dietger's voice was confirmation enough that I looked as bad as I felt. Despite the fact that I had brought down a deer that ventured too close to the roadway and drunk my fill from a vagrant whose luck was at an end, I knew I was not fully healed.

I waved off his concern. In the lamplight, I caught a glimpse of my hand and saw that the flesh had not yet knit closed where it had been flayed to the bone. Perhaps the wild look in Dietger's eyes was well deserved. "I'll be fine."

"Did you find the professor?"

I collapsed into a chair, regarding the cozy fire on the hearth with a shudder. "Yes. So did a hellhound."

The silence told me Dietger took my comment quite seriously. "Did you meet the Wild Hunt?"

"Near enough." I slouched in the chair, uncomfortably aware of the feel of sinew and skin stretching to cover the gashes. I gave him a brief recounting, to which he listened his a mixture of horror and concern.

"So we're left with another mystery," I said. "Which is, what Cuvelier meant by '*de profundis.*'"

"It's part of black vespers," Dietger said quietly. "The service for the dead that's usually said on All Hallow's Eve. It's from the Psalms, one that begins 'Out of the depths…'"

My eyes widened. "Oh shit," I gasped.

Dietger fixed me with a disapproving look. "That's not the next line of the Psalm."

"The depths," I repeated. "The well under the church. That's what this is all about. Whatever's in that box of Jansen's breaks the wardings that the relics in the altar placed on the bones in the well. We've got to get to that damned box and destroy it to seal the well again. And we'd better do it quickly before any more people die."

Dietger paled. "We have to do it tomorrow night."

That was not what my battered body wanted to hear. "Why tomorrow?"

"It's Friday, the saint's day—what the Germans call *Walpurgisnacht.*"

That was the tidbit that had been eluding me. The eve of the feast of St. Walpurga was a night when dark magic ruled, and the Wild Hunt rampaged. Alard and I had always stayed indoors, but I had chalked that up to mortals' fondness for the bonfires that lit the night on May Eve. It was the last triumph of darkness before the coming of spring, a celebration rooted in antiquity.

"Mevr. Geerts told me there have been two more deaths in the parish. She's afraid that if we don't break the power of that bone box before midnight tomorrow, all hell will—quite literally—break loose."

Now that's just a lovely thought. This job went from bad to worse at every turn. I shifted in my chair and saw that the bones of my left hand were finally covered with new, pale flesh. A glance told me that my shoulder was still raw muscle and tendon. Dietger kept his gaze averted, as if seeing me without my flesh was the equivalent of being without clothing.

"Did the good lady have any suggestions on just how we're to do that?" I couldn't help the tartness of my tone. Perhaps an older immortal like Alard would have weathered similar injuries with more grace and had stamina left over to save the world, but I was exhausted and aching, and it put me in a foul mood.

"Father Verhelst will say Mass at sundown when the bonfires are lit," Dieter replied, ignoring my tone. "Just before midnight, the town crier will call curfew, sending people back to their homes and warning them that spirits walk abroad. Mevr. Geerts says Father Verhelst goes to bed early, and the streets will be empty. We just need to get into the church and destroy the bone box before midnight. Mevr. Geerts will make sure the side door to the church is unlocked."

It sounded so simple when he said it that way. My last job, the one that cost Alard and Dietger's father their lives, had sounded simple at the beginning, too. Then things had gone badly wrong. But I had no plan of my own, and I could not fault his thinking.

"How do we do it?" I asked. "How do we destroy the bones?"

Dietger met my gaze, and by now I had apparently healed enough that he did not flinch. "I was hoping you had an inspiration on that."

I wondered if Dietger thought that most of my years with Alard were spent fighting monsters and battling supernatural forces. True, that was part of it. Fortunately for us, those battles had been relatively few and far between. Most of our work involved locating the questionable object, binding its power, and neutralizing the danger by destroying it or returning it. Perhaps we had been inordinately lucky, but the majority of cases had not put us in imminent peril.

"We don't know where Jansen got the box, or what exactly is in it, but if it's calling to whatever is in the well, it could even be slivers of the giant's bones," I speculated. "That's the only thing I can think of that might be powerful enough to disrupt the relics in the altar." I paused, racking my brain to remember all the ways Alard and I had disposed of dangerous items. It was a fairly short list: burning, crushing, submersion, dissection. "Throwing the giant's hand in the river worked in the legend," I said. "Perhaps we could drown it in holy water."

The look on Dietger's face made it clear that he was not fully convinced, but I figured we'd make it up as we went along. The night was far spent, and I was desperate for rest to complete my healing. Dietger showed me to a small room in the cellar his father had kept for Alard, and I collapsed, too tired for nightmares.

❦

I DID NOT RISE until sunset, and I was pleased to find myself wholly healed. That was good because going about in public torn to shreds would have raised uncomfortable questions. Dietger had left fresh clothing for me, along with a brace of rabbits for my breakfast. I had no doubt that he would make use of the drained carcasses for rabbit stew. Much refreshed, I climbed the stairs to find Dietger in the sitting room waiting for me.

"It's begun," he said, staring out the window. At first, the orange glow beyond the glass made me think that I had risen too early. But when I joined him, I could see that dozens of huge bonfires dotted the city streets.

I saw someone raise what appeared to be a body and cast it into the flames. I must have startled, because Dietger chuckled and I turned to him, horrified. "How can you laugh? They're burning someone out there!" *Perhaps someone like me.*

"You're the most sheltered thief I've ever encountered," Dietger replied. "That isn't a person. It's an effigy made from the last stalks of the harvest. Some people plow an effigy like that into the fields in the spring to ensure a good crop, and others hang one in their barns to ward off mice. Burning one of the figures is supposed to get rid of the past year's bad luck."

We waited until tenth bells to go out. The night was cool, but the bonfires at every turn warmed the air so that it felt like summer. I looked around at the people who thronged in the streets. Some gathered around the fires to sing, but more of the songs I heard were bawdy tavern tunes than befitted the night before a saint's day. If the glow of the bonfires didn't keep the waking dead and the Wild Hunt at bay, many of the townsfolk went through the streets beating drums, ringing bells and whacking pieces of wood against solid objects to frighten away the spirits. It felt more like a street festival than a night for dark magic.

St. Walpurgis Church loomed dark against the sky. We circled it twice, walking casually like two gentlemen out for an evening stroll. I eyed the door Mevr. Geerts had agreed to leave unlocked for us and was pleased that it was in a narrow alleyway toward the back of the building, away from prying eyes.

"Did Mevr. Geerts say where Friar Jansen would be tonight? It doesn't matter that Father Verhelst goes to bed early if the Friar is a night owl," I said.

"She overheard the friar telling Father Verhelst that he would be gone in the morning," Dietger said. I could imagine the housekeeper's relief, but suspicion chilled me. *Just where*, I wondered, *was the friar planning to go?* Several possibilities occurred to me, none of them good.

For nearly two candlemarks, we kept a careful vigil outside the church, shifting our location from time to time to avoid curious passers-by, and making sure to spend much of the time separate but within sight of each other. I saw no sign of light or movement in the church itself, although we watched as a lantern's glow traveled from the first floor of the rectory to what was presumably a second-floor bedroom. Around us, the crowd thinned until only the drunks remained, increasing our chances of getting into the church unseen.

Just as the eleventh bell sounded, Dietger and I left our positions and ambled by separate routes to the door at the back of the church. I put my ear to the wood and listened, but even I could make out no sounds within. Carefully, I turned the knob, and when it yielded, I inched the door open, cautious that the hinges remain silent. Nothing stirred.

I could see well in the shadows, but enough moonlight made its way through the stained glass to make it possible for Dietger to move without tripping. We moved through the vestry, alert for the slightest sound. The door to the sanctuary was also unlocked. I went first, my senses on high alert. If we were right and Friar Jansen had brought his bone box to Antwerp to loose the spirits beneath the church, then I feared he would be nearby to see his efforts to completion.

I looked around the darkened sanctuary. The smell of incense lingered from the earlier Mass. Once again, Father Verhelst had neglected to remove the chalice from the altar. But the relic box was not in sight.

We ventured a few steps further, and I caught the smell of fresh blood just as my toe struck something immovable. I looked down to find Father Verhelst's body splayed across the aisle.

Beside me, Dietger gasped. Even in the gloom, I could see that blood soaked the priest's cassock, enough blood to suggest his body had been savaged. We stepped over the dead priest and I saw further evidence of Friar Jansen's handiwork. A circle had been drawn in blood around the altar, and I wondered if the well lay directly beneath.

"Looking for this?"

Friar Jansen stepped from the shadows holding the reliquary aloft. The same light that had glowed in the *kludde's* eyes shone from his, mad and malicious. He had grown thinner just in the time since we had gone to Mass, as if he had barely enough skin to stretch across his bones. His eyes and cheeks were sunken, like something was eating him from the inside. Perhaps it was.

"It's almost time," he said, his mouth stretching in a rictus.

Dietger lunged to the left, while I dove right, toward the reliquary. Dietger was only supposed to draw off the friar, but he tackled him instead. I grabbed for the bone box as the two struggled, not surprised that Jansen was much stronger than he looked. Suspiciously strong, I found as I tried to wrest the box from his grasp, his strength nearly mirrored my own.

I tore the reliquary from the friar's bony fingers. Dietger continued to struggle with Jansen, and the sound of their thrashing echoed in the cavernous sanctuary.

I dared not allow myself to worry about Dietger's safety. The safety of all of Antwerp—perhaps all Europe—could well depend on being able to destroy the damned box before it could loose the shades sealed in the well.

I raised the reliquary overhead and dashed it to the stone floor, expecting that at least the wooden case would shatter. Instead, it merely rolled to one side, and I heard ghostly laughter, taunting me. I tore at the carved latticework, succeeding only in slicing my fingertips. Up close, I could see that its pointed top was open, just a bit, like a mouth.

A glance told me that Dietger was taking a beating at the friar's hands. I ran to the baptismal font and plunged the relic beneath the waters, hoping that Alard was right and that the blessed liquid would not boil the skin from my hands. Bubbles rose, as if I were attempting to drown a living thing, but neither my hands nor the relic were more than wet.

I threw the reliquary to the floor. I had brought a short length of iron with me, and withdrew it from my belt, beating the reliquary with my full strength, yet its deceptively fragile case did not crack. I smelled old, curdled blood, and I remembered what Mevr. Geerts had said about the relic bleeding.

It feeds on death, on blood.

Dietger was clearly losing his battle. Time was running out. I snatched up the reliquary and ran to the front of the sanctuary, taking the chancel steps at a bound. The sound of the crazed laughter grew louder as I approached the bloody circle, and I could hear the hiss of malignant whispers in the shadows as the bound spirits sensed freedom approaching. My gaze was fixed on one thing, the forgotten chalice.

The circle's warding hit me like a physical blow. It might have felled a mortal, but Jansen had been too focused on letting the dead free to worry about keeping an undead out. I set the reliquary on the altar, fearing every second that Janson would appear beside me to thwart my plans.

The silver chalice burned my flesh like a hot poker as I grasped it, and I cried out but did not loosen my grip. I poured the consecrated wine over the reliquary, fighting the pain to channel as much of it into the small opening at the top as I could. My hand shook as the skin charred, blackening from my palm past my wrist.

A high-pitched shriek pierced the gloom of the darkened church. I thought at first Jansen cried out in anger, but I realized that the shrieking came from all around me, loudest from the stairwells that led from the sanctuary down to the levels beneath, down eventually to the well.

Jansen finally freed himself of Dietger and belatedly ran for the chancel. My fear grew as I saw Dietger fall back, unmoving, when the traveling monk released him. The shrieking grew louder, and I took that to be a good sign, although I had no idea whether the bound spirits feared their escape was thwarted or were celebrating their imminent release.

Jansen had reached the chancel steps, his mouth drawn back into a snarl, eyes glowing yellow like the *kludde*. I had poured out the cup of wine, and in doing so, spent myself. Had I not been leaning against the altar, I would have fallen as the last few drops dripped into the reliquary.

Red wine stained the white altar cloth and stung my peeling hand. The wine looked no more sanguinary than any other, providing no clue as to whether its consecration had indeed turned it into god-blood. Ichor oozed from my hand where the burns had not cauterized the skin, mingling with the flood of red. *The blood of the undead, and the blood of the undying, to stop the resurrection of the damned.*

The reliquary exploded in a flash of white light so glaring that I flung my arms up to shield my face and squeezed my eyes tightly closed. The chalice ripped from my hand, taking shreds of skin with it. The bloody circle channeled the blast light upwards toward the windowed dome, smashing the fragile glass and sending a beam into the night sky. All around me, I heard the rattle of bones. Beyond the circle, I heard the mighty rush of wind sweep across the sanctuary, heard Jansen cry out, and heard wooden furnishings tossed about.

Then silence.

I was still conscious, so at least the white light had not cremated me. I opened my eyes and felt all of my exposed skin cracking as if I had ventured too close to a window at noon. The pain from my charred hand was excruciating. But I still existed.

The altar cloth was still white except for the wine's stains, and the chalice lay where I had dropped it, but only a pile of ash remained of the reliquary. The bloody circle was gone. I looked out over the sanctuary. Small tables and furnishings had been swept down the aisles as if carried by a whirlwind, but neither the pews nor the stained glass had been damaged.

Jansen's body lay crumbled at the foot of the chancel steps, his eyes wide but unseeing, skin sunken and yellowed like a long-dead corpse. I did not know what deal he had made with the reliquary, and now I would probably never know, but whatever bargain he had struck failed him.

Fear stuck in my throat as I searched the shadows for Dietger. A figure hunched over him, and I cried out, afraid of some new enemy. The figure turned, and I recognized Mevr. Geerts.

"He's alive," she said, answering my unspoken question. "The icon at the door wept oil earlier. There was a drop left, enough for the worst of his injuries. It's all gone now," she added. She looked at me, taking in my burned skin. "You don't look so good, either."

"You saw what happened?"

Mevr. Geerts smiled. "I hid in the balcony. I couldn't rest without knowing what happened."

I had been a central part of the action, and I still couldn't say for certain what happened. I couldn't quite bring myself to believe that the wine was more than wine, but I had little other explanation. When one dealt with the fabulous every day, at what point did the potentially miraculous stretch credibility? I knelt next to Dietger and was relieved to hear a steady heartbeat and regular breath, though he was certain to be sore and bruised from his fight.

I would try to make sense of things tomorrow, if I ever could. If not, the fact that we survived and that whatever was bound in the well beneath the church remained bound was enough for me. Despite my injuries, I was still capable of one more effort. I lifted Dietger and stood, heading for the door. "It's time to go home," I murmered to him. "It's over, for now. And after we've recovered, we need to visit a flat and a burial vault before our next adventure. I for one, would like to be a little more prepared."

DARK LEGACY

Alard was the best dead man I ever knew.

I stood in front of the door to Alard's mysterious flat in Antwerp, the one he had only mentioned once in our hundred years together, and hesitated with the key in my hand. The door almost felt alive, and there was a strange tingling as I put my hand to the lock. Yes, Alard had bequeathed the key, the apartment, and all its contents to me. Yes, I knew that Alard was truly gone, not only dead and undead, but destroyed for all time. Yet somehow, I knew that the instant I put the key in that lock, Alard's death would be real and final. And though I was over a century old, I wondered if I was really ready to face existence without him.

"Are you sure you're ready for this?" Dietger, my mortal friend, and business partner, was watching me with concern.

I managed a wan smile. "I don't think I'll ever be ready for this."

The lock yielded easily, and the tingling sensation passed as I crossed the threshold and found myself in a darkened room. I lit a lantern, and we stepped inside, locking the door behind us. In our business, it was never a good idea to have your back to the door.

In many ways, it was a typical Antwerp flat. I was surprised because the apartment was far less opulent than I would have expected.

Alard had been over three hundred years old, and a long existence tends to make it easier to accumulate wealth. Alard was my maker, the one who had brought me across into the dark gift, and as much of a father to me as anyone had ever been. In our time together, I knew we had turned quite a profit, which Alard had shared generously with me. I had set aside a tidy sum for contingencies and had assumed that Alard, having lived three times as long, had accumulated at least three times as much. Maybe he had and just chose to live frugally. Whatever his secrets, they were about to be bared to me.

Dietger lit another lamp, and then a third so that the room was illuminated. "Look at those," he murmured.

If I still were breathing, I might have caught my breath. Portraits large and small hung on the walls of the flat's parlor. They spanned the Continent and the past three hundred years, a variety of painters and artistic styles, with fashions as varied as their time and place, yet the face was always Alard's. Blond hair, crisp blue eyes, and slightly crooked nose in an otherwise perfect face, Alard looked like the young aristocrat he had once been, just over the cusp of thirty, before he had been turned by his maker in a debtor's prison.

"Do you know what you're looking for?" Dietger asked.

I shook my head. "No. Alard gave me the key and told me that if anything ever happened to him, I should come here." I smiled sadly. "In a century, you'd think he would have had time to tell me everything, but he didn't. I imagine he had his reasons. I hope the answers are here—I have a lot of questions."

Alard had recruited Dietger's father, Carel, into the "business." Everyone in Antwerp knew Carel—and now Dietger—ran an antiques and curio shop called Vanities. What few realized was that Vanities was far more than it seemed. Alard's real business was finding dangerous magical items that had found their way back into circulation, and removing or destroying them. Vanities served as a convenient front, and it also attracted sellers who might want to sell a troublesome family heirloom, something Dietger was all too happy to oblige.

Dietger resembled his father, with light brown hair and blue eyes. With his shopkeeper manner and charming smile, he seemed an unlikely partner for a dangerous business. I don't know whether or not I looked like my father since I never met the man. I did not resemble Alard. I was wiry and thin-built, with hair that was an unremarkable shade of blond. My eyes were my most memorable feature, blue-gray, the color of the sea before a storm. Other than that, my features were pleasant enough without standing out, a benefit back in my mortal days when I was a jewel thief. Unlike Dietger, I was a very likely partner for dangerous work, which was why Alard had saved me from the guards after a botched robbery and given me the dark gift.

Now Alard and Carel were gone, leaving Dietger and me with final orders to carry on their work. I had to hope that somewhere in this flat, Alard had left me what I needed to know to do just that.

"What are we looking for?" Dietger asked.

I shook my head dumbly. "I have no idea. Before this visit, Alard never brought me to Antwerp in the century we worked together, although occasionally, he left on his own for a few days or weeks at a time. He might have come here at those times, but he never mentioned it."

"Let's see what we find."

Moving through the flat gave me a view of Alard that a century of companionship had not. In one of the portraits, the oldest, he posed with a handsome family: a lovely wife, four healthy-looking children, even a dog. The clothing confirmed what Alard had once told me, that he had been born to nobility. I looked at the face of the young man in the painting. Proud, confident, certain that the world was his to conquer. Yet not long afterward, gauging by his age in the portrait, Alard's father had gone into debt so deeply that Alard had been seized as a surety and thrown into prison. When his maker turned Alard, he saved him from a lingering death in a dungeon. Yet he had cost Alard everything: love, family, and position, in return for near-immortality. It was a steep price to pay.

Together, Dietger and I made a careful search of the parlor. "Alard had interesting friends," Dietger observed wryly.

That was an understatement. We found personal correspondence between Alard and Dante Alighieri, and I wondered if Dante had known what Alard was and sought his input, if not exactly on the nature of hell, then on what dark creatures lay outside most mortals' awareness. A painting by Bosch that I had never seen in any museum hung beside two framed woodcuts by Dürer. A bust of Alard, done in white Italian marble, looked suspiciously like masterworks I had glimpsed in palaces and cathedrals. Everywhere I looked, I saw clues to the man I thought I knew.

"Your master had excellent taste." Dietger was handling an illuminated manuscript with awe. I had no idea whether Alard acquired his treasures by purchasing them, stealing them, or receiving them as gifts, but they revealed a more brooding and introspective side than Alard usually let show, of a man who had never relinquished the perquisites of his former life.

There was a large brass-bound chest with a complex lock to one side of the room. I couldn't help it: I had been a jewel thief far too long. I knelt next to the chest, my fingers itching to work out its secrets. It was a challenge, and in the back of my mind, I could hear Alard's laughter, taunting me to finish the job. Behind me, Dietger continued to work his way through the contents of the flat, occasionally commenting on the value of the find or Alard's exquisite taste. Crystal and silver serving pieces, men's jewelry, beautifully tailored clothing, currency from a dozen kingdoms, Alard stored his precious objects here in an otherwise nondescript flat in a very moderate section of Antwerp.

The lock yielded to my skill, and I lifted the lid. Inside was enough gold to ransom any king in Europe several times over. Atop the gold was a letter in Alard's handwriting, addressed to me.

I rocked back on my heels, flummoxed for the first time in a very long while. We hadn't completed a full search of the flat, but what we had seen so far equaled anything to be found in the most illustrious palaces of Europe, and perhaps Asia too. And I had a sneaking suspicion that the letter in my shaking hands left it all to me.

I read the letter slowly, knowing that it was the last message from Alard that I would ever receive. I read it hearing his voice in my mind, and it comforted me even as it broke my heart.

My Dear Sorren,

I must assume that you are reading this because I have met the final death. You were the last, and best, of the very few whom I brought across. You are my blood-son, and to you, I leave all that I possess.

In this flat, you will find the deed to properties and safe houses across Europe, as well as to the land and building that houses Vanities. You will find valuable items which are now yours to keep or sell as you see fit, and gold enough to allow you to retire a wealthy man, should you wish to do so. In my desk, you will find accounts I have kept at banks across the Continent and Asia. Use them well, and you will never again be in want.

I leave another, darker legacy to you as well, I fear. There is a man who goes by the name of Holmgang. He and I first crossed swords when I was turned. If he is not the one who caused my final death, it is not for lack of trying. I have kept him away from you, but now that you inherit my work, you have become the enemy of Holmgang. Holmgang was a Norse rogue, an undead raider and outcast sorcerer who exacted a terrible price from the Normandy coast three hundred years before I was brought across. My maker broke his army and sent him home, badly damaged. Holmgang never forgave him, and when my maker was destroyed, Holmgang focused his hatred on me. Immortal vengeance has no end. He is not to be underestimated. He will come after you, I fear, now that I am gone, or after your mortal partners. You bear the burden to defend them.

Three items may help you survive. A spae-woven shirt which makes the wearer invisible and impervious to iron, a bone carved with runes, and a spindle whorl—powerful magic for those who know how to weave a spell. Watch for the death horse, and if it comes, call for Secona. She is a spae-wife, and a seiðr woman, strong in the ways of Seiðr. Call her name three times beneath a birch tree, and she will come.

Along with my possessions, you inherit my role with the Alliance, work with which you are already well acquainted. I fear that I may not have shared everything you need to know. A man named Erikonos will find you, and he will explain what I have not. Finally, my blood-son, guard well this apartment. It has been spelled by powerful mages and is a safe place of last resort. Find shelter here when nowhere else is safe.

I have nothing else to give you, Sorren. Be well, and keep my memory.

Alard

Vampires can't cry. We bleed, and it's not pretty. I choked back my tears, unwilling to let Dietger see me covered in blood. I know I didn't fool him, but he was kind enough not to say anything. He had just lost his father. He understood.

Briefly, I recapped the letter. "Death horse?" Dietger asked.

I shrugged. "Alard had a tendency to think he had told me things that he had neglected to mention. This is one of those times."

Dietger let out a long sigh. "What now?"

I looked around the flat. "We finish getting our bearings here, see what else is left, and then it's your turn."

"Somehow, I doubt my father left me a trunk full of gold."

I didn't say anything, but I wasn't so sure. Alard had a generous streak, and Carel had been a trusted partner and something even more rare: a mortal friend. I was certain Alard had taken very good care of him.

"What about Erikonos and Secona?" Dietger's voice jarred me out of my thoughts.

"It sounds like Erikonos will show up in his own time," I replied. "As for Secona… we know how to summon her if we need her."

We spent another candlemark in the flat, continually astounded by the treasures Alard had accumulated, and the evidence that he had known and counted as friends some of the most illustrious men of his long existence. Then we locked up the flat and left. Everything about it made Alard's absence that much more final. I tried not to show how much the loss weighed on my mind.

~

IT WAS LATE when we left Alard's flat, and we had one more place to go before turning in for the night. Carel had left Dietger instructions to "visit" a crypt in Groenplaats, one of Antwerp's old cemeteries. The note had been interestingly vague, but clear about one thing: Dietger was to pay his respects to the crypt, but not to bury Carel there. We were both certain that meant Carel had left his final instructions in the crypt. What those instructions were was anyone's guess.

Groenplaats was in the center of the city, within the city walls, and had been used as a burying ground since the 1200s. I walked among the tombstones and felt the age of the place settle on my shoulders like a mantle. I glanced toward Dietger. He looked uneasy. That was to be expected. We were walking into an ancient cemetery well after midnight, and while I was used to such things, most mortals were not.

Dietger was far too sensible to be jittery about shadows. I was vigilant for another reason. I was quite well aware that the night was full of entities that were not living but not truly dead. In the course of my work with Alard, I had met my share of malevolent specters, hungry ghouls, and a host of other supernatural beings that made my own vampiric nature seem civilized by comparison. We did not need to meet any such creatures tonight, beings that truly deserved the title "monster."

"That's it." Dietger pointed toward an old stone crypt. The small stone building was unassuming, its markings nearly unreadable after many years exposed to the weather.

"Family tomb?" I asked.

Dietger shook his head. "Not to my knowledge. We've buried a few of father's relatives in the last few years, but not here."

It was certainly possible that the crypt was an old family relic. It was also possible, I thought, that Carel had somehow acquired the crypt to serve as a repository. By the look of it, no one had entered in many years. The front door was of solid metal, but the lock, to which Dietger had a key, turned easily.

Inside, there was barely room for the two of us to stand in a tiny vestibule facing four individual "drawers" in which remains could be placed. There were no windows, so we had no fear of discovery when we unshuttered our lanterns for a better look.

"No names," Dietger said, gesturing toward the fronts of the niches. He was correct. Where the names of the deceased should have been carved into the stone or a metal plate affixed, there was nothing. "Do you think that means that no one's actually buried here?"

I shrugged. "One way to find out." Dietger looked a bit green at the idea of opening the niches, but since my turning, death and I have become, if not old friends, then close acquaintances. Personally, I find a long-dead corpse much less bothersome than a fresh one. A pile of rotting cloth, matted bits of hair and clean bones looks little like the person as he or she once appeared. But a fresh corpse is jarring in its emptiness. I have seen enough of both kinds to be sure.

Perhaps it might have taken more than one mortal to wrest open the first niche, but additional strength is one of the benefits of my undead existence. I knew from the moment the niche slid free that there was nothing to trouble Dietger's more delicate sensibilities. No smell of death wafted from the newly-opened space. Instead, we found several large boxes of gold and silver coins, the deed to a house in Flanders, several velvet bags of expertly cut diamonds, and a piece or two of jewelry that to my eye suggested Holbein as its creator. On top of Carel's legacy was an envelope sealed with a wax crest.

Dietger sorted through the unexpected riches with an unreadable expression, and I wondered if I had appeared much the same at Alard's flat. I stood as far back as I could in the tight space, trying to give Dietger privacy. Dietger cracked the seal on the letter and read the letter silently. I was willing to bet that he read it several times for as long as he stood, utterly still, eyes fixed on the parchment. Finally, he sighed and folded it back up, placing it into the niche.

"It's much as you found with Alard," he said quietly. "He's left me a tidy sum—a small fortune, really—along with a safe house in Flanders. In the letter, he commends me to Alard's sponsorship, and failing that, to yours. He reminded me of the importance of the real work behind Vanities—removing the dangerous objects—and begs me to carry on the trust."

"And will you?" That question, unspoken, had hung between us for several weeks. I had already made my decision.

Dietger nodded. "Yes, and not just for father's sake. It's important work, something I'm proud to be part of."

I relaxed, just a little, at his words. I liked Dietger and suspected that, like our fathers, in time we could become friends. I'd had few mortal acquaintances since my turning, and no real friends other than Alard given the peripatetic nature of our business. By now, I was well in control of my hunger, so I did not think I posed a threat to Dietger outside extreme, nearly unthinkable, circumstances. He was familiar, if not entirely comfortable, with being around vampires, so I was reasonably certain he did not intend to cause me harm. Dietger was clever and agreeable, and while he was not a trained fighter, he had shown his mettle. I was optimistic about the future of our partnership.

"Let's have a look at the rest of these niches," I said. One by one, I opened them. We found more treasures, but no further correspondence. I noticed that both Carel and Alard had taken care to leave us wealth in a variety of forms, many of which were highly portable and easily liquidated. The implication that we might need to disappear suddenly and permanently was not lost on me, and from the look in Dietger's eyes, it had not eluded him, either.

"Let's go back to the shop," I said. Dietger lived in a flat above Vanities, while I took shelter from the daylight in a townhome Alard had rented when we arrived in Antwerp. I found myself uneasy and was resolved to see Dietger home safely, though I knew he was well-armed.

Few were about at this hour, and those who were, other than the constable, were well into their cups. If anyone wondered about two gentlemen out for a stroll in the wee hours of the night, they were polite enough not to ask.

"I forgot to mention that we received a package today," Dietger said as we left the cemetery. "You'll have to take a look at it tomorrow. It's a wide chalice—very ornate—and by the look of it, very old."

"Interesting. Any idea why it came to us, or who sent it?"

"It was addressed to father. There was a note inside, with the sender's name. A woman from the northern part of the city. She referred to a prior conversation with father and was sending the chalice as they had agreed. Her note inferred that she had inherited the cup from an elder relative, and she wished it sell it because she believed it gave her 'bad dreams.'"

Something about what Dietger said prickled in the back of my mind, but I couldn't quite gather my thoughts. Perhaps tomorrow, after a day's rest, I would remember. Now, my thoughts were still consumed by what we had found at the flat and in the crypt.

We were nearly back to Vanities when I grabbed Dietger by the arm. "Wait," I cautioned.

Dietger followed my line of sight and frowned. "What in the name of God is that?"

In front of the shop, someone had pounded a wooden pole between the paving stones of the sidewalk. The pole was carved with runes, and atop it was a freshly severed horse's head.

"A niding pole," I replied, my voice flat. I was scanning the area for danger, since the pole was a clear threat. My hearing and sight are much keener than a mortal's, but I sensed nothing, beyond the few stragglers who had gathered around the bloody post.

"I guessed it wasn't a friendly gesture," Dietger said under his breath. "But what does it mean?"

Alard and I had traveled through the northern lands, and I knew that Alard's maker had been Norse, like his enemy Holmgang. From Alard, I had learned about the customs of those wind-swept places and the fearless people who called those places home. Alard had told me stories about the duels and curses, the gods and tricksters. The niding pole had made for a vivid story, but I had never expected to see one.

"It's a curse," I replied tightly. "The death horse. Those runes are insults and spells. The head faces the shop, and the old ones believed that the pole would channel the power of the death goddess up and through the head, directed toward whatever the skull faced. As if that's not bad enough, it desecrates the ground by driving out the land sprites and making it a dead place."

"Land sprites?" Dietger's tone was skeptical.

I fixed him with a glare that I suspected conveyed my thoughts. *Your business partner is a vampire, your store trades in cursed objects, and you've already seen your share of dark magic. And you question that there are sprites?*

"Does it work?" Dietger asked, foregoing his question.

I nodded. "Unfortunately, yes. At least, according to Alard. He didn't remember the old times, but his maker was from those days, when the Vikings preyed on the shores and riverbanks of most of Europe."

"What kind of curse does is cast?" Dietger eyed the niding pole with understandable uneasiness.

I looked at the pole with its bloody burden. "The usual. Death. Destruction. And if that's not bad enough, it made the recipient an outcast from the community."

"So we're supposed to be shunned before we die, or after?"

I met Dietger's gaze and knew his humor was a way of masking his fear. "Perhaps it sounds strange to modern folk, but don't discount the old ways. A niding pole is a potent curse, and there will be others who know what it means. This will cause problems—in addition to the curse itself."

"Can't we just remove the pole?" Dietger's expression begged for an easy answer.

I shook my head. "That won't remove the curse." After what we had learned in Alard's letter, I had no doubt that this was Holmgang's first salvo. "I think we're going to need the *seidr*-woman. And I'm betting that Alard suspected this would happen."

Dietger eyed the drunks and constable who had stopped to stare at the gory pole. "What about them?"

I shrugged. "Let's hope none of them know the old stories, and that Secona will come to us quickly."

We both agreed that summoning Secona was more important than sleep, so Dietger and I set out in search of a birch tree. We found one, finally, and made the invocation.

"What do we do now?" Dietger asked. "Do we wait here? If we go back to the shop, how would she know where to find us?"

It was a good question, and I didn't know what to tell him. Alard's directions had been rather sparse. "I don't know," I admitted. "She'll show up when she shows up—*if* she shows up," I added.

It was still several hours before daybreak, and the night was cold. We headed back to Vanities. The small crowd had dispersed, but someone had marked ugly runes on the door. Neither Dietger nor I wanted to pass the niding pole on the way into the store, so we went around to the back.

I stopped still in my tracks, and Dietger stopped, too. "Can you feel it?" I asked in a whisper.

"I can feel that something's wrong," Dietger said. "I just don't know what."

I have no magic, other than the old power of the dark gift. Yet to me, the ground beneath our feet had changed. It felt as if the ground itself had died, that its "soul" had departed, and what remained was something barren and unholy.

In the alley behind the shop, shadows shifted. Not shadows, but "somethings" that were waiting. Waiting for the accursed. For us. They were hungry. I could feel it in my bones. Among mortals, I was the top predator. But among the ancient immortals, a vampire was hardly more than a long-lived human. The shadows were ancient, as old as the world itself, maybe older. They were far more dangerous than I was.

"Let's go elsewhere," I said.

Dietger gave me a questioning look. "Land sprites?"

"Or something," I replied.

To my relief, the shadows seemed content to stalk the shop. They did not try to follow us. Perhaps they were bound to the niding pole or to the land it cursed. I just knew that until Secona cleansed the land, we were exiled.

We returned to Alard's flat. It was spelled to be safe, and comfortable for a mortal. I left Dietger there and went to feed, trolling the wharfs and the taverns where the cutpurses lurked for sustaining blood. I did not kill. Alard had long ago taught me to take what I needed without killing, to feed lightly from several donors and blur the memories to keep from being remembered. Before I went back, I bought cheese, dried meat, and bread along with a jug of wine for Dietger. I returned in less than a candlemark, anxious to be at rest before dawn, and found Dietger safe and asleep. I placed the food where I knew he would see it. Then I went into one of the windowless interior rooms, and died to the daylight.

I woke at sundown. Dietger had slept nearly as long as I did, though his rising was not tied to the darkness. "Thanks for the food," he said, still chewing a piece of the hard bread.

"I figured that if I was hungry, you would be too," I said. I looked around the flat at all the portraits of Alard. Seeing his face made me miss him even more. Right now, I missed his wisdom. Alard would know our enemy. He would know what to do about the niding pole. He would know how to assure that Secona found us. I knew nothing, except that I had sworn to Alard and Carel that I would protect Dietger. So far, I wasn't doing a very good job.

"Now what?"

I'd been asking myself that question since I had awoken. I still didn't have a good answer. "Perhaps we start at the birch tree," I said slowly, thinking as I spoke. I frowned as I looked at an item on the side table that had not been there the night before. "What's that?"

Dietger gave a half-smile. "That's the chalice the woman wanted us to sell for her. She left it wrapped in a parcel outside the door, and I grabbed it when you came for me. Since I'd already locked up, I put it in my bag," he said, indicating a small satchel he always carried.

I picked up the chalice and looked at it closely. It was wide and shallow, unlike a drinking cup. This looked to me like a ceremonial goblet, although I had little experience with such things. It was old, and it was carved with the same type of runes as the niding pole. Norse runes.

"So the woman said it caused her bad dreams," I mused, turning the goblet in the light of the lantern.

"That's what the note said," Dietger replied.

Bad dreams could come in so many forms. As I turned the chalice in the light, an old memory triggered. "This isn't a drinking goblet," I said quietly. "It's a seething cup."

"A what?"

"A scrying vessel," I replied. "A way to see the future, a type of divination."

"So perhaps it showed the woman what she didn't want to see?" Dietger said, looking closely at the chalice. "Something sad or dangerous, something bad."

"Bad dreams," I repeated. "Maybe the chalice isn't actually cursed. Maybe the woman is, and the chalice showed her what is to come."

"Or perhaps, the chalice is twisted, and it shows lies," Dietger said. "An untruthful scrying vessel would cause the bad luck it showed because people would alter their behavior."

I nodded. "Perhaps. Secona will know."

"If she comes." The question of how to find her, or how to help her find us without sitting night and day beneath the birch tree remained unspoken.

"One thing is certain. We're not going to get any answers hiding in here," I said when Dietger had finished eating. "We need to figure out what damage the niding pole has done for us with the townspeople and to the shop. And we need to find Secona. If the flat is spelled, she may not be able to find us here, so we need to be out there."

I withdrew the spae-woven shirt. "Put this on—please."

Dietger eyed the shirt warily. "Alard left it to you," he said. "Why are you telling me to wear it?"

I gave him a look. "One—it speeds healing. Two—it protects against iron. That rules out a lot of weapons. I'm a vampire. I heal very quickly from everything that doesn't destroy me. You don't."

Reluctantly, Dietger nodded. "All right. What about the other two things, the rune bone and the whorl?"

I grimaced. "No idea. Perhaps Secona will understand their magic and know how to use them. If Alard left them, he must know something about Holmgang's weaknesses that we don't. Until we find Secona, let's start with the woman who sent the chalice."

Alard's flat also included an arsenal of knives, swords and other blades. Dietger and I armed ourselves before we set out. No one appeared to be watching us as we left. We each put our hoods up, hoping that if word of the niding pole had spread, we would be less easily recognizable.

The chalice's former owner had left her address on the letter, and we made our way to a comfortable townhome not far from the center of the city. Lights illuminated the windows, and Dietger climbed the steps and knocked on the door.

A maid answered our knock. After a quiet conversation with Dietger, she disappeared for a moment, then returned to see us in. "The Mistress will see you," she said, ushering us into a comfortable parlor.

I saw nothing remarkable about the parlor. It could have been any well-to-do home in Antwerp. A painting of a man and woman hung over the mantle, our host and hostess. The elegant brocade upholstery complimented satin draperies. The mantle and fireplace were marble, and the tea service was silver.

"You're not the man I spoke with from the antique shop." The woman looked from Dietger to me, with the obvious question unspoken.

"My apologies Mevr. Fontaine. You dealt with my father. I am Dietger, and this is my business partner, Sorren." Mevr. Fontaine had the look of a comfortable Burgher wife. I was willing to bet that her husband was a well-to-do-merchant, and their wealth allowed them luxuries that only nobility and monarchs might have enjoyed not long ago. She sat with a straight spine, shoulders back, head held high, legs just so, the epitome of a very proper lady. Yet I could see the nervous movement of her eyes, smell the fear in her sweat, hear her rapidly beating heart. For all her comforts, Mevr. Fontaine was afraid.

"We would like to know a little more about the chalice, if you please," Dietger said in his most charming manner.

Mevr. Fontaine looked up sharply. "Do you wish to decline the sale?"

Dietger's smile was warm. "Certainly not. Many of the items we handle have troubled pasts." That was putting it mildly. "It helps us match an item to its best new owner if we have a better idea of its provenance," he added.

"You mean how I got it and where it came from—and why I want rid of the damned thing."

Dietger nodded. "Yes. All of those things."

The maid returned with tea. I declined, but Dietger allowed a cup to be poured for him. When the maid had finished serving her mistress and Dietger, Mevr. Fontaine looked up. "I'd like not to be disturbed, Greta. Please close the door when you leave."

Greta made a nod and a curtsey and did as she was bid. Mevr. Fontaine held her teacup in both hands as if it might save her soul. "My husband is traveling, that is why I had to wait until now to deliver the chalice. He knows nothing of this."

"He's not aware of the problems with the chalice, or that you've decided to sell it?" Dietger probed.

"Either. The chalice was part of my inheritance. It came to me only recently, with the death of an aunt. Her family came from Denmark, and it was said—quietly, of course—that she was descended from the *Seiðr*."

"They're sometimes called the spae, or the *seidr*, aren't they?" I questioned, for Dietger's benefit since I already knew the answer.

Mevr. Fontaine nodded nervously. "That's not something I'd like repeated, and if I should hear that it's been said, I will deny it and bring a charge against you, do you understand?"

"Of course," I replied. "But this is between us. Do you believe your aunt had a gift?"

Mevr. Fontaine's teacup shook, and she set it down after a sip to calm her nerves. "I'm a Christian woman, and such things are forbidden."

"I didn't ask if her gift would please the rector. Do you believe it was real?"

Mevr. Fontaine hesitated for a moment, then nodded sharply. "Yes. I do. She was my mother's sister, and while my mother never had the gift, there was always a woman in each generation who did. There was talk in the family, you know, about what they foresaw, or who they healed, or how they took revenge on someone who hurt a relative." She met my gaze. "These were fearsome women."

"I don't doubt it," Dietger replied. "How did you come to have the chalice?"

Mevr. Fontaine was silent for a moment and reached for her cup. In that moment, I knew. "You're the one in your generation, aren't you?" I said quietly.

She startled, nearly dropping her cup, and sloshing a few drops onto the Aubusson carpet. I expected her to deny it, but she pressed her lips together until they paled, and then took a deep breath and raised her head.

"Yes," she said, very quietly. "That's why the chalice worked for me." She looked past Dietger and me, remembering. "I didn't intend to. I told you—I'm a Christian woman."

"But you're also of your aunt's blood," I said. She let out her breath and nodded.

"Yes. I wasn't sure before. But I knew my aunt would never bequeath her chalice to me if she didn't think I had her gift. It was too precious to her. There had been… signs… from time to time." Now that the subject had been broached, she began to speak in a tumble, like in the confessional.

"There were things I knew that I couldn't have known… things I saw happen that hadn't happened yet. I tried to pretend, tried to deny it. My husband knows nothing of this." From her expression, I suspected that he would not approve. "I decided to put flowers in the chalice. But when I filled it…"

"You saw something that frightened you," Dietger finished. Mevr. Fontaine nodded.

"What did you see?"

Mevr. Fontaine did not speak until she had finished her tea and set the cup aside. Once again she took a deep breath, and when she set her hands in her lap, I saw her struggle to unclench her fists. The memory was obviously troubling. "I saw a man in a black cloak with the head of a raven," she said in a voice just above a whisper. "He held a staff and a cord tied with many knots. I saw him untie a knot and a dark spirit was loosed. It seemed to come at me, through the water. I... dropped the chalice."

"Was that the only vision?" I asked gently.

Reluctantly, she shook her head. "No. One night when I was dining alone, Greta had set out the chalice filled with wine. I reprimanded her, but she swore I had ordered it, although I had no memory of doing that."

"And did the vision come again?"

Mevr. Fontaine nodded. "Yes."

"What did you see?" Dietger prodded. Mevr. Fontaine had gone pale, and her breathing was rapid and shallow.

"I saw my death," she said after another long pause.

Dietger and I exchanged glances. "That's why you brought the chalice to Vanities? You thought that perhaps you could alter fate if you no longer had the chalice?"

Mevr. Fontaine's careful façade crumbled. "We all die," she said, swallowing hard. "But this was not the gentle passing of an old woman. If the chalice is correct," she said and had to pause to pull herself together, gathering courage, "I will be murdered."

A movement outside the parlor window caught my eye. Before I could warn either Dietger or Mevr. Fontaine, a sudden force shattered the windows, sending a hail of razor-sharp glass through the room. Shards of glass struck with the force of knives. Dietger slumped from his chair, bleeding profusely from a dozen cuts, bits of glistening glass stuck in his flesh like darts. I suspected I looked much the same, but within a moment, my wounds were already beginning to heal, forcing out the glass where it had lodged.

Mevr. Fontaine sat upright on the sofa, but both her fine clothing and the brocade upholstery was awash in bright red blood. One of the larger shards had taken her in the throat, striking an artery, and even as I rushed to her side, I could feel her heart slowing and her life weakening. There was nothing we could do for her.

A dark cloaked figure stood just beyond the window. His hood peaked in front of him, resembling a raven's face, and his cloak had a black iridescence like a raven's feathers. He held a staff that looked as if it were wrapped in knotted rope, just as Mevr. Fontaine foresaw.

Dietger was back on his feet, and together we charged through the shattered window after the attacker. While Dietger was no soldier, Carel had trained him well with the basics of self-defense and weaponry, and he unsheathed his own blades seconds after I had drawn mine. To my dismay, the cloaked figure leveled his staff at us, and gave a pull on the rope that wound around its tip and hung down nearly to its end, unraveling three of the knots.

Inky shadows untwined themselves from the cord and moved sinuously towards us, graceful as a dancer, sudden as a snake. They took no heed of my blades, slamming me to the ground beneath the spreading limbs of an old tree. Darkness enveloped me. I feared for Dietger, but I could not see him, and it was taking all my immortal strength to fight against the shadow's freezing cold. I heard Dietger scream. I could feel the shadow warring with the Dark Gift. The shadows could not steal my breath or still my heart: that had been done a century ago. I had no body heat save the borrowed warmth of my victims' blood, but what remained from my earlier feeding was stripped away.

Whatever the origin of the shadows, they were superior predators, strong enough to overpower my vampire strength, hungry enough to find the spark of old magic that moved my undead body and leech it from my bones. I could hear the raven-man chanting in one of the Northern languages, and the rhythmic pounding of his staff against the ground seemed to drive the shadows to frenzy.

I was rapidly losing my battle, and I despaired for Deitger. My hands clawed at the dirt beneath me, and my nails tore at the roots of the old tree. "Secona," I shouted with all the energy that remained within me. "Secona. Secona."

There was a flash of bright light, and abruptly, the shadow recoiled. I blinked and the raven-man was gone.

I lay on my back, utterly spent. I was bleeding from gashes that sliced my clothing and tore my flesh. Dietger lay nearby, his clothes stained with blood. He was not moving, but I could hear his heart beating, and I took comfort in that.

Only moments had passed since the raven-man appeared. I was grateful that Mevr. Fontaine's maid was not brave. Presumably, she was hiding somewhere, because she had not yet discovered her blood-soaked mistress and begun screaming. I dragged myself to my feet. Dietger and I needed to vanish before the neighborhood came to find out what had happened.

The woman stood between us and the Fontaine house. She wore a blue cloak with a headpiece of black lambskin trimmed in white rabbit. A mantle covered her shoulders and fell to the bottom of her skirts, inlaid with gems. Around her neck were strings of glass beads, and a large leather bag hung from a belt at her waist. The woman wore ermine gloves and carried a staff set with brass and stone, with the wound skeins of a distaff at the top. I could sense the power that seemed to radiate from her, and I knew I was in the presence of old, strong magic.

"Secona."

She nodded. "Bring your friend. We must leave."

I lifted Dietger effortlessly although he was not a small man. He was pale, and when he did not protest as I lifted him, I knew he was hurt badly.

"The shirt will sustain him for now, but we must get to shelter," she said.

"How quickly can you move?" I asked because had it just been Dietger and me; I could move with vampire speed, much faster than the swiftest sprinter.

Secona laughed. "Faster than your dark gift," she responded. "Where shall we meet?"

"Did you know Alard? His flat?"

"I know the place." Abruptly, Secona disappeared.

A woman's scream pierced the night, and through the shattered windows, I saw that Greta had recovered her wits and come, too late, to her mistress's defense. I mustered the energy to run, hoping that I could sustain the pace long enough to reach Alard's flat. Normally, such a relatively short distance would not be a problem, but I was not at my full strength. While I can't fly, I can levitate, and I've found that I can combine that with running to reach quite impressive speed, but tonight, levitation was beyond my strength. The cuts from the glass had healed quickly, but the gashes from the raven-man's shadow creatures seemed to fight healing, and they were excruciatingly painful. I could not imagine what it must be like for a mortal. Dietger was unconscious, though still alive.

My oath to Carel and Alard to keep Dietger safe drove me to push myself to my limit. When I arrived at Alard's flat, Secona was waiting in the shadows. "You must bid me enter," she said. "Alard's precautions are quite powerful."

I hefted Dietger over my shoulder so that I could use my key. "Secona—I welcome you," I said, and hoped that I was right in trusting her this far. Dietger groaned. I had no choice. I had to trust Secona or Dietger would die.

The flat was dark, but that posed no problem to me. I entered and went straight to put Dietger down on the sofa. Secona spoke a word, and the lanterns lit all at once as the door slammed shut and locked behind us. A chill ran down my spine. Her effortless power left a tingle in the air like a nearby lightning strike.

"Can you heal him?" I stood back, and if she read a challenge in my stance, so be it.

Secona gave me an enigmatic smile but did not answer. Instead of rushing to Dietger's side, as I had hoped she would, Secona made a slow circle of the flat, moving counterclockwise. Three times she circled Dietger, singing to herself as she went. After she completed the third circle, she withdrew an abalone shell from the pouch on her belt and took a handful of dried herbs from another pouch. With a gesture, a spark ignited the herbs and they burned with the scent of juniper and mugwort.

I stood by, my fists clenched, willing myself to be still. I had pushed the thought of my own injuries out of mind, but it angered me that so far, to my eye, Secona had done nothing of substance to save Dietger. Yet Alard had trained me well. Secona was a being of great power, whose nature I did not fully understand. I dared not lose her favor.

Secona stood beside Dietger, still holding her staff. The top of the staff was a distaff, similar to the one Alard had bequeathed to me. Secona unwound a length of knotted cord from her distaff, and laid the cord around Dietger so that it circled his entire body like an outline.

As she moved, she sang softly in a language I did not understand. When she had laid the rope all the way around Dietger, she loosened two of the knots. At first, I thought that a puff of steam or mist sprang from the rope, and then I realized that she had set free two spirits, much like the dark beings that the raven-man had called down on us. I watched as the mist enveloped Dietger, forming an opaque cloud that hovered over him for several minutes. I could not see Dietger through the mist, but I could sense him growing stronger, his heartbeat and breathing becoming steady.

Throughout it all, Secona had not spoken to me or spared me a glance. Now, she beckoned for me to come closer. I stopped just a pace behind her and waited. Secona sang a few words, and the mist unraveled around Dietger and coiled itself around me. I resisted the urge to flee, willing myself to remain still as the cold wisps wound around me. Their dark counterpart had inflicted pain with every touch. These pale tendrils soothed with every contact, sending a strange frisson through me that tingled from the top of my scalp to the soles of my feet.

Another softly sung word and the mist uncoiled, slipping back to its mistress, who bound them once more in the fiber of her distaff. Secona stepped away from the sofa and gestured for me to come closer.

Dietger lay sleeping peacefully. His wounds were gone, as was the blood that marred his clothing. I looked down at myself. My jacket and pants were still torn from where the shadows had attacked us, but the gashes on my arms, legs, and face were healed without a trace.

"Thank you," I said, feeling as ragged as my voice sounded. "What were those… things… that attacked us?"

"Spirits," Secona replied matter-of-factly. "Holmgang is a *Seiðr*. Among our people, the power of a *Seiðr* must be inherited. Holmgang became a *Seiðr* by stealing the power from the one to whom it rightfully belonged. He has killed to take power that does not belong to him, and that makes him outlaw and outcast."

"Did he raise the niding pole against us?" I asked. She nodded. "Those shadow-things he sent against us—we saw something similar in the alleyway behind the store when the niding pole had cursed the ground. Were they land sprites?"

Secona looked troubled. She lowered her hood, and I could see that her hair was flaxen-colored. Even by lantern light, her skin was nearly as pale as mine, and her eyes were icy blue. "They were once land sprites," she said quietly. "A true *Seiðr* does not bind spirits against their will. My spirits serve me willingly."

Her expression grew sad. "Holmgang breaks and twists the spirits he binds, just like the niding pole removes the essence from the land and warps its sprites."

"Alard warned us he would come," I said. I dropped heavily into one of the tall chairs, exhausted. "But he didn't tell us how to fight him."

"What tools did Alard leave you?" Secona asked.

I pointed to the spae-woven shirt that had helped to save Dietger's life. "The shirt, obviously." I looked to her distaff. "There is a bone with runes carved into it and a spindle-whorl. I have no idea what to do with those. And Alard left me a nice collection of fighting knives." Those I knew how to use, but I doubted they would be effective against Holmgang.

"Holmgang will challenge you to a duel," Secona said. "And you must respond to his challenge. Defaulting will allow him to seize your property—and your soul."

I stared at her in shock. "You want *me* to fight *him*? He's as old as my maker's maker. I'm barely a century old—a child, as immortals go."

Secona nodded. "You don't have to destroy Holmgang. You only have to defeat him in a ritual duel."

"What counts as defeat?"

"First blood."

Had I been mortal, I would have broken out in a cold sweat. "I don't know if Alard mentioned this, but I was a jewel thief, not a warrior. I've been practicing since Alard turned me, but I haven't had nine hundred years to perfect my technique. Holmgang was a fearsome warrior before he was turned—and I imagine he's had plenty of practice since then."

"Alard bested him," Secona said. "I was there."

She appeared no older than my own apparent mortal age of mid-twenties, and I recalculated her age by more than three hundred years. "How?" I asked. I'd seen Alard in plenty of fights. He usually won by cleverness or treachery, not by brute force or exceptional skill. In my mortal days, I usually tried to avoid the whole subject by running away or hiding really well. That had worked well for me—until the day it didn't.

"There are rules for the duel, very old rules that have a magic of their own. Holmgang is very proud of his prowess as a warrior and of his strength. He will launch a brutal attack."

"What did Alard do?" I was intrigued now and felt a glimmer of hope. If Alard could survive, possibly I could also.

Secona appeared to bite back a smile. "He seemed to faint dead away. Once he hit the ground, while Holmgang was taken aback, Alard struck him in the ankles with his sword. First blood is first blood."

Oh yes, that sounded like Alard. Rather clever, too. But it was unlikely to work a second time. "Holmgang won't let me get away with that," I replied. "So how do I beat him?"

"You have some things in your favor," Secona replied. "Holmgang mounted the challenge by placing the niding pole. The place of the duel is set by tradition: a three-way crossroads. Mortals would meet at midday; as you are both undead, it must be midnight. Your combat ground is made up of two ox hides staked to the ground with hazel wood, within the confines of a cord. As the challenged, you have the choice of judge. You choose me."

"Absolutely," I said, nodding fervently.

The hint of a smile quirked at Secona's mouth. "I accept. I will prepare the dueling area, and it is my cord that will confine the area."

"Can Holmgang call his spirits?" Dietger asked.

"No," Secona replied. "But neither can I. And as the judge, I am bound by old magic to speak the truth. I cannot call in your favor if you have not won according to the letter of the rules."

My ears pricked up. Secona was giving me a hint. I could win by keeping to the letter of the rules, but not to the intention of the law. I was quite familiar with the gray area in between.

"You may take two blades into the marked area with you. If you step outside the area, you forfeit. You may not try to exhaust your opponent by running in circles or dodging. You must parry," Secona instructed.

"How can I win?" I asked, my head spinning. The budding hope of a moment ago was now crushed.

Secona met my gaze. "You cannot win if you fight against Holmgang's strength. Force him to fight against your strength."

"Can he do magic inside the dueling area?"

Secona shook her head. "No. He may use only what is an essential part of himself."

"What about the niding pole?" Dietger asked. "How do we get rid of that before Sorren and I are run out of town?"

"If Sorren bests Holmgang, I can remove the curse," Secona replied. "Alard left us the means. The runes carved on the bone are the incantation, and the spindle whorl was a gift of mine to Alard long ago. Used with my distaff, it will magnify my power."

"What is Holmgang?" I asked. "You said he was undead. Is he a vampire like me?"

Secona frowned. "Holmgang is undead, but it was the price he paid for his stolen power. He was not brought across as you were, so while he is immortal, it is not from the dark gift. His magic enhances the fighting skills he had as a mortal, but within the challenge ring, he leaves his magic behind, while the dark gift is part of your essence."

"How does Sorren respond to Holmgang's challenge?" Dietger asked. He looked vastly better than when we had arrived, and had found the remaining bread and cheese from the night before.

"I will take your response to the niding pole for you," Secona replied, "and as judge, I will choose the crossroads and time when you fight. Expect the duel to be tomorrow at midnight."

"What can I do to prepare?" I was no duelist, and the very thought of facing Holmgang in single combat seemed overwhelming.

Secona met my gaze. "Feed well. Rest well. And remember—fight to your strengths, not his."

Secona left us after that, with assurances that she would return tomorrow to share the location of the duel. Since Dietger was no longer injured, I slipped out to find my own sustenance and drank more deeply than usual. The night was far spent when I returned. Dietger was sleeping. I went into my windowless room, locked the door and laid down, knowing that even my fear could not resist the dawn's call to sleep.

I awoke after sundown. Dietger was awake and dressed, and I saw that he wore not only his sword but a bandolier full of knives. He looked as worried as I felt, but he said nothing aside from a mumbled greeting.

On the table lay my sword, freshly sharpened. Beside it lay a variety of swords Dietger must have found hidden in the apartment, set out for me to choose my second blade. We discussed the relative merits of each weapon at length, desperate not to talk about the very real threat that faced us in just a few candlemarks.

I could see Dietger's concern in his face, although his brisk manner kept me from commenting. Vanities was his livelihood, his inheritance, and Carel's legacy. I had no intention of allowing Holmgang to take it from him. I knew Dietger kept company with a woman in town, and I suspected he would ask her to marry him before long, ensuring that Vanities would be passed down to another generation. Holmgang's fight was with me, yet Dietger had nearly been killed because of it and stood to lose everything if I failed. I would not let him down.

SECONA CAME TO the door when the city bells chimed the eleventh hour. "I thought you'd be here sooner," I said, unable to keep my frustration out of my voice.

"I am in time," she replied, unruffled. "Come with me."

We traveled in silence to a crossroad on the edge of the city. Holmgang stood on the other side of the three intersecting roads, glowering at me. His distaff stood propped against a large tree. Secona had already prepared the dueling area. Two tanned oxhides marked the combat area, staked to the ground and ringed with the knotted skein from her distaff.

I had spent the last few candlemarks taking a desperate inventory of my skills, and I feared I still came up short compared to Holmgang. I could pick any lock in Belgium, enter a house unnoticed, lift a wallet or a piece of jewelry from a mark without ever attracting attention. I had vampire speed and enhanced senses, and I could levitate a little. None of that seemed useful at the moment.

When I had seen Holmgang outside Mevr. Fontaine's house, he had looked fearsome in his iridescent black cloak and raven-beaked hood. He had set those to the side with his distaff, but even without them, he was an intimidating opponent. He appeared to be in his third decade, with a cloud of fiery red hair and a plaited beard. His eyes were icy blue, and he fixed me with a killing look. I was average height and wiry, good for thievery. Holmgang stood a head taller, and probably was double my weight, with arms that seemed like tree trunks and legs stout as a ship's mast.

He's got a longer reach than I do, and he's too heavy to knock off his feet. I assessed, seeing my opponent's true form for the first time. *If this were a bar, I wouldn't pick a fight with him.* Even at a distance, I could see the battle scars that attested to Holmgang's experience as a warrior. A jagged line cut down from his right eyebrow across his cheek. His hands were covered with small, pale scars, every one of them earned in combat. I was willing to bet the rest of him was covered with scars as well. He looked ready to take me apart, and I still didn't have a plan.

"Enter the combat area," Secona said and brought her staff down hard against the ground. Dietger stood behind her, a silent witness. I drew myself up to my full height, squared my shoulders, and resolved that if my long existence came to an abrupt end this night, I would attempt to die with dignity. Holmgang grinned at me hungrily, and I could guess his intention was to kill me, but not until I had begged for mercy on my knees.

We stepped into the combat area on opposite ends of the oxhides. I gripped my sword two-handed, and inspiration struck. Holmgang had me on strength and reach, but I had the advantage in speed.

Screaming like a berserker, I ran at him with my full vampire speed. Holmgang staggered back, but still managed to block my strike with strength that sent a shock down my arms. He came at me with rage in his eyes, so fast that for a split second, I wondered whether Secona was mistaken about him not being a vampire. I parried, relying on the speed of my reflexes rather than talent. The dark gift gave me the strength to hold my ground, but I knew it would only be a matter of time before Holmgang's skill got through my guard.

I had fought many mortals in my century of existence, and since my turning, won every fight. I had no confidence that I would prevail here. Holmgang was tireless, and I knew that, sooner or later, despite the dark gift's enhanced senses, I would make a mistake. I dared not look toward Secona or Dietger. In a normal fight, I would not mind taking a few gashes, even wounds that would kill a mortal, knowing I would heal despite the pain. Here, I dared not allow a scratch, and I had not come close to inflicting even a nick on my enemy.

Holmgang struck again, with a blow that would have snapped my bones if I had still been mortal. Madness glinted in his eyes, and I knew he would not be satisfied until he finished me. His blows rained down, driving me to the edge of the hide, a boundary I dare not pass.

Holmgang's next swing nearly caught me, and my eyes widened, looking to Secona to see if the strike had drawn blood. It hadn't, but I couldn't expect to be lucky again.

I had strength and stamina, but even my reflexes weren't a match for sheer skill. Holmgang came at me again, sensing his advantage, relentless. He knocked me off balance, at the edge of the boundary, and

I knew that to step foot off the hide was to admit defeat. I did the only thing I could.

I hovered.

I'm usually much better at hovering on the way down than rising up. That's saved me more than once when the need for a speedy exit sends me over a wall or out a window, and my ability to levitate saves me from splattering across the cobblestones. This time, sheer anxiety sent me six feet straight up in the air, and for an instant, Holmgang was caught off guard.

This was my chance. Before Holmgang could adjust, I spun my sword so that I gripped it point down, and fell on him.

My sword sliced against the side of Holmgang's head, opening a bloody wound, nearly taking off his ear. Holmgang reacted, bringing his sword up more swiftly than I expected, spitting me through the abdomen. I heard Secona shouting, heard Dietger curse. The pain was excruciating. I had won by the rules and drawn first blood. But as I lay helpless at the feet of my enemy, I knew how easy it would be for him to remove his sword and finish me with a blow to the heart or a stroke to the neck.

"Stop!" A wave of power swept across us. Now that the duel was officially over, Secona was free to use her magic. Holmgang muttered a potent curse and ripped his weapon free of my gut. I arched in pain, blood soaking the hide beneath me. Holmgang's sword clattered to the ground, and he stalked away, leaving me where I lay. Already, I could feel the dark gift beginning to knit together the grievous wound, but it would be a while until the pain subsided.

"Retract your curse," Secona ordered.

Holmgang gave me a killing look, and then growled words I did not understand. Secona nodded. "Leave here," Secona demanded. "You have challenged and lost. You are outlaw to this place. Do not return, or you are subject to my wrath."

I blinked my eyes once, and Holmgang stood garbed in his iridescent cloak and raven hood, holding his distaff, though I had not seen him move to retrieve them. I blinked again, and he was gone.

Secona held Dietger back until she had lifted the magical boundaries of the dueling area. By then, I was well along with healing, able to sit up by myself, though not fully healed. Dietger rushed over to where I sat. He regarded me with concern. "Can you stand?"

I grimaced. "Give me a few more minutes." I looked toward Secona. "Is it over? Is the curse lifted from the store?"

Secona nodded. "You fought well. Holmgang was sure you would be an easy kill. You used your strengths against him. Not every vampire can levitate, or fly. Obviously, he forgot that some can."

"What happens next?" I asked.

Secona shrugged. "I will go back to where I was and what I was doing before you called to me."

"Will we see you again?" Dietger asked. He offered me a hand up, and I accepted, although I had to grit my teeth against the pain as I pulled myself to standing.

Secona's smile was unreadable. "Perhaps. If the need arises. Alard and I crossed paths on occasion." She met my gaze. "He would have been quite proud of how you handled Holmgang today. Don't think that Holmgang was the only one watching how this challenge played out. Others will note that you bested him. They'll either think twice about challenging you themselves, or lay a more difficult snare."

"That's something to look forward to," I muttered. Then I remembered my manners. "Thank you."

Secona inclined her head in acknowledgment. "You're most welcome." I blinked, and she was gone, as the wind rattled the leaves of the trees nearby.

"Now what?" Dietger asked.

I found that I could walk without limping too badly. "We take care of that damned chalice," I replied. "And then get back to business. Come on. Let's go back to the Vanities. We've got work to do."

VENDETTA (EXCERPT)

"WATCH OUT, CASSIDY!" TEAG'S WARNING WAS A HEARTBEAT TOO late. The dark wraith screeched in fury, and his clawed hand raked across my shoulder, opening four bloody cuts. I ducked out of reach and flung up my left hand with its protective bracelet. The ghostly figure of a large, angry dog appeared by my side, teeth bared, snarling at the wraith.

The ghost dog sprang at the wraith, striking it square on, driving it back so I could get out of the way. It wasn't the first time a soul-sucking creature of death showed up in the break room of my store, but it also wasn't something I had planned on when I opened the velvet jewelry box.

"Cover me!" I shouted to Teag, trying to figure out how fast I could get to a weapon that I could use against the billowing, monstrous shape.

"Go!" Teag said to me. He turned to the wraith with a wicked grin and snatched down a fishing net made of clothesline rope from a hook on the wall. "See how you like this!" he yelled, throwing the net over the wraith.

Normal rope would have gone right through the wraith's dark form. Wraiths are like that – solid when they want to be, insubstantial when you want to hit them. But the magic woven into the net meant it stuck, catching the wraith in a web of power. It wouldn't hold forever, but it could buy us precious seconds, and that delay might be the difference between life and death.

If I'd expected a fight to the death, I would have made sure my weapons were closer. I had to dive for the door to my office and grab my athame from atop my desk. The athame focused my magic, and I opened myself to the powerful memories and emotions that I connected with it, drawing strength. The wraith surged forward, straining at the energy of the rope net that glowed like silver. The ghost dog harried the wraith, snapping at its heels, keeping it occupied.

I swung back into the room and leveled the athame at the wraith, channeling my magic. A cone of blinding white light surged from the athame, and when the cold power struck the wraith, it shrieked and twisted, forced back toward the wall. It looked as if the white light was burning through the wraith, like fire on paper, and with one last ear-piercing scream, the deadly apparition vanished.

The ghost dog looked back at me, wagged its tail, and winked out. I slumped back against the wall, feeling suddenly drained. Magic takes energy, and I was still pretty new at learning to channel mine for big stuff, like fighting off monsters. Then again, with the amount of prac-tice we'd been getting lately, I figured I'd be up to speed in no time.

"Nice net," I said, managing a grin.

Teag returned a tired smile. "Good shooting." His expression grew serious. "You're bleeding."

I sighed and sat down in one of the chairs at the small table, eying the overturned jewelry box mistrustfully. For now, at least, the box seemed harmless. "I didn't move fast enough," I said.

"You weren't expecting an attack," Teag replied.

"I'm beginning to think I should always expect an attack, and be pleasantly surprised when an antique is just an antique, instead of a demon portal to the realms of the dead." The wraith's claws must have taken a swipe at my energy as well as my shoulder, and I hoped that didn't include shreds of my soul as well. Teag retrieved the souped-up first aid kit we keep in one of the cupboards. Unfortunately, we need it a lot. It's not your average office supply store kit. It's got surgical needles and sutures, sterile bandages, prescription painkillers, and antibiotics, plus healing herbs and potions supplied by our friendly neighborhood Voodoo mambo and root workers.

Then again, Trifles and Folly wasn't your average antique store, and Teag and I had a few extra abilities they don't teach in business school.

I'm Cassidy Kincaide, the current owner of Trifles and Folly, an antique and curio store in beautiful, historic, haunted Charleston, South Carolina. The store has been in my family almost since Charleston was founded, close to three hundred and fifty years ago, and we have a big secret to go with that success. We do much more than sell interesting, expensive, old stuff. Our real job is getting dangerous magical items off the market and out of the wrong hands. When we succeed, nobody notices. When we fail, lots of people die.

I inherited Trifles and Folly from my Uncle Evan. Teag is my assistant store manager, best friend, and occasional bodyguard, and Sorren is my silent partner – a nearly six-hundred-year-old vampire who is part of a secret collaboration of mortals and immortals called the Alliance, dedicated to getting rid of items with dark magic before they can hurt anyone. The antiques that don't have any magical juice, Trifles and Folly resells. Those that are just unsettling but not danger- ous, we neutralize so that they won't cause a problem. Items that are magically malicious or so tainted with bad emotions that they will hurt people, we lock up or destroy.

I shrugged out of the shoulder of my shirt and winced as Teag cleaned the deep scratches. "Do you think it'll come back?" Teag asked as he daubed carefully at the damage the wraith had done.

I sighed. "No way to tell until we know more about what it was and why it came in the first place. And that means taking a look at what's in that jewelry box."

Magic runs in my family, and the person chosen to run Trifles and Folly needs all the magic he or she can summon, because we keep Charleston – and the world – safe from things that go bump in the night. My magic is psychometry, the ability to read the history of an object by touching it. Not every object, thank goodness, just those that have been touched by strong emotion or powerful energy. Heartfelt emotion is one of the strongest sources of power. That's why a tattered old dog collar is my protective bracelet – summoning the ghost of my golden retriever, Bo – and my grandmother's mixing spoon is my athame, used handle-side out. Both items have a strong emotional connection for me, and in both cases, the protection of the beings associated with the items resonates enough to fend off some seriously nasty creatures.

The salve Teag smoothed on my cuts included plantain, comfrey, and rose to prevent infection and slow the bleeding. The herbs had been mixed by Mrs. Teller, a powerful root worker, so they carried a supernatural level of healing and protection. Teag covered the scratches with gauze and then pulled out a small woven patch of cloth imbued with his magic, which he taped down over the gauze to keep it in place. Teag is a Weaver, someone who can send energy and intent into woven and knotted fabric. He's also able to weave together strands of information that would elude a regular person, making him an awesome researcher and an amazing hacker.

"Is that one of the patches you made?" I asked, slipping my shoulder back into my shirt.

Teag grinned. "Yeah, you'll have to let me know how that works. The patches are a bit of an experiment right now."

I paused for a moment, focusing on my wounded shoulder. "There's a tingle of magic from the salve and from the patch," I said, paying close attention to what I was feeling. "The cuts don't hurt as much as they did before, and where you bandaged it feels warm… like sunlight on a summer day."

Teag nodded. "That means that the poultice and the patch I wove are speeding the healing and driving out infection." Supernatural predators often had bad stuff on their claws, either poison or a taint that could be as deadly as the cuts themselves.

I went over to the fridge and poured us both glasses of iced tea, made the Charleston way, so sweet the fillings in your teeth stand up and wave. I needed a moment before I took on handling that antique jewelry box, and I figured that Teag wouldn't mind a break either in case something else tried to kill us. Fortunately, the shop was closed, so we didn't have to worry about the safety of customers or our part-time assistant, Maggie.

We drank the iced tea in silence, stealing glances toward the little velvet box on the table. Both of us knew we had to deal with it, and given what we had just survived, neither of us were looking forward to the prospect.

I finished my sweet tea, and couldn't postpone the inevitable. "Okay," I said. "Let's see what was so special about this little jewelry box."

"You feel up to it?" Teag asked.

I gave him a look that didn't need words. "As ready as I'm going to be. And you're supposed to be having dinner with Anthony tonight. That gives us about an hour and a half for me to read the mojo on the jewelry box, get knocked flat on my ass, and come back to my senses without making you late for your date." I was being intentionally flip-pant, but the reality was much more dangerous, and we both knew it.

"Do you think we should wait for Sorren?" Teag asked.

I thought about it for a moment, then shook my head. "Kinda late now, don't ya think?" I asked with a wry half-smile. "Besides, he's in Boston, taking care of whatever-it-was that made him up and leave on a moment's notice. I think I'll be okay. Let's get it over with." I moved my chair closer to the box on the table.

The velvet was worn and faded. It was too big for a ring box, and I wondered if it had originally held a pair of earrings, or maybe a dainty bracelet. The wraith had shown up a few seconds after I opened the box, but as I thought back over what had happened, I realized that the wraith hadn't come *from* the box. That was important, because it meant the wraith hadn't been trapped inside. But why had it shown up at all?

Hard experience taught me to look before I touched. I was also learning to see what I could learn without making contact with an item. Practice was sharpening my ability to use the magic I was born with but had only recently begun trying to control. I held out my hand, palm down, over the faded blue velvet and closed my eyes, concentrating.

The sense of overwhelming loss made me sway in my chair. Second-hand grief welled up in my throat, as tears stung my eyes. Beneath those darker emotions, I felt the remnants of something joyful, sullied now by whatever had been taken away. Dimly, as if in a faded photograph, I saw an image of a couple in their twenties, hand in hand. Then, as I watched, the young man's image faded away to nothing, leaving the woman all alone.

Magical seeing – things like psychometry, clairvoyance, and being a psychic – requires a lot of reading between the lines. I wish it were as clear-cut as it seems on television, where ghosts speak in complete sentences and visions are in high-definition with the volume turned up. In real life, images are distorted, murky, and incomplete. Spirits move their mouths, but often no sound emerges. The little snip of stone tape memory we see leaves a lot of room for interpretation. And that's the problem. When we don't have full information, we have to guess. Sometimes, we're right, and the problem gets solved. Other times, we guess wrong, and someone gets dead.

Then I realized what was causing the extra buzz that my magic had picked up from the velvet-flocked box; this item came with its very own ghost.

In general, my psychic gift of reading the history of objects doesn't give me any special power to see ghosts. Oh, I've seen more than a few ghosts – then again, I live in Charleston, which is one of the most haunted cities in North America. I think it's written somewhere that every house built before 1950 has to be haunted, and every native-born Charlestonian has a yearly quota of ghostly sightings. Given the nature of what we do at Trifles and Folly, seeing ghosts comes with the territory. Some of the spirits have been helpful. Others have been lost, not even sure that they are really dead. And some of those ghosts have been downright pissed off and dangerous.

In this case, the ghost was terrified out of its everlovin' mind.

As I reached toward the box again, my fingers hovering over the velvet, the ghost welled up at me in a rush, so fast that I rocked onto the back legs of the chair, and might have gone over backward if Teag hadn't been standing behind me. Most of the time, ghosts hang back, but this one got right in my face, so to speak, screaming soundlessly, eyes wide with fear.

"Are you okay?" Teag was worried. I gestured to him that I was fine. So far, this ghost wasn't trying to hurt me. It just really wanted to get my attention. Maybe I had been the first living person it had ever had a chance to contact. Or maybe the wraith that had come after Teag and me wasn't really looking for us at all. Perhaps it had a different kind of prey in mind.

That left me stuck between two bad options. I really didn't want to make the level of connection that would happen if I touched or held the jewelry box. It was already clear that the box had a history of tragedy, and if I made contact, I would feel that sad background as forcefully as if I had lived it myself. On the other hand, whoever's spirit was still connected to the jewelry box was in torment, and might suffer forever if I didn't do something about it.

I reached out and picked up the box.

The first image I saw was of pearl earrings; dainty round balls with a lustrous glow, classy and always in style. Judging from the box, and the name of a local jewelry store I knew had gone out of business before 1900, I figured that the gift had been given back in the Victorian period. Then I looked into the box, and I knew for certain. Inside was a dark round circle, braided from brown, human hair.

Gotta love the Victorians; they knew how to make mourning a life-long, high-art spectacle. By modern standards, the old customs seem mawkish, even macabre. But in a time when most families buried as many of their children as they saw live to adulthood, when few people lived past their forties and a lot of folks died young from cholera, smallpox, and other terrors we've since vanquished, and when the Civil War killed half a million young husbands, lovers, fathers, sons, and brothers, our great-great-grandparents had a lot to mourn.

They mourned in style, with whole wardrobes of black crepe clothing, elaborate social rituals and an entire etiquette for grief. On the other hand, these were real people, and their loss was just as real as it is for modern folks. They tried to hang on to the memory of their departed beloveds. Sometimes, they took pictures of the corpse, dressed up in its Sunday best, perhaps the only picture of the person they would ever have. And other times, they clipped a lock or two of hair and plaited it into jewelry, something to remember the person by, or something they could keep with them all the time. These were *memento mori* in the full, original meaning of the word, "to remember death."

The beautiful, ghastly wreath of hair was a piece of Victorian death jewelry.

The vision was sudden and overwhelming.

I was cold, so cold. One moment I had been sweating on a battle- field in Virginia, and the next... the next there was nothing. They say you never hear the bullet that gets you. How could you, when all around you the sound of hundreds of rifles crashes like thunder? I remembered a loud noise, a sharp, sudden pain and then falling into darkness.

And waking up. Only, not really. When I emerged from the dark- ness, my body didn't come with me. Women sobbed. Men pretended that they weren't crying. My little sister fainted and had to be carried from the room. I wanted to tell them I was still there, wanted to tell them how much I loved them, but "I" wasn't "me" anymore. I was up here, and the rest of me was down there, not moving, gray with death.

I thought I had been frightened on the battlefield. That fear paled in comparison to how terrified I was now. I thought that the Almighty would have gathered me to his bosom by now, if I were worthy. I'd heard tell all my life about bright lights and a land of milk and honey. Since I was still here, maybe that bright light wasn't going to come for me. I didn't have words for how afraid I was of what that meant for my immortal soul, so I just stayed where I was, looking for Amelia, my beloved. She always knew how to make sense of things.

Then I saw her. Oh dear Lord, had grief for me done that to her? My pretty Amelia, so young and happy, looked gaunt and frail, hollow- eyed. Her father walked her to the casket, as if she could barely stand. She nearly collapsed, sagging almost to her knees, before he collected her and helped her stand next to me to say good-bye.

I wanted to touch her, to tell her I was near, but I couldn't. And then she leaned over and kissed my forehead, and carefully snipped some of my hair where it was the longest. Hot tears fell on my cold skin, but somehow, I felt them. No one faulted her for weeping. We were going to marry in the spring.

I couldn't go back, and I couldn't go on, so I followed my Amelia home. And since the Almighty didn't seem to want me, I did the best I could, watching over my girl. I had nowhere else to be. She plaited my hair into a memorial wreath, and she wore it on a chain around her neck. And if, when she touched it, she thought she imagined my presence, I was closer than she knew.

Abruptly, I was Cassidy again. I saw time flow by like an old movie. The scene changed, years passed. Amelia died, still grieving her lost love. The hair wreath went into the velvet box that had once held a gift that gave great joy. The young man's ghost remained, too afraid to move on. And then, the shadows came.

This time, I didn't enter the ghost's thoughts as fully as before, except to feel terror in every cell and sinew of my body. After a hundred years of quiet darkness, not exactly heaven but far removed from hell, something appeared in the everlasting night. It was not the Father Almighty.

Like watching a movie with the sound turned off, something I could see but not influence, I saw the wraith stalk the young man's ghost. Tad. His name had been Tad. Thaddeus, maybe, but no one called him that. Just Tad. Lonely, afraid, desperate for company, he had gotten too close the first time, only to lose part of what little he had left to the wraith's hunger. After that, there was terror. Hiding. Fear of being found, of having the last little bit of self destroyed after all these long years. The darkness was so vast. Suddenly, the everlasting night that had seemed to be the enemy became an ally, a place to play a deadly game of hide-and-seek. And finally, the young man's spirit got the answer it had been seeking. There are some things worse than death. Being consumed is one of them.

When I came back to myself, I was screaming. Teag held me by the shoulders, shaking me gently, calling my name. We've done this a lot, unfortunately.

"Come back, Cassidy!" His eyes were worried. I guessed that I'd been pretty far gone. I've never gone so deep into a vision that I haven't been able to find my way back, but there's always a first time. And if there was a first time, it was likely to be the last time.

I nodded groggily, like a drunk sobering up on coffee. The terror and loss of the young man from the vision stayed with me, frightening and sad. "I'm okay," I managed. Teag's look told me that he sincerely doubted that.

Instead of arguing, he pushed another glass of sweet tea into my hand, and waited while I gulped it down. The icy cold liquid shocked me back to myself, and the sugar rushed through my veins like elixir. Only then did I realize I was shaking and sobbing, grieving for two lovers who had been dead for more than a hundred and fifty years.

I dragged the back of my hand over my eyes and took a deep breath to steady myself. Teag waited patiently. "I saw the story behind the memorial jewelry," I said, carefully laying the velvet box aside. "Young lovers. Civil War." Unfortunately, that story was a common refrain with the pieces we often saw at Trifles and Folly, although rarely had the past made such an impact. "I'd expect a piece like that to have a lot of mojo," I added, trying to get my voice to stop quailing. "But there's a ghost attached to it, and the thing we fought off tried to destroy him."

Teag frowned, alarmed. "That monster attacks ghosts?"

I nodded. "Yeah. It took a bite out of him. And I have the feeling that whatever that thing was, it went away, but it's not really gone."

"Then we've got a big problem," Teag said. "Because Charleston is a spookfest, and that monster is going to have an all-you-can-eat buffet if we don't do something about it."

END

Read the full adventure in *Vendetta, A Deadly Curiosities Novel.* You can also continue to follow Cassidy, Teag, and Sorren's adventures in *Trifles and Folly 2.*

AFTERWORD

CHARLESTON, SOUTH CAROLINA is a real place. Some of the landmarks and a few of the historical figures in this book do exist, and some (but not all) of the historical events were real. But the characters and their shops are all a work of fiction. So for example, if you go to Charleston (and I hope you do, because it's a lovely place to visit), you can see the real Charleston City Market and walk down King Street, but you won't find any of the businesses or restaurants I've mentioned by name. Any resemblance to real people or actual businesses is completely coincidental.

Many people in Charleston will tell you that the ghosts, however, are real. My ghosts are fictional, but that's because Charleston has enough of its own already. But don't take my word for it. See for yourself.

I hope you enjoyed the adventures with Cassidy, Teag, and Sorren. If you want more, check out the other Deadly Curiosities Adventures collected in *Trifles and Folly 2*, as well as the full-length novels, *Deadly Curiosities, Vendetta,* and *Tangled Web* available in paperback and e-book. Cassidy has more short stories and novellas coming! Check out the website: www.DeadlyCuriosities.com for the latest news.

ABOUT THE AUTHOR

GAIL Z. MARTIN is the author of *Scourge: A Darkhurst Novel*, from Solaris Books. Gail is also the author of *Vendetta: A Deadly Curiosities Novel* and *Trifles and Folly 1: A Deadly Curiosities Collection*, the latest in her urban fantasy series set in Charleston, SC; *Shadow and Flame* is the fourth book in the Ascendant Kingdoms Saga; *The Shadowed Path* (The first Jonmarc Vahanian Adventures collection), as well as *Iron and Blood* a Steampunk series, and *Spells, Salt, & Steel*, both co-authored with Larry N. Martin.

She is also author of *Ice Forged, Reign of Ash*, and *War of Shadows* in The Ascendant Kingdoms Saga, The Chronicles of The Necromancer series (*The Summoner, The Blood King, Dark Haven, Dark Lady's Chosen*); The Fallen Kings Cycle (*The Sworn, The Dread*) and the urban fantasy novel *Deadly Curiosities* and *Tangled Web*. Gail writes three ebook series: *The Jonmarc Vahanian Adventures, The Deadly Curiosities Adventures* and *The Blaine McFadden Adventures. The Storm and Fury Adventures*, steampunk stories set in the Iron & Blood world, are co-authored with Larry N. Martin.

Gail's work has appeared in over 35 US/UK anthologies. Newest anthologies include: *The Big Bad 2, Athena's Daughters, Heroes, Space, Contact Light, With Great Power, The Weird Wild West, The Side of Good/The Side of Evil, Alien Artifacts, Cinched: Imagination Unbound, Realms of Imagination, Clockwork Universe: Steampunk vs. Aliens, Gaslight and Grimm, Baker Street Irregulars, Journeys, Hath no Fury*, and *A Haven Harbor Halloween*.

Find out more at www.GailZMartin.com, at DisquietingVisions.com, on Goodreads https://www.goodreads.com/GailZMartin, and free excerpts on Wattpad http://wattpad.com/GailZMartin.

Trifles and Folly: A Deadly Curiosities Collection

Trifles and Folly 2: A Deadly Curiosities Collection

By Gail Z. Martin and Larry N. Martin

Jake Desmet Adventures

Iron & Blood

Storm and Fury: A Collection of Storm and Fury Adventures

Spells, Salt, & Steel: New Templars

Spells, Salt, & Steel

Open Season